EMBODYING *Contagion*

HORROR STUDIES

Preface

Horror Studies is the first book series exclusively dedicated to the study of the genre in its various manifestations – from fiction to cinema and television, magazines to comics, and extending to other forms of narrative texts such as video games and music. Horror Studies aims to raise the profile of Horror and to further its academic institutionalisation by providing a publishing home for cutting-edge research. As an exciting new venture within the established Cultural Studies and Literary Criticism programme, Horror Studies will expand the field in innovative and student-friendly ways.

EMBODYING *Contagion*

THE VIROPOLITICS OF HORROR AND DESIRE IN CONTEMPORARY DISCOURSE

EDITED BY SANDRA BECKER,
MEGEN DE BRUIN-MOLÉ AND SARA POLAK

UNIVERSITY OF WALES PRESS
2021

www.uwp.co.uk

British Library Cataloguing-in-Publication Data

A catalogue record for this book is available from the British Library.

ISBN 978-1-78683-690-8
eISBN 978-1-78683-691-5

The University of Wales Press acknowledges the financial support of the Dutch Research Council (NWO).

Embodying Contagion is available as an open access publication
DOI 10.16922/contagion

Typeset by Chris Bell, cbdesign

MIX
Paper from responsible sources
FSC® C013604

Printed and bound by CPI Group (UK) Ltd, Croydon, CR0 4YY

Contents

Acknowledgements

IDEAS, LIKE VIRUSES, are not very effective in isolation. We are indebted to this book's many contributors, including those whose work does not appear in the final manuscript. In particular we want to acknowledge Michelle Green, who played a key role in the book's early development. We are also indebted to the Dutch Research Council (NWO) and to Leiden University Centre for the Arts in Society for their generous financial support of this collection. Many thanks to the fantastic team at University of Wales Press, including our commissioning editor Sarah Lewis, copy-editor Heather Palomino, Dafydd Jones and the rest of the editorial team. Many thanks are also due to Josje Calff and Menno Polak, our external proofreaders.

Above all, we would like to dedicate this book to all those people whose bodies have been pathologised, stigmatised, marginalised and downright endangered by their media, their neighbours and their nations. You deserve better.

The Editors, October 2020

Notes on Contributors

Sandra Becker is a lecturer in the Department of Media and Culture Studies at Utrecht University, the Netherlands. When the work on this collection began, she was in the final stages of her PhD project 'Fathers of the Nation: White Masculinities and Fatherhood in Contemporary US-American TV Series (2001–2016)' in the Department of American Studies at the University of Groningen. Approaching early 2000s TV series such as *Breaking Bad, The Walking Dead* and *The Strain* as cultural-historic artefacts, she analysed their depiction of their white father protagonists against the backdrop of socio-economic and political events and gendered discourses at the beginning of the twenty-first century that paved the way for the election of 'Daddy Trump'. She has published and taught on both the contagious medium television and the concept of toxic masculinity.

Megen de Bruin-Molé is a lecturer in Digital Media Practice at the University of Southampton. She specialises in historical fiction, popular culture and contemporary remix. Her book *Gothic Remixed: Monster Mashups and Frankenfictions in 21st-Century Culture* (Bloomsbury, 2020) explores the boundaries and connections between contemporary remix and its related modes through the lens of monster studies. Since 2016 she has been an editor of the *Genealogy of the Posthuman*, an open-access initiative curated by the Critical Posthumanism Network (*http://criticalposthumanism.net/genealogy/*). Read more about Megen's work on her blog: *frankenfiction.com*.

Peter Burger is assistant professor in the Department of Journalism and New Media at Leiden University. He applies rhetorical perspectives to journalism, narrative folklore and social media discourse, with a special interest in crime stories, fact-checking and disinformation.

Yvonne Karyn Clark is a graduate student at the University of Utah, where she studies critical and cultural approaches to rhetoric of pop-culture media, technology, and space and place.

Elana Gomel is an associate professor at the Department of English and American Studies at Tel-Aviv University. She has taught and researched at Princeton, Stanford, University of Hong Kong and Venice International University. She is the author of six academic books and numerous articles on subjects such as narrative theory, posthumanism, science fiction, Dickens and Victorian culture. As a fiction writer, she has published more than fifty fantasy and science fiction stories and three novels. She can be found at *https://www.citiesoflightanddarkness.com/*.

Astrid Haas is Marie Curie Research Fellow at the Institute of Black Atlantic Research, University of Central Lancashire, UK. Holding a doctorate from the University of Muenster and a postdoctoral degree from Bielefeld University, she taught American Studies at several universities in Germany. Her research covers travel writing, drama and autobiography, the Black and Latinx Diasporas, Gender and Science Studies. She wrote *Stages of Agency: The Contributions of American Drama to the AIDS Discourse* (Winter Verlag, 2011) and *Lone Star Vistas: American, Mexican, and German Travel Narratives of Texas, 1821–1861* (University of Texas Press, 2021). Her current, EU-funded research is entitled 'Black Inter-American Mobilities and Autobiography in the Age of Revolutions (1760–1860)'.

Marouf Hasian Jr is full professor in the Department of Communication at the University of Utah, and is a distinguished professor at that university. He is the author of some twenty books covering critical genocide studies, humanitarian rhetorics, postcolonialism, indigeneity studies, critical legal studies and critical memory studies.

Mica Hilson is an associate professor at the American University of Armenia, where he chairs the English and Communications programme. His research on modern and contemporary literature, popular culture, ecocriticism, and sexuality studies has appeared in numerous journals – including *Pacific Coast Philology*, *The Comparatist* and *Doris Lessing Studies* – as well as many edited collections, including *Security and Hospitality in Literature and Culture* (Routledge, 2016), *The Ethics and Rhetoric of Invasion Ecology* (Lexington, 2017) and *Curricular Innovations: LGBTQ Literatures and the New English Studies* (Peter Lang, 2019).

Madison A. Krall (University of Utah) is a PhD candidate in the Department of Communication exploring how rhetorical norms and practices are related to public perceptions of science, health and the body. Her chapter titled 'Negotiating Public Scientific Regulatory Controversies: Dr Frances O. Kelsey's Productive Postponement of Thalidomide in the United States' is part of the forthcoming edited collection *Reframing Rhetorical History* (University of Alabama Press, 2021) and she has co-authored articles appearing in journals such as *Quarterly Journal of Speech and Health Communication*. Krall teaches rhetoric and health communication courses and is currently writing her doctoral dissertation on the rhetoric surrounding the thalidomide disaster.

Sara Polak (Leiden University Centre for the Arts in Society) is assistant professor in American Studies, focusing on US presidents and the politics of media contagion. She wrote *FDR in American Memory: Roosevelt and the Making of an Icon* (Johns Hopkins University Press, 2021) and co-edited *Violence and Trolling on Social Media. History, Affect and Effects of Online Vitriol* (Amsterdam University Press, 2020). She currently focuses on Trump's Twitter use and online cartoon politics. Polak teaches American literature and regularly comments on US politics and culture in Dutch media.

Angela M. Smith is Associate Professor in English and Gender Studies and Director of Disability Studies at the University of Utah. Her research focuses on body politics in American literature, cinema and popular culture. Her book *Hideous Progeny: Disability, Eugenics, and Classic Horror Cinema* (Columbia University Press, 2011) considers how classic American horror cinema exploits and alters eugenic understandings of disability. She has published in journals such as *Literature and Medicine*, *Post Script* and *College Literature* and in the essay collections *The Matter of Disability* (University of Michigan Press, 2019), *Horror Zone* (I.B. Tauris, 2010) and *Popular Eugenics* (Ohio University Press, 2006).

Priscilla Wald is R. Florence Brinkley Chair of English at Duke University, author of *Contagious: Cultures, Carriers, and the Outbreak Narrative* (Duke, 2008) and *Constituting Americans: Cultural Anxiety and Narrative Form* (Duke, 1995) and co-editor, with Matthew Taylor, of *American Literature* and, with David Kazanjian and Elizabeth McHenry, of the New York University Press book series *America in the Long Nineteenth Century*. She is on the board of the Centre for the Humanities and Medicine at Hong Kong University and co-directs the First Book Institute with Sean Goudie at Penn State. She is working on a monograph entitled *Human Being After Genocide*.

Francis Ray White is a senior lecturer in Sociology at the University of Westminster in London, UK where they teach extensively in gender and sexuality studies and the sociology of the body. Their main research interests are in the discourses of the 'obesity epidemic' as well as questions of fat, queer and trans embodiment. Francis's recent work has been published in the edited collection *Thickening Fat* (Routledge, 2019) and in journals including *Somatechnics*, *Critical Public Health*, *Fat Studies* and *Sexualities*.

Preface

Priscilla Wald

WHEN THE EDITORS and contributors submitted the initial manuscript of *Embodying Contagion*, none of us anticipated we would be making our final revisions during a global pandemic. The experience vividly illustrates many of the issues addressed in the volume, notably how such an event has starkly confronted us with the inequities and injustices that urgently require our attention. We can no longer call for change. At all levels, we have to make it. All of us.

The pandemic should not have taken governments by surprise. We have had considerable warning. In the mid-1990s, mainstream journalism and popular culture became veritably obsessed with what the science journalist Laurie Garrett called *The Coming Plague*. Her 1994 account of what she described in her subtitle as *Newly Emerging Diseases in a World Out of Balance* came out of the 1989 conference 'Emerging Viruses: The Evolution of Viruses and Viral Diseases', held at the end of a decade in which HIV had made its disastrous global rounds, puncturing the sanguinity of the scientific medical establishment in the global North. The eradication of naturally occurring smallpox in the late 1970s, among other epidemiological and pharmacological feats, seemed poised to make the serious threat of communicable disease a thing of the past, but the subsequent decade manifested the prematurity of that promise, and the conference put the phrases 'disease emergence' and 'emerging infection' into widespread circulation.

While the HIV/AIDS pandemic was the most widely known virus to shatter the complacency, it was one among a group of newly identified or resurfacing catastrophic communicable diseases that the participants in the conference identified as part of a social, geopolitical and epidemiological phenomenon resulting from an increasingly global, interdependent and shrinking world. As human beings moved into areas in which human habitation had been sparse or non-existent, they came into contact with microbes to which they were immunologically naïve. As people and goods circulated with increasing ease and frequency, microbes circulated with them and mutated in the process. The film director and producer Wolfgang Peterson began his 1995 medical thriller, *Outbreak*, which chronicles the threat of a viral apocalypse, with an ominous warning from one of the conference organizers, the molecular biologist Joshua Lederberg, that 'the single biggest threat to man's continued dominance on this planet is the virus'.[1]

Writing in a post-conference edited volume, the epidemiologist D. A. Henderson, who had spearheaded the campaign to eradicate smallpox, notes the 'ill-founded complacency about infectious diseases' that had turned the attention of scientific medicine, including the Centers for Disease Control, away from that threat and towards chronic disease. 'It is evident now', he observes, 'as it should have been' in 1969, when the US Surgeon General had declared the threat of communicable disease 'marginal', that 'mutation and change are facts of nature, that the world is increasingly interdependent, and that human health and survival will be challenged, ad infinitum, by new and mutant microbes, with unpredictable pathophysiological manifestations.'[2] The microbiologist Richard M. Krause had issued that warning in 1981 in *The Restless Tide: The Persistent Challenge of the Microbial World*. The problem of disease emergence had to be addressed not just as a problem for scientific medicine and epidemiology; it stemmed from globalisation, development practices and the inequities they exacerbated as well as the environmental devastation they accelerated. Accordingly, the problem had to be addressed through widespread changes in behaviours and practices at the individual, collective and governmental levels.

As the message circulated through scientific publications, mainstream journalism, and popular fiction and film, it produced a set of conventions – a vocabulary, images and storylines – that collectively comprise what I have called 'the outbreak narrative': an account of an outbreak – in its most archetypal and apocalyptic incarnation – that begins in the forests of the global South and travels into the metropoles of the global North, where it threatens humanity with extinction before heroic epidemiologists and other medical professionals in the global North draw on their expertise and the technologies of scientific medicine to save the species. As this story, exemplified by *Outbreak*, proliferated in the mainstream media and popular culture, it shored up faith in scientific medicine as it undercut the message of the need for radical change the conference participants sought to disseminate. And it created a popular sensation that titillated as it terrified.

The proliferation of the outbreak narrative attests to its broad appeal, raising the question of what cultural needs it fills. The essays in this volume address those questions, considering the titillation as well as the terror, the spread of ideas and affects as well as microbes and mutations, the power and danger of bodies in contact, and the fragility and tenacity of social bonds. The bodies circulating through these essays map the contacts of an increasingly interconnected, if often alienating, world. They bear witness to the social, political and economic inequities creating the conditions that turn outbreaks into pandemics.

This timely volume appears in the midst of a confluence of crises that make its vivid analyses undeniable. Certainly, what was once an insufficiently heeded warning can no longer be ignored. We are living the consequences of doing so. But what exactly will change remains unclear. The pandemic and the high-profile case of the police murder of a compliant and hand-cuffed Black man, George Perry Floyd Jr, have brought widespread media attention to structural racism in the US and elsewhere. Writing in June 2020, I am hopeful that the massive protests worldwide will translate into the profound social, economic and geopolitical transformations that are so very long overdue. But how quickly and comprehensively we make those changes remains an urgent question.

I hear the phrase 'when we go back to normal' with deep concern. We cannot – should not – 'go back to normal'. The lesson of the pandemic should teach us that 'normal' is what got us here, and that the natural and social worlds are inseparable. There is no such thing as a natural disaster; our systematic inequities find expression in pandemics as well as catastrophic weather events. Racism, resource exhaustion, global poverty, environmental devastation, climate change: all, as the 1989 conference made clear, are interconnected as well as predisposing factors of pandemics. The outbreak narrative bespeaks a fundamental anxiety, perhaps even antipathy, in humanity's engagement with the idea of 'nature'.

Countless observers over the years have sounded the alarm about humanity's often hostile relation to our environs. The German Jewish philosopher Hannah Arendt noted the curious response to the 1957 Sputnik launch recorded in the media: not 'pride or awe at the tremendousness of human power and mastery', but 'relief about the first "step toward escape from men's imprisonment to the earth"', which is to say toward escape from mortality.[3] If mutation and change are facts of nature, and extinction or evolution are the fate of all species, then the one certainty is that the human future, if there is one, will not resemble its past. It is the insight Robert Neville achieves, in Richard Matheson's 1954 *I Am Legend*, that 'normalcy [is] a majority concept, the standard of many and not the standard of just one man', and that it is he, not the viral vampires he has been fighting, who has become monstrous – and legendary – now.[4]

Neville's insight applies to geopolitical as well as evolutionary change, and the impossibility of disentangling them is evident in the uncannily insightful subgenre of science fiction horror, where the monstrous often trends towards the allegorical and the idea of the human is always just beyond definition. The highly evolved homicidal vegetation of the hybrid genre of science fiction horror in the mid-twentieth century – the 'intellectual carrot' in *The Thing from Another World*, the pod people of *Invasion of the Body Snatchers*, the carnivorous flora of *The Day of the Triffids* – and the familiar hybrid human/virus antagonists that speak in defence of an aggrieved earth in fictional outbreak narratives of the late twentieth century express the latent antipathy Arendt had noted.[5] These demonic adversaries are diagnostic, manifesting a projected hostility in Nature that justifies humanity's ostensible need to dominate our environs. Humankind is in a death match, fighting to survive, which is synonymous with resisting change. But they also diagnose the structural fault lines obscured by the term 'natural disaster' or the displacement of human responsibility onto 'enemy microbes' and other monsters. 'Humanity' is not all-encompassing; the 'human' is a mobile term, and 'us' and 'them' are contingent and contextual. The history of racial colonialism includes the naturalisation of populations, and the genre of science fiction horror, which is often the genre of the fictional outbreak narrative, frequently stages the return of a colonial repressed: a threat to white supremacy.

The term 'Viropolitics' manifests this slippage between the material and the monstrous. While HIV/AIDS demonstrated how catastrophic communicable diseases can remap social relations and geopolitics, the changes resulted from the circulation of both microbes and stories. The essays that follow explore these fundamental entanglements. They show how apocalyptic threats have cycled through journalism and popular culture, with the outbreak narrative rising in response to each potentially catastrophic pandemic, such as the extensive West African Ebola outbreak of 2014–16. But as HIV/AIDS became increasingly less newsworthy, and warnings about the coming plague became sparser in the mainstream media, the viral zombie, a significant focus in the following essays, also underwent a transformation, appearing more frequently as a figure of sympathy, playfulness, even sexiness, as the world acclimated steadily to intensified globalisation.

We were woefully underprepared for COVID-19, and we are similarly not collectively heeding the threat of climate change, which in 2020 hangs more urgently in the air not least because of its role in the rapid global spread of SARS-CoV-2. Apocalyptic narratives – of outbreaks or weather-related disasters – show how anxieties surrounding geopolitical transformation find expression in the more dramatic scenarios of species-threatening events. As these stories titillate us, they shape experience: who, what and where a culture locates its threats, its definitions of 'us' and 'them', its response to other cultures and to the planet.

Apocalypse is about revelation and renewal, and these stories bear witness to how humans incorporate threats to our survival into mythic occasions of rejuvenation – opportunities, that is, to promise the inevitable triumph of humanity over species-threatening events, and, in the process, to affirm humanity collectively as unique, intangible, ineffable: a disembodied concept that is not ultimately subject to the decay or transformation represented by the zombie virus and a force that will ultimately use its distinctive ingenuity to conquer the ravages of Nature in its various meanings and its multiple threats. It is a narrative that dangerously obviates the need for change. The immediate question of how to survive obscures the more challenging question of how we might live responsibly and equitably in a shrinking – and ever more interdependent – world. As in the myths of classical literature, however, disruptions in the natural world signal crises in the social world. Adverse environmental events, such as pandemics, catastrophic weather disasters, and long-term climate change, illuminate the structural violence of a world out of balance and the urgent need for radical social and global transformation. The essays that follow take up these questions as they consider *The Viropolitics of Horror and Desire in Contemporary Discourse*.

Notes

1. *Outbreak*, Wolfgang Petersen, dir. (Warner Brothers, 1995).
2. Donald A. Henderson, 'Surveillance Systems and Intergovernmental Cooperation', in Stephen S. Morse (ed.), *Emerging Viruses* (New York: Oxford University Press, 1993), pp. 283–9.
3. Hannah Arendt, *The Human Condition* (Chicago: The University of Chicago Press, 1958), pp. 1–2.
4. Richard Matheson, *I Am Legend* (New York: Fawcett Publications, 1954), p. 160.
5. *The Thing from Another World*, Christian Nyby, dir. (Winchester Pictures Corporation, 1951); *Invasion of the Body Snatchers*, Don Siegel, dir. (Walter Wanger Productions, 1956); *The Day of the Triffids*, Steve Sekely, dir. (Security Pictures Ltd, 1962).

Embodying the Fantasies and Realities of Contagion

Megen de Bruin-Molé and Sara Polak

FROM *OUTBREAK* to *The Walking Dead*, apocalyptic narratives of infection, contagion and global pandemic are an inescapable part of post-millennial popular culture. Yet these fears and fantasies are too virulent to simply be quarantined within fictional texts; vocabulary and metaphors from outbreak narratives have infiltrated how news media, policymakers and the general public view the world and the people within it. Indeed, popular cultural imaginations of outbreaks seem to have played an important role in responses to the coronavirus outbreak of 2020. In 2008, Priscilla Wald outlined the history of the 'outbreak narrative', emphasising the ways in which the politics of fictions and the fictions of politics have always been intertwined. Wald traces contagion from its early uses in the fourteenth century, where it literally meant 'to touch together', connoting dangerous or corrupting ideas and attitudes: 'Revolutionary ideas were contagious, as were heretical beliefs and practices'.[1] In contemporary contexts, we find narratives in which humans' 'futile efforts to defend themselves against the threat of illness in the daily interactions' are 'made global by contemporary transportation and commerce'.[2] In all instances, contagion serves as 'a principle of classification that displayed the rationale of social organization and was, therefore, the force that bound people to the relationships that constituted the terms of their existence'.[3] Over its long history, the outbreak narrative has transcended the boundaries of any single text or discourse to become myth: 'an explanatory story that is not specifically authored, but emerges from a group as an expression of the origins and terms of its collective identity'.[4] In today's always-in-crisis culture, outbreak is our shared mode of discourse. Riots in Minneapolis following the murder of George Floyd in 2020 seemed to 'suddenly erupt'; the popular discontent that led to the election of Donald Trump has often been read as 'festering under the surface'; when something 'goes viral', it 'spreads quickly'.

That said, each outbreak presents its own challenges and discursive quirks. With this collection of essays about the viropolitics of horror and desire in contemporary discourse, we hope to demonstrate how, in its own unique historical moment, each outbreak has contributed to a larger contemporary obsession with metaphors and modalities of contagion. Understanding these obsessions and their histories can help us to make sense of our current situation, and hopefully to recognise these patterns and prejudices more quickly in future moments of crisis. In particular, we want to place special emphasis on one specific object of the outbreak's viropolitics: the body or bodies that make contagion possible. In this we build on the histories of the contagious body laid out by interdisciplinary scholars like Margrit Shildrick, Sarah Juliet Lauro, Neel Ahuja, Edward P. Comentale and Aaron Jaffe. The interactions between human and non-human bodies form one aspect of this history of contagion, emphasising changing definitions of what it means to be (and be recognised as) human. Coronavirus, for example, has often been linked in the media to bats – animals that have been culturally understood as monsters for centuries. This happened as part of both the SARS outbreak in 2003 and the COVID-19 outbreak in 2019. In the case of COVID-19, many Western journalists incorrectly attributed the source of the virus in humans to bat-eating, and to Chinese 'wet markets' selling exotic animals. A viral video of a woman eating a bat in 'a Wuhan restaurant' seemed to corroborate this story – in reality, it was part of an old series of sensationalist videos from travel vlogger Wang Mengyun, and the video was not even filmed in China.[5] The transmission of coronavirus from non-human to human animals also involved a far more complex chain of global food industries. Regardless of the facts, fantasies of Asian others with 'exotic' and 'uncivilised' eating habits effectively served to demonise and dehumanise them, contributing to a worldwide surge in anti-Asian racism.

Fantasy and myth-making also play an important role in contagion's changing definitions. For Wald, microbial contagions 'take a mythic turn when they are cast as the response of the Earth itself to human beings who have ventured into primordial places they should not disturb'.[6] In the twenty-first century, as Ahuja points out, this mythic turn is further intensified:

> The living body is not only an ecology reproduced by constituent species (think of the life-sustaining work of gut bacteria or the ingested flesh of animals or plants). It is also an assemblage crosscut by technological, economic, and environmental forces (medical technologies, insurance markets, agricultural systems, toxic pollution) that render the body vulnerable as they reproduce its conditions of possibility.[7]

As contemporary science reveals the ways our bodies exist as shifting and sharing ecosystems rather than isolated and inviolate objects, contemporary culture unveils a seemingly endless series of new ways to be, to behave and to belong alongside other bodies. This was revealed with particular poignancy in the wake of the COVID-19 pandemic, which generated an outpouring of new strategies for intimacy and interaction under social distancing, but also prompted new waves of fear and violence towards certain bodies: towards masked bodies, towards unmasked bodies, and towards racialised bodies culturally marked as 'contagious'. The global increase in xenophobia following the pandemic offers all too many examples of this fear and violence in action.[8]

These shifting ways of being in an outbreak and the increased levels of work and labour they demand are also accompanied by other systemic forms of resistance to, and anxiety about, contagion. For Ahuja, the contemporary contagious body is symbolic of 'an anxiety about the dependence of the human body on forces that appear inhuman, even inhumane: medical technologies to extend, optimize, or end life; markets and institutions that unequally distribute resources for sustaining life; environmental processes that support, deprive, or injure bodies'.[9] The contagious body is a body that cannot be neatly quantified: it is a body in flux. Consequently, the contagious body is difficult to market, insure, regulate or reclaim – all of the processes central to twenty-first-century capitalist culture. As Shildrick suggests, in this context:

> vulnerability must be managed, covered over in the self, and repositioned as a quality of the other . . . in western discourse, the notion of the diseased, the unclean or the contaminated is never just an empirical or supposedly neutral descriptor, but carries the weight of all that stands against – and of course paradoxically secures – the normative categories of ontology and epistemology.[10]

Every time we talk about the contagious body, we negotiate the boundaries between bodies that are welcome, bodies that must be confined or silenced, and bodies that must be eradicated. We contribute to the contagion narrative and myth. For instance, during the COVID-19 pandemic, some countries emphasise monitoring body temperatures to detect potential cases, and practically everywhere, workers in the food supply chain have had to continue work as usual. Padmini Ray Murray tweeted about an Indian case of a food delivery service that listed, on the packaging, the body temperatures of the chef, the food packer, and the delivery boy, who might have been in contact with the food.[11] Employing workers' medical data in the interest of reassuring consumers sheltered in place, creates, as Murray suggests a kind of 'data apartheid', through which labourers' data are used not to protect their own health, but to comfort paying customers.

Fantasising Contagion

For ease of reading and teaching, this book is divided into two sections: one emphasising the role of epidemic fantasies in theory and reality, the other focused on epidemic theories and realities in fantasy. Despite this structure, however, we hope it will quickly become apparent that such distinctions are actually quite difficult to make. This collection consequently aims to problematise and deconstruct such binaries rather than reinforcing them. Where previous scholarly work has examined the spread of epidemic realities in horror fiction, the essays in this volume also consider how epidemic fantasies and fears influence realities. Bringing scholarship from cultural and media studies into conversation with scholarship from the medical humanities and social sciences, the collection aims to give readers a fuller picture of the viropolitics of contagious bodies in contemporary global culture. In this we aim to move away from the binary 'two cultures' approach to viropolitics and academic research described by Tim J. Lustig and James Peacock (2013), which addresses the continuing discursive practice, from the mid-twentieth century, of strictly differentiating science and literature/culture.

In this collection we especially want to highlight the persistent intersection of contagion discourse with narratives of fantasy or 'the fantastic'. The fantastic – whether framed as a genre, a mode or a discourse – pervades narratives of outbreak. In academic and journalistic discourse, the fantastical nature of outbreak narratives often results in their dismissal as fanciful or hysterical, and those who spread them as uneducated or delusional. This is not a new perspective on the fantastic. In 1817 the poet and critic Samuel Taylor Coleridge described 'Imagination' as a literary form distinct from and superior to the 'Fancy' that dominated many novels of his time.[12] Many years later structuralist critic Tzvetan Todorov would define the literary fantastic as follows:

> In a world which is indeed our world . . . there occurs an event which cannot be explained by the laws of this same familiar world. The person who experiences the event must opt for one of two possible solutions . . . The fantastic occupies the duration of this uncertainty. Once we choose one answer or the other, we leave the fantastic for the neighbouring genre, the uncanny or the marvelous . . . The possibility of hesitation between the two creates the fantastic effect.[13]

For Todorov, writing almost twenty years after (though largely unaffected by) the publication of J. R. R. Tolkien's landmark fantasy narrative *The Lord of the Rings* in 1954, there is a clear distinction between the interpretation of events privileged in the uncanny (which privileges the supernatural explanation), the marvellous (which privileges the scientific or rational explanation) and the fantastic (which hesitates between the uncanny and the marvellous). This distinction has been highly influential, but has proved unsatisfactory to categorise the wealth of twentieth-century art and narrative that labels itself as 'fantasy', most of which relies heavily on the suspension of disbelief and the acceptance of *another* world, with laws that differ from our own.

Due to the incredibly broad range of modern texts categorised as fantastical, as well as the fact that scholarly interest in this type of fiction is relatively recent, definitions of what fantastical fiction is and implies are varied. For major theorists in the field, it has primarily been a question of genre.[14] In this approach the fantastic is defined as distinct from the science fiction genre, in that fantasy deals with 'the construction of the impossible, whereas science fiction may be about the unlikely, but is grounded in the scientifically possible'.[15] In the introduction to the *Cambridge Companion to Fantasy Literature* (2012), Edward James and Farah Mendlesohn suggest that a hold-all definition of fantasy is ultimately inadequate, and represents a misdirection of effort. Instead, they propose a system where we consider *gradations* of the fantastic, drawing on Attebery's mathematical analysis of fantasy as a 'fuzzy set', or 'a group of texts that share, to a greater degree or other, a cluster of common tropes which may be objects but may also be narrative techniques'.[16]

Regardless of the definition of fantasy that theorists use, or of their theoretical approach, studies of fantasy and the fantastic still tend to focus on texts at the highbrow end of the cultural spectrum. It is generally no longer necessary to defend oneself when embarking on an academic study of genre fiction (fantasy, horror, science fiction), particularly considering the widespread academic interest in the fantastic prevalent from the latter half of the twentieth century, but the distinction between 'serious' and 'trivial' fiction highlighted by Coleridge in 1817 still pervades academic approaches to contagion narrative, much as the distinction between 'reality' and 'fiction' is used to divide those studies which are seen to have a valuable impact on politics and society from those which are purely cultural, that is, trivial or escapist. In this collection, we hope to demonstrate how the fantasies, horrors and desires of even the most trivial contagion fictions can return to shape new realities.

Containing Contagion

In their collection *Diseases and Disorders in Contemporary Fiction*, Lustig and Peacock note that one can, on a societal and cultural level, speak of a 'syndrome syndrome' – the tendency to understand any form of unconventionality or imperfection in individuals and societies as a syndrome, is itself a syndrome plaguing contemporary culture.[17] In the same way, we can see an 'epidemic epidemic' and a 'contagion contagion'. Therefore, to avoid a plague of self-referential contagiousness, a word on terminology: in this book's title and throughout, we often refer to contagion, both in its literal meaning of 'the communication of disease from one organism to another, by close contact', and as a metaphor to denote any kind of spreading. The contagion metaphor is itself highly contagious, and we have often allowed this infectious wordplay to bleed into the language. Although there is clearly also a risk to engaging too unselfconsciously in the very phenomenon that one is also analysing, we have chosen not to restrict ourselves overly in doing so – but caution remains necessary. It is very important to be aware that this metaphor, like any metaphor, carries its own ideological implications. As Lauren Oyler shows in the *New York Times Magazine* article 'When Did Everything Get So Toxic?' (2 October 2018):

> [the] image conjured is one of a passive population, helpless to defend ourselves against the invisible but deadly ideological forces that surround us, corrupting our purity and then turning us into agents of our own destruction . . . The epithet concentrates structural criticism in the symptom, not the cause.[18]

Toxicity is a different metaphor than contagion or virality, but this image of a helpless population under attack from a force that corrupts its purity, and turns it against itself, is the same, as is the notion that any contamination directly implies a risk of complete 'turning' from pure to toxic, from healthy to infected and infectious, from master to slave, and from human to zombie.

Naturally, no book on contemporary bodies of contagion would be complete without this final figure: as a famously 'creolized and creolizing' monster, the zombie has pervaded most of the chapters in this collection in one way or another.[19] Echoing the mythologisation of contagion more broadly, several chapters in this collection offer an extended look at how, in the words of Sarah Juliet Lauro, the zombie serves alternately as 'a metaphor, a symbol, an allegory, a figure, and an icon', all aggregating into the contemporary 'zombie myth'.[20] In fact, zombified 'monsters' make an appearance in our very first chapter, on 'The Krokodil Drug Menace, Cross-Genre Body Horror and the Zombie Apocalypse' (by Peter Burger). But as Lauro points out, reading 'the zombie in the light of its full historical, anthropological, and mythological context suggests how we might rethink other myths and symbols and their sources in order to look at a wider range of unintended significations'.[21] Rather than taking the zombie as either a static figure or a totalising one, each chapter in this collection stops to consider the local, specific and viropolitical implications of the infected, 'zombified' body.

Burger's chapter, which details a number of Russian and European medical reports and news stories about Krokodil – a mysterious drug with allegedly gruesome, zombifying effects – shows how contagion narratives and popular cultural discourse impact news media. Crucially, the existence of the drug remains uncertain, to say nothing of its actual effects. Although they purport to share nothing more than the facts, then, these reports about the spread of Krokodil unwittingly morph into horror stories, made all the more horrifying by their repeated claims to objectivity. Users of Krokodil are constructed as zombified monsters, who are simultaneously victims of a substance that eats them alive, and innately criminal and societal outcasts.

Sara Polak's chapter '"Preparedness 101: Zombie Pandemic" and the Ebola Scare – How the CDC's Use of Zombie Pop Culture Helped Fan a Nationalist Outbreak Narrative' (chapter 2) closely analyses a public information campaign that uses the zombie as a readily available monster of otherness: the Centers for Disease Control's (CDC) Zombie Apocalypse campaign to increase disaster preparedness among the American population. It does not look specifically at implementation, but reads the zombie metaphor that drove the campaign's central text (a comic) in the context of the ideological implications of the contagion metaphor. The chapter shows that contagion has actually been understood by American publics as an exclusionary pretext to 'close the borders' and 'stop flights', in order to 'keep out' Ebola. Implicitly this is read as a call to keep out non-white people – for instance by Donald Trump, whose tweets in response to the Ebola epidemic are analysed in the article, alongside tweets that explicitly link the CDC's zombie comic to the Ebola outbreak narrative.

Despite their inclusion of the zombie, as these chapters demonstrate, the metaphor of zombie-ism is far from the only lens through which we might consider the contagious body. As Wald points out, epidemiology involves 'a fascination not just with the novelty and danger of the microbes but also with the changing social formations of a shrinking world'.[22] At heart, contagion narratives are not about disease at all, but rather about the warring horrors and desires inherent in human and non-human embodiment, networks and contagion vectors in an increasingly risk-averse world, illustrating the 'power and danger of bodies in contact' in a globalised world.[23] Contributors reflect on the many contexts and mediated spaces of contagion throughout this book. When they occur in reports of real events in the real world around us, contagion metaphors introduce narrative schemata from popular culture that are often both hard to miss, and easy to take for granted as 'natural' or ahistorical. Madison Krall, Marouf Hasian Jr and Yvonne Karyn Clark (chapter 3) discuss how the outbreak narrative around the Zika viral outbreak in 2016–17 gave rise in American news media and policy documents to an increasingly strong rhetoric of securitisation and militarisation, echoing the same process that was seen in responses to the 2013–15 Ebola epidemic in West Africa. Their critical praxiological studies approach focuses on determining the specific practical application of policies and guidelines. They also examine how these ways of applying and implementing policies affect the context in which they are introduced, and how the discourse of policy documents, informational leaflets and guidelines influence such processes.

In Angela Smith's chapter, 'An Affectionate Epidemic: How Disability Goes Viral on Social Media' (chapter 4), it becomes evident that contagion and virality are not only matters of horror and disgust, but also of desire. Smith explores the widespread and global affective economy of disability images on social media platforms like Facebook. The chapter analyses the practice of 'like-farming' that invites users to like, share and respond 'Amen' to posts portraying disabled people – often children, usually without their consent, and with a story that is fabricated. Users who do 'like' and share such posts generally do not realise that they are supporting an unethical economic model, but even when they are made aware of this, the affective attraction of spreading such material continues unabated. The desire of many Facebook users to believe that their affirmation is helpful to the disabled person portrayed outweighs their knowledge that the narrative is a forged construction, designed to benefit other people and interests. Cultural contagiousness may sometimes seem positive and affectionate – in this case disability going viral – but can be just as violent as its more explicitly horrific equivalents.

Rounding off the first part of the collection, Francis Ray White employs Judith Butler's theory of resignification to show how obesity has become discursively connected to climate change – first in British policy documents in the early twenty-first century, and subsequently in tabloids and elsewhere. In '"Fatties Cause Global Warming": The Strange Entanglement of Obesity and Climate Change' (chapter 5), White examines how both issues are framed as 'epidemics', suggesting that they share a root cause. In this contagion narrative, fat bodies carry sole or extra responsibility for climate change as agents and harbingers of social, moral and environmental collapse.

These first five chapters concern non-fictional, real-life events, media campaigns and reporting that employ monstrosity and the fantastic narratively and discursively. In the remaining chapters the collection pivots to consider fantastical discourses, where actual zombies, monsters and spectres embody contagion. Sandra Becker's work on viral vampires and anti-intellectualism in '"Time is of the Essence, Doctor": Twenty-First-Century (Post-)Apocalyptic Fiction, White Fatherhood and Anti-Intellectual Tendencies in FX's *The Strain*' (chapter 6), and Megen de Bruin-Molé's analysis of the friendly zombie in 'Killable Hordes, Chronic Others and "Mindful" Consumers: Rehabilitating the Zombie in Twenty-First-Century Popular Culture' (chapter 7), show how the fantastical figure of the zombie changes over time to adapt to the culture in which it is established. Analysing Guillermo del Torro's TV series *The Strain*, Becker argues that the series' narration is underwritten by anti-intellectual tendencies, privileging its main protagonist's role as father over his role as CDC investigator and medical scientist and offering fantasies of evil spirits in place of real-life systematic flaws and threats. Similarly, De Bruin-Molé looks at how late twentieth-century consumption and identity politics have impacted representations of the zombie in popular culture, showing how the rise of the 'sympathetic' or rehabilitated zombie takes neoliberal values to new extremes.

Chapters 8 and 9 each study fictional drama and narrative that specifically focuses on contagious bodies in the context of queerness and of the AIDS epidemic. Mica Hilson's 'Networks, Desire and Risk Management in Gay Contagion Fiction' (chapter 8) examines this dynamic in the context of twenty-first century online gay contagion fiction, which is itself a medium that spreads very easily. Although rarely mentioning AIDS explicitly, the protagonists in the analysed online short stories face contagious health risks that they are ultimately unable to avoid despite their high level of risk management. In comparison to the plethora of zombie stories that follow the neoliberal ideology of self-managed health and survival, Hilson argues, these fictional short stories and their 'complex ambivalence to contagion' shed a more realistic light on contagious risks in our globalised, networked world. Astrid Haas's chapter '"This Long Disease, My Life": AIDS Activism and Contagious Bodies in Larry Kramer's *The Normal Heart* and *The Destiny of Me*' focuses on issues around gay sexuality and AIDS activism, as portrayed specifically through late twentieth-century drama. Haas thereby shows the limits of the dramas' strategy to change societal discourses by reflecting on the discriminatory merging of gay men (with supposedly deformed identities) and IV drug addicts to a contagious, monstrous outsider group threatening the nation at the height of the AIDS epidemic.

Elana Gomel's chapter, 'The Epidemic of History: Contagion of the Past in the Era of the Never-Ending Present' (chapter 10), is something of a cross-over between the two parts. It concerns both historical events that are fictionalised through the addition of fantastical elements, and fantastical narratives that historicise utopian and dystopian visions which might otherwise be lost. Like other chapters in this second half of the volume, it is primarily concerned with explicitly fictional depictions of contagion. Gomel's analysis of post-historical monsters aligns itself with both parts of the collection, however, in that it ties together the zombie *topos* in popular culture and zombie-like figures in historical narrative.

As each of these chapters demonstrates, although contagion can take many different forms, in talking about and narrativising contagious bodies we also fix them momentarily in place, allowing us to symbolically reclaim and regulate them once more. As with other kinds of 'monsters' the contagious body makes a variety of contemporary anxieties manifest (and therefore manageable). Its 'epidemiology turns an outbreak of communicable disease into a narrative', making 'the routes of transmission visible' and helping 'epidemiologists anticipate and manage the course of the outbreak'.[24] This is where fantasies and narratives of contagion meet, mingle with, and supersede real-world fears. In an age where fact and fiction seem increasingly difficult to separate, contagious bodies (and the discourses that contain them) continually blur established boundaries between real and unreal, legitimacy and frivolity, science and the supernatural.

Notes

1. Priscilla Wald, *Contagious: Cultures, Carriers, and the Outbreak Narrative* (London and Durham, NC: Duke University Press, 2008), p. 12.
2. Wald, *Contagious*, p. 4.
3. Wald, *Contagious*, p. 14.
4. Wald, *Contagious*, p. 9.
5. James Palmer, 'Don't Blame Bat Soup for the Coronavirus', *Foreign Policy*, 27 January 2020, *https://foreignpolicy.com/2020/01/27/coronavirus-covid19-dont-blame-bat-soup-for-the-virus/* (accessed 2 July 2020).
6. Wald, *Contagious*, p. 10.

7. Neel Ahuja, *Bioinsecurities: Disease Interventions, Empire, and the Government of Species* (Durham, NC: Duke University Press, 2016), p. viii.
8. HRW, 'Covid-19 Fueling Anti-Asian Racism and Xenophobia Worldwide', Human Rights Watch (HRW), 12 May 2020, *https://www.hrw.org/news/2020/05/12/covid-19-fueling-anti-asian-racism-and-xenophobia-worldwide* (accessed 25 June 2020).
9. Ahuja, *Bioinsecurities*, p. vii.
10. Margrit Shildrick, *Embodying the Monster: Encounters with the Vulnerable Self* (London and Thousand Oaks: Sage, 2002), pp. 68, 70.
11. Ray Murray, Twitter post, 20 April 2020, 4.32 pm, *https://twitter.com/praymurray/status/1252243718725423105/photo/1.*
12. Samuel T. Coleridge, 'Bibliographia Literaria', in Donald R. Stauffer (ed.), *Selected Poetry and Prose* (New York: Modern Library, 1951), p. 156.
13. Tzvetan Todorov, *The Fantastic: A Structural Approach to a Literary Genre* (Oxford: Blackwell Publishers Inc., 1977), pp. 25–6.
14. Kathryn Hume, *Fantasy and Mimesis: Responses to Reality in Western Literature* (New York: Methuen, 1984); William R. Irwin, *The Game of the Impossible: A Rhetoric of Fantasy* (Urbana: University of Illinois Press, 1976); Rosemary Jackson, *Fantasy: The Literature of Subversion* (London: Routledge, 1998); Colin N. Manlove, *The Impulse of Fantasy Literature* (London: Palgrave MacMillan, 1982); Todorov, T*he Fantastic.*
15. Edward James and Farah Mendlesohn (eds), *The Cambridge Companion to Fantasy Literature* (Cambridge (UK): Cambridge University Press, 2012), p. 1.
16. James and Mendlesohn, *The Cambridge Companion to Fantasy Literature*, p. 1.
17. Tim Lustig and James Peacock (eds), *Diseases and Disorders in Contemporary Fiction: The Syndrome Syndrome* (New York: Routledge, 2013), p. 1.
18. L. Oyler, 'When Did Everything Get So "Toxic"?' *The New York Times*, 2 October 2018, *https://www.nytimes.com/2018/10/02/magazine/when-did-everything-get-so-toxic.html* (accessed 5 August 2020).
19. Lustig and Peacock, *Diseases and Disorders in Contemporary Fiction*, p. 3
20. Sarah J. Lauro, *The Transatlantic Zombie: Slavery, Rebellion, and Living Death* (New Brunswick: Rutgers University Press, 2015), p. 4.
21. Lauro, *The Transatlantic Zombie*, p. 25.
22. Wald, *Contagious*, p. 2.
23. Wald, *Contagious*, p. 13.
24. Wald, *Contagious*, p. 19.

PART ONE

EPIDEMIC FANTASIES IN REALITY

1

The Krokodil Drug Menace, Cross-Genre Body Horror and the Zombie Apocalypse

Peter Burger

IN 2011, ALARMING stories about the new drug krokodil started to appear in Western European and American news media. Originating in Russia and neighbouring countries, krokodil is a home-brewed desomorphine-based opiate, associated with horrific images of decaying limbs. For drug chemistry cognoscenti, its name echoes that of alpha-chlorocodide, an intermediate product in the process that turns codeine into desomorphine.[1] The name is more popularly understood, however, as reflecting the fact that it turns the addicts' skin scaly and green, or, alternatively, makes them look as if they have been ravaged by a crocodile's jaws. Gruesome images of krokodil's alleged effects proliferate on news sites, in medical journals, and in YouTube videos, generating thousands of comments. A critique of krokodil discourse in these diverse sites and genres warrants an approach that merges the sociology of social problems with folklore studies.

The krokodil menace is the latest example of society's penchant to construct drug users as monsters. A dominant trope in recent drug discourse is that of the zombie, that is, not the original living dead of Haitian folklore, but the pop culture and Western contemporary folklore zombies that take their cue from George Romero's cannibalistic ghouls. Contaminated and contagious, present-day 'drug zombies' may be black or white, but they are invariably represented as poor and marginalised, even among drug users. The stories told about krokodil and its users – whether vernacular, tabloid, educational or academic – display a strong cross-genre similarity, and ultimately feed the hegemonic narrative that dehumanises drug addicts of low socio-economic status. Merging global news and amusement media discourse and imagery with vernacular discourse, they also exemplify the interconnected and hybrid nature of present-day folklore.

Krokodil is Coming

Known in Russia since 2003, krokodil appeared on the radar of Western European and American news media, medical researchers and drug counsellors in 2011.[2] The latest drug menace was said to be more lethal than any of its predecessors – and it was rapidly moving westwards. I will have occasion to reappraise these claims in subsequent paragraphs, but for the moment I shall stick with the story as it can be traced in news coverage and in the majority of papers in medical journals.

Although news media and medical authorities alike classified krokodil as the latest designer drug, this label, connoting style and affluence, belies its underclass nature. 'Home-brewed', another common epithet, comes closer: krokodil is described as a toxic concoction of codeine, matchstick heads, gasoline, iodine, bathroom cleaner, paint thinner and hydrochloric acid – practices and accounts may vary.[3] Cooked up in kitchen labs, it is injected intravenously by Russian drug addicts too poor to afford heroin. Its effects are understood to be more vicious than those of other drugs. Krokodil is said to be instantly addictive and infallibly lethal. According to a 2011 feature in *Pravda*'s English-language edition, 'Some may take it for five years, but many people die after taking their first dose of this drug'.[4] Users are said to have a one-to-two-year life expectancy, during which time their bodies are eaten away from the inside. News media display, with varying degrees of restraint, their gangrenous limbs and mutilated bodies.

Originally confined to Russia, Ukraine, Georgia and other former Soviet republics, in 2011 krokodil was observed migrating westwards. According to a paper published in the *American Journal of Medicine*, krokodil use 'has been spreading rapidly across Europe'.[5] European news media sounded the alarm: '"Krokodil" killer drug sweeps through Europe', ran a headline on Belgian news site *Het Laatste Nieuws* in October 2011. Employing a striking metaphor that plays on xenophobia and nationalism, the article claimed, 'Already the krokodil rubs its body against the Belgian and Dutch borders'. In the accompanying picture a woman holds up her mutilated forearm, allowing an unimpeded view of its bones and tendons.

Individual cases in Western Europe were first spotted in Germany (October 2011), Norway (August 2012), the Netherlands (March 2013) and the UK (October 2013).[6] Across the Atlantic, unconfirmed reports from Canada (November 2013) were followed by the first 'official' US case in December 2013, a Missouri patient who lost a finger to the drug.[7] In December 2013, too, news media drew attention to the first patient in Mexico, a 17-year-old girl, highlighting the lurid detail that she had injected the drug in her genitals.[8]

In spite of headlines like 'Doctors confirm: Use of flesh-eating opioid drug krokodil is spreading in U.S.', these are, without exception, scattered, individual cases, often unconfirmed or eventually labelled as false alarms by law enforcement and medical authorities.[9] News media initially downplayed this uncertainty, dwelling on the alarmist claims and largely ignoring the retractions. Eventually though, in October and November 2013, the lack of evidence sparked a backlash. Pointing out that the horrific skin lesions found with American patients were probably MRSA infections or other known sequelae of 'ordinary' heroin use, a growing number of US news media slammed the krokodil threat as mere media hype: 'Krokodil concerns lack teeth' (*Newsweek*, 28 October 2013).[10] After 2015, news coverage of krokodil use and dire warnings by health authorities subsided in the US, but they made a fresh resurgence in the UK in 2018, with headlines such as 'Flesh-rotting "zombie" drug Krokodil "has arrived in the UK" – and it's 10 times stronger than heroin' (*The Mirror*, 1 November 2018).[11]

Using material from varied and at first sight disparate media worlds – news sites, medical journals, and YouTube videos and user comments – I will examine the way this purported drug epidemic and its victims were discursively constructed in institutional and vernacular (or 'folk') venues.

The Vernacular Public Sphere

Novelty drug panics have frequently been analysed from a constructionist perspective on social problems.[12] Regardless of their grounding in real-life conditions, these need to be recognised and promoted by claims makers.

The sociology of social problems leads us to expect a mostly top-down process, in which experts, policymakers and other high-status claims makers strive for the acceptance of their claims about the nature and proposed solutions to the new threat.[13] News media usually do not act as claims makers in their own right, but rather transmit the claims of others, adapted to news media formats. Eventually, at the very bottom of this trickle-down model, the claims reach the public.

But this drug epidemic is different. With the coming of Web 2.0, the vernacular public sphere has grown more prominent. In the words of folklorist Robert G. Howard, the vernacular exists 'alongside but apart from institutions', for example in user comments on news sites or in more elaborate forms such as sick jokes and Photoshop humour in response to shocking news.[14] English and communication studies scholar Trevor J. Blank reads these intentionally tasteless responses to death, disaster and scandal as counter-hegemonic: they voice vernacular criticism of the official perspective on these topics, as expounded by mainstream news media.[15] Rather than the deaths themselves, the jokes target the emotionally stifling media coverage. Following Michael Jackson's death, for example, jokes mercilessly spotlighted aspects of his life that news media necrologies piously glossed over: 'Like Michael Jackson always said: Live fast, die young, leave a vaguely Vietnamese looking woman's corpse'.[16]

Despite its subversive potential, Howard cautions that 'it is important to recognize that the vernacular can act to support or contest the institutional, and often it does a little of both'.[17] Most studies of the vernacular web, however, focus on its power to subvert and disrupt, for example fuelling the allegedly social media driven Arab Spring or fostering vaccination conspiracy theories.

The second major characteristic of the vernacular web is its hybridity.[18] Its very existence is vouchsafed by the infrastructure provided by institutions, for example Facebook, YouTube, Twitter, and comments sections on news sites. Expressing its own alternative authority, the vernacular necessarily invokes institutional authority. Institutions, in turn, avail themselves of blogs, Twitter accounts and Facebook pages to project an ethos-boosting grass-roots image. In the case of the alleged krokodil epidemic, I argue, the vernacular and the institutional are meshed to the point where it becomes difficult to say who is taking his cue from whom. Scholarly journals present images borrowed from YouTube videos as medical evidence and zombie metaphors pervade news discourse and users' comments as well as medical discourse. In this collusion, the vernacular web's counter-hegemonic potential is not realised. As I start to try and unpick this tangle, the first thread I will follow is that of drug scare rhetoric.

Drug Scare Rhetoric

Time and again, news media, policymakers and law enforcement personnel discover a drug that is worse than all previous ones. The rhetoric they employ to sell the public on this new menace has been analysed by the American historian of social problems Philip Jenkins. In his book *Synthetic Panics* (1999), Jenkins predicts that each fresh threat will be given a 'catchy label that would lend itself to imaginative permutations in news headlines'.[19] In this respect, krokodil was a journalist's dream come true. A small sample of headlines: 'The drug that eats junkies'; 'The drug that eats you alive'; 'Flesh-eating drug krokodil "could sink its teeth into British addicts", health workers warned'.[20]

The new drug, Jenkins says, will be depicted as more addictive, toxic and harmful than all its predecessors. Numbers are provided to substantiate the claim that we have an 'epidemic' on our hands. The numbers are personified through stories about individuals who suddenly turn extremely violent, or completely ruin themselves. The threat's urgency is enhanced by implicating the new drug in current social problems such as illegal immigration. And, finally: claims makers demonise the new drug's users by comparing them to zombies and other monsters.

A recent US instance of drug scare rhetoric is the prominent 2012 news story of Rudy Eugene (31), a black Haitian-American who was killed by a police officer when he was caught in the act of biting a 65-year-old homeless man's face. He was, according to the Miami police, under the influence of 'bath salts' – like krokodil, a DIY designer drug. In epithets evocative of George Romero-style cannibal zombies, Eugene was labelled the 'Miami Zombie' and the 'Causeway Cannibal' by news media. As it turned out later, Eugene was neither a cannibal (no human flesh was found in his digestive tract) nor a bath salts addict – only marijuana could be detected in his system. Both allegations were used to exonerate the policeman who had shot a frenzied, but naked and unarmed suspect.[21]

Like the paddo and bath salts incidents, cautionary stories about krokodil can be, and have been, employed to support a political agenda. In March 2013, Belgian minister for Social Affairs and Public Health, Laurette Onkelinx, referred to krokodil when she announced a bill to ban legal highs.[22] The extreme case of the monster drug is used to prop up anti-drug policies meant to combat more mundane substances. In a more general sense, monsters, and zombies in particular, are a rhetorical staple of public policy discourse – the institutional as well as the vernacular.

Public Policy Discourse – and Zombies

The Miami police force did not need to invent the zombie label for Rudy Eugene, since this was already firmly established as an explanation for bizarre and violent behaviour. In fact, a study of three major Miami area newspapers reveals that reporters consistently ignored interpretations of Eugene's behaviour in terms of mental illness, focusing instead on influences from outside that carried more cultural resonance.[23] Law enforcement sources favoured craze-inducing narcotics, the explanation that carried most weight among officials. Eugene's girlfriend claimed that he may have been a victim of drink spiking.[24] Her attorney, however, pointed the finger at cannibalism, 'a serious issue . . . very dangerous to the health and well-being of both the cannibal and the victim.'[25] Eugene's Haitian background cued explanations in terms of zombies. Exactly what had turned him into a zombie remained a matter of debate. The US Centers for Disease Control and Prevention (CDC) felt it necessary to publicly deny the existence of a zombie virus.[26]

A year earlier, however, the CDC itself had jumped on the zombie bandwagon, utilising the imaginary threat of a zombie apocalypse to urge citizens to prepare for real-life disasters.[27] Zombie talk also crops up in drug prevention programmes.[28] In 2011, the US Navy issued anti-bath salts posters in which a service member's face appears as a zombie in the mirror ('It's not a fad . . . It's a nightmare'). The Washington D.C. Department of Health ran series of ads showing decomposing teenagers who supposedly used synthetic marijuana or Spice: 'No one wants to take a zombie to the prom'.[29]

This use of zombie references is part of a general surge in popularity of the undead cannibals. During the nineties, but more emphatically since 2001, the number of movies, TV shows, video games, books and academic studies featuring the walking dead has increased.[30] Unlike the elitist, solitary and eloquent vampires, zombies appear as a ragged, incoherent mob. In pop culture as in policy discourse, they exemplify global threats particular to today's risk society, such as illegal immigration, terrorism and pandemics.[31] Unsurprisingly, zombie references also cropped up in Ebola news and rumours during the 2014 outbreak of the disease in western Africa. In one instance, a hoax news site presented a *World War Z* movie still of a black zombie as evidence that an Ebola victim had risen from the dead. Horror movie scenarios bled into concerns about real-world threats. As one medical doctor recalled, looking back on a public hearing:

> Fear during epidemics is based in distrust. People are quick to doubt experts, they criticize health officials for any perceived mistake, and they wonder aloud why more attention is not being paid to worst-case scenarios. As one frightened Texas congressman memorably said, 'Every outbreak novel or zombie movie you see starts with somebody from the government sitting in front of a panel like this saying there's nothing to worry about'.[32]

The word *zombie* triggers a frame for understanding, in which state and society have broken down, and evokes a post-apocalyptic landscape in which only clan solidarity and superior firepower stand between survival and the zombie hordes. Zombies provided both vernacular and institutional krokodil discourse with a ready-made metaphor. Before turning to an examination of krokodil coverage, comments and research, however, we need to look into the nature and history of its most powerful characteristic: more so than any preceding drug scare, krokodil rhetoric stands out because of its strongly visual nature.

Fear and Disgust

As a mediated menace, krokodil is first and foremost a visual, visceral threat: the stark images jump at the viewer from videos and news items. The prominence of the visual is a relative novelty in drug scares, although not unprecedented – remember the 1936 movie *Reefer Madness*, which had actors with contorted faces and postures portraying marijuana addicts. The most striking example of an anti-drug effort that depends on visual shock tactics for its effect, is the 2005 'Faces of Meth' campaign.[33] Displaying paired mugshots of meth addicts before and after they started using the drug, the campaign highlights signs of physical decay such as sores, sunken cheeks and rotten teeth ('meth mouth'). The stereotypical 'meth head' is described as 'white trash' or, again, as a 'zombie': although originally about Haitians, the metaphor can also be used for marginalised white people.[34]

The anti-meth campaign is an instance of 'pedagogical policing', that is, scaring young viewers away from methamphetamine by instilling fear and disgust.[35] To hammer home their message, 'You don't want to become like these people', the pictures have to allow viewers to identify themselves with those depicted. Merely showing the 'after' pictures would not achieve this effect. The images do not just show the meth problem, they could also be said to create it. This is demonstrated by the effects of their use in British news media: in the UK, which unlike the US did not cope with methamphetamine abuse, the same before and after mugshots helped engender a moral panic, which resulted in law reform: in 2007, crystal meth was upgraded from Class B to Class A, even though its use in the UK was 'almost non-existent'.[36] Such is the performative power of these pictures.

Disturbing Content Warning: 'You Cannot UNSEE This'

If the Faces of Meth are repulsive, krokodil images are up several notches on the scale of grossness. Many of these images are available for a general audience: CNN broadcast images of rotting feet and the picture of the woman showing the bare bones in her forearm has been published by news media worldwide. Usually, the images come with a warning. Viewers are protected from some of the most abhorrent YouTube videos about the drug – such as 'The Effects of Krokodil – Real Life Zombies': more than 1.7 million views since November 2013 – by a screen that requests them to log in, confirming they are over sixteen. In these cases, watching these images of human decay becomes a dare, an initiation, or something akin to legend tripping. Many viewers rate these videos as the most abhorrent they ever came across: 'I just watched a cat teach a baby squirrel to purr and then I watched this. I think I ripped my brain. . . That's the most horrifying thing I've ever seen! Nothing even comes close. Nothing . . .'[37]

After watching a video showing a woman with an empty eye socket, whose skull is almost bare, another viewer comments: 'What you will see here is 100-% REAL!!! NOT for kids! DO NOT watch if kids are around!!! From Russia with love. NO other drug is this insanely destructive!!! Keep in mind, you cannot UNSEE this!'[38] Why show these images? The sensation of seeing such images is itself addictive, because they are highly spectacular, and media know that viewers are interested in this kind of image-induced rush. In a typical US news clip (CNN, 11 October

2013: 'Krokodil crosses over to U.S. from Russia') the anchor apologises but insists: 'And I wanna warn you, because some of these pictures here that we're gonna show you, they *are* graphic, but it's important for people to understand how *awful* this is.' In the clip, a medical expert paints the nature of the threat in surprisingly vernacular language: 'It's a zombie drug', says Dr Abhin Singla, introduced as the Illinois doctor who treated krokodil addicts. 'I mean that literally, it kills you from the inside out. If you want a way to die, this is a way to die.'

So why would anyone want to use krokodil? Because of the price, the CNN reporter on the spot explains: '. . . to a heroin addict, there are a few things about the drug that are actually attractive. First of all, it's cheap, about a third the price of heroin.' Dr Singla concurs: 'I think eventually if it stays on the market long enough, you get people that are desperate addicts that can't support their own heroin habit, but can utilize this drug, not really caring about the consequences, and get the same high for a third of the price.' This final expert quote segues into the pay-off, voiced by the reporter: 'But the real price looks like *this* [gloved finger probing gangrenous foot] and the hope is that *these* images are horrific enough to prevent people from using the drug'.[39]

The argument that watching these images may prevent the use of krokodil can also be found – but less prominently – in comments on news items or YouTube videos: 'Sorry if this type of content "upsets" you, however if one person watches this and it causes them to think and not do stupid shyte then it's served some purpose. I made my teen daughter watch this, it gave her the horrors – good'.[40] At first sight, this may look like an instance of pedagogical policing, taking its cue from the Faces of Meth campaign.[41] The difference, however, is that krokodil footage and pictures skip the 'before' stage and dwell on the after-effects of krokodil use. For US and western European audiences, moreover, the majority of images depict foreign nationals: krokodil is invariably described as originating in Russia, and so do most of its victims. The most popular documentary on the subject, VICE's 2012 'Siberia: Krokodil Tears' (9.4 million views to date) is set in a remote part of Russia.[42]

Disgust and distance effectively bar most opportunities for identification with the addicts. In the Faces of Meth campaign, the first of each pair of pictures shows the addict as a deviant – these are mugshots, after all – but not as aliens or monsters. Krokodil imagery, in contrast, turns the addict into a spectacle and provides the audience with a front row seat at the freak-show.

Blaming the Victim

The social and geographical distance between viewer and victim all but precludes empathy. To be sure, a number of commenters do commiserate: 'heartbreaking poor people must be in so much pain'.[43] Some appeal to religion:

> So long as they aren't directly harming anyone but themselves, you should feel sympathy to drug users. It's not like they grew up wanting to be an addict. Many made bad choices that got them addicted in the first place, but most would give anything to quit and be normal. I know many on this site are religious (nothing wrong with that), so I ask you: how would Jesus handle an addict? Would he cast them out or would he offer compassion and try to help?[44]

Yet, analyses like the following remain minority opinions: 'Substance abuse is a disease; it isn't a moral lapse or stupidity'. Or: 'Communities need to start providing safe needles and spaces for users to shoot-up in or detox in as well. There is more help to provide that way than throwing people into jail, or simply allowing them to get sick and die on the streets'.[45]

Many comments are flippant or obscene, wilfully ignoring the pain and suffering of the afflicted: 'This was difficult to masturbate to'.[46] Most, however, are outright condemnatory, blaming the victim, or rather denying the krokodil addicts' victim status. A British commenter:

> We have become a nation sympathetic to drug users as if they are victims . . . As said no one forces them to start. I have the option which I choose not to take because I am aware of the repurcussions [sic], the same as I and everyone else have the option to jump off a bridge. Drug users are only victims of their own ignorance![47]

The addicts have brought it on themselves by sheer stupidity: 'Wow! Anyone dumb enough to ingest a drug made from gasoline, paint thinner & and lighter fluid deserves to die a slow and painful death'.[48] 'When you're just too stupid to say "no" why should anyone else have to pay the bill for your idiocy?? Less than 2 years average survival?? That should cut down some of the demand.'[49]

This blanket condemnation of krokodil addicts is frequently underpinned by a vernacular version of social Darwinism: 'I say health officials should just sit back and let natural selection do its job'.[50] On numerous occasions, addicts are jokingly nominated for the Darwin Awards: 'In the spirit of Charles Darwin, the Darwin Awards commemorate individuals who protect our gene pool by making the ultimate sacrifice of their own lives. Darwin Award winners eliminate themselves in an extraordinarily idiotic manner, thereby improving our species' chances of long-term survival.'[51] A forum user started a topic with the subject line: 'Almost darwin award winner injects weird new drug into her genitals (graphic photos)'.[52]

Hybrid Zombie Discourse

For many commenters, the krokodil addicts evoke as little empathy as the monsters in a video game: they deserve to die, because they are zombies. 'Here it is guys. The start of the zombie apocalypse. The Walking Junkie Dead.'[53] More than a metaphor, the zombie label triggers an entire frame of understanding: it is one of those 'little tacit theories about what exists, what happens, and what matters'.[54] Frames contain an issue's nature, its cause, consequences and preferred solutions. Being zombies, the krokodil addicts' bodies and brains are beyond the reach of medical and psychiatric care. There is only one solution: 'Kill them all!', or, 'Kill it with fire'.

This frame pervades vernacular and news media discourse about krokodil, and can be detected as well in medical publications. The feared krokodil epidemic that eventually did not materialise in Europe and the US was not exclusively a news media or a government creation. Medical doctors seemed as eager to scoop the competition as journalists were. In the rush to claim the nation's or the state's first krokodil patient, they inadvertently fanned the fires of rumour. Interviewed by CBS5, Frank LoVecchio, co-medical director at Banner's Poison Control Center in Phoenix, Arizona, said: 'Where there is smoke there is fire, and we're afraid there are going to be more and more cases'.[55]

The diagnosis of individual krokodil patients in case studies from western Europe and the US is controversial. It is usually based on the assessment of symptoms and patient self-reports, rather than toxicology.[56] The alleged Dutch case of krokodil abuse, for example, concerns a 24-year-old Polish man, who told doctors he had been drinking and sniffing krokodil, which is unusual, given the fact that this is primarily injected intravenously. The man disappeared from the hospital before further examination and treatment could take place. These and similar case studies have been criticised as fear-mongering, based on the absence of laboratory confirmation of desomorphine.[57] A letter to the *American Journal of Medicine* dismissed claims about krokodil in the US as urban legend: '"Krokodil" in the United States Is an Urban Legend and Not a Medical Fact.'[58]

The medical publications are indeed legendary, in the sense that they make claims about extreme, but disputed, cases of human behaviour and disease, and do so using language and images that derive from pop culture, mass media and vernacular sources. The following quote is from a paper in the *American Journal of Therapeutics*: 'It is a modern day man-made Frankenstein-like drug which was manufactured due to the pursuit of drug addicts to make a cheap yet effective narcotic but ended up in creating havoc on its users.'[59]

This feedback loop extends to the use of information and images. Dr Dany V. Thekkemuriyi and his colleagues refer in their article in *The American Journal of Medicine* to *Time* magazine for the oft-repeated mean two-year survival time since first use.[60] Claims about prevalence and spread are often based on inaccurate or obsolete news reports. Maria Katselou and her research team at the Department of Forensic Medicine and Toxicology of the National and Kapodistrian University of Athens, Greece, likewise refer in their paragraph on prevalence and use to online coverage by the *Daily Mail*, *Der Spiegel*, the *New York Daily News* and *USA Today*. Krokodil's defining characteristic, the horrific imagery, too, is implicated in this hybridity.[61]

A Hall of Mediated Mirrors

Contemporary media – vernacular and institutional alike – are awash in images that are shared freely and easily between platforms, genres and individuals. They can be recycled, altered, repurposed and refashioned.[62] In our media-saturated world, representations of deviant behaviour exist in 'an infinite hall of mediated mirrors'.[63] Krokodil is no exception, but it does stand out for the free exchange of images between vernacular, journalistic and scholarly venues.

The Faces of Meth mug shots were produced and spread by institutions. Much of the krokodil imagery, in contrast, is user-generated content of uncertain origin. A case in point is the popular VICE documentary 'Siberia: Krokodil Tears'. The climax of this 25-minute production is the British reporter's meeting with two adolescent krokodil addicts. The boys come across as apathetic and do not display the lesions the viewer had come to expect when, at the beginning of the documentary, the drug's effects were discussed. At this point, footage taken from KAY9X's YouTube channel is spliced into the documentary, without further clarifications as to its origins.

The very same pictures of rotting limbs and bare bones turn up in medical publications. The 2013 Dutch case report by pharmacist Marieke Roskam-Kwint and colleagues at the hospital Gelderse Vallei in Ede recycle stills from a Dutch newscast, that in turn lifted them from an unspecified YouTube video.[64] Two out of five pictures used by Emanuele A. Alves and his international research team to illustrate the effects of krokodil in their article in *Forensic Science International* are sourced to news sites (*International Business Times*, Elmanana.com.mx), one was even taken from a Namibian web forum.[65]

Studying krokodil use in Russia and the Ukraine, Jean-Paul C. Grund and his fellow addiction scholars, Alisher Latypov and Magdalena Harris, belong to the minority of researchers who use YouTube videos and news sources with due caution and in addition to other sources of information, such as consultations with NGO representatives in the region investigated.[66] Given the dearth of ethnographic fieldwork among krokodil users, other sources of information may be necessary to fill the gaps.[67]

Conclusion: The Danger of Off-the-Shelf Metaphors

Stories about the novel drug krokodil are made up of familiar elements from preceding drug scares, but take them one step further. The images are even more horrific, the contributions of the vernacular, the journalistic and the academic even harder to distinguish. The knee-jerk employment of the term zombie, to pick out one of the most salient elements of krokodil discourse, has been criticised before, albeit not in the context of vernacular and institutional hybridity.[68]

In the CNN newscast quoted earlier, an American doctor who has treated patients with krokodil-like symptoms says: 'It's a zombie drug. I mean that literally, it kills you from the inside out.' Strictly speaking, this is apt, because any toxic or infected substance that is injected or ingested could be said to kill you from the inside. However, the word zombie also conjures up the image of the flesh-eating ghouls who devour people from the outside in. The zombie epithet conflates the drug and the addict, and in the process turns the addict into a cannibal threat to humankind.

The zombie label evokes the threat of violence, but in fact even the most garish news stories do not portray these addicts as violent. 'Krokodil' connotes violence, but its first victims are the addicts themselves. The monster metaphor is force-fitted onto a category of persons who risk becoming the victims of (state) violence themselves. Several researchers have argued that the horrendous bodily decay associated with krokodil use is the consequence of persecution and poor health care: police harassment and discrimination, maltreatment in medical facilities and lack of needle exchange or methadone replacement programmes push drug addicts towards the most dangerous kinds of home-brewed opioids.[69] These explanations in terms of drug and health policy effects have been largely ignored by the news media and only gained some traction during the backlash at the end of 2013, when the krokodil epidemic did not materialise on US soil, for example *Newsweek*, 28 October 2013: 'Krokodil Concerns Lack Teeth'.[70]

The zombie metaphor does not inevitably support a political and law enforcement agenda that dehumanises drug addicts and can even be used as an excuse for lethal police violence.[71] In fact, zombie talk and zombie walks have been hailed by social critics as instruments to subvert the hegemony of neoliberal discourse and consumer culture. Recalling its origin as a Haitian slave, the zombie has also been used as a symbol for capitalist and colonial exploitation. The banking crisis has generated a wave of zombie enthusiasm, for example Occupy Wall Street protesters dressing up as zombie bankers.[72]

Krokodil addicts, however, who are predominantly represented as monstrous and alien, have few allies. Vernacular discourse about the drug sometimes hints at conspiracies: 'They are trying to make zombies a reality, through drugs, this is their test subject. First bath salt now this. They are seriously attempting to create a zombie apocalypse, I know I sound silly, but that's what we're headed for'.[73] These suspicions have not developed into a full-fledged counter-narrative, similar to the conspiracy allegations of CIA involvement in the crack crisis in black neighbourhoods.[74]

Krokodil discourse does not appeal to solidarity with fellow humans, but to xenophobic and nationalist fears of a threat to the body politic. The zombie hordes are coming: 'Krokodil In Nogales: Mexican Officials Report Flesh-Eating Drug In City Near Arizona Border' (*Huffington Post*, 2 June 2014); 'Has Krokodil, the Flesh-Eating Street Drug, Made Its Way to the UK?' (Vice.com, 2 October 2013); 'EXCLUSIVE: The sisters who are the first proof that Russian flesh-eating "cannibal" drug Krokodil IS in the U.S.' (*Mail Online*, 5 October 2013); 'Krokodil In Canada: Deadly,

Flesh-Eating "Zombie" Drug Reportedly Arrives North Of The Border In Ontario' (*International Business Times*, 19 November 2013).

The story does not end here: new 'worst drugs ever' keep being introduced on a frequent basis. In 2015, news media discovered a fresh novelty drug that ticks all the boxes. Flakka, or Alpha-PVP, is imported into the US from China, is said to be more addictive than crystal meth and to cause zombie-like behaviour (*The Times*, 12 June 2015: 'Florida swamped with Chinese "zombie" drug').[75] Flakka is 'nicknamed "$5 insanity" and notorious for triggering . . . violent, naked sprees' (*New York Times*, 23 June 2015[76]). The drug's unique selling point – for journalists, at least – is that it reportedly gives its users 'superhuman strength', which may very well prime the use of excessive force to subdue them. In 2017, Manchester and other UK cities suffered a 'zombie spice addicts plague' (*The Independent*, 11 April 2017).[77] One year later, Stoke-on-Trent was coping with the synthetic drug Monkey Dust. According to one police officer, restraining users was like 'dealing with someone who thinks they are the Incredible Hulk'.

The vernacular, according to Howard, 'can act to support or contest the institutional, and often it does a little of both'.[78] In the case of krokodil, it mostly supported the institutional appraisal of the issue. Krokodil addicts have primarily been constructed as Others. Their metamorphosis from humans into monsters, this analysis suggests, was as much discursive as it was drug-induced. In traditional Haitian folklore, zombies are victims first: a magical drug has robbed them of their agency, transforming them into undead slaves. The zombie metaphors of contemporary drug scare rhetoric, however, downplay their victimhood, representing them instead, George Romero-style, as subhuman cannibals.[79]

Notes

1. J.-P. C. Grund, A. Latypov and M. Harris, 'Breaking Worse: The Emergence of Krokodil and Excessive Injuries among People who Inject Drugs in Eurasia', *International Journal of Drug Policy*, 24 (2013), 265–74, 266; M. Katselou, I. Papoutsis, P. Nikolaou, C. Spiliopoulou and S. Athanaselis, 'A "Krokodil" Emerges from the Murky Waters of Addiction. Abuse Trends of an Old Drug', *Life Sciences*, 102/2 (2014), 81–7, 81.
2. Katselou et al., 'A "Krokodil" Emerges', 82.
3. Grund et al., 'Breaking Worse', 266.
4. Grund et al., 'Breaking Worse', 269.

5. D. V. Thekkemuriyi, S. G. John and U. Pillai, '"Krokodil" – A Designer Drug from Across the Atlantic, with Serious Consequences', *American Journal of Medicine*, 127/3 (2014), e1–e2.
6. 'Zelfmaakdrug Krokodil nu ook in Duitsland', *NOS.nl*, 13 October 2011, *http://nos.nl/op3/artikel/303658-zelfmaakdrug-krokodil-nu-ook-in-duitsland.html* (accessed 26 January 2020); K.-L. Lindblad, 'Bad News: People Are Taking Krokodil in Norway', *Vice*, 8 August 2012, *http://www.vice.com/en_uk/read/krokodil-norway* (accessed 26 January 2020); H. M. Roskam-Kwint, S. P. Kruizinga, M. J. H. Kaal and H.-P. R. Bootsma, 'Gevaarlijke Designer Drug "Krokodil" voor het Eerst in Nederland Gesignaleerd. Casuïstische Mededeling', *Pharmaceutisch Weekblad Wetenschappelijk Platform*, 7 (2013), a1328; T. I. Lemon, 'Homemade Heroin Substitute Causing Hallucinations', *African Journal of Psychiatry*, 16/6 (2013), 411; C. Meredith, '"Krokodil" Trend Of Flesh-Rotting Drugs Hits UK (GRAPHIC PICTURES)', *The Huffington Post UK*, 26 October 2013, *http://www.huffingtonpost.co.uk/2013/10/24/krokodil-drug-graphic-pictures-uk_n_4156584.html* (accessed 26 January 2020).
7. J. Davison, 'Krokodil hype: Is toxic "flesh-eating" street drug in Canada?', *CBC News*, 25 November 2013, *http://www.cbc.ca/news/health/krokodil-hype-is-toxic-flesh-eating-street-drug-in-canada-1.2435122?cmp=rss* (accessed 17 September 2014); Thekkemuriyi, John and Pillai, '"Krokodil" – A Designer Drug from Across the Atlantic'.
8. 'Houston girl, 17, is treated for rotting skin after "taking flesh-eating drug Krokodil" in Mexico', *Mail Online*, 3 January 2014, *http://www.dailymail.co.uk/news/article-2532996/First-confirmed-case-Krokodil-Mexico-17-year-old-Houston-treated-addiction-poor-mans-heroin-doctors-thought-STD-rotted-genitals.html* (accessed 26 January 2020); A. Jauregui, 'Mexican Teen Reportedly Injects Krokodil Into Genitals (UPDATED)', *The Huffington Post*, 6 December 2013, *http://www.huffingtonpost.com/2013/12/06/krokodil-mexico-teen-injected-drug-genitals_n_4398102.html* (accessed 26 January 2020).
9. T. Gettys, 'Doctors confirm: Use of flesh-eating opioid drug krokodil is spreading in U.S.', *RawStory.com*, 15 November 2013, *https://www.rawstory.com/2013/11/doctors-confirm-use-of-flesh-eating-opioid-drug-krokodil-is-spreading-in-u-s/* (accessed 26 January 2020). See, for example, in Germany, 'Russische Todesdroge: Bochumer Junkies spritzten doch kein "Krokodil"', *Focus Online*, 14 October 2011, *http://www.focus.de/gesundheit/ratgeber/psychologie/news/russische-todesdroge-bochumer-junkies-spritzten-doch-kein-krokodil_aid_674807.html* (accessed 26 January 2020), and Norway, T. Ustad Stav, 'Ingen beslag av «krokodil» i Tromsø', *nrk.no*, 19 October 2012, *http://www.nrk.no/nordnytt/ingen-beslag-av-_krokodil_-1.8364552* (accessed 26 January 2020).

10. V. Bekiempis, 'Report: Krokodil Concerns Lack Teeth', *Newsweek*, 28 October 2013, *http://www.newsweek.com/report-krokodil-concerns-lack-teeth-1123* (accessed 26 January 2020). See also: V. Bekiempis, 'Why You Don't Need to Worry about "Flesh-Eating" Drug Krokodil', *Newsweek*, 21 October 2013, *http://www.newsweek.com/why-you-do-not-need-worry-about-flesh-eating-drug-krokodil-613*; J. Peters, 'Don't Believe the Hype about the "Flesh-Eating" Drug Krokodil', *Slate*, 18 November 2013, *http://www.slate.com/blogs/crime/2013/11/18/krokodil_desomorphine_don_t_believe_the_hype_about_flesh_eating_drug_krokodil.html*; H. Osborne, 'Russia's Flesh-Eating Krokodil Drug an Urban Legend in UK, US and Canada', *International Business Times*, 21 November 2013, *http://www.ibtimes.co.uk/krokodil-flesh-eating-drug-spreading-usa-canada-524200*; Andy Grimm, 'Suspected krokodil a false alarm', *Chicago Tribune*, 27 October 2013, *http://articles.chicagotribune.com/2013-10-27/news/ct-met-krokodil-hunt-20131027_1_bath-salts-heroin-false-alarm*; A. Haglage, 'Behind the Krokodil Panic', *Daily Beast*, 7 November 2013, *http://www.thedailybeast.com/articles/2013/11/07/behind-the-krokodil-panic.html* (all accessed 26 January 2020).
11. C. Gogarty and T. Davidson, 'Flesh-rotting "zombie" drug Krokodil "has arrived in the UK" – and it's 10 times stronger than heroin', *The Mirror*, 1 November 2018, *https://www.mirror.co.uk/news/uk-news/flesh-rotting-zombie-drug-krokodil-13519348* (accessed 26 January 2020). For a sceptical account of the UK 'krokodile crisis' see E. Goddard and I. Hamilton, 'The toxic impact of drug panics', *The Independent*, 6 November 2018, *https://www.independent.co.uk/news/long_reads/drug-panics-overdose-spice-monkey-dust-krokodil-mental-health-a8541036.html* (accessed 26 January 2020).
12. Philip Jenkins, *Synthetic Panics: The Symbolic Politics of Designer Drugs* (New York: New York University Press, 1999); Craig Reinarman and Harry G. Levine, 'The Crack Attack: America's Latest Drug Scare, 1986–1992', in Joel Best (ed.), *Images of Issues: Typifying Contemporary Social Problems* (New Brunswick: Transaction, 1995), pp. 147–86.
13. See Joel Best, *Social Problems* (New York: Norton, 2008).
14. Robert G. Howard, 'How Counter-Culture Helped Put the "Vernacular" in Vernacular Webs', in Trevor J. Blank (ed.), *Folk Culture in the Digital Age: The Emergent Dynamics of Human Interaction* (Boulder: University Press of Colorado, 2012), pp. 30–55, 45.
15. Trevor J. Blank, *The Last Laugh: Folk Humor, Celebrity Culture, and Mass-Mediated Disasters in the Digital Age* (Madison: University of Wisconsin Press, 2013).
16. Blank, *The Last Laugh*, p. 92.

17. R. G. Howard, 'Electronic Hybridity: The Persistent Processes of the Vernacular Web', *Journal of American Folklore*, 121/480 (2008), 192–218, 205.
18. Howard, 'Electronic Hybridity'.
19. Jenkins, *Synthetic Panics*, p. 184.
20. S. Walker, 'Krokodil: The drug that eats junkies', *The Independent*, 22 June 2011, *http://www.independent.co.uk/news/world/europe/krokodil-the-drug-that-eats-junkies-2300787.html*; K. Alonzo, 'Krokodil, The Drug that Eats You Alive [Graphic Images]', *Guardian Liberty Voice*, 30 September 2013, *http://guardianlv.com/2013/09/krokodil-the-drug-that-eats-you-alive-graphic-images/*; H. Smith, 'Flesh-eating drug krokodil "could sink its teeth into British addicts", health workers warned', *Metro*, 23 March 2014, *http://metro.co.uk/2014/03/23/flesh-eating-drug-krokodil-could-sink-its-teeth-into-british-addicts-health-workers-warned-4674343/* (all accessed 26 January 2020).
21. T. Linnemann, T. Wall and E. Green, 'The Walking Dead and Killing State: Zombification and the Normalization of Police Violence', *Theoretical Criminology*, 18/4 (2014), 506–27.
22. 'Regering voert strijd tegen "legal highs" op', *Het Laatste Nieuws*, 26 April 2013, *http://www.hln.be/hln/nl/957/Binnenland/article/detail/1622571/2013/04/26/Regering-voert-strijd-tegen-legal-highs-op.dhtml* (accessed 26 January 2020).
23. R. E. Gutsche, 'Zombies, Drugs, and Florida Weirdness. "Imaginative Power" and Resonance in Coverage of Miami's "Causeway Cannibal"', *Journalism Studies*, 14/4 (2013), 555–67.
24. Gutsche, 'Zombies, Drugs, and Florida Weirdness', 560.
25. Gutsche, 'Zombies, Drugs, and Florida Weirdness', 562.
26. Gutsche, 'Zombies, Drugs, and Florida Weirdness', 561.
27. D. W. Drezner, 'Metaphor of the Living Dead: Or, the Effect of the Zombie Apocalypse on Public Policy Discourse', *Social Research*, 81/4 (2014), 825–49, 830.
28. B. L. Miller, J. M. Stogner, L. E. Agnich, A. Sanders, J. Bacot and S. Felix, 'Marketing a Panic: Media Coverage of Novel Psychoactive Drugs (NPDs) and its Relationship with Legal Changes', *American Journal of Criminal Justice*, 40/3 (2015), 523–41.
29. Miller et al., 'Marketing a Panic', 537.
30. Drezner, 'Metaphor of the Living Dead', 826–7.
31. Drezner, 'Metaphor of the Living Dead', 827–9; I. Schwartz, 'Chuck Todd: Are Republicans "Overdoing" Rhetoric on Ebola?' *RealClearPolitics*, 19 October 2014, *http://bit.ly/1FqnQd5* (accessed 26 January 2020).

32. J. M. Sharfstein, 'On Fear, Distrust, and Ebola', *JAMA Forum*, 24 February 2015, *http://jama.jamanetwork.com/article.aspx?articleid=2130303* (accessed 26 January 2020).
33. T. Linnemann and T. Wall, '"This is Your Face on Meth": The Punitive Spectacle of "White Trash" in the Rural War on Drugs', *Theoretical Criminology*, 17 (2013), 315–34.
34. Linnemann and Wall, '"This is Your Face on Meth"', 316.
35. Linnemann and Wall, '"This is Your Face on Meth"'.
36. T. C. Ayres and Y. Jewkes, 'The Haunting Spectacle of Crystal Meth: A Media-Created Mythology?', *Crime Media Culture*, 8 (2012), 315–32, 316, 327.
37. Kay9x, 'Krokodil Drug (Rusia's Disaster)A drug that eats junkies', *YouTube*, 25 June 2011, *http://www.youtube.com/watch?v=cM6v-43-1PU* (accessed 26 January 2020).
38. The Real Truth Movement, 'The Effects of Krokodil – Real Life Zombies', *YouTube*, 23 November 2013, *https://www.youtube.com/watch?v=8HLYnl7vEoYT* (accessed 26 January 2020).
39. CNN, 'Krokodil crosses over to U.S. from Russia', *YouTube*, 11 October 2013, *https://www.youtube.com/watch?v=-xF1ejbShZ8* (accessed 26 January 2020).
40. Kay9x, 'Krokodil Drug'.
41. T. Linnemann, L. Hanson and L. S. Williams, '"With Scenes of Blood and Pain". Crime Control and the Punitive Imagination of The Meth Project', *British Journal of Criminology*, 53 (2013), 605–23.
42. Vice, 'Krokodil: Russia's Deadliest Drug (NSFW)', *YouTube*, 17 May 2012, *https://www.youtube.com/watch?v=JsUH8llvTZo* (accessed 26 January 2020).
43. The Real Truth Movement, 'The Effects of Krokodil'.
44. J. Nye, 'Horrific images of drug-users eaten alive by flesh-eating illness caused by homemade heroin substitute that has arrived on American shores in Arizona', *Mail Online*, 26 September 2013, *http://www.dailymail.co.uk/news/article-2432802/Drug-users-eaten-alive-flesh-eating-illness-caused-homemade-heroin-substitute-Krokodil.html#reader-comments* (accessed 26 January 2020).
45. Both: 'Krokodil, The Flesh-Eating Street Drug That Rots Skin From Inside-Out, Expands To Illinois', *The Huffington Post*, 9 October 2013, *http://www.huffingtonpost.com/2013/10/09/krokodil-drug_n_4073417.html?utm_hp_ref=krokodil* (accessed 26 January 2020).
46. The Real Truth Movement, 'The Effects of Krokodil'; see Blank, *The Last Laugh*.
47. Nye, 'Horrific images of drug-users eaten alive'.
48. 'Krokodil, The Flesh-Eating Street Drug', *The Huffington Post*.

49. 'Krokodil, The Flesh-Eating Street Drug', *The Huffington Post.*
50. 'Krokodil, The Flesh-Eating Street Drug', *The Huffington Post.*
51. Darwin Awards, 'History & Rules', *www.Darwin-Awards.com*, *http://www.darwinawards.com/rules/* (accessed 26 January 2020).
52. DigInTheCrates, 'Almost darwin award winner injects weird new drug into her genitals (graphic photos)', *ignboards.com*, 19 March 2015, *http://www.ign.com/boards/threads/almost-darwin-award-winner-injects-weird-new-drug-into-her-genitals-graphic-photos.454426543/* (accessed 26 January 2020).
53. *CNN*, 'Krokodil crosses over to U.S. from Russia'.
54. Todd Gitlin, *The Whole World is Watching: Mass Media in the Making and Unmaking of the Left* (Berkeley and Los Angeles: University of California Press, 2003), p. 6.
55. *http://www.kpho.com/story/23521413/first-cases-of-flesh-eating-drug-reported-in-az* (accessed 26 June 2015).
56. See, e.g., Lemon, 'Homemade Heroin Substitute Causing Hallucinations'; Roskam-Kwint et al. 'Gevaarlijke Designer Drug "Krokodil"'; Thekkemuriyi, John and Pillai, '"Krokodil" – A Designer Drug from Across the Atlantic'.
57. ForensicToxGuy, 'Krokodil . . . not so fast, my friends!', The Dose Makes the Poison, 2 December 2013, *http://dosemakespoison.blogspot.nl/2013/12/krokodil not-so-fast-my-friends.html* (accessed 26 June 2015).
58. M. E. Mullins and E. S. Schwarz, '"Krokodil" in the United States Is an Urban Legend and Not a Medical Fact', *American Journal of Medicine*, 127/7 (2014), e25.
59. T. Oliver, S. J. Gheevarghese, U. Gandhi, Z. Y. Bhat and U. Pillai, '"Krokodil"' – A Menace Slowly Spreading Across the Atlantic', *American Journal of Therapeutics*, 22/3 (2015), 231–3, 231.
60. Thekkemuriyi and Pillai, '"Krokodil" – A Designer Drug from Across the Atlantic'.
61. Katselou et al., 'A "Krokodil" Emerges', 83–4.
62. Jay D. Bolter and Richard Grusin, *Remediation: Understanding New Media* (Cambridge (MA): MIT Press, 1999); Linnemann and Wall, '"This is Your Face on Meth"', 320.
63. Jeff Ferrell and Clinton R. Sanders (eds), *Cultural Criminology* (Boston: Northeastern University Press, 1995), p. 14.
64. Roskam-Kwint et al., 'Gevaarlijke Designer Drug "Krokodil"'.
65. E. A. Alves, J.-P. C. Grund, C. M. Afonso, A. D. Pereira Netto, F. Carvalho and R. J. Dinis-Oliveira, 'The Harmful Chemistry behind "Krokodil": Street-like Synthesis and Product Analysis', *Forensic Science International*, 257 (2015), 76–82.

66. Grund et al., 'Breaking Worse'.
67. R. Heimer, 'Patterns of New Drug Emergence: A Comment in Light of "Krokodil"', *International Journal of Drug Policy*, 24 (2013), 275–7.
68. See, e.g., Drezner, 'Metaphor of the Living Dead'; T. Linnemann, T. Wall and E. Green, 'The Walking Dead and Killing State: Zombification and the Normalization of Police Violence', *Theoretical Criminology*, 18/4 (2014), 506–27; Miller et al., 'Marketing a Panic'.
69. R. E. Booth, '"Krokodil" and Other Home-Produced Drugs for Injection: A Perspective from Ukraine', *International Journal of Drug Policy*, 24 (2013), pp. 277–8; Grund et al., 'Breaking Worse'; R. Hämmig, 'Krokodil' frisst Löcher in den Verstand', *dgs-info Extra. 13. Oktober 2011 – Bochum: Info über Desomorphin/Krokodil für Drogenkonsumenten*. Deutsche Gesellschaft für Suchtmedizin e.V. *http://www.dgsuchtmedizin.de/fileadmin/documents/dgs-info_extra_20111013/R.Haemmig_%E2%80%9Ekrokodil%E2%80%9C_frisst_L%C3%B6cher_in_den_Verstand_.pdf* (accessed 26 June 2015).
70. Bekiempis, 'Report: Krokodil Concerns Lack Teeth'.
71. Linnemann et al., 'The Walking Dead and Killing State'.
72. C. L. Kuhling, 'Zombie Banks, Zombie Politics and the "Walking Zombie Movement": Liminality and the Post-Crisis Irish Imaginary', *European Journal of Cultural Studies*, 20/4 (2017), 397–412.
73. Kay9x, 'Krokodil Drug'.
74. Patricia A. Turner, *I Heard it Through the Grapevine: Rumor in African-American Culture* (Berkeley and Los Angeles: University of California Press, 1993), pp. 180–201; S. Parsons, W. Simmons, F. Shinhoster and J. Kilburn, 'A Test of the Grapevine: An Empirical Examination of Conspiracy Theories among African Americans', *Sociological Spectrum*, 19/2 (1999), 201–22.
75. R. Blakely, 'Florida swamped with Chinese "zombie" drug', *The Sunday Times*, 12 June 2015, *http://www.thetimes.co.uk/tto/news/world/americas/article4467603.ece* (accessed 26 January 2020).
76. D. Levin, 'Synthetic Drug Manufacturing Is an Open Secret in China', *The New York Times*, 23 June 2015, *http://www.nytimes.com/times-insider/2015/06/23/synthetic-drug-manufacturing-is-an-open-secret-in-china/?_r=0* (accessed 26 January 2020).
77. A. Lusher, '"Zombie spice addicts plague" caused by everything we warned you about, claim legal highs ban critics', *The Independent*, 11 April 2017, *https://www.independent.co.uk/news/uk/home-news/spice-legal-highs-zombie-plague-walking-zombies-manchester-legal-highs-ban-psychoactive-substances-a7678931.html* (accessed 26 January 2020).

78. Howard, 'Electronic Hybridity', 205.
79. S. Page, 'Monkey Dust mayhem: the English city reportedly at the centre of a drug-fuelled "epidemic"', *The Conversation*, 6 September 2018, *https://theconversation.com/monkey-dust-mayhem-the-english-city-reportedly-at-the-centre-of-a-drug-fuelled-epidemic-102066* (accessed 26 January 2020).

2

'Preparedness 101: Zombie Pandemic' and the Ebola Scare

How the CDC's Use of Zombie Pop Culture Helped Fan a Nationalist Outbreak Narrative

Sara Polak

FROM 2011 TO 2015 the American Centers for Disease Control and Prevention (CDC) ran an emergency preparedness campaign targeting young adults, called 'Preparedness 101: Zombie Pandemic'. The campaign used the zombie hype – at a highpoint in 2011 since the airing of the television series of *The Walking Dead* in the fall of 2010 – as a vehicle to encourage citizens to think about their own disaster preparedness.[1] The campaign had a few main elements: a website and a blog around the theme of preparing for the 'zombie apocalypse', and most notably: a 'graphic novel', disseminated online.[2] In comic strip form, the CDC narrated a pandemic outbreak of a zombie virus, instructing young adults what to have ready and what to do in the case of a zombie attack, 'or a real disaster' as the site repeatedly stresses.[3]

Toward the end of the period in which the campaign was active, a real disaster did happen, albeit on a different continent: there was an outbreak of the Ebola virus in West Africa (primarily in Ivory Coast, Liberia and

Sierra Leone). Although this was obviously, from a US American point of view, a faraway crisis, a few cases occurred within the United States in the fall of 2014, sparking a veritable Ebola scare in American media, particularly across social media platforms.[4] These two events – the CDC zombie preparedness campaign and the Ebola panic – may seem entirely separate, but on closer inspection they are eerily linked. The Ebola outbreak was employed politically, among others by Donald Trump, to advocate for isolationism and border closures. Social media responses suggest that the CDC, however unintentionally, encouraged and sanctioned this specific reaction through its zombie pandemic comic campaign.

To grasp the subtle mechanism that underlies effects like this one, Steve Shaviro addresses the cultural role zombies take on in representations of 'capitalist monstrosity', concluding that zombies 'present the "human face" of capitalist monstrosity' because they 'are the dregs of humanity'.[5] This idea that zombies represent the gory outliers of humanity is taken up by Gerry Canavan, who uses it as a starting point for his argument that 'the evocation of the zombie conjures not solidarity but racial panic'.[6] This is what both the CDC, presumably inadvertently, and many participants in the 'Ebola scare' across social media platforms, share: they allow for fantasies of zombification (whether or not explicitly linked to Ebola or another 'real disaster') to bleed over into racial panic about infestation and infection by the other. As Canavan notes: 'The audience for zombie narrative, after all, never imagines itself to be zombified; zombies are always other people, which is to say they are Other people, which is to say they are people who are not quite people at all.'[7] A similar dynamic quickly evolved in responses to the COVID-19 crisis: a division was made between lives that need to be protected at all cost and lives that are put to the service of that aim and are more expendable. One of the global triggers for the massive #BlackLivesMatter protests following George Floyd's murder, may have been the painfully black-and-white quality of this division, in the US and elsewhere. This article analyses how the cultural type of the zombie as employed in the CDC comic has impacted how Americans have understood the Ebola epidemic, which in turn has affected popular responses to the crisis.

The CDC comic's narrative is in many ways straightforward. A young white couple, Julie and Todd, watch a scary movie. Julie goes to bed; Todd, and their dog Max, stick around to watch more horror movies. Todd sees a newsflash about a worrying virus outbreak, and decides to put together an emergency kit. This turns out to be extremely fortunate, because it becomes clear in the hours afterwards that a dangerous zombie virus is spreading rapidly. The couple is confronted by their neighbour, an elderly woman who has turned into a zombie, and after a few days of staying locked in their house, they decide to flee to the nearby Safe Zone. Meanwhile researchers at the CDC in Atlanta quickly, and in excellent communication and work spirit, research the virus and create a vaccine, which they have produced and distributed to the Safe Zones. Throughout, standard tropes of zombie narratives come up, such as the escape from the house, by car, with zombies hammering on the windshield, and the arrival at the Safe Zone at a moment when the car has just run out of gas. At the very end, as Todd and Julie congratulate each other on the arrival of the vaccines, the Safe Zone is overrun by zombies – yet another staple of zombie popular culture. At this point, Todd, who has fallen asleep in front of the television, wakes up from his bad dream. Of course, however, he once again starts to compile an emergency kit. This is the comic's explicit moral: all American families should have a regularly checked emergency kit ready in case disaster strikes, for example in the form of a virus pandemic.

It is easy to dismiss comics like this one as merely an information leaflet, thinly veiled as entertainment. It is information packaged as entertainment, as the CDC also says on the accompanying website. The narrative follows a classic zombie apocalypse script. Because of this predictability and the undisguised advice about preparedness and emergency kits, this remains unmistakably a piece of public health communication. However, this text merits serious reading as popular culture, because despite being promotional material from a federal agency, it does, in its careful adoption of the form and conventions of a regular popular cultural text, show something about that culture from a federal agency's point of view. Knowingly or not, the text plays into a dynamic of dehumanising victims of epidemics. This dynamic was evolving around the Ebola crisis during the same years, spurred on via social media, the rising 'Alt-Right', and Donald Trump.

The original intention of the campaign had been to engage new audiences by aligning with their interests:

> Wonder why Zombies, Zombie Apocalypse, and Zombie Preparedness continue to live or walk dead on a CDC web site? As it turns out what first began as a tongue in cheek campaign to engage new audiences with preparedness messages has proven to be a very effective platform. We continue to reach and engage a wide variety of audiences on all hazards preparedness via Zombie Preparedness.[8]

Clearly, it is a way of reaching new audiences with 'all hazards preparedness' – which presumably aims to reach everyone – and apparently it works. The website does not make explicit how this has been measured, but it has clearly been deemed 'very effective' in reaching 'a wide variety of audiences'.

As noted, many cultural objects that are (or dovetail on) popular culture are worth studying because of their very triviality, through which they 'give away' something about the culture in which they exist. Some of these points are obvious and unsurprising. Throughout the story, for instance, a heteronormative, white, able-bodied and middle-class character is visible. Their specifically gendered white middle-class representation of Americanness includes a response to the crisis that is just the 'correct' balance of prudent yet willing to take risks, and self-reliant yet trustful of authority and science. Todd's ability to quickly gather an emergency kit, and their alert response to their infected neighbour, reflects the shape the CDC expects civilians' disaster preparedness to take. It goes without saying that the couple's dog Max will accompany them to the CDC's Safe Zone, and there is a procedure in place to check the dog's health as well as the humans', after which all are equally welcome.

But the comic also reflects, and reproduces, more unusual troubling aspects of the dominant culture in which it 'continue[s] to live or walk dead'. Given the specific shape anxiety sparked by actual epidemics tends to take, particularly in the US, the CDC's use of the zombie figure as a placeholder for any virus outbreak or other disaster is troubling. As is argued elsewhere in this book, mediated words and images can themselves form a metaphorical virus with effects that have a very real impact in people's lives. The CDC's zombie comic did nothing to assuage the fear of Ebola in the US, but instead sparked the notion that a popular cultural zombie scenario was in some sense like the Ebola epidemic. In what sense precisely, and what the implications of such a similarity might be, was negotiated in various ways. However, the basic idea, coming from a federal body, that the Ebola outbreak in West Africa has something to do with twenty-first-century American zombie fantasies, constitutes a frame that in fact helped the newly minted Alt-Right in the US in 2014–15 formulate its core message of othering and exclusion.

The comic and the responses to the Ebola epidemic together closely follow the trajectory Canavan describes in his analysis of zombies as quintessential racial threat, also from the perspective of the State:

> One of the ways the State apparatus builds the sorts of 'preaccomplished' subjects it needs is precisely through the construction of a racial binary in which the (white) citizen-subject is opposed against nonwhite life, bare life, zombie life – that anti-life which is always inimically and hopelessly Other, which must always be kept quarantined, if not actively eradicated and destroyed.[9]

The white heterosexual young Judy and Todd and their dog, clearly embody the 'preaccomplished subjects' that Canavan refers to, and the comic can be seen as a kind of state apparatus that constructs 'a racial binary in which the (white) citizen-subject is opposed against nonwhite life, bare life, zombie life'. As soon as the Ebola epidemic became global news, some users commented on Twitter on the CDC's eerie prefiguration of that epidemic in its comic. The same happened following the start of the COVID-19 pandemic. This specific concretisation of the metaphor was of course not the CDC's intention, but it had nonetheless come to embody this function of 'State apparatus', which employed narrative to protect its constituents, othering 'nonwhite' life in the process. In this chapter I will use conceptual metaphor theory to understand how thinking about one thing in terms of another – the Ebola epidemic in term of zombie culture – affects how the former was politicised on US social media.

Representing Ebola

Marouf Hasian Jr in *Representing Ebola* (2016) gives various examples of popular films and other texts, such as the Hollywood movie *Contagion* (Steven Soderbergh, 2011), that simultaneously tell fictional stories about contagious disease, and 'served as an "infomercial promoting specific national and international agencies while encouraging specific behavior from the public"'.[10] Thus, there was a cultural context in which reality and fiction were often difficult to distinguish, and fiction was used to influence behaviour in the real world. In that context, for a federal body to represent a disease outbreak as a zombie apocalypse logically sets the stage for understanding an actual disease epidemic as a horror story, for consumption by American audiences. The commodification implicit in using a zombie apocalypse as a cautionary tale to entertainingly prepare civilians for a disease outbreak, creates a specific exclusionary narrative frame. This frame offers American civilians an already familiar narrative frame in which to understand real epidemics: not as a collective threat to humanity, but as an attack from actors which have already lost their humanity as a result of being (potentially) infected, and which must in terms of narrative justice be quenched and subjected, in the interest of all involved.

Chapter 6 of that book, 'Anticipating the Ebola Apocalypse and American Mediascapes', opens with the key point that 'Government authorities, public health officials, and journalists who talk and write about the spread of infectious diseases have a difficult time drawing that mythic line that is supposed to exist between providing citizens with adequate warnings and creating moral panic'.[11] Hasian offers ample evidence of this idea in attending to the Ebola epidemic of 2013–15, and clearly shows how many television producers and book authors of journalistic and fictional works on contagious diseases became 'Ebola specialists' in the media. Although the CDC of course comes up in this context, and although Hasian through referring to the 'Ebola Apocalypse' himself introduces discourse from zombie studies, he does not explicitly comment on either the CDC's own crossovers with popular cultural representation of viral diseases, nor does he make the link between Ebola and apocalyptic monsters in the cultural imaginary. *Representing Ebola* does not focus specifically on social media representations of Ebola.

A contagious virus, with horrific lethal symptoms, Ebola quickly came to be perceived as an acute threat to public health and national security, both in US mainstream media and online. Ebola already had a place in the American imagination, premediated by age-old plague narratives, mediations of the HIV/AIDS outbreak in the 1980s, and previous Ebola outbreaks. Narrative contexts in which to frame concrete news of the epidemic abounded in American popular culture, in which contagious disease is often the driving theme, providing suspense through its invisible yet threatening nature, and fascination for its gruesome symptoms. The spectral nature of a pandemic – it is powerful but cannot be seen – and its entertainment value, are particularly traceable in zombie narratives, presumably because they are the most prolific popular cultural representations of othering contagion.[12] Defined in modern popular culture by their non-humanity, zombies' main menace lies in their ability to infect humans, transforming them into their own bleak, dangerous and immoral kind. As such, zombie films provide a ready-made frame of reference in which to understand the Ebola epidemic. This interpretation of Ebola as a zombie virus was quickly developed in the straight-to-DVD movie *Ebola Zombies*.[13]

Ebola on Twitter

I came across the CDC's zombie preparedness comic when I was researching the metaphors US American social media users (particularly on Twitter) most commonly employed when they posted about the Ebola epidemic of 2013–15. In my Twitter research I have aggregated about 309,000 US American tweets that mentioned 'Ebola' from 28 September to 5 October 2014, the week following the discovery of the first case in the US, and 183,000 from 23–29 October 2014. This was done using T-CAT, a tool that captures randomly about 1 per cent of the 'full firehose' of tweets. Because the Twitter API (application programming interface) does not allow for collecting historical Twitter data, I had to rely on existing databases of historical tweets. I used a T-CAT database that contains tweets including the word 'Africa'. As a result all selected tweets include both 'Ebola' and 'Africa'. Following this, I sorted them on the basis of other words they used. There are a couple of obvious themes to be discerned within the collection of other words that 'Ebola' tweets use, including 'zombies' – that is, tweets that use both 'Ebola' and 'zombie'. It is hard to establish precisely what percentage of tweets that mention 'Ebola' also include the word 'zombie', because the sample is selectively limited by the fact that all these tweets also include the word 'Africa'.[14] Nonetheless, even within this specific sample there are thousands of tweets that use both 'Ebola' and 'zombie'. It is important to consider this specific genre of responses to the Ebola epidemic together with the CDC's comic about a zombie outbreak, as a warning for disease outbreaks, because such connections are culturally very easily made. The number of tweets referring to the Ebola outbreak as a 'zombie' attack/outbreak/apocalypse shows that the connection was indeed often made.

There were various memes, no doubt mostly in jest – although, as I will discuss, no less troubling because of that – which posed as news of Ebola victims who had arisen from the dead. This link, in the context of pop culture and classical outbreak narratives, is all too obvious. Ebola easily lends itself to being imagined as a zombie virus. It has gruesome effects on the affected body and spreads quickly, though probably less quickly than the visceral fascination its gory aspect arouses. Ebola shares many other aspects with cultural imaginations of zombie viruses. For one thing, Ebola affects black bodies primarily, and zombies have a notorious historical link to African enslaved people, dispossessed and turned into a mindless, but threatening horde.[15] The fact that both are conceptualised as highly contagious viruses also shapes their supposed similarity. In 'Metaphors We Live By', linguists Lakoff and Johnson have shown that through conceptual metaphors, pre-existing mental images can structure linguistic expressions and basic cognitive routes. In an extension of that theory, Thibodeau and Boroditsky explore how the choice of conceptual metaphor structures reasoning, by comparing participants' responses to a text about crime in a city, framed in different metaphors, for instance as a 'beast preying on' the city (animal metaphor) or a 'virus infecting' the city (disease metaphor).[17] They conclude that animal metaphors are correlated with more repressive measures, while disease metaphors correlate with measures that provide care. To think of Ebola victims through the metaphor of zombies – monsters of sorts – presumably affects the nature of responses, in the direction of repressing or excluding the affected.

Priscilla Wald has extensively theorised the cultural and political implications of the virus metaphor, coining among others the term 'outbreak narrative', to think through the narratives of communicable disease outbreaks as related by media and other involved actors. One important aspect, Wald notes, is that outbreak narratives can be more infectious metaphorically than the actual virus whose spread they narrate, and also that outbreak narratives must be treated as stories that affect 'which social structures and whose beliefs, poverty, prejudices, and personalities become the focus of analysis, as well as who is included in the "we" who might have been better off had the virus not been identified'.[18] The metaphors and ensuing narrative units (narremes) driving outbreak narratives are clearly influential and ideologically charged, and will usually focus on the interests not of the virus's victims, but of those presumably threatened by virus carriers.

Although her book *Contagious: Cultures, Carriers, and the Outbreak Narrative* was published in 2008, well before the large 2013–15 West-African Ebola outbreak occurred, and just before social media were used widely enough to be useful to researchers in providing an impression of how groups of people responded to the threat online, Wald discusses the mythological aspects of the Ebola virus based on earlier outbreaks. The Ebola-specific outbreak narratives Wald attends to clearly tend towards treating Ebola as a zombie-like virus, more so than other outbreak narratives.[19] Richard Preston also clearly invokes zombie discourse to describe the Ebola virus in his journalistic account *The Hot Zone* (1995). Here Ebola is 'a dweller in blood' and a virus that 'can seem neither quite alive nor quite unalive'.[20]

Ebola is a viral disease with gruesome bodily symptoms that in 2013–15 affected mainly black people, whose contagiousness could easily be framed as focused on turning presumably mainly white Americans into their own abject kind. This often obviously racist narrative found fertile soil as a result of ages of premediation through narratives of monstrous virus spreaders. This type of narrative has a long history in the American cultural imagination, particularly with regard to enslaved, dispossessed and wounded Africans, who, in the Haitian voodoo tradition, were cast, and conceived of themselves, as zombie-like wanderers.[21] Most tweeted zombie metaphors employed to talk or joke about Ebola are white-supremacist, or clearly tend in that direction. They do not interact primarily with the actual circumstances of the Ebola outbreak, but with pre-existing narrative traditions and cultural preconceptions. They closely stick to the schema Sarah Lauro has outlined in her consideration of 'zombie runs', which are 'geared to the participant who identifies not with the living dead but with the human who must outrun the zombie horde'.[22]

This claim, that American pop culture and politics are invested in the idea that American citizens are having to outrun a zombie horde, is clearly echoed in other areas of popular discourse. A great deal of Ebola discourse on Twitter, and zombie discourse that pertained to the fear of Ebola entering or spreading in the United States, revolved around running from the horde of carriers, supposedly eager to spread their disease. In such tweets one observes a classical replay of the Patient Zero narrative Wald outlines. In Patient Zero narratives, the first identified case of a disease outbreak is cast as a malignant actor who is consciously infecting others with their disease. For instance, as one famous user tweeted on 15 October 2014 'Screw Thomas Duncan for lying on a medical evaluation and entering the U.S. after knowingly having direct contact with numerous Ebola victims'.[23] The patient is named, shamed, criminalised, and assumed to have acted intentionally to infect others. Thus 'Patient Zero', in the case of actual disease scares, allows for the construction of a 'narrative of survival' as we know it from contemporary zombie fiction. Of course, even if the narrative of healthy people fighting the disease through 'escaping' super-spreaders is usually presented as a case of necessary self-protection, it is also a narrative that justifies exclusion. Patient Zero's presumed evil intentions are instrumental in legitimising this step. The popularity of narratives of 'outrunning the zombie horde' aligns with the construction of and animosity towards Patient Zero figures.

From my sample of tweets that use 'Ebola' and 'Zombie' it is difficult to pick out the most 'representative' examples. But based on the thousands of tweets that use both words (in the actual tweet itself, not the user name, biography or other paratext) included in my sample, I conclude that in most cases the tweets are 'jokes' that play on the fascination with zombies, and the combination of that fascination with the objectification of actual victims of the Ebola virus. Many tweets for instance include an obvious hoax containing an image of a black zombie, adapted from a still taken from *World War Z* (2013).[24] Those tweets come with texts such as 'Africa Confirms 3rd #Ebola Victim Rises From the Dead, Releases Picture of First "Ebola Zombie" Captured' or 'Liberia Turns Into Zombie Movie as 2 Ebola Victims Supposedly Rise from the Dead'. While those messages are often clearly hoaxes, and indeed an article that explained that it was a hoax was itself highly popular, it gives a sense of the way in which zombie fascination, as well as images from zombie movies, are linked to and shape the imagination of Ebola in online popular culture.[25] In terms of Richard Grusin's notion of premediation, a great deal of recent zombie discourse as offered in movies such as *Contagion* or *World War Z*, actually prepared US dominant culture for the reception of an Ebola outbreak in those terms.[26] Arguably, the CDC's *Preparedness 101: Zombie Pandemic* acted as a government-sanctioned version of that premediation.

Such processes of premediation are always already politically charged. Tweets that tickle readers with the similarities between Ebola and an enduring popular cultural favourite confirm what Lauro and Wald have argued: the subject position in both the outbreak narrative and the concomitant zombie fantasy is reserved for the people running away from it; the victims or zombies are objects made to stare at. Beyond that, this type of imagery and the anxiety and visceral responses they excite, have been employed politically to disrupt. Social media expressions of often anonymous, under-the-radar users spread these messages, seemingly in order to spur distrust and antagonism in US American society.

One particular, non-anonymous, but loudly heard Twitter voice in this chorus was that of Donald Trump – not yet at the time a presidential candidate. This account was of course both amplified strongly, and it is representative of a common US American response to the epidemic. In September 2014, when a Liberian tourist was diagnosed with Ebola in Texas, the disease moved to the forefront of attention in American politics, news and social media. Donald Trump bought into the Patient Zero

Myth, by tweeting: 'The Ebola patient who came into our country knew exactly what he was doing. Came into contact with over 100 people. Here we go – I told you so!'[27] Trump implies that the patient did, in a real-life performance of the zombie scenario, maliciously travel to the US to meet as many as possible in order to spread the disease.

Trump sent out around a hundred tweets about Ebola in that same period, often stressing the importance of protecting the US border in order to keep out Ebola, and deriding Obama for 'allowing' the disease to affect the US ('President Obama has a personal responsibility to visit & embrace all people in the US who contract Ebola!', 15 October 2014).[28] In doing so, Trump created and contributed to a hype on social media that was clearly intended to disrupt support to affected regions, and international diplomatic and other processes, foreshadowing the America First mentality that has since become a key element of US politics. As I have argued elsewhere, the Ebola scare, like other social media storms (e.g. around Gamergate, and the Birther movement) can be seen as events through which Donald Trump and the collectives now considered part of the Alt-Right – often actually conjured up as a result of such social media storms – found their voice on social media.[29] As such, the criminalisation and zombification of Ebola victims, be it as a joke or as a Trumpian allegation, particularly organised around alleged illegal border-crossing, can itself be seen as a prefiguration of the Trump presidency. Medially, social network sites are the places where Alt-Right communities have been forged and grown, and, ideologically, the particular narrative of Ebola victims infecting the country from the inside is easily linked both to earlier notions of the 'enemy within'. That enemy (usually the left) allegedly infected American society and corrupted it from within.[30] This narrative fits with the conservative perception of Ebola as primarily a threat for the US, which Obama – as part-African himself – did not sufficiently protect the American people from.

In the early days of the COVID-19 outbreak in the US, too, Trump, by then US president nearing the end of his first term, pounced on the opportunity to frame a Patient Zero – this time not an individual, but 'the Chinese' in general – as malignant and guilty. Trump's framing of the coronavirus as a 'Chinese virus' fits his previous eagerness to stress Ebola's exotic origins. Trump's eagerness to blow up the fear of Ebola in 2014, under Obama, is diametrically opposed to his fervour in 2020 to deny the seriousness of COVID-19. However, the basic reflex to interpret this as a reason to 'stop flights' and otherwise block routes that might carry non-American or non-white people into the US, is the same – as is the desire to portray the CDC as inadequate and untrustworthy. Nonetheless, the metaphors and images that the CDC employed in its zombie preparedness campaign, fit strangely comfortably with Trump's binary discourse, which seems itself inherited from a fantasy universe.

CDC and *The Walking Dead*

The CDC's *Zombie Pandemic* comic conforms both with Lauro's claim that we now identify with those outrunning the zombie horde, at least in the case of some though not all zombie others, and also with Trump's posing as such in response to Ebola. In establishing how the comic relates to the Ebola epidemic, it is important to evaluate its place among similar cultural texts, and to understand how it interacts with the emergence of the social media sphere as a space in which political constituencies take shape.

Generally speaking, the CDC's graphic novel seems highly aware of its own mediality and interaction with popular culture: it is because of the horror movies that Todd presumably has his zombie apocalypse dream, with a stock ending of being overrun by a horde of zombies, and Julie and Todd get their information about what is going on through radio and television, but their basic knowledge of zombie ontology, as well as disease outbreaks, comes apparently from popular culture, like the horror movies they watch. The dream framework effectively stresses that the comic's core narrative is a remediation of popular zombie culture. It only takes on the characteristics of a premediation when an actual disease outbreak in the real world is understood in the context of that pre-existing story. That this did happen, with this particular comic, is shown in tweets like: 'CDC provided Ebola info in 2011: CDC – Blogs – Public Health Matters – Preparedness 101: Zombie Ap... – @CDCemergency http://blogs.cdc.gov/publichealthmatters/2011/05/preparedness-101-zombie-apocalypse/'.[31] Of course this is a joke, but the point that the CDC's fictional zombie outbreak is directly applicable to the Ebola outbreak works because it can be taken to imply that the CDC extradites Ebola victims from humanity and shifts them to zombie status.

Furthermore, the comic premediates potential real outbreaks in the sense that it wants to portray and put right the public's idea of the CDC's real policies and the workings of federal emergency response in general, compared to the fictional imagination that *The Walking Dead* and others put forward. This is true even if the material is also to some extent ironic and self-conscious, explicitly dovetailing on the success of *The Walking Dead* and intended to be cool, and interact with popular culture, at a time when the popularity of *The Walking Dead*, as well as other zombie franchises, were peaking. Arguably, the CDC *had* to do something around the zombie hype, in part because in the first season of *The Walking Dead* the CDC's headquarters in Atlanta is the setting of the final two episodes, and the centre plays a crucial role in the narrative, and also in the narrative of other contemporary movies, such as *Contagion* (2011).

As Timothy Melley argues in *The Covert Sphere: Secrecy, Fiction, and the National Security State*, American citizens do not have much access to the operations of US federal services, and therefore rely on fiction to shape their imagination of these agencies. Melley studies cases of national security agencies, which actually operate largely in secret. As such, cultural texts that offer a sense of how secret services work, like spy movies, and television series such as *Homeland*, *The Americans* and *24*, are most clearly within the scope of his analysis. For most citizens to get a sense of the workings of the CIA or the FBI, they need those films and series, and, as a result, the fictional cinematic texts operate in lieu of journalistic storytelling.

Although the Centers for Disease Control and Prevention do not occupy the position of a federal service without regular democratic transparency that is specific to secret services, Melley's claim that fictional representation is the main avenue towards shaping a popular imagination available to the general public, does also extend to the CDC. Even though it is not part of the spectacle of secrecy that Melley associates with the intelligence services, it does offer a kind of spectacle of incomprehensibility in Giorgio Agamben's sense.[32] The CDC's work is both fascinating and scientific, and specialised enough to invite clichés of brilliant scientists who do incomprehensible science in a hyper-technological setting, to save the country and world from threats the rest of us could hardly have imagined. *The Walking Dead*'s portrayal of the CDC in the first season largely buys into that image. It portrays science as completely incomprehensible to 'normal' people, and the brilliant-yet-morose white male scientist in charge of all this, as teetering on the brink of madness. The series' main characters are caught with him in the agency's headquarters. Both the group of survivors led by Rick Grimes (Andrew Lincoln) and

Dr Edwin Jenner, the scientist (Noah Emmerich), embody the prototypical pre-accomplished – white – subjects that the fictional State in the series sets out to protect. Almost to their own detriment, since it is practically impossible to leave the building. This protection from infestation by the other, even to one's own detriment, is presented as a rational endgame choice from the perspective of the CDC – if there is nobody left to responsibly take charge of the centre, it should not exist.

This type of imagination of how the CDC works, and how it would work in a situation of irrevocable and overwhelming disaster, is closely aligned to what one would expect on the basis of Melley's analysis of the workings of fictional representations of federal agencies like the CIA or the FBI. It is understandable, then, that the CDC, which can be more transparent about its workings and which has a concrete stake in being trusted in its communication with the public, wants to offer its own impression of what it is doing, and what it would do in dystopic future scenarios. After all, the image *The Walking Dead* offers is perhaps not anti-science, but it does capitalise on the supposedly inscrutable nature of scientific research, and on fantasies about mutually exclusive interests of individuals and the population as a whole, which also come into play, for example, in the debate about vaccination programmes for children. This is, as the vaccination debate shows, a dispute that easily transforms into either exaggerated reverence, or mistrust, and even outright rejection of science.

Like the secret services for security, the CDC is understandably regarded as an agency involved on the one hand in inaccessible research, and on the other in the opaque, even manipulative, machinations of managing public health. One obvious reason to mistrust it is that it does not only fight disease and work to improve public health, it also is in charge of communicating about this. As doing that can directly influence public health, particularly in the context of contagious diseases and the contagion of mass anxiety, there is a logical potential for duplicity in its communication. The fear here, presumably, would be that it can be good from the CDC's point of view not to create panic, for instance in a country receiving people from a geographical region affected by a contagious disease, when for individuals in the receiving area panic could be justified, because to them there is a risk involved. It is understandable, then, that agencies like the CDC both have a strong presence in fictional narratives, and also, that they are easily integrated in conspiracy theories of 'deep government' that falsely reassures 'the people'.

Conclusion

Particularly after the portrayal in the first season of *The Walking Dead*, it made communicative and narrative sense, that the CDC – which gets its public image more from popular fiction featuring the centre than from its own often invisible work – chose to offer its own take on how to prepare for, and battle, the zombie apocalypse. To do so in the form of a graphic novella pays tribute to the origins of *The Walking Dead*, which of course originally is a black-and-white comic, created and written by Robert Kirkman, which first came out in 2003. Moreover, by presenting preparedness advice in the form of a comic strip, it is possible to combine a high degree of accessibility of information with entertainment value. Whereas the majority of public health advice texts are perceived as dry or boring, the graphic novella form increases the chances of engaging a young audience.

The comic obviously has good intentions in its effort to rewrite the story of a zombie epidemic so as to give a sense of how civilians and the CDC would or should act. However, in doing so, it also strengthens the pre-existing metaphor by which people are turned into 'zombies' through Ebola and other contagious diseases that affect black people in the first place. The CDC is a federal agency, dedicated to research and applying the power of science in emergency public health situations. While I do not think readers take the threat of a zombie apocalypse as presented in the comic too seriously, the mental connection is nonetheless reinforced, and to some extent officially authorised.

Social media responses to the Ebola epidemic of 2013–15 show how the CDC's use of the zombie metaphor is actually problematic, in light of the Ebola 'scare' in the United States, which erupted, mainly, on social media platforms. Hasian's discussion of Arjun Appadurai's 'mediascapes' and 'ideoscapes' as they evolved in the unfolding of the Ebola epidemic, show how American popular culture in a sense premediated the Ebola epidemic, so that it was, when it occurred, already highly present, both as a narrative and in terms of images, in the US American imagination.[33] Where Hasian attended in detail to films that represent Ebola and other virus outbreaks, and to television and other traditional news media's framing of the epidemic, I have additionally explored the dynamics in which Ebola was specifically connected to zombie discourse and narratives in the specific process of 'going viral' online.

Although the pun here is of course intentional – and there are many alluring opportunities – I have tried to be as literal and un-metaphorical as I can, because I want to argue that the conceptual metaphors used to describe the Ebola epidemic, particularly online, but elsewhere too, are key to understanding the fascination and scare surrounding the Ebola epidemic. This can be seen for instance in the popular notion of the 'Ebola apocalypse' Hasian refers to, and the metaphor – 'Ebola patient IS zombie' – seems to play a central role in ensuring the fascination of American audiences, both to news and social media references to the epidemic.[34] The same fascination with zombies is employed, clearly, by the 'Preparedness 101: Zombie Pandemic' campaign to inform the public about preparedness for real disease outbreaks or other hazards. The many tweets that have jokingly noted that the Zombie campaign was the CDC's disguised preparation for the Ebola epidemic, show how easily the equation can be reversed to 'Zombie IS Ebola patient'.

However, while the comic seems to engage critically to some extent with its own role in society and the agencies and institutions that usually shape the CDC in the cultural imaginary, the campaign also misses important points. For one thing, the decision to allow the website to 'live or walk dead' after the campaign's ending, has implied that, in the wake of the 2013–15 Ebola epidemic, the graphic novel suddenly revived, but in a way in which it was not intended. Although the link between Ebola victims and zombies is obviously made by many regardless of the *Zombie Pandemic* preparedness comic, those who were aware of it could easily attribute meaning to the coincidence so that it became a premediation of the actual epidemic, or rather of the way the Ebola scare played out in the USA. This was further enabled by the fact that a disease scare produced by hardly any actual victims on American soil remained an outbreak narrative rather than an actual outbreak.

Clearly, the CDC understands, at least on some level, and plays with the force of the zombie metaphor. The joke about Zombie Preparedness 'living or walking dead on a CDC website' wittily links the key characteristic of zombies to one of the central issues around online communication: do you leave it online even if it is no longer current or relevant? It might seem an inconsequential issue, and as a researcher of course I am glad that it has been left online, but ironically, the zombie metaphor here can be carried further than was probably foreseen. The campaign came back to life as a result of the resonances with the Ebola epidemic in a now-malignant form, often both criticising the CDC and dehumanising potential Ebola victims.

Thus, the Centers for Disease Control and Prevention have been naïve in assuming that the zombie metaphor could be harmless. The cultural discourse and narratives that this metaphor plays into in a social media context are heavily ideologically inflected with racism and nativism, as Priscilla Wald has shown for outbreak narratives in general. When coming from the CDC, phrases like 'The rise of zombies in pop culture has given credence to the idea that a zombie apocalypse could happen' have a self-fulfilling quality. Of course, no actual zombie apocalypse could happen, but the fact that the CDC is hypothetically addressing it facilitates and legitimates the metaphor. The ideological interests and desires that underlie the fascination with hordes of undead aliens, out to infect 'us' with their abject condition, are unaccounted for, but were quickly picked up by Donald Trump and early exponents of the nascent Alt-Right. The zombie metaphor in this context is a medially attractive way to dehumanise real victims. And Ebola as a disfiguring viral disease already has a history of being discursively linked to horror and zombies. On Twitter, the comic came to be an obvious reference point for how 'even the government' knew that the Ebola epidemic was really a zombie attack. Of course, this was mostly done in jest, but that does not make it innocent or harmless. As such, the CDC with its 'playful' campaign to warn Americans to be prepared for outbreaks and other disasters, presumably accidentally, played into a popular cultural fascination with Ebola that was politically actively used by others to fan the flame of xenophobia.

Notes

1. CDC, 'Zombie Preparedness', Centers for Disease Control and Prevention (CDC), Office of Public Preparedness and Response, 11 October 2018, *https://www.cdc.gov/phpr/zombie/index.htm* (accessed 30 January 2020).
2. CDC, 'Zombie Preparedness Graphic Novel', Centers for Disease Control and Prevention (CDC), Office of Public Preparedness and Response, 11 October 2018, *https://www.cdc.gov/phpr/zombie/novel.htm* (accessed 30 January 2020).
3. Written by Maggie Silver; Art Direction by James Archer; Pencilled and Inked by Bob Hobbs; Digital Colour by Alissa Eckert; Lettering & Layout by Mark Conner.
4. Marouf A. Hasian Jr, *Representing Ebola: Culture, Law, and Public Discourse about the 2013–2015 West African Ebola Outbreak* (Madison: Fairleigh Dickinson University Press, 2016), p. 144.
5. S. Shaviro, 'Capitalist Monsters', *Historical Materialism*, 10/4 (2002), 281–90, 288.

6. G. Canavan, '"We are the Walking Dead": Race, Time, and Survival in Zombie Narrative', *Extrapolation*, 51/3 (2010), 431–53, 433.
7. Canavan, '"We are the Walking Dead"', 432.
8. CDC, 'Zombie Preparedness'.
9. Canavan, '"We are the Walking Dead"', 433.
10. Hasian Jr, *Representing Ebola*, p. 145.
11. Hasian Jr, *Representing Ebola*, p. 131.
12. Esther Peeren, *The Spectral Metaphor: Living Ghosts and the Agency of Invisibility* (New York: Palgrave Macmillan, 2014).
13. *Ebola Zombies*, Samuel Leong, dir. (Wild Eye, 2015).
14. *https://github.com/digitalmethodsinitiative/dmi-tcat/wiki/FAQ* (accessed 30 January 2020).
15. Edward P. Comentale and Aaron Jaffe (eds), *The Year's Work at the Zombie Research Center* (Bloomington: Indiana University Press, 2014), p. 31.
16. George Lakoff and Mark Johnson, *Metaphors We Live By* (Chicago and London: University of Chicago Press, 1980, 2003).
17. P. H. Thibodeau and L. Boroditsky, 'Metaphors We Think With: The Role of Metaphor in Reasoning', *PLoS ONE*, 6/2 (2011).
18. Priscilla Wald, *Contagious: Cultures, Carriers, and the Outbreak Narrative* (London and Durham, NC: Duke University Press, 2008), p. 263.
19. Wald, *Contagious*, pp. 43–4.
20. Wald, *Contagious*, pp. 81, 85.
21. Sarah Lauro, *The Transatlantic Zombie: Slavery, Rebellion, and Living Death* (New Brunswick: Rutgers University Press, 2015), p. 27.
22. Lauro, *The Transatlantic Zombie*, p. 2.
23. TmarTn, Twitter post, 15 October 2014, *https://twitter.com/TmarTn/status/522442071907774466* (accessed 30 January 2020). According to the date of access, this tweet has received 1,770,000 followers, 60 Retweets, 230 Likes.
24. *https://www.hoaxorfact.com/Paranormal/2-ebola-victims-in-african-village-rise-from-the-dead-hoax.html* (accessed 30 January 2020); Hoax or Fact, Twitter post, 9 October 2014, *https://twitter.com/HoaxOrFact/status/520167224628109312* (accessed 30 January 2020).
25. *https://www.hoaxorfact.com/Paranormal/2-ebola-victims-in-african-village-rise-from-the-dead-hoax.html* (accessed 30 January 2020).
26. Richard Grusin, *Affect and Mediality After 9/11* (London: Palgrave Macmillan, 2010).
27. Donald J. Trump, Twitter post, 3 October 2014, *https://twitter.com/realDonaldTrump/status/517805743056359424* (accessed 30 January 2020).

28. Donald J. Trump, Twitter post, 15 October 2014, *https://twitter.com/realdonaldtrump/status/522394479429689344* (accessed 30 January 2020).
29. Sara Polak and Daniel Trottier (eds), *Violence and Trolling on Social Media: History, Affect, and Effects of Online Vitriol* (Amsterdam: Amsterdam University Press, 2020).
30. See, e.g., Dinesh D'Souza, *The Enemy at Home: The Cultural Left and Its Responsibility for 9/11* (New York: Doubleday, 2007); David Neiwert, *Alt-America: The Rise of the Radical Right in the Age of Trump* (New York: Verso Books, 2017), p. 74.
31. #2AinNJ, Twitter post, 2 October 2015, *https://twitter.com/ReviveLiberty/status/517693226136768512* (accessed 2 October 2014).
32. Timothy Melley, *The Covert Sphere: Secrecy, Fiction, and the National Security State* (Ithaca: Cornell University Press, 2012), pp. 94–9.
33. Hasian Jr, *Representing Ebola*, p. 142.
34. Thibodeau and Boroditsky, 'Metaphors We Think With'.

3

The Zika Virus, Ebola Contagion Narratives and US Obsessions with Securitising Neglected Infectious Diseases

Madison A. Krall, Marouf Hasian Jr
and Yvonne Karyn Clark

IN THIS PARTICULAR chapter we extend the work of Priscilla Wald and others who have written about how the circulation of 'outbreak narratives' impact the ways that many social agents write or talk about infectious diseases, including avian flu, H1NI, Ebola and the Zika virus. Within the last several years the World Health Organization (WHO) has had to declare that global communities were having to deal with some 'public health emergencies of international concern (PHEIC)'.[1] For example, WHO Director-General Margaret Chan recalled the PHEIC for Zika virus infection on 18 November 2016, and on 18 May 2018 the WHO Emergency Committee convened for its first meeting under the International Health Regulations (IHR) to decide whether the most recent Ebola outbreak in the Democratic Republic of the Congo constituted a PHEIC.[2] Instead of viewing this as reason enough to spend billions of dollars on infrastructures that might help with the prevention, and long-term containment of these diseases, many participants in what we call 'outbreak debates' insisted on finding less costly, emergency preparedness schemes that justified certain types of foreign health interventionism.

It will be our contention that the application of critical 'praxiological studies' will put on display the ways that US obsessions with militarising rhetorics and securitising discourses impact infectious disease containment efforts. If, as Michel Foucault once argued, plagues are forms of real or imagined disorders, then it is imperative that we pay attention to the myriad ways that infectious diseases are treated – figuratively and literally – as militarised or 'bioterrorist' threats that are linked to disciplines, crimes, memories of contagion, disorders, and living and dying.[3]

Critical 'praxiological studies' are materialist types of studies that illustrate how particular theories are actually put into practice in contentious debates about public health 'emergency' or 'security' settings. For example, a critical praxiological study might investigate the ideological reasons why US health communities constantly wrote and talked about 'health security' and the need to declare 'war' on infectious diseases like Ebola, and then proceeded to send troops overseas during the 2014–16 West African outbreak in order to win victories against these microbial enemies or disease vectors. Were American military forces interested in extending their spheres of influence at the same time that they aided Liberians or others who suffered from Ebola?

An example of a critical praxiological study would be when social scientists and humanities scholars study how the circulation of particular interpretations of PHEIC guidelines are used to rationalise interventionism or non-interventionism. Unlike others who might take-for-granted the truth value of claims that are made about infectious diseases, causes or cures, we focus on the 'truth effects' that go into the constitutive, co-production of epistemes that become parts of larger ideological formations – what Foucault called a *dispositif*. Foucault used the term *dispositif* to refer to the large physical, institutional or administrative apparatuses that are used by social groups or societies to produce and maintain particular knowledge structures – related to Bruno Latour's object-oriented *dingpolitik*.[4] Priscilla Wald's notion of outbreak narratives has affinities with our critical commentaries on the need for praxiological studies.

Some authors of earlier praxiological studies have noted that the declarations of any public health emergency, especially in international contexts, do not occur in any ideological vacuum, and that public health officials often have to balance helpful consciousness-raising with the dangers that come from crying wolf too often. While we realise that elite and public declarations of war may help get the attention of Washington, DC politicians, praxiological studies highlight how the select uses of war or security frames – especially during times of war – carry risks.

As we will argue in more detail below, characterising Zika viruses as monsters that have to be fought as if they were zombies, or using phantasmagoric images of Zika victims, may deflect attention away from the structural, material and long-term issues that influence how diseases like Zika are diagnosed and treated by local groups, nation-states or international communities. It is no coincidence that those who search for quick fixes to infectious disease problems oftentimes use military and security frames so that they can declare emergencies, win 'wars' against diseases, and then go home.

We are obviously not the first researchers who have studied how the use of select media frames, and the deployment of particular cultural imaginaries, have influenced the epistemic and epidemiological treatment of the Zika virus. Nerlich, McLeod and Burgess, in 2016, provided interdisciplinary communities with an assessment of how a few Anglo-American blog posts used strategic metaphoric framing of Zika.[5] During this same period Dredze, Broniatowski and Hilyard investigated how various Twitter debates put on display various public communities' understanding of the Zika crisis.[6] Several years later Ribeiro, Hartley, Nerlich and Jaspal highlighted how Brazilian media outlets used 'war frames' – both during and after the 'end' of the Zika outbreak – to deflect attention away from the links that could be made between poverty, regional inequality and gender inequities.[7]

In this chapter we will be arguing that our own praxiological studies of US military and securitising frameworks of Zika viruses support many of the conclusions that appeared in these earlier assessments. It will be our position that an analysis of American popular culture and US scientific communities' representations of Zika virus show the problematic nature of some magnification of risks and some promotions of public health security strategies. These popular and scientific representations, intentionally or unintentionally, oftentimes echo and mimic the positions of those who worry about everything from imaginary zombies to actual foreign terrorists. We contend that while some of these cultural or scientific frames did indeed allow various US and international audiences to visualise how Zika was a *flavirus* transmitted to humans by different mosquitoes that could be managed and contained, other ideological frames surfaced to supplement, or supplant, those managerial rhetorics that involved zombification or monstering.[8]

At this point we need to explain that our understandings of the representational processes associated with zombification have been influenced by Lorenzo Servitje and Sherryl Vint's edited collection *The Walking Med: Zombies and The Medical Image*.[9] We view zombification and its causes as part of the shift away from 'the supernatural to the biological realm of viral infection and human scientific interference', and see praxiological studies of zombification as investigating these interferences. In infectious disease contexts zombies are no longer merely sources of public entertainment, and studies of zombification become a 'critical tool with which to explore the limitations of scientific and medical knowledge'.[10] We are conscious of the problematic nature of some of this monstering and zombification, and yet we feel that we have to attend to the ways that societies treat the zombie as a figure of contagion that 'speaks to our ongoing fears of global pandemic and to recent outbreaks'.[11]

While some zombification – with images of fast-moving zombies – effectively shows the speed with which social structures are overwhelmed by said contagion, others use zombies to get across their counter-terrorist, counter-insurgency or bioterrorist messages. Some of this zombification provides more heat than light, especially in situations where militaristic monstering metaphors become a part of pervasive modes of scientific communication that are then being shared with public audiences.[12]

Instead of improving scientific literacy, and instead of inviting publics to pay far more for needed health-care infrastructures to combat many types of infectious diseases or emerging diseases, spikes in coverage of the 'war on Zika' oftentimes reflect how groups, like mothers or children, are vilified, to the point where those who suffer from Zika are hurt by the circulation of these monstering representations.

Our praxiological review reveals how in some cases even well-intentioned disseminators of information about the Zika virus often (re)produced problematic, graphic and emotive images of newborn babies with serious birth defects in popular culture representations and other rhetorical materials that appeared in scientific journalistic coverage of Zika.[13] In other cases, health planners and other practitioners wrote about the potential bioterrorist usages of the Zika virus or they conflated infectious disease threats and military terrorist threats. The research question that needs to be asked by critical investigators is whether the use of these war frames – that admittedly helped with the funding for anti-Zika campaigns and consciousness-raising efforts – proved to be too costly a venture? How much of this zombification helped public health care planners, and how much of it deflected attention away from some other environmental or epidemiological causes of the spread of the Zika virus? Did this appropriation of select cultural frames in infectious disease contexts tell us more about the popularity of the global war on terrorism, or more about zombification voyeurism, than it did about how best to combat the Zika virus?

In order to help answer those types of queries the rest of this chapter will be divided into four sections. The first portion of the chapter provides a brief commentary on the role that framing studies play in praxiological studies of infectious diseases like the Zika virus. The second segment illustrates how crafters of American popular press representations, between 2015 and 2017, used monstering or securitising techniques as they commented on the similarities that purportedly existed between wars that had to be fought against Zika viruses and terrorist foes. The uses of these frames helped magnify the perceptual existential dangers for anxious US audiences who did not want their families to suffer. They did not want American communities to suffer in the same way that Brazilian families had suffered from the Zika virus, and they did not want to see any non-interventionism in the 'war' on Zika.

In the second section we also note how mass-mediated representations of the Zika virus circulated in the mainstream presses, as well as in the alternative outlets that could be found on the web. The third section complements this by highlighting how authors of scientific articles – even those that complained about epidemiological misinformation – may have also contributed to the zombification and securitisation of the Zika virus. While masquerading as forms of scientific literacy, or attempts to provide practical critiques of problematic popular press representations, these scientific frames of the Zika virus oftentimes reified the very ideological formations that they were critiquing. In the concluding fourth section we comment on the heuristic value of praxiological analyses while also noting how this extends the work of others who have worried about the use of zombification, military metaphors or the public health securitisation of infectious diseases.

The Role of Framing in the Constitutive Creation of Problematic Zika Perceptions

Even though they have used different methodologies, both social scientists and humanities scholars have been concerned about the role that framing plays in scientific literacy and public health planning for the containment of infectious diseases. As Baruch Fischhoff noted, the labeling of risks does impact their perceived outcome, and several scholars have sought to better understand how mediated representations impact public perceptions of Zika, the regulation of bodies, and public health interventionism.[14] In their study 'Frequency of Risk-Related News Media Messages in 2016 Coverage of Zika Virus: Risk-Related News Media about Zika', for example, Sell et al. learned that public concerns surrounding Zika were possibly increased as a result of the large percentage of news stories with risk-elevating messages, such as 'mosquito-borne transmission, potentially catastrophic birth defects, and potential spread in the United States'.[15] Their conclusions were supporting existing research that public perception regarding risk increases in part, based on skewed news media articles about the dangers of infectious disease outbreaks. As it pertains to social media, Seltzer et al. determined that the majority of Instagram posts between May and August 2016 contained unclear or misleading information about Zika, with the majority of images expressing 'fear and negative sentiment'.[16] They were worried about the further circulation of problematising public perceptions, given the high volume of misinformation or incomplete information that was being shared with diverse audiences.

In some cases, studies have reviewed not only representations of the Zika virus, but commentary on vaccines and other preventive measures as well. Regarding public views on the mass-mediated transmission of the seminal human trial of a vaccine for Zika, Hilgard and Jamieson discovered there was a significant, though short-term, increase in the confidence people had in science, suggesting 'that it is possible to bolster the credibility of science when science provides uncontroversial solutions to problems covered by the media'.[17] As highlighted by Lazear, Stringer and De Silva, the driving force for discovering such vaccines and antivirals, in keeping with the majority of the current Zika virus literature, is the desire by the public to 'combat ZIKV infection' because of alarmed perceptions regarding ZIKV's association to microcephaly.[18]

Humanities scholars who have studied these Zika frames are worried about not only the spread of misinformation about Zika but the ideological and material aspects of these portrayals. Although Brazil would be the first nation in the Western Hemisphere to experience a large-scale spread of Zika during autumn 2015, critical scholars interested in the cultural, social, legal, military and security dimensions of infectious diseases critiqued how communities in dozens of other countries were representing cases of Zika infection. As Ribeiro, Hartley, Nerlich and Jaspal have recently noted, those who were involved with the construction of particular mediatised 'frames' could have investigated how this outbreak had something to do with a host of social and gender inequalities, but instead, officials and media agenda setters in places like Brazil decided to characterise the reaction to the early 2016 response to the Zika outbreak as a declaration of war.[19] Given the horrific nature of the death toll that came from the earlier Ebola outbreak of 2013–16 it was understandable why those who worried about the effects of the spread of the Zika virus might write about the anxieties of those who worried about losing 'the war' against this epidemic that took the lives of thousands in Sierra Leone, Liberia and Guinea.[20] Were they dealing with Zika but seeing Ebola? If Yanbi Andrea Wang and Michele Barry's *Los Angeles Times* article from 9 February 2016, entitled 'Zika Outbreak Bears an Eerie Resemblance to the Spread of Ebola' gives any indication of the problematic way in which Ebola discourse was mapped onto Zika, then we can presumably offer that yes, they likely were.[21]

In the next section we extend our analysis by showing how Zika mass media representations that circulated in the popular culture tried to magnify the significance of the spread of this disease by monstering and securitising Zika.

The Circulation of Zika Media Representations Between 2015 and 2017 and the Monstering of the Zika Virus

On mainstream and social media websites Zika has been categorised as a security threat in myriad ways, and we would argue that one of the most popular ways to characterise Zika involved the use of monstering techniques. For example, some online bloggers, like those using the popular video sharing website YouTube, announced the early arriving threat with direct language in titles such as 'ZIKA ZOMBIES CONFIRMED IN AFRICA' and 'Survivors of Zika Virus Mutate into Zombies Want to Eat Doctors', producing frames that sutured together Zika contagion frames with zombie rhetorics.[22]

Media coverage of the Zika virus and this monstering spiked between 2015 and 2017, but this would not be the first time that infectious diseases would be zombified. As Sara Polak noted in chapter 2, the Centers for Disease Control and Prevention (CDC) launched their zombie preparedness website, their blog and their Facebook campaign to spread the word in 2011.[23]

Ali S. Khan, head of the CDC's Office of Public Health Preparedness and Response, stated during an interview with *The Atlantic* that: 'The rise of zombies in pop culture has given credence to the idea that a zombie apocalypse could happen. In these scenarios, zombies would take over entire countries, roaming city streets eating anything living that got in their way. The proliferation of this idea has led many people to wonder: How do I prepare for a zombie apocalypse?'[24]

This would not be the first time that members of public cultures heard these types of dire messages. As Marina Levina once remarked, monsters have historically served 'as illustrations of the fallibility of nature – diseases, viruses, and pandemics, as opposed to the will of God or other supernatural forces'.[25] Given this historical backdrop, it was necessarily surprising that in a world where publics worried about the Avian Flu, Ebola and other diseases, fears of pandemics (e.g. the coronavirus (COVID-19) pandemic) would be linked to zombies. Our praxiological study of some of this zombification of Zika in US presses between 2015 and 2017 reveals that there were at least three main strategies or sub-frames that were used in the production of these *epistemes*. The first, almost ubiquitous, rhetorical technique, involved the mention of microcephaly. The second strategy involved linking talk of vaccines or cures to the containment of mythic monsters, while the third zombification strategy focused on the supposed 'biting' similarities that existed in zombie and Zika scenarios.

Given the neurological features of the human brain, the rhetorical leap to zombies is sometimes easy to make. After all, microcephaly is a disorder that can be represented in non-clinical ways, permitting those in the popular culture to comment on how an infant's head is significantly smaller than average and is linked to abnormal brain development in the womb.[26] International presses in 2016 carried countless stories of how Brazilian families had to cope with microcephaly, impacting everything from sanitation programmes to Olympic planning, but these were just some of the places where global audience texts and visualities honed in on perceived microcephaly dangers. For example, many mass media outlets reported on how knowledgeable experts were saying that the Zika virus, if contracted by a pregnant woman, may cause microcephaly in the infant being carried. Margaret Chan, the World Health Organization (WHO) Director at the time of the initial Zika outbreak, told reporters that there was only circumstantial evidence of Zika causing microcephaly, but the evidence that infectious disease researchers had in their possession was 'suggestive and extremely worrisome'.[27]

The oftentimes eugenical characterisations of infants with microcephaly quickly morphed into commentaries that assumed that this was a form of monstering that needed to be prevented, in much the same way that one might prepare for the zombie apocalypse. The possibility of a microcephaly connection to Zika spurred some, like Eddie Cole, to write articles about some of these symbolic linkages. In his 2016 article, Cole took content from *Reuters* and argued that while 'health officials haven't explicitly stated that Zika will cause people infected with it to rise from their graves and hunt down the living . . . it kinda sounds like it will'.[28] In addition, Cole claimed that officials advising women to avoid pregnancy until more is known about the virus were 'afraid of zombie babies'.[29]

Mainstream newspapers were not the only outlets that participated in this zombification. Sydney Lupkin, a journalist writing for *Vice News*, also covered the connection to the birth defect for *Vice*'s news coverage website. Lupkin wrote that while the disease can be fatal, those contracting Zika and suffering from the secondary symptom of the disease (microcephaly), could survive, although those with microcephaly would likely have 'developmental issues'. These developmental issues rhetorically (if unfairly) connect the Zika virus and microcephaly survivors to zombies, monsters often represented as brain dead.[30] Microcephaly was covered in depth by many news sources, and a critical purposive sample of some mainstream newspapers shows that the *New York Times* had fourteen articles (out of over one hundred articles on Zika broadly) specifically covering the dangers of Zika as connected to birth defects in depth between 2016 and 2018.[31]

Other outlets carried similar representations. *Quora*, a website branded as 'a place to share knowledge and better understand the world',[32] commonly posted news blog posts that allowed individuals to ask and answer questions. Unsurprisingly, the question 'Will Zika virus bring the long-awaited zombie apocalypse?' began an online debate between microcephaly in 'unborn children' and milder 'rashes' in adults. The comment thread ends on the following note:

> Actually once we are told harmless lil [sic] zika [sic] was only a minor rash . . . then . . . then . . . then . . . Now they are saying it eats memory . . . learning . . . motor skills . . . eyesight . . . hearing . . . causes bad headaches . . . and next???? Zika now may stay with you till death. and [sic] slowly eat your brain away ttill [sic] you suffocate to death while paralyzed . . . ZIKA ZOMBIES.. [sic] OR. [sic] ZICKIES.[33]

The lack of clarity in media representations over what are the risks and side effects of the Zika virus contributes to the problematics that we alluded to in the earlier portions of this essay. Many websites, including *Business Insider* and the Zombie Research Society, similarly covered Zika and its connection to microcephaly while downplaying the effects on adults contracting and spreading the disease.[34]

The spread of the disease heightens the monstrous and threatening nature of Zika, which is connected in these infectious *epistemes*, and this spurs some communities' demands for a vaccine or a cure for the virus. Similar to countless other apocalyptic representations that circulate in mainstream or popular culture venues, zombie Zika epidemics can create the impression that there is no feasible 'cure' that can stop the spread of the virus. Cole argued that the lack of a vaccine or pharmaceutical cure gives a sense of déjà-vu of Ebola as, referencing *Reuters* once more, 'We've got no drugs and we've got no vaccines'.[35]

Talk of vaccines and cures might seem innocent enough, but during a Global War on Terrorism (GWOT) talk that begins with the spread of infectious disease containment can quickly lead to discussions of militarisation, securitisation and potential bioterrorist threats. Writers Tom Miles and Ben Hirschler also make the connection to Ebola, a disease with its own allegedly monstrous and militarised connections, and they point to the spurring of a 'hunt' for a vaccine. Readers might assume that the Zika virus epidemic came new to the biological world in 2015. And these impressions may be created, in spite of the fact that the WHO cites Zika as first discovered in Uganda in 1947.[36] Miles and Hirschler also comment on the related topic of 'mutation', a concept that is also connected to zombies, since one problem with a possible vaccine is the fact that the disease could be 'evolving' in ways that hinder vaccine efficacy.[37] Mutations are often said to interfere with everything from Ebola containment to counter-zombie strategising.

In the same way that commentary on microcephaly was used to magnify familiar health risks to growing numbers of the population, this talk of vaccines, zombies and Zika could be used to critique treatments and governmental plans for containment. The lack of a vaccine means that only the 'flu like' symptoms of the disease can be treated 'with rest and fluids plus over-the-counter pain medications'.[38] The issue over treatment caused the Zombie Research Society to criticise both the WHO and the CDC, as they argued that the organisations were 'fumbling the handling of a dangerous virus.'[39] Some contributors to social media or mainstream media outlets tried to argue that preparation for an adequate response to Zika was in its infancy, but, as noted above, this was the type of disease that researchers knew about long ago. More than a few mentioned the 1947 discovery of Zika in Africa, and how, only in 2015, when the threat of Zika spreading from Brazil, to Latin America and the Caribbean (and therefore Florida and the rest of the United States), American decision makers finally seemed to show any concern. This 'leap to the Western Hemisphere' prompted the WHO to belatedly declare that the Zika virus outbreak could now be 'categorized as a "public emergency of international concern"'.[40]

This monstering of the Zika virus also impacted the ways those in popular cultures or mainstream presses wrote or talked about 'patient zero' and the initial spread of the Zika virus. After all, one primary way the Zika virus spreads internationally is through the bite of a mosquito and the movements of infected individuals. In May of 2015 when the epidemic gained international attention, the *Atlantic* reported that more than 200,000 had been infected by Zika, mostly from mosquitoes.[41] Given the fact that zombie aficionados oftentimes note how zombies can infect their victims via biting, or an exchange of bodily fluid, we can understand why some pundits would want to focus attention on the ways that the Zika virus might affect an unborn child in the womb. In the same way that fans of zombie movies might note the rapidity of moving zombie threats, one might note how the spread of the Zika virus was rapid, crossing the borders of more than twenty countries by May of 2015. The WHO was claiming that all of the 'Americas' are at risk to the spread of the disease, and by May of 2017 the virus spread to dozens of countries throughout the Americas, 'and all 50 U.S. states'.[42]

The potential reasons for the rapid transmission of Zika (not unlike zombie transmissions) was a major topic of discussion. One observer noted that the 'virus likely arrived via infected travellers, who were bitten by local mosquitos'.[43] Stobbe noted that the Zika infectious sweep 'across Latin America and the Caribbean in 2015 and 2016' via unaware travellers prompted the United States Food and Drug Administration (FDA) to require blood banks to screen for the disease to prevent furthering the spread via blood transfusions. However, similar to the issue surrounding possible vaccines, there is 'little bang for the buck in Zika blood testing'.[44] Advisers to the FDA have noted that if there is no cheaper solution to testing for Zika in the United States, the screening should largely be abandoned.

All of this talk of the Zika virus and zombie threats is understandable in popular cultural contexts, but what do we do when scientific journalists, scientists and others within scientific communities use similar literal and figurative analogies as they declare 'war' on Zika?

Scientific Press Coverage of the Need for 'War' Against the Zika Virus

Sorenson, Jordan and LaDeau recently remarked that the way 'science is communicated' – particularly the components of science that are emphasised to members of the community, i.e. framing – can have an impact on 'how individuals respond to the implications of this science'.[45] The framing of the Zika virus (commonly referenced as ZIKV) in scientific press coverage in the public health domain of the United States has a significant impact on public understandings of ZIKV with regards not only to its transmission, but also with respect to how the public can effectively 'combat' and contain this 'fatal' disease through individual prevention strategies and collective efforts guided by varying government agencies. Dealing with the Zika virus is, therefore, even in scientific communities, a matter of individual security and safety. Note, for example, how scientists or scientific journalists can comment on how a mother acting in sanitary ways can prevent microcephaly. This can be configured as a national 'health security' issue as well.

The securitisation and militarisation of the Zika virus is relatively apparent in the titles and headings of many of the articles or the contents therein that appeared in the scientific press coverage of ZIKV between 2014 and 2018. For example, *Science Magazine*, a publication of the American Association for the Advancement of Science, showcases this militarisation explicitly in its December 2016 issue, with a news article in the infectious disease section entitled 'One Year Later, Zika Scientists Prepare for a Long War'. Written by Gretchen Vogel, the article highlights the fact that researchers are still uncertain of the risks surrounding Zika and that they are concerned that an additional wave of 'birth defects' should be anticipated. Vogel further reminds readers that 'The virus is now firmly *entrenched* [emphasis added] in Latin America, which is already *battling* [emphasis added] several other mosquito-borne diseases'.[46] The author of that same article underscored the similarities and differences that existed between the United States and other Zika-affected countries, such as Colombia and Brazil. Clare Wilson, a contributor to *New Scientist* magazine, employed similarly militarised language in her February 2016 article, entitled '7 Ways the War on Zika Mosquitos Could Be Won'.[47] Jeanette Ferrara, an author for *Scienceline* – a project of the Science, Health and Environmental Reporting Program at NYU – asked if there was 'An Easy Solution to the War on Zika?' in her article under the same title.[48] A praxiological review of these articles illustrates how many members of the scientific journalistic community viewed their own participation in the 'war' against Zika as something that involved more than mere rhetoric. Oftentimes the main issue was not whether this was a war, but how it needed to be fought.

The content of the scientific press coverage is also overwrought with implicit and explicit war framing and scientific configurations of the Zika virus that work to engage readers in the ongoing war with the 'fatal' disease. Mirroring the US approach to the COVID-19 virus, fighting Zika thus becomes a moral imperative, where scientists, doctors, lay persons and others work together to control the spread of this infectious disease. In Wilson's *New Scientist* article the rhetoric is more implicit, since she highlights that the US population is an international body responsible for funding research and organising 'international efforts to *combat* [emphasis added] mosquitos'.[49] Wilson shares the following tweet from Brazil's president Dilma Rousseff: 'We must wage war against *Aedes aegypti*, the vector of dengue, of chikungunya and of Zika'.[50] Was this simply a figure use of militarised metaphors, or was Brazil's leader asking for interventionism that resembled the militaries' interventionism during the 'West African' Ebola crisis?

These types of references not only bring together Brazilian and American warriors who fight against Zika, they also help reify the idea that military and security communities have some of the same concerns that should also occupy the attention of scientific communities. The use of this type of discourse and framing magnifies not only the dangers but also the number of social agents involved in these wars. In a special article released by *Bayer Research Magazine*, entitled, you guessed it, 'The War on Mosquitoes', Bayer researchers' aims to 'stem Zika, malaria, and dengue'[51] are highlighted, with their efforts reviewed and glorified. It matters a great deal that this dramatised way of representing the Zika virus is presented by Dr Kurt Vandock, Senior Scientist of Environmental Science in Bayer's Crop Science Division in the United States, a former Captain in the United States Army. Vandock, who was deployed to many Middle Eastern locations during Operation Enduring Freedom in Afghanistan, is quoted in the magazine article twice. After referencing how many people he saw suffering from the diseases transmitted by mosquitoes, such as malaria, Vandock shares the following quote (with respect to the mosquitoes): 'These hordes of blood-sucking insects are more dangerous than any *enemy army* [emphasis added]. Over the past decade, the population and geographical range of *Aedes aegypti* have exploded globally.'[52] At the close of the article, in which Bayer scientists' approaches to the Zika-carrying mosquitoes take centre stage, Vandock adds: 'Every army is vulnerable in some way, and that applies to the black and white squadrons of mosquitoes – you just have to know how to *attack* [emphasis added] them'.[53]

Those who adopt critical, praxiological vantage points would invite readers to pay special attention to several points in this typical scientific commentary. First of all, note the ways that descriptions of the work of Bayer scientists seem to echo some of the claims about bites that appeared in the popular cultural or mainstream press literatures that we critiqued earlier in the chapter. Second, note the recursive, ideologically loaded nature of this commentary about the Zika virus. Readers are learning how to wage wars on multiple fronts, where the vectors that are responsible for the spread of Zika are anthropomorphised into human threats that resemble terrorists. Regardless of whether the primary focus is on fighting a war on mosquitoes or a war on Zika, it is clear that audiences are supposed to take for granted the moral and military imperatives of waging the war, both figuratively and literally. As well as the involvement of military personnel.

In spite of claims being made about reducing misinformation and the need for both objectivity and for accurate epidemiological information, much of this scientific press coverage is also fraught with the language of monstrosity that appears to build on the contagion and outbreak narratives that Priscilla Wald has mentioned.[54] In *The Public Library of Science* (PLOS) blog article, written by Brigitte Nerlich, Carmen McLeod and Steven Burgess, the threat of the mosquito is made vividly apparent, with the authors expressing, in their piece titled 'Frankenflies Sent to Defeat Monster Mosi: Zika in the English Press', their perceptions of the current Zika debates. In one key ideological fragment, they did not hesitate to take advantage of the media's obsession with war metaphors:

> A coalition of the willing has unleashed a surge of *Frankenflies* at the frontline of the *War on Zika*. *Armed* with a genetic payload, the *airborne troops* will carry out a precision strike against a rogue group of Mozzys that harbor the virus. Proponents argue by clearing the

> ground of hostile flies they will be able to degrade the operating capability of virus and *neutralize the threat* of the current Zika insurgency in Brazil and beyond. However, critics claim this shock and awe approach will prove ineffective in the face of Mozzy *guerilla tactics*, with flies able to go to ground through reliance on egg dumps hidden in native territory. Further there are concerns that despite advances in precision molecular *bombing*, this *nuclear option* could result in collateral damage; or at worst further de-stabilize the situation, allowing an axis of airborne pathogens to *invade the territory*, potentially leading to the emergence of new, more dangerous *weapons of mass infection* [emphasis added throughout].[55]

This satirical blending of the language of warfighting against Zika with counter-insurgency abroad imitates the discourse of securitising the US homeland. What's more, the militaristic terminology from the quote (i.e. war on Zika, neutralise the threat, guerrilla tactics, and invade the territory) both amplifies and takes advantage of the rhetorical figurations that are circulated in popular press outlets. The potent fragments that go into the constitutive formation of these securitised Zika *epistemes* reify the notion that there are all types of pathogens that have to be fought, regardless of whether they involve combat against infectious vectors or terrorists on battlefields.

What adds even more layers of sedimented epistemic knowledges to the formation of a massive militarised *dispositif* are the ways that these authors proceed to complement their discussion of 'Frankenflies' with the monstering of Zika victims, a rhetorical tactic similar to the one Peter Burger identified in his work on the demonisation of krokodil drug users in chapter 1. In these scientific journal conversations we hear once more about how microcephaly is caused by Zika and about the mothers who may or may not choose to carry their affected foetuses to term.

These commentaries should be viewed as examples of Zika monstration. Just as Nerlich, McLeod and Burgess point out the popularity of war metaphors that appear in key commentaries on the Zika virus, author Aura Bogado went beyond the coverage of clinical commentary in her description of how some sources depicted young children with microcephaly. Categorised as a science piece, Bogado's *Grist* news article, entitled 'Zika, Tropical Medicine, and Infant Monsters of the Third World', explains that the babies who are born with microcephaly are described in the English news media as 'strange', 'deformed', 'terrible', and individuals with 'shrunken heads'.[56] She elaborated by noting that she believed that 'profound fear' had everything to do with the ways that these infants were represented as potential monsters.[57]

These US worries – that sometimes included commentaries on abortion, reproduction and the economics associated with Zika planning – were expressed in ways that replicated the rhetorics that appeared in Brazilian press outlets. The framing mechanisms used by journalists in Brazil infuriated both pro-natalists and organisations that cared about women's reproductive rights when they tried to circulate this missive:

> In the battle against Zika, five governments in the Americas, Colombia, Jamaica, Dominican Republic, Ecuador and El Salvador, have recommended in official publications that women in reproductive age [*sic*] should avoid pregnancy . . .[58]

What began as a discussion of the possible spread of the Zika virus turned into more complex conversations on everything from abortion to the transnational policies of many Central American or South American countries.

From a critical vantage point the framing of infants as disposable may be an unintended by-product of the circulation of dehumanising, monstrous language that is used to describe babies born with microcephaly. Sarah Schuetze, whose work was cited by Bogado, explains it best – the visual appearance of the babies born with microcephaly is the real perceptional threat associated with the spread of the Zika virus, and the spread of these anxieties was one of the key reasons that led to resonance of the militarised, securitised, dehumanising language dominating the scientific press coverage between 2014 and today.[59] It was not always clear that the public health containment of Zika need not involve treating babies as monsters.

Conclusion

After reviewing these popular culture, mainstream press and scientific journalistic discussions of Zika, readers can readily understand why we worry about the potential persuasive impact of these interrelated Zika virus representations. During late autumn 2016, members of the World Health Organization finally felt that they could announce that the Zika crisis no longer needed to be labelled as an international medical emergency. However, this announcement did not end the circulation of commentaries about the war on the Zika virus or the securitisation of these particular infectious disease concerns. Ribeiro, Hartley, Nerlich and Jaspal recently averred that 'the cartography of Zika' frames that circulated in Brazil in 2016 and 2017 often treated the spread of the Zika virus as an issue of 'biomilitarism' that needed to be handled by women whose preventive actions could help contain the spread of the Zika virus.[60] Armed with governmental emergency rhetorics that focused on "vector eradication", these short-term Brazilian strategies deflected attention away from more structural and material factors that had everything to do with long-term sustainable public health policies.

Our praxiological approach puts on display how both popular cultural representations of Zika and scientific journalistic coverage of this disease also involved the melding together of counter-terrorist discourses with public health eradication commentary in American press outlets. Instead of commenting on the need for billions of dollars for infrastructural preparation for everything from sanitation to vaccines, most of the Zika monstering attention seemed to be on magnifying the dangers so that publics would see the merits of warfighting on several domestic and international fronts.

Given the complexity of twenty-first-century calls for 'public health security' and the 'emergency' management of diseases such as Ebola or Zika, there are myriad materials and symbolic factors that go into the discovery, diagnosis, treatment and containment of infectious diseases. And, while no two disease rhetorical constructions are alike, in many instances critical studies of these rhetorics can show how similarities exist in the racialised and gendered dimensions of these Zika representations.

It is problematic enough that this zombification of the Zika virus appears on social media platforms, but our contribution makes the point that some of these same monstering *epistemes* circulated and drifted across forums and into more mainstream outlets or scientific venues. This helped create a situation where social agents in several forums were spreading similar messages about Zika victims, root causes of the virus and select Zika policy measures.

That said, we do not want to give the impression that the usage of all of these varied monstering rhetorics has escaped the attention of other interdisciplinary scholars. As critical readers might imagine, the use of this dominant 'war' framing – that oftentimes marginalised the importance of spending billions on public health infrastructures of sanitation – was also picked up by those scholars who realised that some hegemonic framing was being used to escape partial responsibility for the appearance and spread of the Zika virus.[61] Other academics, activists and journalists have noted that experts, civil sanitation workers and politicians needed to share some of the responsibility for the spread of these fears, and they have produced counter-narratives that underscored the role that poverty, absence of refuse collection, shortage of water and social inequality played in the spread of the Zika virus.

Sadly, interest in trying to understand the causes of the Zika virus waxes and wanes, and having substantive, lengthy and just debates about these issues is no easy matter. Regardless of the initial cries of Zika zombies that were prompted by the fear of microcephaly, worries of a lack of a vaccine, and concerns about the explosive spread via mosquito bites, it seems that interest in Zika in the mainstream media has largely waned through 2017 into 2018. As of 2 May 2018, the CDC provided a possible answer: including the states and territories, the total United States 'presumed symptomatic' Zika viral infections reported, totals only 1,118 cases.[62] This is a far cry short of the reports from Brazil, estimating over 200,000 cases.[63] However, perceptions matter, and the 'war' framing of the Zika virus magnifies these threats in ways that resonate with those who are more than willing to believe in securitised or militarised ways of handling monstrous infectious diseases. With many in the US comparing the COVID-19 pandemic crisis to a war, we presume that a critical tracing of the outbreak narrative around the COVID-19 disease outbreaks in American news media and policy discourse will demonstrate that the cogent rhetoric of securitisation and militarisation is here to stay.

Notes

1. WHO, 'IHR Procedures concerning public health emergencies of international concern (PHEIC)', World Health Organisation (WHO), 2019, *https://www.who.int/ihr/procedures/pheic/en/* (accessed 29 April 2019).
2. WHO, 'Statement on the 1st meeting of the IHR Emergency Committee regarding the Ebola outbreak in 2018', World Health Organization (WHO), 2018, *https://www.who.int/news-room/detail/18-05-2018-statement-on-the-1st-meeting-of-the-ihr-emergency-committee-regarding-the-ebola-outbreak-in-2018* (accessed 29 April 2019).
3. Michel Foucault, *Discipline and Punishment: The Birth of the Prison* (New York: Vintage Books, 1975), p. 198.

4. Bruno Latour, 'From Realpolitik to Dingpolitik: How to Make Things Public. An Introduction', in Bruno Latour and Peter Weibel (eds), *Making Things Public: Atmospheres of Democracy* (Cambridge (MA): MIT Press, 2005), pp. 1–31.
5. Brigitte Nerlich, Carmen McLeod and Steven Burgess, 'Frankenflies Sent To Defeat Monster Mosi: Zika in the English press', *PLOS*, 15 March 2016, *http://blogs.plos.org/blog/2016/03/15/frankenflies-sent-to-defeat-monster-mosi-zika-in-the-english-press/* (accessed 16 May 2018).
6. M. Dredze, D. A. Broniatowski and K. M. Hilyard, 'Zika vaccine misconceptions: A social media analysis', *Vaccine*, 34/30 (2016), 3441–2.
7. Barbara Ribeiro, Sarah Hartley, Brigitte Nerlich, and Rusi Jaspal, 'Media coverage of the Zika crisis in Brazil: The construction of a "war" frame that masked social and gender inequalities', *Social Science & Medicine*, 200 (2018), 137–44.
8. We see these as related terms that are representing similar phenomenon, i.e. zombies are a type of monsters, and monstration is the larger term. For further explication of this differentiation, see Jennifer Rutherford, *Zombies* (New York: Routledge, 2013), pp. 1-24.
9. Lorenzo Servitje and Sherryl Vint (eds), *The Walking Med: Zombies and the Medical Image* (University Park: The Pennsylvania State University Press, 2016).
10. Review of Lorenzo Servitje and Sherryl Vint (eds), *The Walking Med: Zombies and the Medical Image* (University Park, 2016): Andrew Peter Godfrey, 'The Ethical Zombie', *The Comics Grid: Journal of Comics Scholarship*, 7/1 (2017), 1–9.
11. Servitje and Vint, *The Walking Med*, pp. xii–xiii.
12. Brendon M. H. Larson, Brigitte Nerlich and Patrick Wallis, 'Metaphors and Biorisks: The War on Infectious Diseases and Invasive Species', *Science Communication*, 26/3 (2005), 243–68.
13. Science journalists traditionally work for magazines, newspapers and digital news services etc. and their job is to convey science news to the lay public.
14. B. Fischhoff, 'Risk Perception and Communication Unplugged: Twenty Years of Process', *Risk Analysis*, 15/2 (1995), 137–45, 141.
15. T. K. Sell, C. Watson, D. Meyer, M. Kronk, S. Ravi, L. E. Pechta, K. M. Lubell and D. A. Rose, 'Frequency of Risk-Related News Media Messages in 2016 Coverage of Zika Virus: Risk-Related News Media Messages about Zika', *Risk Analysis* (2018), 1–11.
16. E. K. Seltzer, E. Horst-Martz, M. Lu and R. M. Merchant, 'Public sentiment and discourse about Zika virus on Instagram', *Public Health*, 150 (2017), 170–5.

17. Joseph Hilgard and Kathleen Hall Jamieson, 'Does a Scientific Breakthrough Increase Confidence in Science? News of a Zika Vaccine and Trust in Science', *Science Communication*, 39/4 (2017), 548–60, 557.
18. H. M. Lazear, E. M. Stringer and A. M. De Silva, 'The emerging Zika virus epidemic in the Americas: Research priorities', *Journal of the American Medical Association*, 315/18 (2016), 1945–6.
19. Ribeiro et al., 'Media coverage', 137.
20. G. Mitman, 'Ebola in a Stew of Fear', *The New England Journal of Medicine*, 371 (2014), 1763–5.
21. Y. A. Wang and M. Barry, 'Zika outbreak bears an eerie resemblance to the spread of Ebola', *Los Angeles Times*, 9 February 2016, *https://www.latimes.com/local/lanow/la-oe-0209-wang-barry-zika-ebola-20160209-story.html* (accessed 29 April 2019).
22. PumpingMiddleAge, 'ZIKA ZOMBIES CONFIRMED IN AFRICA', *YouTube*, 25 February 2016, *https://www.youtube.com/watch?v=jqjAm8F7BBM* (accessed 30 April 2019); J. Straw, 'Survivors of Zika Virus Mutate into Zombies Want to Eat Doctors', *YouTube*, 6 March 2017, *https://www.youtube.com/watch?v=lVNVYe7tJ4k* (accessed 30 April 2019).
23. CDC, 'Zombie Preparedness', Centers for Disease Control and Prevention (CDC), Office of Public Preparedness and Response, 11 October 2018, *https://www.cdc.gov/phpr/zombie/index.htm* (accessed 15 May 2018).
24. C. Good, 'Why did the CDC Develop a Plan for a Zombie Apocalypse?', *The Atlantic*, 20 May 2011, *https://www.theatlantic.com/politics/archive/2011/05/why-did-the-cdc-develop-a-plan-for-a-zombie-apocalypse/239246/* (accessed 14 May 2018).
25. Marina Levina, *Pandemics and the Media* (New York: Peter Lang, 2015), p. 63.
26. Mayo Foundation for Medical Education and Research, 'Microcephaly', *Mayo Clinic*, 26 April 2018, *https://www.mayoclinic.org/diseases-conditions/microcephaly/symptoms-causes/syc-20375051* (accessed 14 May 2018).
27. T. Miles and B. Hirschler, 'Zika virus set to spread across Americas, spurring vaccine hunt', *Reuters*, 25 January 2016, *https://www.reuters.com/article/us-health-zika-idUSKCN0V30U6* (accessed 15 May 2018).
28. E. Cole, 'A Virus That Sure Sounds Like It Causes The Zombie Apocalypse Is Spreading Across The Americas', *Brobible.com*, 2016, *https://brobible.com/life/article/zika-virus-zombie-apocalypse-maayybe/* (accessed 14 May 2018).
29. Cole, 'A Virus That'.
30. Sydney Lupkin, 'Here's What You Should Know About the Zika Virus', *Vice News*, 29 January 2016, *https://news.vice.com/article/heres-what-you-should-know-about-the-zika-virus* (accessed 15 May 2018).

31. 'Health: Zika Virus Search', *The New York Times*, *https://www.nytimes.com/news-event/zika-virus* (accessed 15 May 2018).
32. 'Will Zika virus bring the long waited zombie apocalypse?', *Quora*, January 2016, *https://www.quora.com/Will-Zika-virus-bring-the-long-waited-zombie-apocalypse* (accessed 15 May 2018).
33. 'Will Zika virus bring', *Quora*.
34. L. Ramsey, 'A wacky conspiracy is circulating about Zika and GMOs – and it needs to stop', *Business Insider*, 30 January 2016, *http://www.businessinsider.com/zika-virus-conspiracy-theory-2016-1* (accessed 15 May 2018); L. W. Boyd, 'Zika Virus Adapts Itself for the USA', *Zombie Research Society*, 9 February 2016, *http://zombieresearchsociety.com/archives/28315* (accessed 15 May 2018).
35. Cole, 'A Virus That'.
36. 'The history of the Zika virus', World Health Organization (WHO), 2019, *http://www.who.int/emergencies/zika-virus/timeline/en/* (accessed 15 May 2018).
37. Miles and Hirschler, 'Zika virus set to spread'.
38. Lupkin, 'Here's What You'.
39. Boyd, 'Zika Virus Adapts Itself'.
40. J. Belluz, S. Tubrin and G. Barton, 'The Zika Virus, explained in less than 3 minutes' [video], *Vox*, 2 February 2016, *https://www.vox.com/2016/2/2/10890210/zika-virus-explained* (accessed 15 May 2018).
41. E. Yong, 'How Zika Conquered the Americas', *The Atlantic*, 24 May 2017, *https://www.theatlantic.com/science/archive/2017/05/how-zika-conquered-the-americas/527961/* (accessed 15 May 2018).
42. Yong, 'How Zika Conquered'.
43. Lupkin, 'Here's What You'.
44. M. Stobbe, 'Study Finds Little Bang for the Buck in Zika Blood Testing', *Associated Press*, 9 May 2018, *https://www.usnews.com/news/us/articles/2018-05-09/study-finds-little-bang-for-the-buck-in-zika-blood-testing* (accessed 29 April 2019).
45. A. E. Sorenson, R. C. Jordan and S. LaDeau, 'Reframing communication about Zika and mosquitos to increase disease prevention behavior', *Cogent Environmental Science*, 3 (2017), 1–10, 1.
46. G. Vogel, 'One year later, Zika scientists prepare for a long war', *Science*, 354/6316 (2016), 1088–9.
47. C. Wilson, '7 ways the war on Zika mosquitoes could be won', *New Scientist*, 2 February 2016, *https://www.newscientist.com/article/2076078-7-ways-the-war-on-zika-mosquitoes-could-be-won/* (accessed 16 May 2018).

48. J. Ferrara, '7 ways the war on Zika mosquitoes could be won', *Scienceline*, 2 February 2016, *http://scienceline.org/2016/05/an-easy-solution-to-the-war-on-zika/* (accessed 16 May 2018).
49. Wilson, '7 ways the war'.
50. Wilson, '7 ways the war'.
51. 'The War on Mosquitoes: Bayer Researchers Aim to Stem Zika, Malaria and Dengue', *The Bayer Scientific Magazine*, 30 (2016), 94–9.
52. 'The War on Mosquitoes', 99.
53. 'The War on Mosquitoes', 99.
54. Priscilla Wald, *Contagious: Cultures, Carriers, and the Outbreak Narrative* (London and Durham, NC: Duke University Press, 2008).
55. Nerlich, McLeod and Burgess, 'Frankenflies Sent'.
56. A. Bogado, 'Zika, tropical medicine, and infant monsters of the third world', *Grist Magazine*, 11 February 2016, *https://grist.org/science/zika-tropical-medicine-and-infant-monsters-of-the-third-world/*, accessed 16 May 2018.
57. Bogado, 'Zika, tropical medicine'.
58. Ribeiro et al., 'Media coverage', 141.
59. Sarah Schuetze, 'The Zika Virus: What We're Really Talking About', *The Society Pages*, 2 February 2016, *https://thesocietypages.org/girlwpen/2016/02/02/the-zika-virus-what-were-really-talking-about/* (accessed 16 May 2018).
60. Ribeiro et al., 'Media coverage', 137–44.
61. See Ribeiro et al., 'Media coverage', and Larson, Nerlich and Wallis, 'Metaphors and Biorisks'.
62. CDC, '2017 Case Counts in the US', Centers for Disease Control and Prevention (CDC), 24 April 2019, *https://www.cdc.gov/zika/reporting/2017-case-counts.html* (accessed 15 November 2019).
63. R. Lowe, C. Barcellow, P. Brasil, O. G. Cruz, N. Alves Honorio, H. Kuper and M. Sá Carvalho, 'The Zika Virus Epidemic in Brazil: From Discovery to Future Implications', *International Journal of Environmental Research and Public Health*, 15/96 (2018), 1–18.

4

An Affectionate Epidemic

How Disability Goes Viral on Social Media

Angela M. Smith

> Why do we feel so bad when seeing handicapped people or animals? How can that terrible and exhausting feeling be overcome?[1]

THIS INQUIRY ON the Quora website imagines disability as an emotional problem for non-disabled spectators, as if they 'catch' the imagined sad state of disabled people and then wish to feel better. Online texts frequently cater to this emotional susceptibility, emphasising disabled people's supposed helplessness, and then delivering uplift by showing disabled people 'overcoming' their supposed limitations, being normalised (treated, prostheticised, cured), or being 'helped' by non-disabled people. The emotional pay-off is evident in the titles of popular online videos: 'Tear-Jerking Moment Caring Dad Carries Disabled Son Outside So He Can Feel the Rain on His Skin'; 'This Disabled Woman Needs Help. Watch the Dog's Reaction . . . I'm Crying!'; 'Little Boy with Prosthetic Legs Is A Real Inspiration To All'; 'These Guys Did Something for a Disabled Veteran That'll Make You Smile'; 'Try Not To Cry Watching This Boy With Autism At A Coldplay Concert'. As I have argued elsewhere, the circulation of such texts indicates an *affection* for disability, insofar as their subjects, themselves apparently 'affected' by a condition or impairment, emotionally affect viewers – eliciting fondness, tenderness or love – and thus incline viewers to feel 'affectionate' toward (their conception of) disabled people.[2]

A particular kind of Facebook post features photographs of disabled or sick individuals captioned with emotive descriptions of a health struggle or some kind of stigmatisation. These 'like-farming' posts call viewers to 'like' to affirm the pictured individual, 'share' to counteract negative treatment, and/or type 'Amen' to produce cure. Those who respond confirm their belief in the sadness and degradation of disability and gain the satisfying experience of ameliorating suffering with compassion and prayer. Because these images call viewers to share for a noble cause, they may 'go viral'.[3] But those who share are duped. The images are stolen and framed with fabricated names and stories, and as they proliferate to others' newsfeeds, they draw advertisers or purchasers to the originating site or facilitate a profitable scam.[4] In this process, disability becomes metaphorically and affectively contagious, travelling amongst social media users who 'catch' it and pass it along.

This article examines the usefulness of considering the affective circulation of 'like-farming' posts as viral or contagious. Doing so risks construing disabled or sick people, the subjects of the images, as contagious threats. But it can also reveal the role of respondents in passing on ableist affection or affectation, leaving them feeling good while harming and debilitating disabled people. The metaphor of virality also allows respondents to redirect the ableist effects/affects of like-farming images. Family members relocate pathology from their objectified child to the 'sick' like-farmer who circulates and profits from the stolen image. Disability activists depict the spread of such images as a kind of pornography, indicting both the profiteers and the consumers who gain pleasure from viewing and spreading the images. And disabled Twitter users generate their own disruptive content for virally affecting disability images. Each response mutates the virus, the affective substance of the disability encounter, calling out ableist affection and disseminating alternative disability affects.

Ableist Affection: Sharing the 'Love'

> 'No one will share this'.
> – Popular caption for like-farming images

Like-farming posts on Facebook feature images of apparently sick or disabled people – often children or young women – and urge users to help by sharing, liking or typing 'Amen'. A small dark-eyed child in a white collared shirt and dark overalls, propped up by someone's hand, is framed by the words, 'I have Down Syndrome. Can I Get Your 1Like and Amen Share If Your [sic] Not Ashamed of Me'. A young bilateral above-elbow amputee poses in a short dress, beneath a post reading, 'No one will Share this [followed by a series of sad or shocked emojis]. Because she is Disabled. Type Amen'. A close-up of a young woman with a facial birthmark is captioned '1 Like = Beautiful. Say YES if she is beautiful. God loves our Souls!' A bald-headed girl kneels in a ring of pompoms, wearing her cheerleading uniform; the caption invites viewers to '"Share" to tell her she's beautiful' and 'Pray for her to beat cancer'.[5]

These images presume the degraded or pitiful status of sick or disabled people, associating them with shame or sadness and implying they are not loved. They exhort viewers to counter this undesirable affect and affirm the individual's value by sharing and typing 'YES' or 'Amen', sometimes suggesting that doing so will generate money for a cure. Users thus perceive themselves as 'catching' the disabled person – an ostensibly supportive act, as in 'catching' someone who is falling – and then virtually and virtuously passing them on, so that others can also 'help' mitigate their disabled state.

Such affirmation constitutes a ritualised act designed to contain and segregate potentially threatening difference. These acts echo the social and religious prohibitions discussed by anthropologist Mary Douglas. Douglas contends that rules and rituals around, for instance, particular foods or sick or menstruating people do not only serve hygienic concerns but facilitate social cohesion, organising persons and objects into bounded categories and excluding or containing liminal elements and bodies.[6] Julia Kristeva interprets these ritual taboos as processes of psychic and social abjection, both a fascinated approach toward and a protective warding off of threats to individual and social wholeness.[7] In turn, Priscilla Wald contends that these rituals of prohibition continue to motivate contemporary social and medical procedures ostensibly designed to protect against microbial contagion.[8]

In-person or online encounters with disability thus constitute atypical bodies as liminal and pollutant entities, troubling emblems of physical and mental variability and vulnerability. Disabled bodies appear mired in an abject state of 'suffering and horror', and the non-disabled individual, confronted with and 'touched' by the disabled other, works to wrest their own 'clean and proper' self from the encounter.[9] This extrication relies on social rituals or conventions: approaching the disabled person, making overtures of pity or assistance or charity, proffering prayers for rescue and cure. Writes Eli Clare, 'Strangers pat me on the head. They whisper platitudes in my ear, clichés about courage and inspiration. They enthuse about how remarkable I am. They declare me special.'[10] Some make unsolicited donations, like the passer-by who flipped a coin into activist Mary Lou Breslin's cup, splashing her with coffee.[11] People also leap to 'help'. Chris Hewitt recalls:

> Once I was sitting at the foot of a flight of steps when two guys appeared and without a word picked me up in my chair and carried me to the top. When I had recovered from my amazement I said, 'Excuse me, I know you meant well, but I was only waiting for a friend. Would you please carry me back down now?'

And people enact what Trisha Sprayberry calls 'Can I pray for you?' encounters, like the woman who tells her, 'I saw you over here in your wheelchair and saw you trying to reach that can of olive's [*sic*] from the shelf. I thought, well bless her heart . . . I thought that I'd offer my prayers and that I may help you heal your body'.[13] Clare comments, 'Strangers offer me Christian prayers or crystals and vitamins, always with the same intent – to touch me, fix me, mend my cerebral palsy, if only I will comply. They cry over me, wrap their arms around my shoulders, kiss my cheek.'[14] Having completed these ablutions, they extract from the interaction their own comparatively whole and agential self.

As well as performing social rituals designed to tame and contain the disabled body and to ward off its potential contagion, individuals seek an affective boost from their disability encounter. Silvan Tomkins's affect theory offers the useful concept of affective 'scripts' or '*sets of ordering rules*' that guide affective responses to particular stimuli and interactions, shaping their 'interpretation, production, and control of scenes'.[15] For Anna Gibbs, Tomkins's affect theory valuably 'specifies which affects are likely to be called up in response to which others and why'.[16] Erving Goffman's *Stigma* also illuminates the social rules of the encounter between 'the normal' and 'the person he is normal against', including the affirmation of normalcy for the former and the likely outcome of 'shame' for the latter.[17] In these interactions, then, non-disabled people follow an internalised script designed to manage perceived threat and transform it into a pleasing affective experience for themselves, with minimal regard for the experience of the disabled person.

Social media users who engage with like-farming images similarly enter into the kind of stimulus-affect-response script described by Tomkins: they view and read (stimulus), they perceive those depicted as sad or suffering and feel pity (affect), and they click to like or share (response). While the posts solicit uplift for those pictured, the affective benefit in fact passes to those who like or share. Their willingness to publicly affirm an ill or atypical body as 'beautiful' – especially when they're told no one else will – enlivens and inspires them, thus distancing them from the ostensibly passive, incapable body pictured. The affective script strips agency from the disabled person, making it difficult for them to alter the emotional exchange. Clare writes, 'After five decades of these kinds of interactions, I still don't know how to rebuff their pity, how to tell them the simple truth that I'm not broken'.[18] Nonetheless, precisely through engaging the rhetoric of virality, contagion or sickness, individuals and groups do seek to disrupt ableist affection online, in some cases by renaming such affection as itself pathetic and pathogenic.

Pathogenic Profit

> [C]hildren with disabilities and birth defects seem to get the most traffic.[19]

The word *contagion*, meaning 'the communication of disease by direct or indirect contact', also signifying 'the ready transmission or spread as of an idea or emotion from person to person', derives from the Latin *contagionem*, 'a touching, contact'.[20] In turn, *virality* signifies dangerous contact: the Latin *virus* connotes 'slime', 'poison', or 'ooze'.[21] Contagion and virality are thus fraught disability metaphors. Historical associations of disability with communicable diseases such as leprosy or polio haunt rhetorical constructions of disabled people – and people of colour, poor people and immigrants – as potential contaminants in the national or social body. Rhetoric of contagion often serves racist, xenophobic and imperialist ends, such that 'contagion most often comes to be associated with danger and undesirability – a racialized, pathological threat to be neutralized, eliminated or cured'.[22] These ideas shape everyday encounters with disabled people: for instance, blogger Samantha Connor describes a mother who quickly hurries away her child, explaining, 'I don't let him talk to people in wheelchairs, they might have diseases'.[23] Recent representations of autism as an epidemic similarly reflect a fearful, pathologising view of disability and neurodiversity, as noted by Hannah Ebben: 'A narrative of contagion suggests that autism is a thing that one can "catch" like a virus, which adds to the conception of autism as a thing alien to human bodies.'[24] The association of disability with contagion thus risks stigmatising disabled people as repugnant and debilitating to the social body, as in like-farming posts that construct non-contagious embodiments as innately bad, sad and unpleasant states to be kept at arm's length.

A problem of the viral metaphor for like-farming images, then, is its perpetuation of ableist associations of disabled bodies as carriers of potentially contagious pathologies. This demonisation echoes the social rhetoric around biological viral contagions described by Priscilla Wald, where the language of 'index cases', 'superspreaders' and 'Patient Zeros' transforms particular individuals 'from victims to agents – and embodiments – of the spreading infection'. For Wald, this projection of sinister agency onto victims of circumstance implicitly forecloses 'more effective, just, and compassionate responses both to a changing world and to the problems of global health and human welfare'.[25]

While Wald seeks to challenge the cultural construction of viral victims as agents, new-media scholars express concern about describing online dissemination as 'viral' precisely because it elides human agency in spreading viral content. Henry Jenkins, Sam Ford and Joshua Green note that the term 'viral' emerged to differentiate older 'top-down hierarchies of the broadcast model' from the internet's 'integrated system of participatory channels' and rapid circulation: 'one of the most common explanations [for the "viral" term] is that media content now disseminates like a pandemic – spreading through audiences by infecting person after person who comes into contact with it'. They continue:

> The term 'viral' first appeared in science fiction stories, describing (generally bad) ideas that spread like germs . . . [T]he viral is linked to the 'irrational', the public is described as 'susceptible' to its 'pull', and participants become unknowing 'hosts' of the information they carry across their social networks.

Thus, in 'viral marketing', as in early versions of Hotmail, 'People communicated and – in the process – sent along a marketing message, often without realizing it had happened'.[26] But the viral model reductively suggests all such communication is harmful. Jenkins insists 'Participation . . . is not a disease and should not be treated like one. To do so is to denigrate not just the act but the people doing it – that is, us'.[27] It also ignores the active role individuals play in passing content along. Jenkins et al. assert that virality fails to describe 'situations in which people actively assess a media text, deciding who to share it with and how to pass it along' and the extent to which 'their choices, investments, agendas, and actions determine what gets valued'.[28] Yet internet users' continued embrace of the viral metaphor is itself a kind of agency. It suggests people gravitate to the viral as the most useful figuring of how being online *feels*. Conducting online transmission is experienced as a kind of touching, an encounter or outreach that can affect, impinge on and even alter the self.

Taking seriously the concerns of Wald and Jenkins, then, I contend that using 'virality' as a lens for like-farming posts can help us see the transmission of ableist pleasure as both socially/ritually choreographed and individually managed. We may also take up Limor Schifman's distinction between viral *communication as transmission* – a direct transmission of information – and viral *communication as ritual*, 'the construction and representation of shared beliefs'.[29] For instance, discussing advertisements that describe autism as an epidemic and instruct people how to detect 'signs' of autism, Ebben contends that such ads 'train our perception' in the 'recognition of abnormality'. These ads might appear as a straightforward transmission of information. But Ebben also asserts that those thus trained then actively spread pathologising concepts of autism, in what we may recognise as a ritualistic affirmation of ableist beliefs: 'As the power of knowing autism is productive, although we are constantly on the lookout for indexical signs, we enact their object, autistic contagion, ourselves.'[30] The viral or epidemic metaphor thus risks pathologising neurological difference but can also be redeployed to viscerally figure and problematise the spreading of such reductive understandings. This version of virality construes those who spread such images as distributors and beneficiaries of affective excitement – fear, alertness, pleasures of recognition – and as active producers of 'knowledge' that causes harm to disabled people by devaluing difference as deficiency. The viral metaphor for like-farming images thus allows the redistribution of responsibility for spreading ritualised, ableist responses onto those who benefit from, rather than are harmed by, their diffusion.

Therefore, the viral metaphor not only aptly conveys the proliferation of ableist affection *via* like-farming posts but intervenes in that spread by relocating the source of the viral 'problem'. Family members of like-farming victims often use this strategy, aiming to convince unaware users of like-farming's pathological nature. They distinguish between what users *think* they are passing along – calls for help and prayers for ill or disabled people – and what is *actually* being passed along – stolen images of their loved ones, exploited for the profit of like-farmers. They believe that if people understand that they are victims of a scam, and that their ignorance causes harm to vulnerable individuals, they will stop spreading the virus.

For instance, in 2012, Terri Johnson discovered an image of her daughter, Katie, who has Down's syndrome, circulating on Facebook, accompanied by the words, 'This is my sister Mallory. She has down [sic] syndrome and doesn't think she's beautiful. Please like this photo so I can show her later that she truly is beautiful.' Friends and family searched online to find the posts and reveal the deception. The original post was eventually removed, although Johnson estimates her daughter's image had already been seen by 5.5 million people.[31] Another parent, 'Katie', discovered a like-farming scam using a picture of her son Connor, lying in a hospital bed with EEG wires taped to his head. The caption laments, 'Nobody Cared to Pray for Farnando [single-tear emoji] Can He Even Get Your 1Like, Amen, and Share. [crying emoji]'. Like Johnson, Katie found it difficult to stop the image circulating:

> I spent the majority of the evening pleading with my Facebook friends to help me report the pictures and its spammers so it would be taken down. As I spread the word on everyone's newsfeed, I was tagged in a post – yet another spammer had posted my boy's picture with the same caption. By nightfall, I couldn't keep up with all the like farmers that were exploiting social media goodwill in asking for prayers for my child whom they'd never met – all for their monetary gain. My son's stolen photo had gone viral, and there was very little I could do about it.[32]

A current Facebook search for 'Pray for Farnando' shows that Connor's image still circulates and that the text about 'Farnando' also appears alongside photos of other children.[33]

These mothers' attempted disruptions of like-farming texts rely on – but also invert – the logic of virality, pathos and pathology exploited by the original posts. *Pathos* signifies 'the quality or power . . . of arousing feelings of pity, sorrow'; something is *pathetic* when it 'causes or evokes pity', but also when it is 'miserably or contemptibly inadequate'.[34] The notion of suffering also inflects the combining form *patho-*, signifying 'disease', as in *pathogenic*, meaning 'producing disease'.[35] All these connotations attach to the disabled/sick people in like-farming posts: they are ill and/or suffering, they are 'inadequate' and needing help or affirmation and they thus evoke viewers' pity. Liking and sharing both presume and act against these bodies' 'pathogenic' qualities: the possibility of 'catching' the abjection or negativity of these apparently unfortunate conditions.

Family members seek to relocate this pathogenic affect from their loved ones to the like-farmers themselves. Courtney Westlake, for instance, writes of having her baby daughter's image stolen for an 'Amen + share' post. She writes, 'Here's what you're actually doing when you type Amen or share the photo on your wall: 1. You're exploiting what is most likely a stolen image of a child whose family has no idea it is being used. 2. You're making the owners of the page that posted it or the twisted people who stole the photo and created the post a whole lot of money.' Westlake's rhetoric redirects pity from the fabricated image toward those who've actually been exploited, while constructing like-farmers themselves as pathogenic, spreading a morally diseased profiteering practice. Most of Westlake's commenters express shock, vowing to never again click on such images. Writes one, 'I have shared and typed "Amen" on posts like these, and I am truly sorry for any harm I may have caused by doing so. I only meant to be helpful. Thank you for the helpful information and I won't be sharing posts like these anymore.' Comments another, 'I'm so sorry for all the one's [*sic*] I have forwarded. I did not know how it was being used. I will not post or share again of these precious children.' Many focus on the victimisation of the vulnerable, stating, 'It is appalling that people make money off of our sick children', and 'Someone exploiting the most vulnerable, I have no words'.

For others, however, the pathogenic affect Westlake seeks to redirect remains conflated with the 'pathetic' objects of the posts' imagery: writes 'iessandra', 'Occasionally I would type amen – then one day I decided to look at the person's site that the request came from. I was horrified!!! The photos on that person's timeline were grotesque, horrible, maimed, mutilated bodies – absolutely sickening. And I went to one other person's FB page and the same thing. Sick, sick people.!' These responses suggest that while the pleas of those hurt by like-farming may impede the images' viral spread, they do not significantly alter the rhetorical conventions around sick or disabled people. As Beth Haller and Jeffrey Preston write, citing Susan Wendell, 'This frame also implies a distinct shame attached to disability, that being seen publicly is upsetting and disabled people must be protected from this experience.'[36] After these interventions, then, like-farming itself may be understood as a harmful contagion but the conception persists of disabled and sick people as only shamed victims. With the ableist 'affectionate' script revealed as a scam, the only alternative response to depictions of disability or illness appears to be horror, and the impulse is to exclude such images entirely.

Moreover, the intervention doesn't always work. Some of Westlake's commenters observe that even after being educated about like-farming, their friends continue to share. One writes, 'I have warned my FB friends about these scams but it doesn't seem to sink in. You just can't help the gullible.' Another states, 'sadly, 90% of the people on my Friend list are ignorant and just plain stupid . . . they won't listen . . . Even though I've shared this with them.' Some of the commenters themselves are reluctant to surrender their encounters with these posts. One asserts, 'Be kind and accept the prayers of that hurting child. Even if the picture is stolen and baby is not [*sic*] longer with us here on earth and in our lives does not mean a prayer from an honest person will not [*sic*] be wasted.' Says another, 'I wonder if we didn't like or comment on it, but just prayed and shared it, if the scammed results would still apply. Prayer TRULY does work!'[37] These statements hold fast to the ritualistic power of passing along the image, raising questions as to how else we might intervene in the viral spread of ableist 'affection' and to what extent metaphors of contagion can reimagine disability affect in the social media sphere.

Catchy Metaphors: Inspiration/Pity Porn

The strategic labelling of uplifting disability images as 'inspiration porn' – and the comparable term 'pity porn' – offers another intervention into the spread of affective ableism. The concept of 'inspiration porn' was popularised by the late Australian disability activist and comedian Stella Young. In her 2014 TED talk, Young invokes images of children running on prosthetic legs captioned 'Your excuse is invalid' or 'The only disability in life is a bad attitude', commenting:

> [T]hese images – there are lots of them out there – they are what we call inspiration porn. And I use the term 'porn' deliberately, because they objectify one group of people for the benefit of another group of people. So in this case, we're objectifying disabled people for the benefit of nondisabled people. The purpose of these images is to inspire you, to motivate you, so that we can look at them and think, 'Well, however bad my life is, it could be worse. I could be that person.'[38]

Young contends that the conventions of inspiration porn also shape offline encounters, as when a woman tells her, 'I see you on the train every morning and I just wanted to say it's great. You're an inspiration to me.'[39] Such interactions, Young asserts, affectively oppress disabled people. They presume their innately abject or shamed state while also requiring them to express or perform optimism, and they recast the depressing effects of discriminatory systems as a personal state of mind, all to cheer up non-disabled spectators. To stem this viral spread, Young suggests, '[N]ext time you're tempted to share that picture of an adorable kid with a disability to make your Facebook friends feel good, just take a second to consider why you're really clicking that button.'[40]

The term 'inspiration porn' works in similar ways to family members' castigation of like-farmers. It condemns affecting representations believed true or harmless by revealing them as cynical acts of objectification for others' gain. Like the commenters on Westlake's page, those confronting the term realise that while they thought they were spreading something *good* to uplift disabled and sick people, they have been spreading something *harmful* that exploits disabled and sick people.

But unlike familial interventions, 'inspiration porn' directly indicts consumers. It makes explicit the pleasurable pay-off to those who share, explaining ongoing attachment to sharing even after being educated about like-farming. If sharers imagine themselves as helpful benefactors, and if aggrieved family members instead read them as unwittingly deceived scam victims, 'pity/inspiration' rhetoric construes them as wilful exploiters of disabled bodies for their own enjoyment. The liking or sharing of disability images becomes an implicitly sexualised transaction in which users click to 'purchase'; exchange likes and shares for the thrill of 'helping'; and aggrandise the self at the expense of the fetishised disability object. And since viewers not only consume or 'catch' these disability images but also pass them on, they constitute both consumers *and* distributors of this ostensibly degraded genre.

The construction of online ableist images as 'porn' relies at least implicitly on associations of pornography with contagion and pathology, including sexually transmitted disease. As the term is invoked by disability activists to *condemn* pity/inspiration images and perhaps encourage their extinction, it also evokes historic and recent constructions of pornography as an 'epidemic' that brings ill health to the social body.[41] Thus, while it valuably draws attention to the agency and complicity of those who 'spread' this material, it perhaps also aligns critique of ableism with condemnations of (sexual) porn as 'unhealthy', inherently morally degraded or politically retrograde. Such moral crusades have long been used to control the bodies of gender, sexual and racial/ethnic minorities, as well as those of disabled people, constructing marginal identities and practices as threats to normative health and morality.[42] Thus, while the 'porn' label can usefully critique non-disabled disseminators of inspiration/pity porn, its negative associations might also land on already vulnerable bodies. Like the resignifications of fatness in terms of environmental influence discussed by Francis Ray White in chapter 5, which may still perpetuate notions of fat bodies as diseased and morally weak, this usage of 'porn' rhetoric risks reinforcing perceptions of disabled people as either passive and exploited or perverse and dangerous.

Nonetheless, the 'inspiration porn' label suggests a potentially productive commandeering of the language of crisis and moral panic. Construction of inspiration porn as an 'epidemic' may help viscerally convey it as damaging and requiring urgent amelioration. Moreover, the authorship of the term alters a power imbalance: Young's label and its viral uptake constitutes a 'talking back' by disabled activists that reconfigures the ableist affectionate script. Even though it may be supported by a reductive view of porn, the term still imagines the ostensibly undesirable body ('no one will share this') as in fact deeply *desired* (even as it is exploited and fetishised). It thus makes way for oppositional disabled self-representations. Haller and Preston note that Young's talk inspired the Facebook page 'This is what disability looks like', which describes itself as 'featuring images of people with disabilities that do NOT pander to sentimentality, inspiration and/or paternalism'.[43] It is these kinds of self-authored images that can displace viral pity/inspiration and generate alternative affective scripts.

Viral Mutation: Disability Affect

The affective interventions considered thus far seek to change the emotional experience of consumers of disability images. Those who share like-farming images conceive of themselves as charitable saviours of sick or disabled people, while purchasing a safe distance from the potentially contagious stigma of disability. The parents of sick or disabled children try to interrupt this spread by recasting sharers as naïve disseminators of harmful material. And activists use 'pity/inspiration porn' labels to indict consumers as both users and distributors of an objectifying genre that caters to their own pleasures. Both interventions seek to stop the spread of pathetic or pathological concepts of disability, but the former reconsolidates views of disabled people as passive and exploited objects, while the latter may perpetuate associations of disabled people with contagious deviance.

As noted above, however, the authorship of the 'inspiration porn' label by disabled people interrupts simplistic objectification of disabled figures. When disabled people assert and circulate their own emotional experiences and responses, they reroute ableist affect and create new, potentially viral, affections. In so doing, they constitute the kind of 'queer diaspora' defined by Jasbir Puar in terms of 'affectionate networks or lines of affiliation'. Puar contests conventional uses of contagion 'in relation to unwanted and afflicted bodies', insisting instead that 'all bodies can be thought of as contagious or mired in contagions: bodies infecting other bodies with sensation, vibration, irregularity, chaos, lines of flight that betray the expectation of loyalty, linearity, the demarcation of who's in and who's not.'[44] Kelly Fritsch and Anna McGuire also imagine contagion, which impels 'both social responsibility and collective action', as 'a productive site through which to engage a queer/crip biosocial politics'. They assert that it 'provides the grounds for provocative encounters and exchange' as it both 'produces pathologies *and* nurtures communities of solidarity'.[45] Ebben notes that, in the case of the autism 'epidemic', 'the conscious *act* of declaring oneself autistic would stand for a queer/crip desire of the undesirable'.[46] And Beth Ferri declares, '[V]iruses can . . . be understood as exhibiting a kind of dangerous adaptability and/or even a menacing queer desire.'[47] These latter perspectives invoke the concept of 'cripping', the revelation and remaking of ableist structures by nonconforming bodyminds.[48]

Rather than seeking primarily to shut down virality, then, disabled subjects' uptake of affective exchange generates new viral or contagious content. In the 1994 documentary film *Vital Signs: Crip Culture Talks*

Back, for instance, performance artist Mary Duffy, born without arms, narrates how she rebuffs ableist affective impositions:

> I have a little card which I use for these occasions. You know, it's a response for somebody, for example, whom I may choose to ignore at the post office. I'm addressing an envelope and they come along and say, 'Isn't it marvelous what they can train you to do nowadays?' And I don't respond to them, so they try and gather a crowd and say [more loudly], 'Isn't it marvelous what they can train them to do nowadays?' And so I get to take out this card, my little red card [gestures with foot], which I hand out to everybody at the post office – or pedal out, I suppose you'd say – and it says, 'As a proud disabled woman, I find your comments and questions regarding my disability as obstreperous, unwelcome . . ., as well as downright insensitive . . . Please turn over'. And on the back it says, 'This card is saturated with a noxious substance. Both your hands will fall off in the next 24 hours'. [Laughs] And nobody ever gets the joke, you know? But I like it. It's my defense in a hostile world.'[49]

Duffy's card re-scripts conventional disability encounters, revealing the ableist affection beamed at her as 'obstreperous, unwelcome . . . insensitive' and 'hostile'. Duffy also denies the distancing that ableist affection seeks, exploiting the older idea of contagion or virality as 'a kind of poison' by telling card-holders they have been contaminated with radical impairment. When ableist interlocutors take Duffy's card, they become scripted actors in *her* drama. Duffy narrates her own affective experience and controls the effect/affect she has on witnesses, asserting a 'menacing queer' humour.

When disabled individuals and groups become agents in or narrators of affective encounters, they can orchestrate (and 'go viral' with) alternative affects and emotions. For instance, one of the like-farming posts mentioned above features a photo of a young woman with a facial birthmark, captioned, 'Say YES if she is beautiful!' The woman is Crystal Hodges. Her image was stolen from a blog post in which she explains and destigmatises her 'port wine stain', discusses her treatments, critiques intrusive responses ('People have even argued with me, telling me it's not a birthmark, and that I have something like skin cancer or something contagious') and encourages acceptance of differences.[50] But her attempt to rewrite ableist reactions is undercut when her image is used to sustain fearful and pitying responses, as Hodges explains:

> A group on Facebook with nearly 2 million followers has been using a photo of mine without my knowledge or consent – a photo that I took (just a selfie!) barely 20 minutes after a painful laser treatment on my facial birthmark. In addition to using my photo, they added text that says, '1 Like = Beautiful'. . . as well as their personal logo. My name and permission were not included in this process, nor was my story, a link to my blog or website.[51]

Hodges states that her image has now been shared by at least five different Facebook groups; in one, with 30 million-plus followers, her image has 'over 256,000 "likes", 1,000 shares and over 13,000 comments'.[52]

Hodges links the online sharing of her image to real-life scripts imposed on her, including the assumption her difference is contagious. She notes her education in deferring to others' emotional needs: 'When people would stare . . . my mom is the one who taught me to smile at them. Maybe the staring person is having a bad day and needed a smile to lift their spirits.'[53] But she insists on her right to control her story and its affective outcomes: 'I don't want my photo to go viral without the story being told. I want people to know my story – but not with the purpose of gaining sympathy. I want my story to be known in attempts of educating other people, and in hopes of motivating a cultural change in how "different" people are treated.'[54] Hodges thus seeks to change online and real-world affective scriptings of people with atypical appearances.

Such blog and website commentaries usefully redirect popular views of disability and can make news: Hodges's narrative appeared in *Today*, *People*, *The Telegraph* and *The Sun*. But disabled people also contest virality in spaces where their utterances can 'go viral', that is, can be actively liked and shared in the same way as Facebook posts or tweets. One Twitter scenario offers an apt example. On 22 September 2014, Ken Jennings, former *Jeopardy* champion, tweeted, 'Nothing sadder than a hot person in a wheelchair'.[53] The tweet shares elements with like-farming posts, assuming disability as a degraded and pathetic state that 'saddens' witnesses. However, because the tweet was more mocking than ostensibly charitable or affectionate, it drew criticism as 'awful' and 'insensitive'.[56] On seeing the tweet, Paralympian Joshua Cassidy responded with a different kind of affecting disability image, re-tweeting Jennings's comment alongside a photo of himself, beaming happily, arms outstretched and draped with medals.[57] In 2018, the tweet was reactivated by disabled Twitter users in the same ironic and subversive spirit. Annie Segarra retweeted Jennings's 'Nothing sadder than a hot person in a wheelchair' beneath an image of her posing in her chair, wearing dark red lipstick, a blue blazer and blue knee-socks with a short plaid skirt. Segarra's tweet read, 'Cry about it, babe' and carried the hashtag #HotPersonInAWheelchair.[58] The hashtag caught on, spawning a wave of images of people in wheelchairs, showcasing a variety of postures, body types and settings. People presented themselves in formal dress, casual-wear, costumes, lingerie and naked. They grinned, smiled shyly, or looked fierce or thoughtful. In her tweet, Elizabeth Jeannel kissed her wheelchair-using partner while draped in a rainbow flag, stating, 'Idk [I don't know] she looks pretty happy to me [shrug emoji]'.[59]

The #HotPersonInAWheelchair tweets invoke Jennings's emotive phrase 'Nothing sadder' in order to reject it. They assert alternative emotions through performing or articulating happiness, fierceness or 'hotness', a term connoting attractiveness, self-confidence and potency. Tweeters also contest normative concepts of 'hotness': for instance, Michaela Oteri wrote, 'Yes, I am **fat AND** hot'.[60] The Representation Project articulates several of the hashtag's affective interventions, retweeting an image of activist Lizzie Kiama in her chair, arrayed in brightly coloured headwear, lipstick and layered tulle skirt, with the statement 'Inspired by . . . activists posting under #HotPersonInAWheelchair (and [angry-face emoji] infuriated that we live in a society where they have to defend their beauty, existence, and joy)'.[61] Some tweets turn 'sadness' back onto Jennings himself, as in Segarra's original 'Cry about it, babe' and in assertions that his *ableism* is sad or pathetic. The emphasis on 'hotness' also reframes this alternative set of disability affects in relation to sexual and inspiration/pity porn. Geoff Trappett, Paralympian and founder of advocacy organisation Inclusion Moves, wrote, 'Was wondering why my Twitter feed resembled softcore porn. Glad I looked for an answer. Sometimes terrible comments inspire greatness!'[62] The comment complicates the 'pity/inspiration porn' trope and embraces the pornographic as a potential viral mode of alternative disability affect and desire. Several other Twitter hashtags have contested stereotypical disability representations.[63] But, like #DisabledJoy, #HotPersonInAWheelchair particularly engages the affective realm. Making news on sites such as the *BBC* and *The Guardian*, the hashtag trended enough to 'go viral' with affective scripts explicitly opposed to pity or inspiration.[64]

If we conceive the viral as an online phenomenon driven by dominant, ableist, emotional scripts, we can also imagine ways of rewriting those scripts and their contagion rhetoric. Calling on disabled people to spread the love, #HotPersonInAWheelchair participates actively in affective social-media contagion, displaces viral ableist affection and circulates diverse, exciting disability affects. It also orients disabled affect towards members of the disability community, facilitating new scripts for disabled affective experience and expression and exemplifying the kind of 'collective agency in a networked culture' that Jenkins feared might be elided by the viral metaphor.[65] These tweets thus help enact a world in which disabled people wrest control of communicable disability affects, exceeding ableist transmissions and 'touching' viewers in unpredictable ways.

Notes

1. 'Why Do We Feel So Bad', *Quora*, *https://www.quora.com/Why-do-we-feel-so-bad-when-seeing-handicapped-people-or-animals-How-can-that-terrible-and-exhausting-feeling-be-overcome* (accessed 30 April 2018).
2. Angela M. Smith, 'Dis-Affection: Disability Effects and Disabled Moves at the Movies', in David T. Mitchell, Susan Antebi and Sharon L. Snyder (eds), *The Matter of Disability: Materiality, Biopolitics, Crip Affect* (Ann Arbor: University of Michigan Press, 2019), pp. 118–43.
3. On how emotional appeals contribute to virality, see J. Berger and K. L. Milkman, 'What Makes Online Content Viral?' *Journal of Marketing Research*, 49/2 (2012), 192–205; L. L. Henke, 'Breaking Through the Clutter: The Impact of Emotions and Flow on Viral Marketing', *Academy of Marketing Studies Journal*, 17/2 (2013), 111–18; M. Guerini and J. Staiano, 'Deep Feelings: A Massive Cross-Lingual Study on the Relation Between Emotions and Virality', preprint version of *WWW 2015* 'Web Science Track' paper, *https://arxiv.org/abs/1503.04723* (accessed 26 May 2018).
4. For online columns explaining like-farming, see D. Gross, 'On Facebook, Clicking "Like" Can Help Scammers', *CNN*, 22 January 2014, *http://www.cnn.com/2014/01/21/tech/social-media/facebook-like-farming* (accessed 8 August 2017); J. Abel, 'Like-Farming Facebook Scams', *Consumer Affairs*, 22 April 2015, *https://www.consumeraffairs.com/news/like-farming-facebook-scams-look-before-you-like-042215.html* (accessed 26 May 2018); L. Lenz, 'That Viral Photo of a Baby with Disabilities is Likely a Money-Making Scam', *The Daily Dot*, 10 August 2016, *https://www.consumeraffairs.com/news/like-farming-facebook-scams-look-before-you-like-042215.html* (accessed 23 April 2018).

5. Because these posts are often removed, it is difficult to identify stable online sources. The first image does not currently appear online. The others appear on posts about the problem of like-farming, although they can also crop up again on Facebook. See C. Charles, 'Facebook Page "Sowter Daisy" Shows Why You Shouldn't Type Amen on a Post', *That's Nonsense*, 21 November 2016, *http://www.thatsnonsense.com/facebook-page-sowter-daisy-shows-why-you-shouldnt-type-amen-on-a-post/* (accessed 26 May 2018); C. Hodges, 'My Photo Went Viral on Facebook for the Wrong Reason', *The Mighty*, 21 May 2015, *https://themighty.com/2015/05/woman-responds-when-port-wine-stain-photo-goes-viral/* (accessed 26 May 2018); and Gross, 'On Facebook'.
6. Mary Douglas, *Purity and Danger: An Analysis of Concepts of Pollution and Taboo* (New York: Routledge, 2002 [1966]).
7. Julia Kristeva, *Powers of Horror: An Essay on Abjection*, translated by Leon S. Roudiez (New York: Columbia University Press, 1982).
8. Priscilla Wald, *Contagious: Cultures, Carriers, and the Outbreak Narrative* (London and Durham, NC: Duke University Press, 2008), pp. 13–14.
9. 'Suffering and Horror' is the title of one of Kristeva's chapters. The term 'clean and proper' (in relation to the body or self) is a translation of the French term 'propre'.
10. Eli Clare, *Brilliant Imperfection: Grappling with Cure* (Durham, NC: Duke University Press, 2017), p. 6.
11. Joseph Shapiro, *No Pity: People with Disabilities Forging a New Civil Rights Movement* (New York: Three Rivers Press, 1994), p. 19.
12. Chris Hewitt, 'Sticks and Stones', in Bob Guter and John R. Killacky (eds), *Queer Crips: Disabled Men and Their Stories*, 2nd edn (New York: Routledge, 2014), pp. 14–15.
13. T. Sprayberry, 'The Can-I-Pray-For-You Encounter', The Mobility Resource, 23 September 2013, *https://blog.themobilityresource.com/blog/post/the-can-i-pray-for-you-encounter* (accessed 26 May 2018).
14. Clare, *Brilliant Imperfection*, p. 6.
15. Silvan Tomkins, 'Script Theory and Nuclear Scripts', in Eve Kosofsky Sedgwick and Adam Frank (eds), *Shame and Its Sisters: A Silvan Tomkins Reader* (Durham, NC: Duke University Press, 1995), pp. 179–95, 181.
16. Anna Gibbs, 'After Affect: Sympathy, Synchrony, and Mimetic Communication', in Melissa Gregg and Gregory J. Seigworth (eds), *The Affect Theory Reader* (Durham: Duke University Press, 2010), pp. 186–205, 188.
17. Erving Goffman, *Stigma: Notes on the Management of Spoiled Identity* (New York: Simon & Schuster, 1963), pp. 6–7.
18. Clare, *Brilliant Imperfection*, pp. 5–6.

19. Lenz, 'That Viral Photo'.
20. 'Contagion', Random House Unabridged Dictionary, 2018; 'Contagion', *Online Etymology Dictionary*, 2010, *http://www.dictionary.com/browse/contagion* (accessed 30 January 2020).
21. 'Virus', Random House Unabridged Dictionary, 2018, *http://www.dictionary.com/browse/virus* (accessed 1 June 2018).
22. K. Fritsch and A. McGuire, 'The Biosocial Politics of Queer/Crip Contagions', *Feminist Formations*, 30/1 (2018), vii–xiv.
23. S. Connor, 'Pity Porn – It's a Headf**k, My Friend', *The Stringer*, 12 October 2014, *http://thestringer.com.au/pity-porn-its-a-headfk-my-friend-8822#* (accessed 1 June 2018).
24. H. Ebben, 'The Desire to Recognize the Undesirable: De/Constructing the Autism Epidemic Metaphor and Contagion in Autism as a Discourse', *Feminist Formations*, 30/1 (2018), 141–63, 150.
25. Wald, *Contagious*, p. 3.
26. Henry Jenkins, Sam Ford and Joshua Green, *Spreadable Media: Creating Value and Meaning in a Networked Culture* (New York: New York University Press, 2013), pp. 17, 19–20.
27. Frank Rose, 'Henry Jenkins on "Spreadable Media", why fans rule, and why "The Walking Dead" lives' [interview with Henry Jenkins], *Deep Media*, 17 January 2013, *http://www.deepmediaonline.com/deepmedia/2013/01/henry-jenkins-on-spreadable-media.html* (accessed 31 May 2018).
28. Jenkins et al., *Spreadable Media*, pp. 20, 21.
29. Shifman here draws on James Carey, *Communication as Culture* (New York: Routledge, 1989); Limor Shifman, *Memes in Digital Culture* (Cambridge (MA): MIT Press, 2014), pp. 60–3.
30. Ebben, 'The Desire to Recognize', 153, 155.
31. T. Shepherd, 'Social Media Stole My Daughter's Identity', News.com.au, 26 October 2012, *http://www.news.com.au/technology/facebook-stole-my-disabled-daughters-identity/news-story/9f77d1cd91ff00363a5c21f9a5bc1bc6* (accessed 14 May 2018). An image of the original post can be found in 'Why You are Already in a Facebook Like Farm', *Koozai*, 6 August 2013, *https://www.koozai.com/blog/social-media/you-are-a-like-farm/* (accessed 9 April 2019).
32. Katie, 'Sharing is NOT Caring: The Exploitation of Children on Facebook', Red Stick Moms Blog, 5 January 2017, *https://batonrouge.citymomsblog.com/sharing-is-not-caring-the-exploitation-of-children-on-facebook/* (accessed 1 June 2018).
33. For instance, a public Facebook post by Avery's Angels Gastroschisis Foundation drew attention to another post that attached the 'Farnando' text to

a different photo, since removed. Avery's Angels Gastroschisis Foundation, 'Alert: Please Report This!!', *Facebook*, 8 January 2017, *https://www.facebook.com/averysangels/posts/10154957008249874* (accessed 9 April 2019).

34. 'Pathos', Collins English Dictionary – Complete and Unabridged 10th edition (HarperCollins Publishers, 2018), *http://www.dictionary.com/browse/pathos*, 30 January 2020. 'Pathetic', Random House Unabridged Dictionary, 2018, *http://www.dictionary.com/browse/pathetic*, 30 January 2020.
35. 'Pathogenic', The American Heritage Stedman's Medical Dictionary, *http://www.dictionary.com/browse/pathogenic*, 30 January 2020.
36. Beth Haller and Jeffrey Preston, 'Confirming Normalcy: "Inspiration Porn" and the Construction of the Disabled Subject?' in Katie Ellis and Mike Kent (eds), *Disability and Social Media: Global Perspectives* (New York: Routledge, 2017), pp. 41–56, 44.
37. C. Westlake, 'Why You *Shouldn't* "Type Amen and Share" Posts of Sick Children', *Courtney Westlake* (blog), 7 January 2016, *http://www.courtneywestlake.com/why-you-shouldnt-share-posts-of-sick-children/* (accessed 1 June 2018).
38. S. Young, 'I'm Not Your Inspiration, Thank You Very Much', *TED Talk*, April 2014, *https://www.ted.com/talks/stella_young_i_m_not_your_inspiration_thank_you_very_much* (accessed 18 May 2018).
39. S. Young, 'We're Not Here for Your Inspiration', *ABC News*, 2 July 2012, *http://www.abc.net.au/news/2012-07-03/young-inspiration-porn/4107006* (accessed 14 May 2018).
40. Young, 'We're Not Here'.
41. Politicians, religious groups, activists and advocates have described pornography with the language of 'pandemic', 'epidemic' and 'public health crisis'. See, for instance, 'Porn in US "A Public Health Crisis"', *The Telegraph*, 16 May 2014, *https://www.telegraph.co.uk/news/worldnews/northamerica/usa/10835994/Porn-in-US-a-public-health-crizis.html* (accessed 31 May 2018); F. Brown, 'Utah Gov. Gary Herbert Signs Resolution Calling Porn a "Health Hazard"', *CNN*, 19 April 2016, *https://www.cnn.com/2016/04/18/health/utah-governor-porn-resolution-health-hazard/index.html* (accessed 31 May 2018); and M. Rezac, 'What Can Priests Practically Do to Combat the Porn Epidemic?' *Catholic News Agency*, 19 December 2017, *https://www.catholicnewsagency.com/news/what-can-priests-practically-do-to-combat-the-porn-epidemic-44881* (accessed 31 May 2018).
42. For example, see Nayan Shah, *Contagious Divides: Epidemics and Race in San Francisco's Chinatown* (Oakland: University of California Press, 2001); Wald, *Contagious*; Jeffrey A. Bennett, *Banning Queer Blood: Rhetorics of Citizenship, Contagion, and Resistance* (Tuscaloosa: University of Alabama Press, 2015);

Neel Ahuja, *Biosecurities: Disease Interventions, Empire, and the Government of Species* (Durham, NC: Duke University Press, 2016).

43. Quoted in Haller and Preston, 'Confirming Normalcy', p. 52.
44. Puar borrows the term 'queer diaspora' from David Eng. Jasbir K. Puar, *Terrorist Assemblages: Homonationalism in Queer Times* (Durham, NC: Duke University Press, 2007), pp. 172–3.
45. Fritsch and McGuire, 'The Biosocial Politics', vii, ix.
46. Ebben, 'The Desire to Recognize', 159.
47. B. A. Ferri, 'Metaphors of Contagion and the Autoimmune Body', *Feminist Formations*, 30/1 (2018), 1–20, 6–7.
48. In an overview of the term 'crip', including its reclamation by disability activists and artists, and its uptake by disability scholars, Victoria Ann Lewis notes the term's sonic and affective impact: 'its quick burst of Anglo-Saxon roughness', its status as an 'affectionately ironic . . . identification', its association with 'disability cool', and its 'pride and panache'. Victoria A. Lewis, 'Crip', in Rachel Adams, Benjamin Reiss and David Serlin (eds), *Keywords for Disability Studies* (New York: New York University Press, 2015), pp. 46–8.
49. *Vital Signs: Crip Culture Talks Back*, David Mitchell and Sharon Snyder, dirs. (Fanlight Productions, 1998).
50. C. Hodges, 'Birthmarks and Laser Treatments', 19 April 2013, *http://www.thetravelinchick.com/2013/04/before-going-through-treatment.html* (accessed 28 May 2018).
51. C. Hodges, 'The Face that Went Viral', 24 August 2014, *http://www.thetravelinchick.com/2014/08/the-face-that-went-viral.html* (accessed 28 May 2018).
52. Hodges, 'The Face'.
53. Hodges, 'Birthmarks'.
54. Hodges, 'The Face'.
55. Ken Jennings, Twitter post, 22 September 2014, *https://twitter.com/KenJennings/status/514125105426071553.*
56. C. Ledbetter, 'Ken Jennings Of "Jeopardy!" Fame Tweets Awful Wheelchair "Joke"', *Huffington Post*, 22 September 2014, *https://www.huffingtonpost.com/2014/09/22/ken-jennings-wheelchair-joke_n_5864374.html* (accessed 29 May 2018); A. Weisman, '"Jeopardy!" Champ Ken Jennings Under Fire for Insensitive Wheelchair Tweet', *Business Insider*, 23 September 2014, *http://www.businessinsider.com/jeopardy-champ-ken-jennings-awful-wheelchair-tweet-2014-9* (accessed 29 May 2018).
57. Joshua Cassidy, Twitter post, 25 September 2014, *https://twitter.com/JoshCassidy84/status/515150910818111488.* Cassidy's tweet and all #HotPersonInAWheelchair tweets are reprinted with authors' permission.

58. Annie Segarra, Twitter post, 21 April 2018, *https://twitter.com/annieelainey/status/987846312761675776.*
59. Elizabeth Jeannel, Twitter post, 23 April 2018, *https://twitter.com/jeannelzabeth/status/988468250576130048.*
60. Michaela Oteri, Twitter post, 24 April 2018, *https://twitter.com/Ogrefairy/status/988860783865065472.*
61. The Representation Project, Twitter post, 23 April 2018, *https://twitter.com/TheRepProject/status/988510175542759424.*
62. Geoff Trappett, Twitter post, 28 April 2018, *https://twitter.com/InclusionMoves/status/990441385093312512.*
63. To name just a few: #DisabledAndCute, #CripPunk, #DisaBodyPosi, #ActuallyAutistic, #WheelchairLife, and #InvisibleIllness.
64. 'How #HotPersonInAWheelchair is Fighting Hate on Twitter', *BBC News*, 7 May 2018, *http://www.bbc.com/news/disability-44004823* (accessed 28 May 2018); F. Ryan, 'Surprised to See a Hot Woman in a Wheelchair?' *The Guardian*, 7 May 2018, *https://www.theguardian.com/society/shortcuts/2018/may/07/surprised-to-see-a-hot-woman-in-a-wheelchair-if-so-examine-your-prejudices* (accessed 28 May 2018).
65. Frank Rose, 'Henry Jenkins on "Spreadable Media"'.

5

'Fatties Cause Global Warming'

The Strange Entanglement of Obesity and Climate Change

Francis Ray White

IN AUGUST 2004 the following report appeared in the mostly fictional tabloid paper *Weekly World News*:

> Fat people's sweat is changing weather patterns, scientist claims.
>
> The huge amount of sweat produced by fat people is causing floods, hurricanes and severe weather all over the world, a leading scientist has discovered. What's more, the large amounts of perfume, lotions, aftershave and other chemicals used by obese folks destroy the ozone as they vaporize and contribute to global warming.
>
> Dr. Edward Millidge, a leading climatologist, believes we're reaching a crisis point . . . While the average person only begins to sweat with mild exertion, obese people routinely sweat while doing nothing more than watching TV . . .
>
> There are things obese populations could do to minimize their impact on weather patterns, such as wearing appropriate clothing, exercising

> regularly in an air-conditioned building, and limiting the use of lotions and such. 'These are just Band-Aids though', says Dr. Millidge. 'The only real solution is to lose weight before they destroy the earth.'[1]

The story was nestled alongside tales of a Jesus-shaped love-bite with healing powers and George W. Bush's alien abduction, and one could assume the credibility of each to be roughly comparable. Fast forward half a decade though, and the framing of fat people as a form of environmental contamination was hitting the real headlines as *The Sun*'s front cover proclaimed, 'fatties cause global warming'. This time it was not their sweat that was the problem, but fat people's 'excessive' energy consumption; 'providing extra grub for them to guzzle adds to carbon emissions that heat up the world, melting polar ice caps, raising sea levels and killing rain forests'.[2]

Perhaps these stories should be dismissed as (albeit cruel) novelty items, not to be taken too seriously. However, while they certainly occupy the sensationalist fringe, accounts of the entanglements of obesity and climate change have been articulated and rearticulated in books, articles and reports across medical, popular scientific and policy discourse over the past fifteen years. The headline above, for example, was part of the widespread media coverage of an article by researchers Phil Edwards and Ian Roberts.[3] In 2007, the UK government's Foresight Report *Tackling Obesities: Future Choices* dubbed obesity 'the climate change of public health' and Health Minister Alan Johnson claimed obesity was, 'a potential crisis, on the scale of climate change'.[4] In 2019, obesity and climate change appeared as the subject of a major Lancet Commission report entitled *The Global Syndemic of Obesity, Undernutrition, and Climate Change*.[5]

The aim of this chapter is not to investigate the veracity of these claims, or determine whether fatties really do cause global warming; nor is it to question the reality of climate change.[6] Rather, with recourse to Judith Butler's (1993; 2004) politics of resignification, what follows is an attempt to understand the discursive sleights of hand that have allowed obesity and climate change to become entangled, and for the links between them to appear legitimate and almost common-sensical. The second aim is to offer a critique of the fat bodies these links produce. Medicalized discourses of the 'obesity epidemic' already constitute fat bodies as contaminated (infected by fatness, diseased) and contagious (spreading infection, bringing bodily and social death).[7] The question here is how the entanglement of obesity and climate change exacerbates this proximity of fat bodies to pollution, contagion and death. Drawing on an analysis of over one hundred iterations of obesity/climate change discourse the chapter will show that while accounts of the links between obesity and climate change appear to be wildly divergent – the respectability of the Lancet Commission a far cry from the lurid headlines of the *Weekly World News* – ultimately they converge around removing the contamination of fatness, seldom straying far from the demand that fat people 'lose weight before they destroy the earth'.

Analysing Obesity and Climate Change

My analysis was conducted using a sample of 112 written pieces that made links between obesity and climate change.[8] Fifty-one were from academic journals, fifty-two from media sources and a further nine from popular science and health websites, all published between 2004 and 2019 and ranging in length from short opinion pieces and contributions to letters pages, to full peer-reviewed academic articles and books. My sample was initially gathered via online searches, and then by following up references in both media and academic articles and repeating this until no new significant sources emerged. The sample is, inevitably, not exhaustive, but it is large enough to reveal consistent themes across time. Notably, the vast majority (88 per cent) of the academic articles were from medical, health or specialist obesity journals, rather than environmental science journals. This speaks both to the fields in which the obesity/climate change link has most salience or credibility, and to the relative absence of discussion about differing political or practical approaches to climate change. The sample also almost exclusively talks about 'obesity', or 'overweight and obesity' ('fatties' notwithstanding) reflecting a dominant medicalised lexicon around body weight, as well as the implication that the normative body is slender and uncontaminated by fatness.[9] 'Fat' and 'fatness' are used throughout this chapter to signal the contested status of 'obesity' as a neutral term, and to distinguish between the sample texts and the analysis.[10]

Analysis of the construction of link(s) between obesity and climate change in the sample yielded three key variants: obesity is *like* climate change; obesity *causes* climate change; and obesity and climate change have *shared drivers*. The 'like' variant (23 per cent of the sample), is concentrated in 2007–8, especially around the Foresight Report and its media coverage, and is the only theme not to feature significantly in academic articles. The 'causes climate change' (43 per cent) and 'shared drivers' (34 per cent) variants are similar in that they are represented throughout the years 2004–19, however there is little media coverage of the shared drivers approach compared to the other two variants. Whilst distinct, the three variants inevitably overlap in certain respects, for example in the promotion of 'solutions' that will solve both obesity and climate change simultaneously such as reducing car use and the consumption of energy/carbon dense food. While there is not scope here for a full discussion of the 'solutions' presented in the articles, the centrality of weight loss across all three variants will be considered later in the chapter.

Underpinning the analysis is Judith Butler's theorisation of the 'resignification of discourse'; namely, the idea that as discourses performatively produce the objects of which they speak, but never in a way that can be fixed or final, it is possible to subversively reiterate those discourses in order to transform or 'resignify' them. Butler's intention is that such resignifications are deployed to rob existing significations of their shaming or injurious power, and to 'extend the norms that sustain viable life to previously disenfranchised communities'.[11] This is very much the spirit in which resignificatory politics have been taken up within fat activism and scholarship. The work of Kathleen LeBesco (2004), for example, applies Butler's theory to the resignification of fat subjectivity as a response to fatphobia, much in the manner that Butler discusses the resignification of 'queer'.[12] However, the relevance of this theory to thinking about obesity and climate change draws more from Butler's acknowledgement that resignification in itself does not necessarily serve social justice, but can as easily apply to reappropriations of discourse that deepen abjection or exclusion.[13] Indeed, the current dominant discursive construction of fatness as 'epidemic', with the attendant implication of a spreading contagion, can be thought of as the legacy of previous successful resignifications of 'obesity'.[14]

When discussing the conditions necessary for a successful resignification, Butler argues one will succeed,

> not because an intention successfully governs the action of speech, but only because that action echoes prior actions, and accumulates the force of authority through the repetition or citation of a prior, authoritative set of practices.[15]

This criterion is useful in terms of evaluating why some formulations of the link between obesity and climate change 'take hold' and go largely uncontested, while others do not. Butler further offers a way to understand what is at stake when the fat body is (re)configured through the link to climate change when she attempts to establish the criteria that distinguish between 'good' and 'bad' resignifications. She argues we must, 'make substantive decisions about what will be a less violent future, what will be a more inclusive population' and ask of a resignificatory move, 'what forms of community have been created, and through what violences and exclusions have they been created?'[16] Drawing on this guide for recognising and evaluating resignifications, the following discussion will outline the characteristics of each variant of the obesity/climate change link, highlighting the discursive conditions that have made each possible and attending to any significant differences between academic and media iterations, and finally move on to identify the kinds of fat bodies they discursively produce.

'A Potential Crisis on the Scale of Climate Change'

The first type of link made between obesity and climate change hinges around framing them as phenomena that are somehow 'like' each other in terms of scale or severity, as was seen in the media reporting surrounding the Foresight Report in 2007. 'Obesity "as bad as climate risk"' was how the BBC put it, while the *Independent* went with, 'obesity is as serious a threat as climate change' and the *Times* said, 'Obesity crisis "on the same scale as global warming"'.[17] The Foresight Report reviewed the causes, extent and potential policy approaches to obesity in Britain and forecasted that by 2050 fifty per cent of women and sixty per cent of men in the UK would be obese, with the yearly 'financial impact to society' pegged at £45.9bn.[18] The Report's major innovation was to draw heavily on a 'systemic' frame which understands the causes of population-wide weight gain to lie beyond the individual.[19] Specifically it draws on the concept of the 'obesogenic environment'. An obesogenic environment, as Colls and Evans argue, 'situates the "causes" of obesity in a body's relationships and interactions with particular (physical, social and cultural) "environments"' and is commonly characterised as one which inhibits physical exercise, but makes 'junk' food highly available, thus increasing the likelihood of population level weight gain.[20]

It is this environmental explanation for obesity which allows the Foresight Report to forge a link between obesity and climate change in terms of their 'like-ness'. The Report first makes the analogy in its introduction, which states: 'obesity, like climate change, is a complex problem but it is not insoluble'.[21] The link is then elaborated in a special section titled 'obesity – "the climate change of public health"?' which suggests a 'number of parallels' between the two:

> Both are complex in causation and solution, with questioning of the evidence, yet they both demand firm and swift action . . . Failure to act at an early stage is already having significant and undesirable consequences . . . The policy discourse is vibrant but is not yet being matched by a requisite, measurable change in the right direction by society, governments and the economy . . . There is a danger that the moment to act radically and coherently will be missed.[22]

The 'like-ness' here ultimately coheres around the idea that obesity and climate change require 'tackling' (as the title of the report suggests) before the 'undesirable consequences' occur. The Report does not have to explicitly elucidate what those consequences are, nor what 'change in the right direction' might entail. This is because specific understandings of obesity as a problem that needs solving are already established and working as instances of Butler's 'prior authority'. Thus a novel and seemingly credible link between obesity and climate change is made possible on the basis of already-authorised accounts of both as inexorably worsening problems that require public action.[23]

If the Foresight Report itself relies on existing significations of obesity to make the 'like-ness' of obesity and climate change intelligible, then the media coverage of it does so doubly. The analogy with climate change was disproportionately prominent in the media due to the widespread reporting of Alan Johnson's comments at the report's launch, namely:

> We cannot afford not to act. For the first time we are clear about the magnitude of the problem. We are facing a potential crisis on the scale of climate change and it is in everybody's interest to turn things round.[24]

The nature of this 'potential crisis' is never explored. Will obesity bring on the same apocalyptic outcomes as climate change – widespread environmental degradation and the end of life on earth? The point here is that the exact 'likeness' does not require further articulation to make a kind of sense. Michael Gard argues that in much 'obesity epidemic' discourse, 'there are no rules; like the distracting wave of the magician's hand, any idea can be made to fit with any other idea so long as the reader can be diverted and dazzled by the spectre of death'.[25] Casting obesity and climate change as 'like' one another performs precisely this sort of trick.

However, contra Gard, it may also be the case that there are *some* rules and attempts to assert the 'like-ness' of obesity and climate change are challenged in some of the commentary around Foresight (if not in news reports which largely just reiterated Johnson's comments). A letter to *The Independent* exemplifies the main counter-discourse articulated in the media. It argues, 'how utterly absurd of the Government to equate the threat of obesity with climate change. Obesity is a disease of decadence seen mainly in the so-called developed world.'[26] Similarly, Max Hastings writing in the *Daily Mail* contends that 'each of us can far more readily address our weight than we can global warming'.[27] These responses assert that *unlike* climate change, obesity is subject to individual control. As such, what they are contesting is the systemic, 'obesogenic environment', account of the causes of obesity, and instead they rely on an individualising frame. As Rich and Evans note, 'within this discourse, individuals are deemed largely responsible for their own health and for "making healthy choices" as if they were free of structural and cultural constraints'.[28]

While recourse to individualising frames may indicate that 'obesogenic environment' accounts of obesity have failed as resignifications of existing, arguably more hegemonic, explanations, they do not substantially alter the way in which either discourse constructs the fat body. The likening of obesity to climate change sensationalises and intensifies existing constructions of the fat body as diseased, deathly, burdensome that circulate in wider discourses of the obesity 'epidemic'.[29] Just one lone article (Basham) questions the analogy on the grounds that obesity itself is neither 'epidemic' nor of crisis proportions.[30] Thus even when the obesogenic environment version of the analogy is repeated but refuted, fat bodies are still constituted as having been contaminated by fatness because they were individually unable to resist the temptations of greed and/or sloth.

'Fatties Cause Global Warming'

Where claiming obesity is 'like' climate change does not suggest any direct connection between the two phenomena, the second variant, summarised nicely by *The Sun* as 'fatties cause global warming', forges a link that makes one responsible for the other. The argument rests on the idea that, as

Phil Edwards and Ian Roberts, two of the central architects of this approach, contend, 'increasing population adiposity will result in an increase in GHG [greenhouse gas] emissions'.[31] This is because 'total food energy consumption increases as BMI increases' and 'because of the additional fuel energy needed to transport heavier people'.[32] Edwards and Roberts's widely cited and widely reported-on article is a modelling exercise that compares the food and fuel energy consumption of a 'normal' weight population to an 'overweight' population, the former based on UK rates in the 1970s and the latter on predicted body mass index (BMI) distribution in 2010. Their conclusion is that 'increased population adiposity, because of its contribution to climate change from additional food and transport GHG emissions, should be recognized as an environmental problem'.[33]

The way Edwards and Roberts construct obesity as directly contributing to climate change is not only mirrored in other academic arguments of this type[34] but has generated 86 per cent of the 'fatties cause global warming' media and popular science coverage in the sample. Edwards and Roberts's work has been heavily criticised by Gallar for its 'complete arbitrariness', and by Evans for relying on 'anecdotes and (cultural and racial) stereotypes rather than evidence'.[35] Edwards and Roberts do indeed make some spectacular claims, for example those in a completely unreferenced article in *New Scientist* (2007). It confidently asserts, 'obese people eat about 40 per cent more in terms of calories than their lean counterparts', something they cite as 'evidence' in subsequent work.[36] Edwards and Roberts also make some bold assertions when they calculate car travel-related greenhouse gas emissions by assuming, 'that all individuals with BMI <30 kg/m^2 use an average small car (e.g. Ford Fiesta) and that individuals with BMI >30 kg/m^2 use a car with more internal space (e.g. Ford Galaxy)'.[37] What is problematic about this is not just Edwards and Roberts's failure to draw on any empirical data on food consumption or BMI and car use (especially how those factors intersect with socio-economic class), not to mention their fantastical imaginings of the physical dimensions of people with a BMI of thirty, but that their arguments were so readily and widely repeated in both the media and subsequent academic work on the topic. The question is why, or rather how, their arguments appear to have made 'sense'.

Referring back to Butler's metrics for resignificatory success, Edwards and Roberts's (re)deployment of obesity as an 'energy imbalance' in part enables their claims to pass as credible. They invoke the energy-in/energy-out thesis wherein, as they put it, 'body fat accumulates when the amount of energy we eat as food exceeds the amount of energy we use moving around', and heavily reference the ways 'energy' comes into play in fat people's lives: 'energy is required in order to overcome inertia and the greater the mass the more energy is required'; 'heavy people consume more energy' and 'require 16% more food energy'; 'wearing a heavy body is like driving around in a gas-guzzler. A heavy person must consume more food energy just to maintain a constant body weight.'[38] They even reference 'Newton's first law of motion' to explain the 'inertia' of fat flesh in terms of 'basic physical laws'.[39] Energy-in/energy-out explanations are not only familiar as common-sense explanations of weight gain and loss but, as Gard and Wright argue, they rehearse widely held ideas that 'the body is governed by scientifically verifiable laws'.[40] Furthermore they echo the 'energy saving' lexicon of discourses of environmental friendliness. Hence, by framing the issue as one of 'energy', Edwards and Roberts reiterate powerful and familiar discourses which allow the idea that obesity causes climate change to accumulate the 'force of authority'.

The 'fatties cause global warming' discourses, perhaps more than the other variants of the obesity/climate change link, foreground particular constructions of fat bodies which also contribute to the intelligibility of their arguments. As the quotes above suggest, fat people are positioned as voracious consumers, best illustrated by the repeated use of the term 'guzzler' in Edwards and Roberts's work – 'a heavy body is a gas (food) guzzler'; 'say no to global guzzling' – and in multiple media articles which quote Edwards saying 'moving about in a heavy body is like driving around in a gas guzzler'.[41] 'Guzzling' conjures the greed and uncontrolled appetites often associated with fat bodies, but perhaps more perniciously it casts that 'guzzling' not just as a failure of will, but of biology; the fat body is unable not to 'guzzle'. The attention to how much food goes into fat bodies in the 'fatties cause global warming' variant articles is complemented by recurring references to what comes back out. While the *Weekly World News* (2004) highlights 'fat people's sweat', so Gryka et al. note that while all humans 'produce CO_2 during respiration . . . due to the fact that CO_2 production is proportionate to body mass, heavier individuals produce more'.[42] Carbon dioxide is not the only climate-destroying substance fat bodies produce. Several articles follow through, as it were, fat bodies' excessive food consumption to their prodigious waste production. Roberts notes, 'greater food consumption means more organic waste, which produces methane as it decomposes'.[43] Michaelowa and Dransfield similarly warn that 'higher food consumption will automatically lead to a higher generation of solid and liquid human wastes', and their diagram showing 'the greenhouse gas emissions impacts of an increase in human body weight' factors in 'waste volume increase'.[44] Fat studies scholar Lesleigh Owen suggests this is typical of the way abject bodies are 'defined by an exaggeration of their relationships with orifices'. She argues this applies in specific ways to fat bodies:

> They are considered more biological, more tied to their processes, their orifices. Fat people, who are, the story goes, universally out of shape, sweat more. They also supposedly eat more, in fact, fat persons serve as visual shortcuts for gluttony. They certainly excrete more.[45]

By drawing on this construction these articles cast bodies as not just contaminated by fatness, but fat bodies as a source of contagion, actively polluting not only themselves, but the planet as well. Hence the audacious and spurious claim that 'fatties cause global warming' is made possible and intelligible.

'Common Systemic Drivers'

Rather than blaming fat people for global warming, the third variant of the obesity/climate change link lays the blame for both at the feet of a third party. In these explanations obesity and climate change are positioned as the side-effects of, variously, the 'big food' industry, global agriculture, fossil fuels and/or capitalist economic development.[46] Arguments of this type have proliferated in the academic literature since 2005. At that time, for example, Paul Higgins looked to 'societal dependence on oil' and subsequently automobiles for producing both climate change, and the 'obesity epidemic'.[47] Similarly, Faergeman blames 'burning fossil fuels' and says this 'is the major source of greenhouse gases, but it also makes pervasive physical inactivity possible'.[48] Both Higgins and Faergeman highlight 'energy-out' deficits as causing obesity, following the 'energy imbalance' model previously discussed. However, Faergeman also addresses the 'energy-in' side, noting, 'similarly, modern agriculture's enormous production of livestock contributes substantially to greenhouse gas emissions, and it is the source of many of our most energy-rich foods'.[49]

Some of the most developed forms of this argument come from Australian researchers Garry Egger and/or Boyd Swinburn.[50] In their book *Planet Obesity* (2010) they attribute the existence and growth of both obesity and climate change to 'economic growth having overshot its sweet spot'.[51] They argue that we have hit a 'catastrophic sour spot' where several interconnected aspects of human and economic development have turned and ceased to produce positive outcomes and 'obesity is the signal of this change'.[52] Swinburn is also the co-chair of the Lancet Commission that produced the 2019 Global Syndemic report, a highly elaborated iteration of the shared drivers variant and ambitious systemic account of obesity. The report makes the novel claim that the global pandemics of obesity, undernutrition and climate change 'constitute a syndemic, or synergy of epidemics, because they co-occur in time and place, interact with each other to produce complex sequelae, and share common underlying societal drivers . . . [of] food and agriculture, transportation, urban design, and land use'.[53] The report is the subject of all but one of the media articles deploying the shared drivers link between obesity and climate change, despite there being almost twice as many academic articles in this category than the other two combined. This absence of media discourse in itself may be evidence of a level of failure of the shared drivers approach's attempt to resignify the connection between obesity and climate change. Unlike the 'fatties cause global warming' link, it cannot lean on the authority (and familiarity) of the dominant individualising frame of obesity.

The Lancet Commission report did generate some mainstream media coverage: however, the media reporting does not faithfully reiterate the report's central thesis. Throughout the report the Commission use the WHO Food and Agriculture Organization's definition of 'malnutrition in all its forms', which is to say malnutrition as 'including obesity, undernutrition, and other dietary risks'.[54] The report is very intentional about this, explicitly saying these are the terms that need to be deployed in order to produce policy that addresses both obesity and climate change (and undernutrition). The report states:

> Thinking in Global Syndemic terms will allow actors to focus on common systemic drivers that need common actions. The Commission recommends that all actors frame their commitments and actions on the SDGs [sustainable development goals] in syndemic and systems terms to show their inherent connectedness and systemic origins. For example, defining the problems using terms like malnutrition in all its forms and The Global Syndemic.[55]

In the media coverage of the report, however, the syndemic is invariably named as being made up of 'obesity, *malnutrition* and climate change', malnutrition, rather than 'undernutrition'.[56] Thus, where the report attempts to authorise a new signification of obesity as a form of malnutrition, the way they are reported as separate entities suggests a failure of that resignification outside the sphere it originated in. Gillborn et al. offer a possible explanation of this when they describe malnutrition as 'an issue that is difficult to attribute to personal responsibility rather than state failings'.[57] As the 'fatties cause global warming' variant shows, individualised, personal responsibility accounts of obesity are readily (nay, enthusiastically) repeated in the public sphere, whereas approaches, such as the 'syndemic', which frame obesity as a type of structural (and sometimes state) failing, still do not appear to have the requisite citational legacy or prior authority to effect a successful resignification.

While the individualising frame is highly problematic in terms of the fat body it produces, it would be an error to see the systemic framing of the 'shared drivers' approach as in some way kinder or less exclusionary. For example, the Lancet Commission defines the 'malnourished', and thus fat body as 'an abnormal physiological condition caused by inadequate, unbalanced, or excessive consumption of macronutrients or micronutrients'.[58] The body here shares many characteristics with the pathological entity shaped by the 'fatties cause global warming' discourses. The shared drivers articles also construct fat bodies as manipulable, passive and as having 'caught' obesity from the toxic environment. The Lancet Commission describes obesity as 'a symptom of deeper, underlying systemic problems', and as 'sequelae' – conditions produced by disease.[59] Egger and Swinburn argue, 'rising population levels of obesity are a sign that something is awry in the modern Western lifestyle', and cast fat people as the 'beacon' for rising levels of chronic diseases.[60] In each case the fat body is produced as having been infected or contaminated by obesity.

Perhaps the most evocative of these comes from Egger and Dixon's article which asks whether obesity and global warming are 'similar "canaries" in the same "mineshaft"?'[61] They argue that trying to fix either obesity or climate change without addressing their shared drivers is 'like trying to resuscitate an asphyxiated canary while leaving untouched the mineshaft that caused the asphyxiation'.[62] Fat bodies in this formulation are bodies that have succumbed to the 'obesogenic environment'; they are the doomed, dead canaries serving as a warning to the rest of humanity. Like the climate-change-inducing bodies of the second variant, these fat bodies also lack control, not because of their unbridled appetites, but because they have been unable to exert the requisite 'rationality and self-discipline' required to stay or get thin in the midst of such abundance.[63]

'The Only Real Solution . . .'

The association of fat bodies with contagion and death is not the only one to cut across all variants of the obesity/climate change link. By means of a conclusion, this final discussion will briefly consider how it is that, despite the complexity of some of the arguments put forward linking climate change and obesity, good old-fashioned weight loss is ultimately the grand plan for thwarting the fat-fuelled apocalypse. The logics that equate fatness with accelerated environmental collapse, legitimate the often-made argument that 'thinner is better to curb global warming'.[64] Phil Edwards's contribution to this debate was to claim 'the main message is staying thin. It's good for you, and it's good for the planet.'[65] Some researchers go so far as to recommend the specific amount of weight loss – Gryka et al., who even title their article 'global warming: is weight loss a solution?' propose 'a 10kg weight loss of all overweight and obese in the UK', which would 'account for over 1% of the CO2 emission reduction target by 2020'.[66]

What is perhaps surprising is that the emphasis on weight loss is as prevalent in the articles taking a systemic approach as it is in those above making individualising arguments. Egger and Swinburn, for example, acknowledge that diets and exercise have failed to have an impact on obesity levels, and likely won't in an obesogenic environment. All the same, they go on to advocate weight loss and, by offering up smug diet book aphorisms such as 'think of movement as an opportunity, not an inconvenience', strongly suggest it is down to the individual to lose weight.[67] As Anna Kirkland notes, this is contradictory because 'the environmental approach to fighting obesity is supposed to be collective, not responsibilizing. Responsibilizing individuals is not really environmental in the obvious sense of the word.'[68]

The Lancet Commission almost respond to this criticism, and yet, via a discursively convoluted strategy, still manage to endorse weight loss as something in fat people's interests. First they offer a critique of weight bias and stigma that reflects those originating in fat activism.[69] Excitingly, this seems to suggest such critique has acquired the 'force of authority through the repetition or citation of a prior, authoritative set of practices' required to effect a successful resignification.[70] However, the report then redeploys this critique to reinforce both the medical surveillance of fat people, and the imperative to lose weight characteristic of dominant (anti)obesity discourses. Their key weapon is the testimony of the one member of the Commission, Patty Nece, who has 'the experience of living with obesity'.[71] The weight-bias she has experienced in healthcare settings is used as evidence that stigma can 'account for the lack of recognition of obesity as a serious medical problem that deserves care'.[72] She then recounts her experience of stigma-free care where, 'because I have now received intensive science-based treatment from an obesity specialist – one who supports rather than judges me for my condition – I am managing my weight effectively'.[73] When fat studies scholar Le'a Kent states that the fat body is only ever 'invoked under the sign of its own erasure (whether through dieting or through death)',[74] she perfectly sums up the repentant fatty role Nece is apparently compelled to play here – defined by and subject to the medical gaze, and wholly engaged in the eradication of her own contaminating fatness.

Throughout this chapter the analysis has attempted to show how, in various ways, it has been discursively possible for obesity and climate change to be linked in popular and medical/scientific discourses. The overwhelming and somewhat bleak conclusion is that when Butler's criteria for assessing resignifications in terms of 'what will be a less violent future'[75] are applied to the links between obesity and climate change, there seems to be only an intensification of the associations of fat bodies with ideas of contamination – fat bodies as both contaminated and contaminating, and fatness more abstractly as something spreading like contagion and infecting the environment. Fat bodies by this logic embody contagion. However, if there is a more hopeful conclusion to be drawn it might be that dominant meanings of obesity are always in flux, never finally fixed, and will always be subject to further resignifications.

Notes

1. D. Fanatia, 'Fat People's Sweat is Changing Weather Patterns, Scientist Claims', *Weekly World News*, 30 August 2004, 47.
2. B. Jackson, 'Fatties Cause Global Warming', *The Sun*, 21 April 2009.
3. P. Edwards and I. Roberts, 'Population Adiposity and Climate Change', *International Journal of Epidemiology*, 38 (2009), 1137–40.

4. Foresight, *Tackling Obesities: Future Choices – Project Report*, 2nd edn (London: Department of Innovation Universities and Skills, 2007), p. 72, *http://www.foresight.gov.uk/Obesity/17.pdf* (accessed 29 August 2019).
5. B. Swinburn et al., 'The Global Syndemic of Obesity, Undernutrition, and Climate Change: The Lancet Commission Report', *The Lancet*, 393 (2019), 791–846.
6. For arguments debunking such claims, see M. Gallar, 'Obesity and Climate Change', *International Journal of Epidemiology*, 39/5 (2009), 1398–9; Michael Gard, *The End of the Obesity Epidemic* (London: Routledge, 2011); Elaine Graham-Leigh, *A Diet of Austerity: Class, Food and Climate Change* (Winchester: Zero Books, 2015); Julie Guthman, 'Excess Consumption or Over-Production?: US Farm Policy, Global Warming, and the Bizarre Attribution of Obesity', in Michael Watts, Richard Peet and Paul Robbins (eds), *Global Political Ecology* (London: Routledge, 2011), pp. 51–66; C. Russell et al., '"Fatties Cause Global Warming": Fat Pedagogy and Environmental Education', *Canadian Journal of Environmental Education*, 18 (2013), 15–33.
7. See Michael Gard and Jan Wright, *The Obesity Epidemic: Science Morality and Ideology* (London: Routledge, 2005); S. Gillborn, G. Rickett, T. Muskett and M. Woolhouse, 'Apocalyptic Public Health: Exploring Discourses of Fatness in Childhood "Obesity" Policy', *Journal of Education Policy*, 35/1 (2020); Le'a Kent, 'Fighting Abjection: Representing Fat Women', in Jana E. Braziel and Kathleen LeBesco (eds), *Bodies out of Bounds: Fatness and Transgression* (Berkeley: University of California Press, 2001), pp. 130–50; F. R. White, 'Fat, Queer, Dead: "Obesity" and the Death Drive', *Somatechnics*, 2/1 (2012), 1–17.
8. Sections of this analysis were previously published in: R. White, 'Undesirable Consequences? Resignifying Discursive Constructions of Fatness in the Obesity "Epidemic"', in Corinna Tomrley and Ann K. Naylor (eds), *Fat Studies in the UK* (York: Raw Nerve Books, 2009), pp. 69–81. Reproduced here with the publisher's permission.
9. For a similar construction of disabled bodies, see chapter 4 in this volume: Angela M. Smith, 'An Affectionate Epidemic: How Disability Goes Viral on Social Media', in Sandra Becker, Megen de Bruin-Molé and Sara Polak (eds), *Embodying Co*ntagion: The Viropolitics of Horror and Desire in Contemporary Discourse (Cardiff: University of Wales Press, 2021), pp. 85–106.
10. Marilyn Wann, 'Foreword', in Esther Rothblum and Sondra Solovay (eds), *The Fat Studies Reader* (New York: New York University Press, 2009), pp. xii–xiii.
11. Judith Butler, *Undoing Gender* (London: Routledge, 2004), p. 225.

12. Judith Butler, *Bodies That Matter: On the Discursive Limits of 'Sex'* (London: Routledge, 1993), p. 223.
13. Butler, *Undoing Gender*, p. 223.
14. See J. Eric Oliver, *Fat Politics: The Real Story Behind America's Obesity Epidemic* (Oxford: Oxford University Press, 2006); White, 'Undesirable Consequences?'.
15. Butler, *Bodies That Matter*, pp. 226–7.
16. Butler, *Undoing Gender*, p. 224.
17. 'Obesity "As Bad As Climate Risk"', *BBC News*, 14 October 2007, *http://news.bbc.co.uk/1/hi/health/7043639.stm* (accessed 29 August 2019); M. Woolf, 'Obesity is as Serious a Threat as Climate Change, says Minister', *ndependent on Sunday*, 14 October 2007, *http://www.independent.co.uk/news/uk/politics/obesity-is-as-seriousa-threat-as-climate-change-says-minister-396842.html* (accessed 29 August 2019); 'Obesity Crisis "On the Same Scale as Global Warming"', *The Times*, 15 October 2007, *https://www.thetimes.co.uk/article/obesity-crisis-on-the-same-scale-as-global-warming-q8zkk53vnjh* (accessed 29 August 2019).
18. Foresight, *Tackling Obesities*, p. 5.
19. E. Rich and J. Evans, 'Fat Ethics – The Obesity Discourse and Body Politics', *Social Theory and Health*, 3 (2005), 341–58, 350.
20. R. Colls and B. Evans, 'Making Space for Fat Bodies?: A Critical Account of "the Obesogenic Environment"', *Progress in Human Geography*, 38/6 (2014), 733–53, 736.
21. Foresight, *Tackling Obesities*, p. 17.
22. Foresight, *Tackling Obesities*, p. 72.
23. See Gard and Wright, *The Obesity Epidemic*; Oliver, *Fat Politics.*
24. Woolf, 'Obesity is as Serious a Threat as Climate Change'.
25. Gard, *The End of the Obesity Epidemic*, p. 28.
26. 'Letters: Obesity and Climate Change', *The Independent*, 16 October 2007, *http://www.independent.co.uk/opinion/letters/letters-obesity-and-climate-change-396985.html* (accessed 29 August 2019).
27. M. Hastings, 'Modern life is blamed for obesity, but whatever happened to willpower?', *Daily Mail*, 18 October 2007, *http://www.dailymail.co.uk/debate/columnists/article-488238/Modern-life-blamed-obesity-happend-willpower.html* (accessed 29 August 2019).
28. Rich and Evans, 'Fat Ethics', 352.
29. Gillborn et al., 'Apocalyptic Public Health', 8.
30. P. Basham, 'Who Are You Calling Fat?', *The Independent*, 23 October 2007, *https://www.independent.co.uk/life-style/health-and-families/health-news/obesity-epidemic-who-are-you-calling-fat-397647.html* (accessed 29 August 2019).

31. Edwards and Roberts, 'Population Adiposity', 1140.
32. Edwards and Roberts, 'Population Adiposity', 1138.
33. Edwards and Roberts, 'Population Adiposity', 1139.
34. See A. Michaelowa and B. Dransfeld, 'Greenhouse Gas Benefits of Fighting Obesity', *Ecological Economics*, 66/2–3 (2008), 298–308; A. Gryka, J. Broom and C. Rolland, 'Global Warming: Is Weight Loss a Solution?', *International Journal of Obesity*, 36/3 (2012), 474–6; J. Squalli, 'Is obesity associated with global warming?', *Public Health*, 128/12 (2014), 1087–93.
35. Gallar, 'Obesity and Climate Change', 1398; B. Evans, 'Climate Change and the Politics of Fatness', *Environmental Politics*, 21/2 (2012), 335.
36. I. Roberts, 'Say no to global guzzling', *New Scientist*, 194/2610 (2007), 21; Edwards and Roberts, 'Population Adiposity', 1137.
37. Edwards and Roberts, 'Population Adiposity', 1138.
38. Ian Roberts and Phil Edwards, *The Energy Glut: The Politics of Fatness in an Overheating World* (London: Zed Books, 2010), pp. 11, 46; Edwards and Roberts, 'Population Adiposity', 1140; Roberts and Edwards, Energy Glut, p. 56.
39. Edwards and Roberts, 'Population Adiposity', 1138.
40. Gard and Wright, *The Obesity Epidemic*, p. 38.
41. Roberts and Edwards, *The Energy Glut*, p. 136; Roberts, 'Say no to global guzzling', 21. See 'Obesity Causes Global Warming, Say Scientists', *Mail Online*, 21 April 2009, *https://www.dailymail.co.uk/sciencetech/article-1172249/Being-fat-causes-global-warming-say-scientists.html* (accessed 29 August 2019); R. R. Britt, 'Are Fat People Destroying Earth?', *Livescience.com*, 21 April 2009, *https://www.livescience.com/7704-fat-people-destroying-earth.html* (accessed 29 August 2019); Jackson, 'Fatties Cause Global Warming'.
42. Gryka et al., 'Global Warming', 474.
43. Roberts, 'Say no to global guzzling', 21.
44. Michaelowa and Dransfeld, 'Greenhouse Gas Benefits', 302, 299. See also page 300 reproduced in Garry Egger and Boyd Swinburn, *Planet Obesity: How We're Eating Ourselves and the Planet to Death* (Crows Nest: Allen and Unwin, 2010), p. 54; Francis Delpeuch, Bernard Maire, Emmanuel Monnier and Michelle Holdsworth, *Globesity: A Planet Out of Control?* (London: Routledge, 2009), p. 151.
45. L. Owen, 'Monstrous Freedom: Charting Fat Ambivalence', *Fat Studies*, 4/1 (2015), 1–13, 5–6.
46. See also R. An, M. Ji and S. Zhang, 'Global Warming and Obesity: A Systematic Review', *Obesity Reviews*, 19/2 (2018), 150–63.

47. P. Higgins, 'Exercise-Based Transportation Reduces Oil Dependence, Carbon Emissions and Obesity', *Environmental Conservation*, 32/3 (2005), 197–202, 197.
48. O. Faergeman, 'Climate Change and Preventative Medicine', *European Journal of Cardiovascular Prevention and Rehabilitation*, 14 (2007), 726–9, 726.
49. Faergeman, 'Climate Change', 726.
50. See G. Egger, 'Dousing our Inflammatory Environment(s): Is Personal Carbon Trading an Option for Reducing Obesity – and Climate Change?', *Obesity Reviews*, 9 (2008), 456–63; G. Egger and J. Dixon, 'Obesity and global warming: are they similar "canaries" in the same "mineshaft"?', *Medical Journal of Australia (MJA)*, 193/11–12 (2010), 635–7; G. Webb and G. Egger, 'Obesity and climate change: can we link the two and can we deal with both together?', *American Journal of Lifestyle Medicine*, 8 (2014), 200–4; B. Swinburn et al., 'The Global Syndemic of Obesity'.
51. Egger and Swinburn, *Planet Obesity*, p. 17.
52. Egger and Swinburn, *Planet Obesity*, pp. 69–70.
53. Swinburn et al., 'The Global Syndemic of Obesity', 791.
54. Swinburn et al., 'The Global Syndemic of Obesity', 791.
55. Swinburn et al., 'The Global Syndemic of Obesity', 835.
56. See J. Christensen, 'To Fix Climate Change, Fix the Obesity and Starvation Epidemics, Reports Say', *CNN.com*, 27 January 2019, *https://edition.cnn.com/2019/01/27/health/obesity-climate-change-undernutrition/index.html* (accessed 29 August 2019); F. Lawrence, 'The Way We Eat is Killing Us – and the Planet', *The Guardian*, 28 January 2019, *https://www.theguardian.com/commentisfree/2019/jan/28/global-food-killing-humans-planet-climate-change-obesity* (accessed 29 August 2019); A. Matthews-King, 'International Treaty Needed to Stop "Big Food" Industry Driving Obesity and Climate Change, Report Says', *The Independent*, 28 January 2019, *https://www.independent.co.uk/news/health/big-food-treaty-agriculture-industry-obesity-climate-change-sugar-tax-a8747176.html* (accessed 29 August 2019).
57. Gillborn et al., 'Apocalyptic Public Health', 14.
58. Swinburn et al., 'The Global Syndemic of Obesity', 795.
59. Swinburn et al., 'The Global Syndemic of Obesity', 797.
60. Egger and Swinburn, *Planet Obesity*, pp. 39, 70.
61. Egger and Dixon, 'Obesity and global warming' 635–7.
62. Egger and Dixon, 'Obesity and global warming', 636.
63. Julie Guthman, 'Neoliberalism and the Constitution of Contemporary Bodies', in Esther Rothblum and Sondra Solovay (eds), *The Fat Studies Reader* (New York and London: New York University Press, 2009), pp. 187–96, 193.

On the expectation that properly managed neoliberal bodies will avoid contagion, see also chapter 8 in this volume: Mica Hilson, 'Networks, Desire and Risk Management in Gay Contagion Fiction', in Sandra Becker, Megen de Bruin-Molé and Sara Polak (eds), *Embodying Contagion: The Viropolitics of Horror and Desire in Contemporary Discourse* (Cardiff: University of Wales Press, 2021), pp. 181–96.

64. E. Landau, 'Thinner is Better to Curb Global Warming, Study Says', *CNN.com*, 2009, *http://edition.cnn.com/2009/HEALTH/04/20/thin.global.warming/index.html* (accessed 29 August 2019).
65. Landau, 'Thinner is Better'.
66. Gryka et al., 'Global Warming', 476.
67. Egger and Swinburn, *Planet Obesity*, pp. 102–4.
68. A. Kirkland, 'The Environmental Account of Obesity: A Case for Feminist Skepticism', *Signs: Journal of Women in Culture and Society*, 36/2 (2011), 463–85, 467.
69. Swinburn et al., 'The Global Syndemic of Obesity', 796.
70. Butler, *Bodies That Matter*, pp. 226–7.
71. A further dimension here is Nece's membership of the board of the Obesity Action Coalition, a non-profit lobbying organisation whose patrons include representatives of the weight-loss industries. Swinburn et al., 'The Global Syndemic of Obesity', 796.
72. Swinburn et al., 'The Global Syndemic of Obesity', 797.
73. Swinburn et al., 'The Global Syndemic of Obesity', 796.
74. Kent, 'Fighting Abjection', p. 136.
75. Butler, *Undoing Gender*, p. 224.

PART TWO

EPIDEMIC REALITIES IN FANTASY

6

'Time is of the Essence, Doctor'

Twenty-First-Century (Post-)Apocalyptic Fiction, White Fatherhood and Anti-Intellectual Tendencies in FX's *The Strain*[1]

Sandra Becker

'POST-APOCALYPTIC FICTION has been moved to our Current Affairs section', states the photograph of a sandwich chalkboard that went viral on social media. Half a year after its initial posting, it had been shared more than 118,000 times by 12 June 2017. The origin of this by now viral message was a Facebook post by a small bookstore in Massachusetts called *The Bookloft* two days after the 2016 US presidential election, with a comment stating 'In case you need a laugh ...'.[2] Although this initial post was merely meant as a jest in light of Donald J. Trump's victory in the presidential race, the board of the *Bulletin of the Atomic Scientists* adjusted the iconic Doomsday Clock to two-and-a-half minutes before midnight only two months later due to serious concerns.[3] The time on the symbolic clock reflected an earnest apocalyptic fear for humanity's fate in the wake of the Trump presidency. With the newly elected president's denial of human-caused global warming, the scientists rated the chances for humanity's self-eradication, and the potential annihilation of all life on earth, to be just as likely as at the height of Cold War nuclear fears in 1953.[4] Similar to the 'Marches for Science' on 22 April 2017, the board of the *Bulletin of the Atomic Scientists* thereby tried to reorient public discourse towards immense, scientifically proven threats of climate change to human kind in a post-truth age marked by wide and thriving questioning of experts and anti-intellectualist refrain from scientific facts.

Five months later, on 1 June 2017, Donald Trump announced the United States' withdrawal from the 2015 Paris Climate Agreement, confirming these scientists' concerns. This in return led the higher education satire page *Academia Obscura* to repost said photograph of *The Bookloft*'s sandwich chalkboard under the heading 'the university library modernization project is coming along nicely'. At the same time, scientific studies like the Special Report SR15 published by the Intergovernmental Panel on Climate Change (IPCC) highlight the disastrous effect of a potential 1.5-degree Celsius rise of the global temperature since the time of the nineteenth-century industrial revolution.[5] The report, which came to be known as the 'Doomsday Report', spurred global protest movements such as the Extinction Rebellion or the global school strikes for climate and their so-called 'Friday's for Future'-marches, but also a wider panic leaving people wondering: *How long will humanity have left until its post-apocalyptic fictions turn into reality?*[6]

While (post-)apocalyptic films and TV series have been used since the Cold War era to channel and make sense of fears that accompany technological advancements, nuclear bombs, radioactivity, globalisation and xenophobic fears of invasions by Others via monsters like Godzilla, alien attacks, narrations of epidemics and zombie hordes, this chapter will particularly focus on the role ascribed to science and scientists in the FX-produced (post-)apocalyptic TV series *The Strain* (2014–17).[7] In particular, I argue that *The Strain* is a very timely product that displays an anti-intellectualism which echoes Donald Trump's apocalyptic administration policies; both before and in the 2020 COVID-19 pandemic. Anti-intellectualism should thereby be understood as an attitude 'opposing or hostile to intellectuals or to an intellectual [or scientific] view or approach' that is part of the cultural history of the US and 'subject to cyclical fluctuation'.[8] Proclamations of 'virulent anti-intellectualism' or more recent warnings of a global 'virus of anti-intellectualism often called "fake news" or "post-truth" politics' should accordingly not be regarded as entirely new phenomena, but rather as contemporary articulations of this cyclically returning anti-intellectualism; with the small exception that anti-intellectualism has started to 'go viral' and spread across the world in this globalised, social media-dominated age.[9]

Drawing from Richard Hofstadter's cultural-historic analysis, sociologist Daniel Rigney identifies three forms of anti-intellectualism in the United States: (1) 'religious anti-rationalism', which rejects reason as cold and emotionless and 'expresses the fear that nothing is sacred in the land of the critical thinker', (2) populist anti-elitism that questions the use of higher education and rejects '[t]heory-driven agendas' in favour of 'the hard school of human experience', historically represented by presidents Andrew Jackson and Theodore Roosevelt, and (3) 'unreflective instrumentalism', which values 'technical reason and the rational calculation of reward and cost' in its support of capitalist profit.[10] The latter two aspects of populist anti-intellectualism, prominently represented by president Trump and the Republicans since 2017, and unreflective instrumentalism, that rejects scientific explanation and research in favour of hands-on approaches and inventions of weapons, will be central to the following analysis.[11] The cable TV series *The Strain* and its monstrous (post-)apocalyptic storyworld will be approached as cultural artefacts that operate on the 'structure of feeling' of the early twenty-first century United States and help understand the coming into being of the present 'conjuncture'.[12]

This chapter aims to show the series' narration of this kind of anti-intellectualism by focusing on two central elements of FX's TV series adaptation of Chuck Hogan's and Guillermo del Toro's novel trilogy *The Strain* (*The Strain*, 2009; *The Fall*, 2010; *The Night Eternal*, 2011), namely its central white father/scientist protagonist and del Toro's aim to re-gothicise its inspirational work by Richard Matheson.[13] The first part of the chapter will focus on the analysis of *The Strain*'s white father protagonist, Ephraim Goodweather (Corey Stoll), and his failure as a father due to his obsession with work and his liaisons with female colleagues. Aside from his meagre performance as father, it is precisely his job as medical investigator at the US Center for Disease Control (CDC), that makes it impossible for him to achieve the status of authoritarian, fatherly leader of survivors. The second part of the chapter will then contextualise the anti-intellectual tendencies of the TV series' narrative with regard to Guillermo del Toro's officially stated effort to reconcile the series' inspirational work, Richard Matheson's novel *I am Legend* (1954), with classic Gothic narrations, such as Bram Stoker's *Dracula* (1897), and Eastern European folkloric tales.[14]

The FX's horror drama TV series *The Strain* (2014–17; four seasons) produced by Mexican filmmaker Guillermo del Toro, Chuck Hogan, and earlier *Lost*-showrunner Carlton Cuse, unfolds the story of a vampiric virus outbreak that starts in New York City and turns the whole US east coast into a monster-dominated, dystopian society, against which the series' protagonists, CDC investigator Ephraim Goodweather and his fellow New York survivors, try to fight back in order to save humanity. Whereas the series was initially supposed to become FX's equivalent to AMC's zombie post-apocalypse hit TV series *The Walking Dead*, the outbreak narrative takes centre stage in *The Strain*.[15] In this, the series not only stands out from *The Walking Dead* (AMC, 2010–present) and its spin-off series *Fear the Walking Dead* (AMC, 2015–present), but also from other post-apocalyptic series that centre their plotlines around virus-related zombie or vampire plagues. *The Strain*'s focus on epidemic response measurements and investigations of the causes of the virus outbreak and of ways to fight it is atypical for zombie/vampire-focused (post-)apocalyptic TV series of the early-2000s and rather to be found in exclusively epidemic/pandemic-centred series of that time, like *The Last Ship* (TNT, 2014–18) or *12 Monkeys* (Syfy, 2015–18).

The critical potential that lies in *The Strain*'s focus on the virus outbreak and CDC measures is, however, impaired by the series creators' attempt to reconcile the idea of infected vampire/zombie hordes originally laid out by Richard Matheson in his 1954 novel *I am Legend* with Bram Stoker's vampire lord *Dracula* and Eastern European tales of vampirism. Not only do infected humans undergo bodily transformations in *The Strain* into hair- and nose-less feral creatures, but this combination also mystifies the origin of the virus to an evil strain of vampirism represented by the Master and his own-willed servant and former Nazi officer, Thomas Eichorst (Richard Sammel). In this respect, the show also differs from other zombie TV series and films of the early twenty-first century, which otherwise saw an 'increasingly normative zombie viropolitics', that shifted the bodily difference towards manageable, non-human behaviours, as Megen de Bruin-Molé demonstrates in chapter 7.[16]

Nevertheless, even though *The Strain* stands out from other epidemic- or zombie-centred TV series and films, the show's extreme form of genre mixing as well as its timely character can best be understood when incorporated in the larger body of early-2000s post-apocalyptic TV series and wider twenty-first century post-apocalyptic US pop culture. As implied by the work that this chapter's approach to Raymond Williams's concept of 'structure of feeling' is based on, it is being assumed that the TV series just as film 'is a particular medium within the general tradition of drama' and that it is thus a cultural-historic source for the dramatic conventions of a time, reflecting on the particular structure of feeling of that period.[17] On this basis, the different aspects that are being foregrounded in *The Strain*'s narration, such as the outbreak narrative, white fatherhood and science can be understood as part of the time-specific dramatic conventions, that allow for interferences on the structure of feeling at the beginning of the second decade of the early twenty-first-century United States. While having to rely on certain genre tropes and iconographies in order for the text to be legible to a wider audience, it is hence this particular articulation of certain aspects of the genre and the specific combination of these that gives an insight into both the timely dramatic conventions and the structure of feeling.

In her recent attempt to formulate a genre definition for post-apocalyptic movies, film scholar Emma A. Harris stresses that it is necessary to consider post-apocalyptic film as a hybrid genre that features elements from the genres of horror, sci-fi, fantasy and religious eschatology narratives:

> [P]ost-apocalyptic fiction does not sit altogether easily as part of science fiction or horror. It contains too many examples of estrangement for the former, and too many examples of cognition for the latter. It is based on social chaos by its very premise, but this leads to the disruption or destruction of the natural order as well . . . The hypothesis suggested by the terms used in trade press is that post-apocalyptic fiction developed as a sub-genre of both science fiction and horror, but can also be regarded as a separate hybrid genre . . . which by its very nature interrelates to a number of generic patterns and tropes.[18]

Harris furthermore mentions iconographic elements and tropes such as post-catastrophe cities in ruins, abandoned cars as leftovers of civilisation, and small struggling communities as well as zombies/vampires, but also traces generic patterns such as 'a privileging of the traditional and rural, conservatism and religion, heroic redemption versus cannibalistic barbarity, carnal desires and monstrous acts, [and] technology as powerful but dangerous'.[19] Her findings correlate with other scholarly analyses, which observed that post-apocalyptic movies – in contrast to twenty-first-century post-apocalyptic literature – particularly feature the element of conservatism and the re-establishment of a lost, traditional social order with regard to race, gender and family structures.[20] While anti-intellectualism is not limited to conservative-minded individuals per se, 'ideological conservatives' levels of trust in the scientific community' have been found to 'have decreased gradually since the early 1990s'.

This turn towards traditional values and patriarchal power structures prevalent in post-apocalyptic films can also be extended to the early-2000s cable channel produced 'Quality TV' or 'Complex TV' series, whose narrations are mostly centred around white, heterosexual, middle-aged father protagonists who adhere in their portrayal of fatherhood to patriarchal notions by stressing the role of breadwinner and hard-working men.[22] *The Strain* does not pose an exception to this trend with its white father lead character Ephraim Goodweather. The centrality of the series' white, scientist/father protagonist is indeed emphasised in the synopsis of the series on the FX's website, whose first sentence states that '*The Strain* tells the story of Dr Ephraim Goodweather, former head of the Center for Disease Control, Canary Team in New York City'.[23]

As the following analysis will show, the series additionally lays emphasis on non-progressive elements by concentrating the outbreak narrative of the vampiric virus particularly on white nuclear families and the deficiencies of the scientific staff of the CDC, above all the team leader of the investigation, Ephraim Goodweather. While the white nuclear family is being made a central point of the narration via the mechanisms of the virus, by having its infected, zombie-like feral vampires first attack (and thereby infect) their loved ones, it is in particular its main protagonist's actions in response to the epidemic that are constantly being questioned and commented on by other characters – whether it is his performance as MD or father. Comments on Goodweather's profession, his education and scientific approach to contain the virus outbreak thereby particularly reflect the series' anti-intellectual tone.

This constant questioning of its main protagonist is further intensified by the early-2000s Quality TV series' typical underlying element of 'melodramatic mode'; a feature that can likewise be found in the contagious film genre of disaster movies.[24] In her analysis of Stephen Soderbergh's 2011 Hollywood blockbuster *Contagion*, Despina Kakoudaki defines this mode as a time-structuring element of the narrative similar to other modes like the epic, tragic or realist, and calls for its recognition as being more than simple emotional excess:

> To recognize the melodramatic mode, then, we have to see it not as overlay but as substrate, as the foundation upon which all the other narrative and dramatic elements are built. To study how the melodramatic mode is activated in a text we can follow just one of its tendencies, its penchant for constructing space for alternative

> outcomes, which also draws the traumatic or tragic events of everyday life into a melodramatic promise. When the bare facts of suffering are transposed into a narrative context where actions and tensions are negotiable, and in ways they are not in real life, the story creates the impression of choice, the impression of alternative outcomes.[25]

Thus, although the newly introduced seriality and linked melodramatic mode of early-2000s Quality TV series allow for the exploration of a complex, large-scale narration that covers, in the case of *The Strain*, both the unfolding apocalypse and the post-apocalyptic struggle for survival, as well as story backgrounds on the Master and Abraham Setrakian in Eastern Europe, it is specifically the element of 'moral legibility' that stresses 'responsibility and response', which is being highlighted by the underlying melodramatic mode of the series.[26]

In the case of *The Strain*, it is this unique combination of conservative values of nuclear family and patriarchal ideals of fatherhood paired with an extreme questioning of moral legibility of its scientist father protagonist that makes Ephraim Goodweather more prone to fail than other CDC investigators, like *Contagion*'s Dr Erin Mears (Kate Winslet) or the character of CDC virologist Dr Edwin Jenner (Noah Emmerich) in AMC's hit series *The Walking Dead*, who has a short appearance before he takes his life due to his failure to find a cure.[27] Having to fight not only a virus, but a vampiric strain of virus that originates from pure evil wandering on earth way before the eighteenth-century story of Jusuf (whose body still serves as the Master's vessel at the beginning of the series) and is prone to join forces with all other evil powers, such as Nazis and rich corporate leader capitalists, like the chairman of the Stoneheart Investment Group, Eldritch Palmer (Jonathan Hyde), adds a specific mythical and fantastic layer to *The Strain*'s narrative. This fantastic layer, a mix of supernatural horror and ancient, mythical spirituality, constantly undermines Dr Goodweather and his team's efforts to analyse and fight the epidemic by means of science.

The Devaluation of Medical Sciences and Goodweather's Missing Leadership Qualities

Three years after the last novel of the trilogy had been published and with two novels already having been transformed into a comic book series by Dark Horse Comics, the TV series' adaptation of Guillermo del Toro's and Chuck Hogan's *The Strain* premiered on the Fox cable channel FX in July 2014. The poster for the first season shows a woman's face, her left eye being held open by a hand with blue medical gloves for the viewer not to miss a thin, light worm emerging from under her skin and making its way out of the white of her eye ball. It thereby highlights and combines the two main themes of the series, the medical/scientific aspect and the worm-transmitted virus and vampirism, which is helped to spread in New York City by a crucial solar eclipse that occurs in episode six, 'Occultation' – and is in a second poster version shown as part of a big and round, red-surrounded vampire's head. The fact of a partial solar eclipse and an actual Ebola case in NYC in October 2014 – with a similarly worm-like virus – only weeks after the last episode of the first season aired, helped the series gain public attention and might have helped attract more viewers to watch its second season. What this coincidence definitely did was to add a conspiracy theory vibe to the TV series; a feature that resonates with the series' overall anti-intellectual tendencies, promoting distrust in medical doctors, such as in its own main protagonist, Dr Ephraim Goodweather.

Goodweather is introduced to the audience as main character in the very first episode, 'Night Zero'.[28] The MD and leading investigator of the CDC Canary team NYC is shown rushing to a counselling meeting with his soon-to-be ex-wife, Kelly (Natalie Brown). Having been delayed by his work, he arrives ten minutes too late to the meeting and the audience soon learns from both Kelly and the counsellor that this is a common pattern for him: Ephraim – or short Eph, as he is called by other characters in the series – had indeed been late for four out of six meetings and it becomes obvious that it is primarily due to his obsession with his job, which he puts before his family, that his marriage has failed.

In the midst of the counselling session, he is called to JFK Airport to lead the response to a mysterious deadly disease outbreak on an aeroplane arriving from Berlin. After a short argument with Homeland Security over who is in charge of a seemingly 'dead plane' arriving from abroad, the doctor wins by stating: 'You don't like terrorists? Try negotiating with a virus. A virus exists only to find a carrier and reproduce. That's all it does and it does it quickly. It has no political views, it has no religious beliefs, it has no cultural hang-ups and it has no respect for a badge.'[29] Dr Ephraim Goodweather and his colleague, Dr Nora Martinez (Mía Maestro), thereafter enter the aircraft wearing hazmat suits. Once inside the plane, they document every step with their helmet cameras.

At first it seems that all two hundred and ten passengers and crew members are dead, but by surprise four of them suddenly wake up, not remembering what happened after landing in New York City. While the survivors are transferred to a temporary quarantine tent, the two doctors are able to trace 'bio prints' in the plane using a UV flashlight. It leads them to the cargo area of the aircraft, where they ultimately discover the source of the strange deadly disease, a parasitic worm, which strongly resembles – as mentioned before – microscopic pictures of the Ebola virus. A pile of earth with more worms in it, which Nora finds, helps them trace the parasites to a large wooden box, which looks a lot like a huge coffin with handmade carvings. The viewer will learn over the course of the first season that this is the home of the master vampire, coming from Europe to spread the vampiric virus in order to take over the New World.

What stands out in these scenes is the visual emphasis on emergency and medical sciences conveyed by the hazmat suits that Dr Goodweather and Dr Martinez are wearing, together with their other scientific equipment, like UV lights, tweezers and helmet cameras, which deliver green-grey coloured, CSI-like footage to nearby computer screens of a colleague. The element of emergency is highlighted by typewriter sound-introduced names of locations and a ticking clock, stating for example 'JFK Airport' or 'Taxiway Foxtrot 21:15:01', and thereby indicates the time passed since the Master and its vampiric virus touched ground in New York City. These details appear in the right corner of the screen after every change of location throughout the whole series; the time element though is dropped over the course of the first season.

This visual accentuation of the medical scientific emergency is, however, in stark contrast with the overall distrust and questioning of the medical scientific staff. This is, for example, portrayed in the reaction of the surviving passengers, who – believing instead in the news of some online leaked documents, which blame the deadly end of the flight on an alternative cause – insist on leaving the quarantine area.[30] The rock star Gabriel Bolivar (Jack Kesy), attorney Joan Luss (Leslie Hope) and husband and father Ansel Barbour (Nikolai Witschl) retreat to home care, despite exhibiting already clear signs of a severe infection, such as extreme paleness, bloodshot eyes, tooth- and headache, and ringing in the ears. All four survivors still vehemently refuse to see a doctor, when implored by their loved ones at home to go to the hospital to get help (e.g. the conversation of Joan Luss with her nanny Neeva).[31] While the series' narration ultimately condemns the patients' shared rejection of medical treatment by having them attack and spread the virus onto their loved ones, their joint decision in the first place reflects a distrust in science and expert knowledge that audiences are already familiarised with in the post-truth, social media-dominated real world with a strengthened anti-vaccination movement in the USA. This indirect point of critique in *The Strain* is therefore likely to go undetected by viewers.

The infected patients' rejection of medical aid and distrust in the CDC doctors, which calls into question the effectiveness of medical science practices and staff, is complemented by verbal attacks on Goodweather and his medical profession, for example by FBI agents. Arrested for appearing on ambiguous footage from a hospital surveillance cam, which shows how the doctor kills the vampire-turned former flight captain, Doyle Redfern (Jonathan Potts), and performs an unofficial autopsy on his dead body, Goodweather is accused by a very aggressive FBI agent of simply talking 'bullshit'. The FBI agent shows no sign of respect for Goodweather as a person, nor for his profession, by shouting: 'I don't give a shit who you are or what fancy medical school you went to . . .'.[32] Similar disrespect is also exhibited by pawnshop owner and vampire hunter, Abraham Setrakian (David Bradley), who travels to JFK airport seeking to warn the CDC officials about the supernatural, viral threat – as mentioned in the title quote of this chapter. In one of the first occasions that the doctor and Setrakian are alone, driving together in Goodweather's car, Setrakian calls him 'romantic and non-pragmatic'.[33] Later, on teaming up with Nora and Setrakian to fight the rapidly spreading plague, Setrakian finds even more denigrating words for the doctor, leaving no doubt about his disapproval of the medical scientific approach to contain the outbreak. Being attacked by Goodweather that his plan to stop the plague by simply killing the master vampire does not make any 'biological sense', Setrakian counters snappishly by pointing to a shelf behind Goodweather:

> I have verified the observations of these authors with my own experience. Those that are inaccurate, I have discarded. This is your scientific method, no? At every turn, everything I have said has proven to be correct. Is that not true? If you wish to defeat this evil, you must trust me. I understand it, you do not![34]

Here two typical elements of populist anti-elitist anti-intellectualism become obvious: first, the rejection of higher-education-based knowledge and status since both the FBI agent and Setrakian reject 'fancy medical school'-knowledge and foreground the more valued 'own experience'-based wisdom; and, secondly, the tendency to make particularly male intellectuals appear effeminate by calling Goodweather's approach to fight the Master and his vampire subjects 'non-pragmatic and romantic'.[35]

Taking a clear verbal stand against Goodweather's medical approach and lingering superiority complex of the natural sciences, Setrakian's behaviour towards Goodweather – and likewise, the overall series' narration – suggests that the doctor does the best job when focusing on his role as father and protector. This is, for example, the case in the very last episode of the first season, when Setrakian prepares both Ephraim Goodweather and his son Zack (Ben Hyland; from season two on, Max Charles) with silver blades for the planned attack on the master vampire. Clearly appreciating the picture of father and son united in the battle against evil in front of him, Setrakian states: 'Since the beginning of creation, boys have hunted beside their fathers. This is nothing different.'[36]

However, having learned at the beginning of the first episode about Ephraim Goodweather's shortcomings as a father and his obsession with his work, it is less of a surprise that he falls back into old habits. After the failed attempt to kill the Master in the finale of the first season, Goodweather states at the beginning of season two that: 'The ground game isn't for me . . . Seeing as how as a vampire hunter I'm total shit, I'm gonna go back to being a doctor'.[37] This return to scientific research in order to try and develop an anti-virus and potential bio-weapon against the viral plague slowly spreading over the city boundaries of NYC turns out to have a fatal impact on Goodweather's life, resulting in him losing both his son and his colleague and lover, Nora Martinez, over the second season.[38] In said episode, Goodweather's son Zack is being taken away from his father by his vampire-turned mother, who fights and kills Nora during the attempt to get her son back into her custody. This plot turn comes as a retribution blow, since it was due to Goodweather's affair with Nora Martinez that he lost focus on his family and his ex-wife Kelly. In contrast to her ex-husband, Kelly, the primary school teacher and mother of Zack, is portrayed to be very caring and good with children in her job, when with her son (e.g. shown to watch the solar eclipse together in the episode 'Occultation'), or even later as vampire when the Master makes her take care of his group of so-called 'feelers' (blind children turned vampires with exceptionally good hearing and smelling skills).[39] Having received only limited information on the epidemic and the suggestion to leave New York City and go to her mother in Vermont from Goodweather, Kelly lacks the protection of her husband and her nuclear family unit and gets infected with the worm-like virus when trying to fight off her vampire-turned boyfriend Matt (Drew Nelson).[40] It is already with regard to these decisions and actions that the series' main protagonist's moral legibility and identity as an intellectual is brought into question, suggesting that he should have put more effort into saving his family first before focusing on his job.

The underlying melodramatic mode and timely structuring of the narration brings in another component that adds to this, namely his affair with his colleague Nora Martinez. After finding Zack alone at home trying helplessly to fight off a vampire who had entered from outside, Goodweather sends his son off with Setrakian and the group of survivors to the safe space of the pawnshop, promising that he will make sure to return with his wife, stating: 'My son isn't growing up without a mother'.[41] Nora and Ephraim stay at the old family house of the Goodweathers to clean up and wait for Kelly to return home. In spite of their actual plan and with both of them feeling emotionally vulnerable, Nora and Eph start to get intimate in Kelly's and Ephraim's former bedroom. Being caught red-handed on the bedroom floor by a friend of Kelly's, who comes along to check on Zack and her – condemning Ephraim's selfish affair in the midst of an unprecedented epidemic by stating that 'in all your concerned state, you still find time to screw on the rug' – Goodweather swears again: 'I love my wife. She's the mother of my son. I'd do anything to find her.'[42] The sequencing of these scenes bluntly shows that it is the timely structuring of the melodramatic mode – and not alone the affair in itself – that is framing Goodweather's decisions and resulting behaviour as morally unacceptable. Having Kelly return for Zack in the season finale and killing Nora in the attempt to get her son back into her custody therefore almost seems to be a righteous stroke of fate.

A similar working of the melodramatic mode paired with an unforeseeable plot twist, which ends in more disaster and punishment for *The Strain*'s main protagonist, occurs in season three. Having once more lost sight of his family and son and instead engaged in an affair with hacker Dutch Velders (Ruta Gedmintas), with whom he is studying the communication system of the vampires amongst each other and with the Master, Ephraim Goodweather is falling back into his love for science and women. Trying to get back Zack, but not doing enough to save his whole family, Goodweather is confronted with his wrongdoings once more when fighting Kelly in the season finale. Fearing for his life and that of his son, he kills Kelly in front of Zack's eyes, which results in the latter activating an atomic bomb at the Statue of Liberty that was placed there by the Master. This crucial event that helps the vampires to fully take over NYC and the whole east coast in the dusty, dark aftermath of the explosion, is triggered by Ephraim's false, too rational, too little family-oriented actions. *The Strain*'s finale of season three accordingly unites the melodramatic mode's time structuring of the narrative, which puts Goodweather's actions and morals into question, with the element of anti-rational anti-intellectualism, which – even though not religiously motivated – clearly supports the conservative values attached to the ideal of the white, nuclear family.

The anti-intellectual tendency of the third season is furthermore reinforced by Goodweather's affair with Dutch Velders, which interferes with her ailing love relationship with the younger, rat exterminator Vasily Fet (Kevin Durand) – mostly called by his surname Fet. Fet's practical knowledge about extermination, the natural behaviour of the city's vermin, and, moreover, his rejection of an architecture scholarship at Cornell University to the annoyance of his own father, depict him in stark contrast to the CDC doctor – whom he usually simply calls 'Doc'.[43]

The series' finale, however, offers its main protagonist, in line with these conservative values and post-apocalyptic story patterns, a last chance for 'heroic redemption' for all his shortcomings and wrongdoings. Primed by aforementioned exterminator Fet, who reminds Eph of a talk over breakfast with the deceased Abraham Setrakian and his 'way of inspiring you [Eph]' and urges him to give Zack another chance, Goodweather takes the lead in 'The Last Stand' against the Master.[44] He also reassures to do good by his short-time lover, Dutch Velders, whose re-awoken love interest in Vasily Fet led her to beg Goodweather to help spare his life; without foreseeing the doctor giving his life instead.[45]

In this, the final episode of *The Strain* offers its main protagonist a last chance to prove that his own mindset has changed over the course of the four seasons, away from him insisting on science and towards his role as father and practical fighting skills. The first aspect, the change of his attitude towards science since the outbreak of the plague, is illustrated by having him recall the said breakfast conversation with Abraham Setrakian. In a flashback, the audience sees a former Goodweather emphatically stating: 'I'm an epidemiologist. I understand disease etiology, modes of transmission, rates of infection. It's really a question of math.'[46] His statement is brushed aside by the old Setrakian saying 'we are not fighting math; we are fighting *strigoi*'.[47] The vampire hunter furthermore warns him that his lost marriage, job and wife are only the beginning and that 'this fight may, in the end, cost you everything'.[48] Setrakian thereby appeals to (1) a turn away from science towards fantastical myth and spiritualism as well as (2) an intuitive, altruistic action of fatherly authority and protection. Having come to fully understand the meaning of Setrakian's words, Goodweather changes the plan without telling anyone, thereby making sure that Fet and Velders can be reunited and have a future together. Instead of Vasily Fet, who was supposed to help kill the Master by detonating yet another nuclear bomb miles below Manhattan in the tunnel system (a plan based, of course, on the practical knowledge of the underground system by the exterminator himself), Goodweather jumps into the elevator, reunites with his son, and in a shared family effort kills the Master and the two of them. With that the series' finale underscores once more the series' framing of fatherhood and experience- and emotion-based intuition as superior to epidemiology, math, rationalism and, overall, science.

Anti-Intellectualism and Re-Gothicising of Richard Matheson's Idea of the Vampire Horde

This valuation/devaluation-bias exhibited in *The Strain*'s narration, which indicates a favouring of the biological role of the father and protector over Goodweather's scientific profession, supports the argument of the series' prevailing theme of anti-intellectualism as well as the story's relation to the acclaimed 'vampire novel of the century', Richard Matheson's 1954 book *I am Legend*.[49] While the appearance and physiological design of Guillermo del Toro's stinger-equipped vampires recall the aesthetics of other monsters of del Toro's Hollywood movies, such as *Pan's Labyrinth* (2006) or *Hellboy* (2004, 2008), as well as Ridley Scott's *Alien* movies and their monsters with xenomorphic inner mouths, the concept of the vampire-zombie horde goes back to Matheson.[50] As Edward P. Comentale and Aaron Jaffe note in their introduction to *The Year's Work at the Zombie Research Center*:

> Richard Matheson's *I am Legend* extended the conceptual overloading of the undead by bridging vampire and zombie . . . In effect, zombies in this period provide the generic clearinghouse and switching station for the undead as such – submerging the literary inheritance of the gothic and the ghost inside other kinds of fringe monstrosities, co-opting legally unprotected pulpy things from beyond, from outside, from underground – including the H-Zombies from the

> Caribbean and West Africa, as well as aliens, other autonomous things from outer space, and mutated walking cadavers from the underground pulps.[51]

In other words, Richard Matheson's groundbreaking work was not only to merge vampire and zombie in his novel, but to thereby demystify the classic gothic vampire tale by providing a viral explanation. Guillermo del Toro, in contrast, does it the other way around in *The Strain*: he re-gothicises the vampire mob by relating it to Bram Stoker's *Dracula* (1897) represented by the master vampire in control of the minds of his subject, fellow vampires. The addition of Eastern European folkloric tales is among other things reflected in the flashbacks to Abraham Setrakian's youth in Romania and his grandmother, whom he affectionately calls *bubbeh*, as well as in the term *strigoi* for vampire.[52]

While an explanation for this re-gothicisation could be del Toro's general fascination with horror stories (see his Bleak House in LA), childhood nostalgia for *Dracula* and horror stories, or twenty-first-century 'Pop Goth', it is noteworthy that del Toro himself commented on the 'arrogance of science' in a 2011 interview with the online magazine *Wired*.[53] Asked about his inspiration to write a (post-)apocalyptic vampire tale like his novel trilogy *The Strain*, del Toro replied:

> Originally, I wanted very much to try and present the origins of the vampire plague in very modern terms. And then little by little, with each book, go back to finding the spiritual in the biology and finding the biology in the myth. I feel like science and religion are like a Möbius strip. When you dig deep enough into religion, you find science to explain it, and when you dig deep enough and long enough into science you find things that are unexplained. And I wanted very much for the books to come full circle . . . For example, if I was writing *Dracula* right now, how would I deal with the arrogance of science? Because science is very, very arrogant. And I thought, 'Well, the best way to deal with that is with an epidemic'.[54]

Even though it would be false to take del Toro's statement about the 'arrogance of science' and the unexplainable about certain matters in science as a proof for an intentional choice of adding anti-intellectualist tendencies into the story of *The Strain* or to put him as a Mexican filmmaker, who moved to the US not before his thirties, on a level with a native-born representative of the US-American anti-intellectualism tradition, by incorporating the element of the questioning of science in combination with the white father/scientist focus, and the melodramatic mode, the TV series adaptation does ironically indeed convey a strong anti-intellectual message. Other than in the novel trilogy, though, which links the master vampire to stories about admonished angels in *The Night Eternal* (2011), the religious aspect addressed in the above quote from del Toro has not been integrated in FX's TV series adaptation.[55] While not featuring the novel series' original element of religious anti-rationalism, the other two kinds of anti-intellectualism traced by Hofstadter and Rigney in US-American cultural history can be found in *The Strain*'s series adaptation; despite the fact that other scholars suggest a more positive reading of the critical stance taken by del Toro towards science, human arrogance and the fragility of civil society.[56]

Next to the anti-elitists' doubting and criticising of scientific approaches and professionals (discussed in the first part of the chapter), the anti-intellectual narrative elements furthermore bear resemblance to the tradition of unreflective instrumentalism as described by Hofstadter in his discussion of the ongoing celebration of inventor and businessman Thomas A. Edison:

> [T]he most impressive illustration arises from a comparison of the American regard for inventive skill as opposed to skill in pure science. Our greatest inventive genius, Thomas A. Edison, was all but canonized by the American public, and a legend has been built around him. One cannot, I suppose, expect that achievements in pure science would receive the same public applause that came to inventions as spectacular and as directly influential on ordinary life as Edison's.[57]

Similar to his comparison of the celebrated Edison to the obscured, less valued Yale professor Josiah Willard Gibbs, who developed the theoretical foundation for modern physical chemistry, *The Strain*'s anti-intellectual narration acknowledges pragmatic, scientific knowledge-based inventions more than medical laboratory research. Hence, while the lethal anti-virus that Ephraim Goodweather and Nora Martinez develop in season two receives little acknowledgement and soon loses its effectiveness, Goodweather's idea to use portable UV lights in order to go out protected at night or the *strigoi* communication disruptor operating on the basis of microwaves, which he invents together with Dutch Velders (his later 'colleague' and lover), receive more appreciation and acknowledgement amongst the other members of the group of survivors.[58]

This pattern of recognising and valuing technological inventions over scientific work fits into today's scientific mistrust promoted amongst others by Donald Trump and his political administration, who ignore scientists' warnings about anthropogenic global warming as mere fake news or Chinese invention and favour 'alternative facts' over scientifically proven data and facts, while supporting sci-fi dreams of a manned mission to Mars.

Conclusion

In a playful turn on the title quote 'Time is of the essence, doctor', this chapter has shown in its analysis of the FX TV series *The Strain* that the series reflects the current 'structure of feeling' of populism-driven anti-intellectualism and confusion over alternative facts in the US (and more broadly in the Western, industrialised world). It suggests that not science and rationalism, but intuitive action and paternalism are able to stop the apocalypse – relating therein to both current conservative, anti-intellectualism in the United States and Donald Trump's self-promotion as authoritarian fatherly leader (or 'Daddy Trump') who takes action.[59]

While adding this specific component of anti-intellectualism to post-apocalyptic popular culture narrations, its general theme of a plague-induced apocalypse also fits the general trend of what film scholar Dan Dinello has termed 'the contagious age', in which contemporary anxieties about viral terrorism (see *Unlocked*, 2017), precarious (work) life experiences and the 'complexity of our present' are translated into viral narrations of (post-)apocalyptic, dystopian storyworlds.[60]

Not only do *The Strain*'s anti-intellectual tendencies form part of a wider trend in vampire-centred US pop culture and Hollywood movies featuring younger imaginations of Professor Abraham van Helsing in *Van Helsing* (2004) or rich vampires with sparkling skin as a substitution for politically powerful ruling lords in the *Twilight* saga (as for the movies, 2008–2010), they also support a populist anti-intellectualism – particularly due to the series creator's attempt to re-gothicise the story of its inspirational work *I Am Legend*.[61] Making an evil monster into the source of an epidemic equally mystifies climate change caused natural disasters in other recent movies such as in the 2014 film *Godzilla* (dir. Gareth

Edwards), in which a Godzilla-like ancient creature is made responsible for an earthquake that causes a meltdown in a Japanese nuclear power plant.[62] It thereby turns the original 1954 movie's message (Gojira, dir. Ishirō Honda), namely that Godzilla has been awoken by the atomic bombs dropped on Hiroshima and Nagasaki, upside down.[63] According to the 2014 movie version by British director Gareth Edwards – just as del Toro, again no US-American native – the atomic bomb tests in the Pacific in the 1950s did not awake the ancient monsters, but are said to have been used to fight them. This flight into fantastic and mystique (or religious) explanations for current dangers and uncertainties that scholars detected to be a widespread trend in US popular culture in the post-9/11 era, can also be traced in the US population with 49 per cent of average Americans and 77 per cent of white evangelic Protestants believing 'the severity of recent natural disasters [to be linked] to the biblical "end times"' according to a 2014 report on attitudes towards climate change by the Public Religion Research Institute (PRRI).[64]

The flight into these fantastic storyworlds full of ancient evil spirits and monsters as well as the questioning of scientific knowledge in *The Strain* support the populist anti-intellectual discourses and their denial of real-world viruses and toxins, produced by humans and set free via human-caused global warming.[65] A similar phenomenon could also be observed in the COVID-19 pandemic, in which Donald Trump vehemently rejected wearing a face mask as recommended by leading epidemiologists and instead fled into calling the virus an evil 'invisible enemy'. This rhetorical tactic simultaneously allowed him to dismiss his responsibility, since 'nobody could ever have seen something like this coming', and to declare himself a 'wartime president' in 'our big war'.[66] Storyworlds and real-life rhetorics filled with the fantastic, evil and mysterious thus help to further push scientific facts into viral discourses of fake news and the realm of abstruse fantasies of pompous scientists. The popularity of *The Strain* and the 2014 *Godzilla* movie and their use of the fantastic should consequently not alone be regarded as means for making current threats tangible and manageable, but as equally supporting the dangerous trend towards anti-science sentiments and populist anti-elitist anti-intellectualism.[67] It is this negative attitude towards science and scientific facts that is prevalent in times of Donald Trump's presidency in the United States and empowered right-wing populist parties in Europe and Brazil in their shared rejection of human-caused global warming and climate change.[68] With that the series is symptomatic of the 'structure of feeling' in the early twenty-first-century United States, which is marked by a bleed-through between reality and fantasy. It is above all the fantastic that both the TV series' storyworld of *The Strain* and real-life discourses turn to when evoking apocalyptic metaphors and mythical explanations for scientifically proven phenomena like viral epidemics and climate change.

Notes

1. The title quote is taken from the first episode of *The Strain*. In the respective scene, pawnshop owner and former vampire hunter, Abraham Setrakian, pays a visit to Ephraim Goodweather and his team of the CDC Canary Team NYC at their press conference at the JFK Airport and warns them about the vampiric virus outbreak and the importance of taking swift measures to contain the outbreak. I, however, am using this quote here metaphorically in order to shift attention to the implications of the time of production and airing of audiovisual drama TV series and particularly of the imagination of post-apocalyptic horror stories – both with regard to monsters and heroes. *The Strain*, 'Night Zero', Guillermo del Toro, dir. (FX, 29 July 2015).
2. The Bookloft, 'In case you need a laugh . . .', *Facebook*, 10 November 2016, *https://www.facebook.com/434847149875233/photos/a.469008116459136.122829.434847149875233/1501154866577784/?type=3&theater* (accessed 8 July 2019).
3. Meaning the board members of the 1945-founded non-technical academic journal on science and public affairs invested in educating about nuclear weapons, climate change, and diseases. See *http://thebulletin.org/*.
4. J. Sinclaire, 'Watch the Doomsday Clock Announcement', *The Bulletin of the Atomic Scientists*, 23 January 23 2017, *https://thebulletin.org/2017/01/watch-the-doomsday-clock-announcement/* (accessed 8 July 2019).
5. IPCC, *Global Warming of 1.5°C: An IPCC Special Report on the impacts of global warming of 1.5°C above pre-industrial levels and related global greenhouse gas emission pathways, in the context of strengthening the global response to the threat of climate change, sustainable development, and efforts to eradicate poverty*, V. Masson-Delmotte, P. Zhai, H.-O. Pörtner, D. Roberts, J. Skea, P. R. Shukla, A. Pirani, W. Moufouma-Okia, C. Péan, R. Pidcock, S. Connors, J. B. R. Matthews, Y. Chen, X. Zhou, M. I. Gomis, E. Lonnoy, T. Maycock, M. Tignor and T. Waterfield (eds), Intergovernmental Panel on Climate Change (IPCC), 2018, *https://www.ipcc.ch/site/assets/uploads/sites/2/2019/06/SR15_Full_Report_High_Res.pdf* (accessed 8 July 2019).

6. D. Wallace-Wells, 'Time to Panic', *The New York Times*, 16 February 2019, *https://www.nytimes.com/2019/02/16/opinion/sunday/fear-panic-climate-change-warming.html* (accessed 8 July 2019).
7. Stephen D. O'Leary, 'Apocalypticism in American Popular Culture: From the Dawn of the Nuclear Age to the End of the American Century', in John J. Collins, Bernard McGinn and Stephen J. Stein (eds), *The Encyclopedia of Apocalypticism*, vol. 3 (New York: Continuum, 1998), pp. 392–426, 401–3.
8. The underlying definition is quoted after the Merriam Webster Online Dictionary, while the observation on its cultural tradition and cyclic nature is based on Richard Hofstadter's seminal work on anti-intellectualism in American life: 'Anti-intellectualism', *Merriam Webster*, *https://www.merriam-webster.com/dictionary/anti-intellectualism* (accessed 8 July 2019); Richard Hofstadter, *Anti-Intellectualism in American Life* (New York: Alfred A. Knopf, 1963), p. 6.
9. J. W. Frick, 'Anti-intellectualism and Representations of "Commonness" in the Nineteenth-Century American Theatre', *The Journal of American Drama and Theatre*, 9/2 (1997), 1–22, 1; M. A. Peters, 'Anti-intellectualism is a virus', *Educational Philosophy and Theory*, 51/4 (2019), 357–63, 361.
10. D. Rigney, 'Three Kinds of Anti-Intellectualism: Rethinking Hofstadter', *Sociological Inquiry*, 61/4 (1991), 434–51; for religious anti-rationalism, see 436–41, 438; for populist anti-elitism, see 441–4, 442; for unreflective instrumentalism, 444–7, 444; Hofstadter, *Anti-Intellectualism in American Life*, p. 291.
11. S. Tesfaye, 'America hits peak anti-intellectualism: Majority of Republicans now think college is bad', *Salon*, 11 July 2017, *https://www.salon.com/2017/07/11/america-hits-peak-anti-intellectualism-majority-of-republicans-now-think-college-is-bad/* (accessed 4 July 2019). The author would like to stress that the anti-intellectual tendencies found in the analysis of the TV series differ – though not completely distinguishing themselves – from other concepts of anti-intellectualism, such as Thomas M. Nichols's proclamation of *The Death of Expertise* due to 'a Google-fueled, Wikipedia-based, blog-sodden collapse of any division between professionals and laypeople'. The form of anti-intellectualism tendencies found in *The Strain* furthermore vary from the problematic growth of what Phil Brown termed 'popular epidemiology' (2007, p. xvii), which – together with slow, industry-influenced regulations for environmental protection around the globe – leads to a questioning of the power of science, as addressed by Soraya Boudia and Nathalie Jas in their edited collection *Powerless Science? Science and Politics in a Toxic World* (2016). Thomas M. Nichols, *The Death of Expertise: The Campaign against Established*

Knowledge and Why it Matters (New York: Oxford University Press, 2017), p. 3; Phil Brown, *Toxic Exposures: Contested Illnesses and the Environmental Health Movement* (New York: Columbia University Press, 2007), p. xvii; Soraya Boudia and Nathalie Jas (eds), *Powerless Science? Science and Politics in a Toxic World* (New York: Berghahn, 2016).

12. Raymond Williams, 'Film and the Dramatic Tradition', in Raymond Williams and Michael Orrom (eds), *Preface to Film* (London: Film Drama Ltd, 1954), pp. 25–41, 33.
13. Guillermo del Toro and Chuck Hogan, *The Strain* (London: HarperCollins, 2011 [2009]); Guillermo del Toro and Chuck Hogan, *The Fall* (London: HarperCollins, 2011 [2010]); Guillermo del Toro and Chuck Hogan, *The Night Eternal* (London: HarperCollins, 2011).
14. Richard Matheson, *I Am Legend* (London: Hachette UK, 2011; New York: Fawcett Publications, 1954); Bram Stoker, *Dracula* (London: Signet Classics, 1996 [1987]).
15. E. T. VanDerWerff, 'The Strain was supposed to be FX's Walking Dead. What happened?' *Vox*, 30 July 2017, *https://www.vox.com/culture/2017/7/30/16059374/the-strain-episode-2-recap-blood-tax-dutch* (accessed 6 July 2019).
16. See chapter 7 in this volume: Megen de Bruin-Molé, 'Killable Hordes, Chronic Others and "Mindful" Consumers: Rehabilitating the Zombie in Twenty-First-Century Popular Culture', in Sandra Becker, Megen de Bruin-Molé and Sara Polak (eds), *Embodying Contagion: The Viropolitics of Horror and Desire in Contemporary Discourse* (Cardiff: University of Wales Press, 2021), pp. 159–78.
17. Williams, 'Film and the Dramatic Tradition', pp. 25, 33.
18. E. A. Harris, 'The Post-Apocalyptic Film Genre in American Culture: 1968–2013' (unpublished PhD thesis, University of Leicester, 2016), 53f., *https://lra.le.ac.uk/bitstream/2381/38758/1/2016HARRISEHPHD.pdf* (accessed 24 June 2019).
19. Harris, 'The Post-Apocalyptic Film Genre in American Culture', 54–5.
20. Elizabeth Abele, 'Last Men Standing: Will Smith as the Obsolete Patriarchal Male', in Elizabeth Abele and John A. Gronbeck-Tedesco (eds), *Screening Images of American Masculinity in the Age of Postfeminism* (Lanham, MD: Lexington Books, 2016), pp. 187–202, 189; M. Broderick, 'Surviving Armageddon: Beyond the Imagination of Disaster', *Science Fiction Studies*, 20/3 (1993), 362–82, 362; Harris, 'The Post-Apocalyptic Film Genre in American Culture', 148ff.; Barbara Gurr, 'Masculinity, Race, and the (Re?)imagined Frontier', in Barbara Gurr (ed.), *Race, Gender, and Sexuality in Post-Apocalyptic TV and Film* (London: Palgrave MacMillan, 2015), pp. 31–44, 36. For

the exceptional findings of progressive elements in post-apocalyptic literature, see Claire P. Curtis, *Postapocalyptic Fiction and the Social Contract: We'll not go home again* (Lanham, MD: Lexington Books, 2010).

21. M. Motta, 'The Dynamics and Political Implications of Anti-Intellectualism in the United States', *American Politics Research*, 46/3 (2018), 465–98, 469.
22. Janet McCabe and Kim Akass (eds), *Quality TV: Contemporary American Television and Beyon*d (New York: I.B. Tauris, 2007); Jason Mittell, *Complex TV: The Poetics of Contemporary Television Storytelling* (New York: New York University Press, 2015).
23. Fox Networks, 'About the Show' [*The Strain*], *Fox Networks*, *https://fxplus.fxnetworks.com/the-strain/article/about-the-show-5b577c5b798f8c001a1bee3d/* (accessed 8 July 2019).
24. See Linda Williams, 'World and Time: Serial Television Melodrama in America', in Christine Gledhill and Linda Williams (eds), *Melodrama Unbound: Across History, Media, and National Cultures* (New York: Columbia University Press, 2018), pp. 169–83.
25. Despina Kakoudaki, 'Melodrama and Apocalypse: Politics and the Melodramatic Mode in *Contagion*', in Christine Gledhill and Linda Williams (eds), *Melodrama Unbound: Across History, Media, and National Cultures* (New York: Columbia University Press, 2018), pp. 312–24, 316.
26. Kakoudaki, 'Melodrama and Apocalypse', p. 317.
27. Moreover, neither the narration of *The Walking Dead* nor its spin-off *Fear the Walking Dead* takes into account the reasons for the pandemic outbreak, and instead they primarily focus on the post-apocalyptic chaos and struggle for survival. In the short amount of screen time that is granted to Dr Jenner in *The Walking Dead*, the series' audience only learn that '[i]t's day 194 since wildfire was declared and 63 days since the disease abruptly went global' ('Wildfire', S01E05). Even though the spin-off starts with its protagonists' lives shortly before and during the first hours of the disease outbreak, even less information is given on the cause and nature of the epidemic. *The Walking Dead*, 'Wildfire', Ernest R. Dickerson, dir. (AMC, 13 May 2012).
28. The title of the first episode of FX's TV series *The Strain*, 'Night Zero', mixes the term 'night', which can be read as a metaphor for the vampiric virus, and 'zero' as in 'zero hour', a term used to describe the scheduled beginning of an event, as e.g. a military operation, or as in the notorious 'patient zero'-narrations of virus outbreaks. *The Strain*, 'Night Zero'.
29. The character of the doctor as well as the series as a whole thus do not recognise the unclear rhetorical boundaries between terrorism and viruses that exist in the real world. As State Department official Richard Haas emphasised

in 2001, when stating that '[l]ike a virus, international terrorism respects no boundaries . . .'. Richard Haas quoted in D. Dinello, 'The Contagious Age: Overwhelmed by Vampires, Viruses, and Zombies in the 21st Century', *Pop Matters*, 7 September 2011, *https://www.popmatters.com/148166-the-contagious-age-overwhelmed-by-vampires-viruses-and-zombies-2495957745.html* (accessed 28 June 2019); The Strain, 'Night Zero'. The novel version of *The Strain*, in which the Master chooses Ground Zero as his residency, on the contrary, can be read to address this issue of blurred boundaries of terrorism, attacks on US ground via aeroplanes and/or from within. See Simon Bacon, '"This Is Something New . . . or – Something Very, Very Old": *The Strain* Trilogy in Context', in Deborah Shaw, Ann Davies and Dolores Tierney (eds), *The Transnational Fantasies of Guillermo del Toro* (New York: Palgrave Macmillan, 2014), pp. 63–82, 73–4.

30. *The Strain*, 'The Box', David Semel, dir. (FX, 5 August 2015).
31. For the conversation with Neeva, see *The Strain*, 'Runaways', Peter Weller, dir. (FX, 26 August 2015).
32. *The Strain*, 'Occultation', Peter Weller, dir. (FX, 9 September 2015).
33. *The Strain*, 'Runaways'.
34. *The Strain*, 'For Services Rendered', Charlotte Sieling, dir. (FX, 16 September 2015).
35. Rigney, 'Three Kinds of Anti-Intellectualism', 442.
36. *The Strain*, 'The Master', Phil Abraham, dir. (FX, 29 October 2015).
37. *The Strain*, 'BK, NY', Gregory Hoblit and Guillermo del Toro, dirs (FX, 17 September 2015).
38. *The Strain*, 'Night Train', Vincenzo Natali, dir. (FX, 10 November 2016).
39. *The Strain*, 'Occultation'.
40. *The Strain*, 'Loved Ones', John Dahl, dir. (FX, 8 October 2015).
41. *The Strain*, 'The Disappeared', Charlotte Sieling, dir. (FX, 30 September 2015).
42. *The Strain*, 'The Disappeared'.
43. *The Strain*, 'Occultation'.
44. For the quote, see the character of Vasily Fet in *The Strain*, 'The Last Stand', J. Miles Dale, dir. (FX, 6 October 2017).
45. *The Strain*, 'The Last Stand'.
46. *The Strain*, 'The Last Stand'.
47. *The Strain*, 'The Last Stand'.
48. *The Strain*, 'The Last Stand'.
49. A. Flood, 'I Am Legend is named vampire novel of the century', *The Guardian*, 3 April 2012, *https://www.theguardian.com/books/2012/apr/03/i-am-legend-vampire-novel-century* (accessed 27 January 2020); Matheson, I Am Legend.

50. *Pan's Labyrinth*, Guillermo del Toro, dir. (Telecinco Cinema/Estudios Picasso/Tequila Gang/Esperanto Filmoj/Sententia Entertainment, 2006); *Hellboy*, Guillermo del Toro, dir. (Columbia Pictures/Revolution Studios/Lawrence Gordon/Lloyd Levin Productions/Dark Horse Entertainment, 2004); *Hellboy II:* 'The Golden Army', Guillermo del Toro, dir. (Relativity Media/Lawrence Gordon/Lloyd Levin Productions/Dark Horse Entertainment, 2008); *Alien*, Ridley Scott, dir. (20th Century Fox/Brandywine Productions, 1979).
51. Edward P. Comentale and Aaaron Jaffe, 'Introduction: The Zombie Research Center FAQ', in Edward P. Comentale and Aaron Jaffe (eds), *The Year's Work at the Zombie Research Center* (Bloomington: Indiana University Press, 2014), pp. 1–58, 48.
52. Setrakian lovingly recalls his Romanian grandmother: 'I learned the legend of this creature from my *bubbeh*, my grandmother, when I was eight years old. She's the one who told me silver could harm them.' *The Strain*, 'For Services Rendered'.
53. Justin D. Edwards and Agnieszka Soltysik Monnet, 'Introduction: From Goth/ic to Pop Goth', in Justin D. Edwards and Agnieszka Soltysik Monnet (eds), *The Gothic in Contemporary Literature and Popular Culture: Pop Goth* (New York: Routledge, 2012), pp. 1–18, 2; A. Watercutter, 'Guillermo del Toro Talks Vampires, Giant Monsters and the "Arrogance of Science"', *Wired*, 16 November 2011, *https://www.wired.com/2011/11/interview-guillermo-del-toro/* (accessed 28 June 2019).
54. Watercutter, 'Guillermo del Toro Talks Vampires'.
55. For an analysis of the religious component in the novel trilogy and its critical potential beyond religious anti-rationalism, see Simon Bacon, 'Toxic Fundamentalism: The Strain (del Toro and Hogan, 2014–17)', in Simon Bacon (ed.), *Toxicity: A Companion* (Bern: Peter Lang, forthcoming).
56. See Keith McDonald and Richard Clark, *Guillermo del Toro: Film as Alchemic Art* (New York: Bloomsbury, 2014).
57. Hofstadter, *Anti-Intellectualism in American Life*, p. 25.
58. For the work on the lethal anti-virus in season two, see *The Strain*, 'BK, NY'; *The Strain*, 'By Any Means', T. J. Scott, dir. (FX, 24 September 2015); *The Strain*, 'Fort Defiance', Guy Ferland, dir. (FX, 1 October 2015); *The Strain*, 'The Silver Angel', J. Miles Dale, dir. (FX, 8 October 2015). For the use of portable UV lights, see *The Strain*, 'Creatures of the Night', Guy Ferland, dir. (FX, 23 September 2015). For the *strigoi* communication disruptor in season three, see *The Strain*, 'Madness', Deran Sarafian (FX, 29 May 2017); *The Strain*, 'Do Or Die', Vincenzo Natali, dir. (FX, 12 June 2017).

59. References to Donald J. Trump as 'Daddy Trump' are mentioned in the following international publications: Angela Nagle, *Kill All Normies: Online Culture Wars from 4chan and Tumblr to Trump and the Alt-Right* (New York: Zero Books, 2017), p. 54; J. D. Mayer, 'Big Daddy Trump', *The American Interest*, 25 August 2016, *https://www.the-american-interest.com/2016/08/25/big-daddy-trump/* (accessed 28 June 2019); E. Wehling, 'Daddy is Home', *Kronen Zeitung*, 22 January 2017, *https://static1.squarespace.com/static/555908b8e4b02f3bca056c41/t/58868241bebafb413c1156de/1485210185741/KRONE.pdf* (accessed 24 June 2019).
60. Dinello, 'The Contagious Age'; Dan Hassler-Forest, *Science Fiction, Fantasy and Politics: Transmedia World-Building Beyond Capitalism* (London: Rowman & Littlefield, 2016), p. 163; Matthias Nilges, 'The Aesthetics of Destruction: Contemporary US Cinema and TV Culture', in Jeff Birkenstein, Karen Randell and Anna Froula (eds), *Reframing 9/11: Film, Popular Culture and the 'War on Terror'* (New York: Continuum, 2010), pp. 23–33, 30. As for the mentioned movie, see *Unlocked*, Michael Apted, dir. (Di Bonaventura Pictures/SRA Productions/Silver Reel/Bloom/Lipsync Productions, 2017).
61. Sorcha Ní Fhlainn, *Postmodern Vampires: Film, Fiction, and Popular Culture* (London: Palgrave Macmillan, 2019), pp. 180, 231. As for the mentioned movies, see *Van Helsing*, Stephen Sommers, dir. (Sommers Company/Stillking Films, 2004); *Twilight*, Catherine Hardwicke, dir. (Temple Hill Entertainment/Maverick Films/Imprint Entertainment/DMG Entertainment, 2008); *The Twilight Saga: New Moon*, Chris Weitz, dir. (Temple Hill Entertainment/Imprint Entertainment/Sunswept Entertainment, 2009); *The Twilight Saga: Eclipse*, David Slade, dir. (Temple Hill Entertainment/Maverick Films/Imprint Entertainment/Sunswept Entertainment, 2010); *The Twilight Saga: Breaking Dawn*, Part I and II, Bill Condon, dir. (Temple Hill Entertainment/Sunswept Entertainment, 2011/2012).
62. *Godzilla*, Gareth Edwards, dir. (Legendary Pictures, 2014).
63. *Gojira*, Ishirō Honda, dir. (Toho Studios, 1954).
64. Mark Gallagher, *Action Figures: Men, Action Films, and Contemporary Adventure Narratives* (New York: Palgrave Macmillan, 2006), p. 198; Lincoln Geraghty, *American Science Fiction Film and Television* (New York: Berg, 2009), p. 103; Frances Pheasant-Kelly, *Fantasy Film Post 9/11* (New York: Palgrave Macmillan, 2013), p. 4; Robert P. Jones, Daniel Cox and Juhem Navarro-Rivera, *Believers, Sympathizers, & Skeptics: Why Americans are Conflicted about Climate Change, Environmental Policy and Science*. Findings from the PRRI/AAR Religion, Values, and Climate Change Survey (Washington (DC): Public Religion Research Institute, 2014), *http://www.prri.org/wp-content/*

uploads/2014/11/2014-Climate-Change-FINAL1-1.pdf (accessed 8 July 2019).

65. T. Smedley, 'The Poisons Released by Melting Arctic Ice', *BBC.com*, 17 June 2019, *http://www.bbc.com/future/story/20190612-the-poisons-released-by-melting-arctic-ice* (accessed 8 July 2019).
66. J. Shafer, 'Behind Trump's Strange "Invisible Enemy" Rhetoric', *Politico*, 9 April 2020, *https://www.politico.com/news/magazine/2020/04/09/trump-coronavirus-invisible-enemy-177894* (accessed 2 July 2020).
67. See Tzvetan Todorov, *The Fantastic: A Structural Approach to a Literary Genre* (Oxford: Blackwell Publishers Inc., 1977), pp. 25–6; O'Leary, 'Apocalypticism in American Popular Culture'; Rigney, 'Three Kinds of Anti-Intellectualism', 441–2.
68. B. Plumer and C. Davenport, 'Science Under Attack: How Trump Is Sidelining Researchers and Their Work', *The New York Times*, 28 December 2019, *https://www.nytimes.com/2019/12/28/climate/trump-administration-war-on-science.html* (accessed 17 January 2020); H. Escobar, 'Brazil's New President has Scientists Worried. Here's Why', *Sciencemag.org*, 1 January 2019, *https://www.sciencemag.org/news/2019/01/brazil-s-new-president-has-scientists-worried-here-s-why* (accessed 17 January 2020).

7

Killable Hordes, Chronic Others and 'Mindful' Consumers

Rehabilitating the Zombie in Twenty-First-Century Popular Culture

Megen de Bruin-Molé

IN POPULAR CULTURE studies we are in the middle of what one might melodramatically term a zombie epidemic. Undead figures permeate the global mediascape. David McNally offers a list of the varied ways in which, at the start of the twenty-first century, fantastical monstrosity has slowly but aggressively emerged from the margins of genre fiction into the public and popular spheres, becoming part of real-world discourse as well as fictional.[1] During this period '*Pride and Prejudice and Zombies* rocketed up bestseller-lists, and seemingly endless numbers of vampire- and zombie-films and novels flooded the market'.[2] The undead monster has seeped into political discourse as well. In 2009, *Time* magazine declared the zombie 'the official monster of the recession', and in 2017 the *New Statesman* featured an undead Theresa May on its front cover, beneath the headline 'The Zombie PM'.[3] Dan Hassler-Forest describes how 'the figure of the undead' has become '[i]nstantly recognizable to general audiences, yet flexible enough to serve both as a legitimate monster and as the punchline to a bad joke'.[4]

Clearly the zombie is an incredibly versatile, and thus incredibly varied, symbol. In this chapter, I want to try to pin down this very broad, very popular figure in the context of contagion and epidemic anxiety, and examine whether our general assumptions about the zombie, as our culture's 'only modern myth', are still accurate in practice.[5] How has the zombie been understood in a popular and political context, and how is it commonly understood today? In particular, how has our changing understanding of the politics of illness, individual autonomy and belonging impacted how we depict the zombie? To answer this question while still attempting to acknowledge the zombie's incredible versatility, in this chapter I identify three branches of contemporary zombie fiction across a variety of popular media. The first involves the familiar 'zombie horde', which harkens back to the identity politics of late twentieth-century horror and symbolises the fear of invasion from a monstrous, 'infectious' outside force. These mindless monsters still dominate Western popular imagination. The more recent 'friendly', self-aware zombie, epitomised by characters like Kieran Walker from *In the Flesh* (2013–14) or Melanie from *The Girl with All the Gifts* (2014), reveals a subtler consideration of what it means to be physically or socially different, through metaphors of quarantine and chronic illness.[6] Though there are certainly earlier examples of intelligent zombies (Dan O'Bannon's 1985 film *The Return of the Living Dead* being one often-cited example), this strand of zombie fiction has also evolved in relation to late twentieth-century trends and identity politics, particularly the rise of the sympathetic monster.[7] Most interestingly, in the final part of the chapter close readings of popular zombie fictions like *iZombie* (2015–19) and *Santa Clarita Diet* (2017–19) help us to consider how the figure of the zombie might develop in the future. In these texts the zombie is no longer a mindless or marginalised figure, but is instead a mindful, mainstream consumer.

The zombie has a controversial history in Western myth and fiction, lifted from African and Caribbean folklore related to the transatlantic slave trade. As a figure whose body and will are literally co-opted by another human, the earliest zombie is already symbol of colonialism and capitalism gone wrong. Since these early days, the zombie has developed additional significance, and has appeared in many different contexts. Often, it is an inherently contradictory figure. Sarah Lauro argues that the Haitian zombie is 'an allegory of slavery that is at the same time historically connected to . . . revolution'.[8] For Seth Morton, and elsewhere Jack Halberstam, the zombie is an example of 'bare life' – a person who is not classed as a person, or upon whom a restrictive brand of personhood is imposed.[9] Another common reading of the contemporary zombie is as a symbol of mindless consumerism and the effects of global capitalism.[10] This last reading is embodied most famously in George Romero's 'mallrats' from *Dawn of the Dead* (1978), milling aimlessly through the retail spaces they occupied with equal mindlessness when they were alive.[11] As Stacey Abbott argues, however, the contemporary zombie is 'a bricolage of influences, responding to shifts and changes within the nature of the horror genre'.[12] Today's zombie has no single genealogy or point of origin.

There are still a few characteristics that unite contemporary zombies. Susan Behuniak highlights cannibalism as one frequently recurring trait.[13] This cannibalism is not always specifically brain-focused, but a key qualifier of the contemporary zombie is that it literally lives off other people, consuming human flesh to sustain its unnatural life. As McNally argues, this 'emphasis on consumption, on eating flesh, was central to the displacement of the zombie-labourer', or slave, that dominated earlier, folkloric interpretations of the zombie.[14] The present-day zombie's literal cannibalism implies metaphorical or social cannibalism as well, and facilitates the characterisation of zombies as 'crazed consumers'.[15] And unlike the earliest zombie narratives, in which we might expect to find instances of magic or other supernatural origins, twenty-first-century zombies are usually created by a virus or other pathogen, classified primarily in 'natural' or scientific terms.[16] It is thus through an analysis of the zombie's viropolitics – the way this figure evokes metaphors of disease and methods for its containment within a socio-political discourse of otherness and consumption – that we can best analyse the zombie's appearances in contemporary popular media.

Chronically Other: From the Killable Horde to the Friendly Zombie

Zombie viropolitics can be dramatically different from text to text. In one strand of contemporary fiction, for instance, the zombie is portrayed as a mindless horde: a global pandemic or invading force that threatens the total collapse of civilisation. Consider the *World War Z* film adaptation (2013) or AMC's *The Walking Dead* (2010–present).[17] Such stories often assign specific physical characteristics to the zombie, summarised by Behuniak as 'Romero's trope' – after George Romero, director of the influential zombie films *Night of the Living Dead* (1968), *Dawn of the*

Dead (1978) and *Day of the Dead* (1985).[18] In such narratives, the zombie's trajectory takes it from 'lack of self-recognition', to 'failure to recognise others, cannibalisation of living human beings, the exponential spreading of this plague, the resulting horror of those still unafflicted, and the zombie's overwhelming hopelessness that makes death a preferred alternative to continued existence'.[19] Horde zombies are unthinking, inhuman monsters, who consume without question or goal, and who the narrative's heroes are framed as justified in killing. In these narratives, to be 'infected' disqualifies one from being human or having human rights, and the zombie is used as a de-humanising metaphor for groups of people considered 'threatening' to Western civilisation: immigrants, enemy combatants, the poor, and so on. As Gastón Gordillo writes, 'This detritus of zombie corpses epitomizes the trope of the killable horde, made up of bodies that are so dangerous, uncontrollable, and devoid of humanity that they *have* to be murdered "in self-defense"'.[20] Gordillo applies this zombie trope to various political scenarios, suggesting for instance that 'What is terrifying about Palestinians, as Ben Stein put it in the case of Missouri, is their mere existence, their "scary selves," which "arms" them with an "incredible" power: the power to instill fear on [sic] the powerful'.[21] Killable hordes represent an ineffable otherness: the collapse of *our* civilisation as *we* know it, prompted by an unstoppable drain on the nation's citizens and resources.

In a markedly different but increasingly dominant strand of fiction, we find individual, 'friendly' zombies who are able to contain their otherness, and who are at least partially reintegrated with human society. These zombies suffer from what we might call 'chronic otherness', or socio-political difference framed through a medical discourse of infection, disease, and treatment. Just as the category of 'chronically ill' separates healthy bodies from unwell ones, the category of 'chronically other' separates the socially normal from the socially abnormal. This framing reflects the tendency in cultural studies to read zombies, like other fantastical monsters, as markers of 'cultural, political, racial, economic, [or] sexual' difference, which ideally encourage discussions and re-evaluations of civil rights in the popular sphere.[22] While the 'killable horde' demands extermination, the viropolitics of the friendly zombie are often enacted through the narrative of chronic illness, which necessitates medical treatment and therapy. 'Chronically ill' zombies are subjected to diagnostic care including regular medication, mobility aids, and make-up or other beauty products to hide symptoms, allowing the zombie to 'pass' as living, healthy and human. In Mira Grant's 2010 novel *Feed*, the main character struggles with the discrimination she faces as a sufferer of retinal Kellis-Amberlee, a dormant version of the zombie supervirus that will 'amplify' upon death, or on contact with the active strain.[23] Her disease is incurable, and will eventually turn her into an infectious zombie, but she manages her condition through medication and through careful use of Personal Protective Equipment (PPE) that is often as much for others' benefit as her own. For instance, she wears dark sunglasses both to protect her light-sensitive zombified eyes, and to protect herself from others' discrimination at the sight of them.[24]

Similarly, in the BBC series *In the Flesh* (2013–14), Kieren Walker is a rehabilitated zombie, suffering from what the NHS has dubbed 'Partially Deceased Syndrome' or PDS.[25] Kieran is given make-up and contact lenses to help him look human, and his treatment includes a combination of therapy and medication. He receives medication in the form of daily injections of a fictional drug called Neurotriptyline (administered into the spinal column at the back of the neck), and his therapy includes the regular repetition of the phrase: 'I am a Partially Deceased Syndrome sufferer and that is not my fault'.[26] These treatments parody both traditional methods for the management of chronic illness, and the inefficacy of such methods to deal with the feelings of exclusion, depression and social isolation such illness can produce. In narratives like *Feed* and *In the Flesh*, infection takes on a more sympathetic meaning: the zombie subject is quite literally a terminal patient, chronically ill and treated as disabled. The zombie remains a potential disease vector, but succeeds in managing their illness and 'living' an undead life. In this case, the zombie's viropolitics are personal, exploring how someone who is marginalised within the dominant culture can potentially escape social isolation and become 'recuperated'.

In a number of these friendly zombie fictions, portrayals of zombies explicitly advocate a progressive identity politics. That is, they condemn the way society treats marginal or 'chronically other' people as unhealthy or monstrous. For instance, in *In the Flesh* the rural community of Roarton struggles to accept Kieran as a rehabilitated zombie. Because Kieran is also bisexual, however, they also struggled to accept him while he was alive. Kieran's status as a bisexual man is related to his status as a PDS sufferer on a number of occasions, particularly because the one is indirectly the result of the other: isolated and bullied as a teen, Kieran committed suicide before being resurrected as a zombie. Kieran's secret lover Rick also suffers a premature death, and likewise returns as a zombie. Unlike Kieran, however, Rick is initially in denial about both his sexuality and his own status as a PDS sufferer. He tries to placate his intolerant father by miming life, and heterosexual masculinity, as closely as possible. Tragically, when Rick finally does embrace his identity, his father murders him. By tying this murder to Rick's identity as a gay man, as well as a zombie, *In the Flesh* is able to equate these two injustices and create a sense of sympathy for the zombie on political grounds.

The figure of the 'friendly zombie' has been tied to many other expressions of identity politics, including those of gender, class and race. In the 2016 film adaptation of *The Girl with All the Gifts*, for example, Melanie – a Black zombie child who has lived her life in a detention centre – forms a strong bond with her white teacher, Miss Helen Justineau. By the end of both film and novel their roles are reversed; Miss Justineau is the captive and Melanie is free. Crucially, the film flips the races of these two characters. In the novel Melanie is white, blonde, and blue-eyed, and Miss Justineau is Black; 'dark brown, like the wood of the trees . . . whose seeds only grow out of the ashes of a bushfire'.[27] Fans and critics were quick to pick up on the significance of this change, particularly in light of the zombie as a postcolonial and posthuman figure. Linking the British film to US politics, one reviewer at BlackGirlNerds.com wrote:

> With a black student, white teacher it's still a story of learning to behave, but a *different* story of learning to behave. It's not a metaphor for learning the skills of adulthood anymore, it's a metaphor for learning to fit in a white world, for learning to talk like they do and act like they do . . . I can't imagine a more anti-Trump, anti-Sessions, anti-everything-2016-came-to-be moment.[28]

Depictions like this one merge the 'foreign infection' narratives of the horde zombie category with 'chronically other' label that cultural studies ascribes to the monster, essentially creating models of multiculturalism and tolerance in which one should live alongside monsters without one group fully assimilating the other.[29] Margrit Shildrick describes this model as *immunopolitical* rather than viropolitical: a relationship that 'contests the discourse of the self's immunity to the other'.[30] Given that many friendly zombie narratives come from a literary or middlebrow (rather than pulp) horror context, their politically correct framing is perhaps unsurprising. In essence, these narratives suggest we should approach the chronic otherness of the zombie with tolerance and coexistence, rather than destruction or forced integration.

'Friendly' zombies also differ from horde zombies in that they are not mindless, whether in terms of their inner lives or their consumer practices. These chronically other characters are fully self-aware. Moreover, they are often uncannily capable of managing their own desires and urges. In this they are a visible reflection of what Oren Ergas describes as the 'mindfulness revolution' in Western culture, where participants are invited to assert control over their lives by 'paying attention' to their 'bodies, breath, actions, speech' and so forth.[31] This is a practice increasingly advocated not only at an individual level, but also within major Western corporations and educational systems as a means of coping with the stress and alienation of everyday life.[32] From this perspective, the friendly zombie very aptly embodies the shift discussed throughout the rest of this book – a 'subjective turn' in the West that signals a blurring between the intangible, religious or supernatural and its 'relations with education and science'.[33] The zombie is a supernatural figure, but its cultivation of its own humanity in these texts reveals much about our assumptions about the nature of personhood and identity formation. Within this metaphor, the zombie is not able to cure their otherness, but through the mindful way it polices its own bodily boundaries it is able to avoid spreading the zombie contagion, and may even be restored to full personhood in the eyes of the audience or reader.

Most friendly zombies balk at consuming human flesh, though some still feel cravings for it. Kieran does not eat anything at all – though he regularly pretends to eat human food at his parents' request.[34] Even in a feral state, however, he is able to resist the urge to kill and consume.[35] In *The Girl with All the Gifts* zombies can 'eat any kind of meat', and Melanie happily subsists on grubs before her first taste of human flesh.[36] Even following her escape from the facility where she was raised, Melanie takes life reluctantly, and only in self-defence. Though these zombies are represented as individuals, then, their motivation for avoiding cannibalism is relational. Neither Kieran nor Melanie wants to hurt the people they love. Both are ironically 'mindful' consumers, who are aware of the harm their consumption creates, and who, through this awareness, can subsequently escape the cycle. They are mindful that their zombie-ism is dangerous to those around them, and take steps to address and contain their urge to consume.

Mindful Consumers

Both strands of contemporary zombie fiction I have discussed so far, the 'killable horde' and the 'friendly zombie' other, offer socio-political models for dealing with those outside or peripheral to the dominant community. The latter category in particular is recognisable across contemporary narratives of horror and monstrosity. As Fred Botting and Dale Townshend have argued, popular horror 'relies on an increasingly fragile and insubstantial opposition between human and Gothic monster'.[37] Physically monstrous characters often take on the role of the hero, unjustly ostracised from society for their physical deformities. Conversely, human characters who seem conventionally normal are often revealed to have a violent and amoral 'monster' buried within their psyche. Jeffrey Weinstock frames the situation as follows:

> What follows from this decoupling of monstrosity from appearance is an important cultural shift that aligns monstrosity not with physical difference, but with antithetical moral values. Monstrosity thus is reconfigured as a kind of invisible disease that eats away at the body and the body politic, and manifests visibly through symptomatic behaviour.[38]

This fear of the invisible monster is acutely manifested in contemporary narratives of the virus, and of the environmental (as opposed to the nuclear) apocalypse. Such narratives represent a world in which 'evil is associated not with physical difference, but with cultural forces that constrain personal growth and expression'.[39] In essence, monstrosity in popular fiction is whatever threatens the individualistic, neoliberal subject.

Following this trend, in the US a new kind of 'friendly zombie' narrative has recently become popular, which again displays its own distinct viropolitics, and falls even more clearly within the contemporary politics of the monstrous highlighted by Weinstock, Botting and Townshend, and Cohen than the examples I have given above. In our twenty-first-century culture of friendly monsters, the monster is increasingly framed as an 'average', liberal humanist individual – a figure which has, of course, 'historically been constructed as a white European male'.[40] An increasingly normative zombie viropolitics can now be found across many genres and media platforms. Examples include romantic dramas, like the 2009 novel *Breathers: A Zombie's Lament* and the 2013 film *Warm Bodies* (preceded by a 2010 novel), sitcoms like the 2017 Netflix series *Santa Clarita Diet*, and television crime procedurals like *iZombie* (The CW, 2015–19) – all starring straight, white, middle class, Western, and otherwise 'average' or normative zombies.[41] There are many possible explanations for the 'whiteness' of the contemporary friendly zombie, though I would suggest that the monster's absorption by mainstream publishing and production industries is at least partly to blame. Representation, hiring practices and imagined audiences in each of these industries are hampered by a long history of conservative and racist structural biases. In any case, these privileged zombies are not framed as meaningfully 'other' in their viropolitics. Rather than serving as a ritualistic demarcation between the self or nation and the monstrous outsider, these monsters instead 'dramatise the profound senses of corporeal vulnerability that pervade modern society, most manifestly when commodification invades new spheres of social life'.[42] Rather than dehumanising the other outside the community, in these narratives the horror is directed inward, to the twin 'monsters' of modernity that cannot be escaped or destroyed, and must be embraced and ethically managed: *capitalism* and *consumerism*.

In a 2005 review of the state of consumer culture theory, Eric Arnould and Craig Thompson suggest that, from one perspective, the consumer market plays a positive role in identity politics, providing 'consumers with an expansive and heterogeneous palette of resources from which to construct individual and collective identities'.[43] More than ever before, we define ourselves through the things we buy, and the ways in which we buy them. Since this review, it has also become abundantly clear that the market plays a dominant role in our self-definition. While we (as individual agents) construct our identities by consuming certain things in a particular way, at the same time 'the market produces certain kinds of consumer positions that consumers can choose to inhabit'.[44] This system ultimately constricts our patterns of consumption, and reduces our range of possible identities. To be a consumer is thus to consume a particular self-ideal, produced by a normative market. In recent years, this cycle has most commonly been linked with neoliberalism: 'the *rationality of contemporary capitalism* – a capitalism freed of its archaic references and fully acknowledged as a historical construct and general norm of existence'.[45] In this framework, individuals judge themselves by their ability to compete with other individuals. This naturalises the idea that each individual can fairly compete by buying or selling labour – the physical work of oneself, or of others.

Crucially, in addition to these individualistic effects, neoliberalism also produces 'certain kinds of social relations, certain ways of living, certain subjectivities' at the wider, cultural level.[46] In this world, the market is 'a natural reality' – individuals are encouraged to constantly build themselves into newer and better versions, more capable of competing in a global market.[47] This is the labour of (un)life, where 'chronic otherness' is the new norm, and personal irregularities or inadequacies must be eternally managed and improved on, rather than unequivocally banished or embraced. As many critics have pointed out, this model can be applied very well to the figure of the undead, though the monster of choice has traditionally been the vampire. McNally, drawing on Karl Marx's own undead metaphor, argues that 'fantastic depictions of global capitalism as a vampire-system that extracts and sells body-parts capture something very real about the economic universe we inhabit'.[48] In an interesting twist on the history of the zombie, who has gone from mindless worker to mindless consumer, this mainstream variety of the friendly zombie is often framed as a newly *mindful* or liberated consumer.

The Netflix series *Santa Clarita Diet* takes this metaphor to its logical extreme in the way it frames its protagonist's self-actualisation through consumption. Joel and Sheila Hammond are both defined by their consumption patterns, but in contrasting ways. Human Joel's careful, frugal consumption is pathologised in the series, used as a comedic sign of his fragile mental state. In a scene from the pilot episode, Joel has a nervous breakdown in a department store while trying to replace a faulty toaster oven. His failure to consume is related to his perceived failure to take care of himself and his family, both of which are comically framed as equally important – 'maybe I shouldn't care about toaster knobs, or being responsible', he exclaims.[49] In contrast, becoming a zombie revitalises Sheila, allowing her to become who she has 'always wanted to be', largely by taking away her impulse control.[50] From her transition in the show's first episode, Sheila consumes what she wants without inhibition – food, drugs, sex, cars, clothes, and (of course) other people. Sheila's consumption is framed as a sign of her liberation, particularly in that she consciously consumes 'poorly', or against mainstream trends and conventions. Sheila's consumption is mindful in that it represents a radical act of self-care. As a result of her newfound ability to consume according to her own, individual whims, Sheila becomes *more* lively, confident and attractive after her transition, prompting her neighbours to ask what her secret is.

Interestingly, the mainstreaming of the zombie in this and other popular texts is often accompanied by its sexualisation, and the zombie is increasingly constructed as a desirable (as well as a desiring) figure. In *Santa Clarita Diet*, Sheila's attractiveness and sex drive increase once she becomes a zombie, drawing the attention of both her husband and other men.[51] In other friendly zombie texts like *Warm Bodies* and *iZombie*, the zombie's pale unblemished skin, dark eye make-up and casually fashionable clothes suggest a rock star before they do the walking dead. The *Warm Bodies* film adaptation taps into this subcultural aesthetic explicitly, aging down its protagonist (known only as 'R') and playing on Emo 'hoodies, skinny jeans, and eyeliner' standards of attractiveness. In Isaac Marion's 2010 novel, R is framed as more conventionally well-groomed, though not undesirable:

> [D]eath has been kinder to me than some. I'm still in the early stages of decay. Just the grey skin, the unpleasant smell, the dark circles under the eyes. I could almost pass for a Living man in need of a vacation. Before I became a zombie I must have been a businessman, a banker, a broker or some young temp . . . because I'm wearing fairly nice clothes.[52]

Though the zombie's newfound 'sexiness' certainly seems to have endeared it to mainstream audiences, this mainstreaming of zombies, their bodies and their consumption arguably weakens their power as a symbol of society's 'real' monsters, specifically those whose difference is 'cultural, political, racial, economic, sexual'.[53] More problematically, in many such texts the violence previously reserved for the killable horde is now displaced onto humans, whose only crime is often one of circumstance. In some cases this even means that the positions of zombie and human in texts like *In the Flesh* or *The Girl with All the Gifts* are flipped, with the zombies as the socially privileged class and the humans as victims and marginalised others. *Santa Clarita Diet* plays with this problem, with Joel agonising over how to help Sheila kill 'ethically' – that is, only killing people who have earned a death penalty (from the Hammonds' perspective). Given the biases of the US ecomonic and criminal justice systems, however, this leads to several false starts before they are able to find a suitable victim. Ironically, Sheila's prey often comes from her immediate peers and neighbours: a police officer, a real estate agent, a group of white supremacists, and other people who abuse their privileged position within racist and capitalist systems. In *Breathers*, the adult zombie narrator Andy Warner is living a stable but unsatisfying existence as a dependent and legal minor under the custody of his parents. Once he inadvertently consumes human meat, it leads him to reconsider his submissiveness to accepted systems of zombie regulation. Eventually, his cannibalism – framed as a natural urge rather than a monstrous one – becomes his empowerment. He dismembers and eats his parents, who have threatened to turn him in to the government, and escapes on a killing rampage.

This violence is disproportionate. Andy is already dead, and in seeking to increase his own comfort and well-being he will kill many more people. These murders are framed as justified from Andy's perspective, however, since it will mean he has the chance to live (and consume) autonomously:

> It's not that I don't feel bad about what I've done to my mother and father. But up until recently, I expected to rot away. And anything I had to lose had already been stolen from me. Then I meet Ray and fall in love with Rita and I feel like I have something to exist for again. I have something that matters. And my parents were going to take that away from me because of ten thousand dollars and a few acts of civil disobedience.[54]

When framed in the light of capitalism and neoliberal competition, Andy's reasoning is made more palatable: he is only preserving his individual liberty and dignity, through which all manner of violence becomes justified. Though violence and cannibalism have long been common features of the zombie in popular entertainment – *Breathers* in particular makes a pointed statement about the link between dehumanisation, violence and social justice – the justification of violence in these kinds of 'mindful' zombie narratives takes on a more ominous resonance, particularly because its protagonists are only different, monstrous and maligned from an individualistic and neoliberal point of view, not from the perspective of their socio-political circumstances relative to others in the narrative. While the violence across these friendly zombie narratives is framed as cathartic and empowering, then, in creating sympathy for the privileged it also serves to distract from the real violence, and real victims, of capitalism.

Normalising Consumption

In neoliberal friendly zombie texts like those discussed above, the zombies are often 'mindful' of what they consume, rationalising their consumption but never directly questioning or condemning the practice of consumption itself. In combination with their privileged socio-economic positions, this can encourage a nihilistic or apathetic reading of any activist or anti-capitalist actions their stories otherwise promote. The privileged zombie's attitude towards mindful consumerism echoes the real-world use of mindfulness as a coping mechanism among Western corporations and consumers. Erika L. Rosenberg, for instance, argues that mindfulness can help consumers address both 'the nonconscious psychological processes that are exploited by corporations and advertisers to shape consumer preferences', and the 'underlying life dissatisfaction and the need for fulfilment that might be temporarily satisfied by consumption activities'.[55] In other words, though they are helpless to undermine consumption itself, consumers can minimise the unease and exploitation of the system by directing their efforts into mindful or ethical consumption practices. Ironically, as Bee Scherer and Jeff Waistell point out, this (mis)use of mindfulness as a coping mechanism actually 'detracts from its main purpose in Buddhism of attaining insight and cultivating compassion (for example by alleviating poverty through wealth distribution)'.[56] The original function of mindfulness is thus 'not ethically neutral', instead actively *challenging* capitalist values of 'economic materialism, competitiveness, and individualism'.[57]

The community of zombies in the TV series *iZombie* can be read from a 'friendly zombie' perspective, as a metaphor for coming to terms with chronic illness, or even with chronic otherness. The show also contains horde zombies – sentient zombies who have gone too long without brains, and are permanently transformed into monsters. The appropriately named protagonist Olivia 'Liv' Moore is a young medical resident, who is personally and financially successful, healthy and able-bodied, white, cis and conventionally attractive. She is infected one night at a boat party, undergoing a physical transformation as a zombie that essentially entails becoming paler and adopting an 'alternative' (i.e. popular subcultural) clothing style. Unwilling to risk infecting others, Liv abandons her promising career as a surgeon, breaks off her wedding engagement, and goes to work as a coroner's assistant, where she won't need to kill for the brains she needs, but can instead steal them from the dead. Eventually, Liv discovers that the zombie's ability to absorb the memories and personalities of the dead by eating their brains can also help her to solve their murders. This forms the main premise of the show, and every week Liv eats the brains of a new victim, partially assuming their identity in order to catch their killers. Again, however, the titular 'monster' is not marginal in any conventional, socio-political sense. The show makes it very clear that her initial state of isolation is the result of her own self-doubt, rather than her infection, as she has a strong and constantly supportive network of friends who are happy to accept her in her new zombie form.

Instead we might consider Liv as a final an example of this newly 'mindful', privileged zombie in popular fiction. Through her role as a crime-solving zombie, Liv is able to come to terms with her need to consume brains, finding new meaning, and new confidence, in her monstrosity. In *iZombie*, the proper antidote to infection and monstrosity is a particularly literal form of 'mindful' consumerism: awareness of the origins of what one consumes – in this case brains – combined with an effort to minimise one's harmful consumption and balance it with humanitarian generosity. Rather than using the zombie and its 'chronic otherness' as a socio-political metaphor for marginalised people, however, *iZombie* presents the zombie as an explicit metaphor for whiteness, capitalist exploitation and mainstream consumer practices.[58] Peter Dendle describes how 'the essence of the zombie at the most abstract level is supplanted, stolen, or effaced consciousness; it casts allegorically the appropriation of one person's will by another'.[59] In *iZombie*, the situation is flipped: the zombie's need to consume human flesh becomes a metaphor for the 'disease' of Western consumer culture and capitalism, in which the fortunate prey on the less fortunate.

Liv's humanitarian actions, as she literally sees and feels alongside the victims of her consumption and acts to bring these people retroactive justice, are contrasted with that of other individuals and corporations throughout the series. In season one, Blaine, the zombie who infected Liv, runs a black-market empire, kidnapping and murdering people (from homeless teens to astronauts) so he can sell their brains – and their memories – to his wealthy clientele. In season two, Liv and other 'good' zombies are pitted against Max Rager, the energy drink corporation that first created the zombie virus, and which still manipulates it for profit. Another zombie business harvests its brains from terminal patients in Nepal, through a hospital owned by its billionaire founder.[60] In the show's later seasons, Liv faces off against a zombie prophet who wants to ensure free brains for all . . . by leading a zombie apocalypse. In another narrative arc a group of zombies form a collective to protect themselves from humans, which includes a food production centre and a private army. It is soon revealed that the memory-free paste they eat is made largely from the brains of enemy combatants in the Middle East, killed during the zombie army's various privateering excursions.[61] At the end of the third season, this organisation uses their exposure as a zombie front to hold the country hostage, demanding the 'voluntarily' donated brains of the dead in exchange for their containment of the virus.[62]

Good zombies, in contrast, ensure that they only consume ethically sourced brains – but again, 'ethical' consumption is only ever defined in contrast to these examples of unethical consumption. *iZombie* does reveal some of the 'work' of capitalism, not only in terms of the harm 'bad' zombie consumption can do, but in the way it links even good consumption to the literal bodies of its victims. Liv prepares and eats most of her brains in the morgue kitchen, often with the body of the deceased in the background. This marks Liv's consumption as intimately and intentionally related to the bodies that sustain her. Of course, this preparation process is also presented in a colourful cooking show montage, which reframes the dead body as a morbidly attractive object of consumption. Despite *iZombie*'s status as a CW network show with relatively diverse casting practices (as well as some legitimate narrative efforts to champion diversity and equality), Liv's assumption of the minds and mannerisms of the people she consumes can still result in uncomfortably flippant stereotypes and appropriations. Early in the first season, for instance, Liv eats the brains of Sammy Wong, a man of Asian descent, and comically discovers that she knows Kung Fu.[63] In other moments the deceased's identity is played for laughs or fetishised as a commodity object, as in a season five episode where Liv eats the brains of a drag queen, preparing these as a rainbow jelly Pride cake.[64] In these moments the focus is overwhelmingly on the spectacle of Liv's consumption, and on Liv as a cis, straight, white woman with the privilege of sampling 'exotic' identities for the audience's entertainment (and her own).

By placing its focus on mindful consumption, *iZombie* and similar texts (*Breathers*, *Santa Clarita Diet*, *Warm Bodies*) draw the focus away from capitalist consumption as a negative practice in itself. They present their privileged zombie subjects as average and socially unremarkable, and normalise their monstrous consumer practices as a cannibalistic 'diet' that can be managed through neoliberal force of will. McNally discusses the limitations of the zombie extensively in *Monsters of the Market*, asserting that zombie narratives 'at their best, tend to offer a critique of consumerism, not capitalism – one that fails to probe the life-destroying, zombifying processes of work in bourgeois society'.[65] Hassler-Forest describes a similar state of affairs, in which the zombie is 'frothing with anticapitalist energy', though 'lacking any kind of program for a postcapitalist alternative'.[66] The zombie, like other contemporary monsters, is being slowly co-opted by a neoliberal consumerist discourse. In many ways, this means that it is more of a 'modern' monster than ever before. In the age of global capitalism, and of increasing nationalism and intolerance across Europe and the US, this justification of 'mindful' consumerism, exploitation and violence feels uncomfortably relevant. The viropolitics presented by this new zombie figure invite resignation and regulation, rather than anxiety or revolution. The neoliberal or 'postcapitalist' zombie narrative not only attempts to convince us that there is no use fighting against our identity as capitalist subjects, it also reassures us that if we only do it right, the monstrosity of capitalism and consumerism is nothing to be afraid of. The underlying implication, of course, is that consumerism and capitalism are *not* inherently oppressive, destructive and marginalising 'diseases', and that it is possible to mitigate the suffering our consumption causes others. This framing is possible because the focus in mindful zombie narratives is on the malady of the privileged capitalist subject, not on capitalism's victims and others. Zombies like Sheila or Liv no longer serve to represent the fear of infection or otherness from outside the community, instead signifying a monstrous and unalterable sameness within. As McNally argues: 'What is most striking about capitalist monstrosity . . . is its elusive everydayness, its apparently seamless integration into the banal and mundane rhythms of quotidian existence'.[67] Now even the zombie has been infected by it.

Notes

1. David McNally, *Monsters of the Market: Zombies, Vampires and Global Capitalism* (Chicago: Haymarket Books, 2012), p. 1.
2. McNally, *Monsters of the Market*, p. 1.
3. L. Grossman, 'Zombies Are the New Vampires', *Time*, 9 April 2009, *http://www.time.com/time/magazine/article/0,9171,1890384,00.html?imw=Y* (accessed 10 September 2014); see the issue's featured article by S. Heffer, 'The humbling of Theresa May', *New Statesman*, 26 June 2017, *http://www.newstatesman.com/politics/uk/2017/06/humbling-theresa-may* (accessed 28 June 2017).

4. Dan Hassler-Forest, *Science Fiction, Fantasy and Politics: Transmedia World-Building Beyond Capitalism* (London: Rowman & Littlefield, 2016), p. 156.
5. Gilles Deleuze and Félix Guattari, *Anti-Oedipus: Capitalism and Schizophrenia* (New York: Continuum, 2004), p. 368.
6. Mike R. Carey, *The Girl with All the Gifts* (London: Orbit, 2014); *The Girl with All the Gifts*, Colm McCarthy, dir. (UK, Warner Bros Pictures, 2016).
7. Cf. Catherine Spooner, *Post-Millennial Gothic: Comedy, Romance and the Rise of Happy Gothic* (London: Bloomsbury Publishing, 2017) and Jeffrey Andrew Weinstock, 'Invisible Monsters: Vision, Horror, and Contemporary Culture', in Asa Simon Mittman and Peter J. Dendle (eds), *The Ashgate Research Companion to Monsters and the Monstrous* (Farnham: Ashgate, 2013), pp. 275–89.
8. Sarah J. Lauro, *The Transatlantic Zombie: Slavery, Rebellion, and Living Death* (New Brunswick: Rutgers University Press, 2015), p. 7.
9. Seth Morton, 'Zombie Politics', in Edward P. Comentale and Aaron Jaffe (eds), *The Year's Work at the Zombie Research Center* (Bloomington: Indiana University Press, 2014), pp. 315–40, 327; M. de Bruin-Molé, 'Our Zombies, Ourselves: A Lecture with J. Halberstam', *Frankenfiktion.com*, 4 February 2015, *http://frankenfiction.com/our-zombies-ourselves-a-lecture-with-j-halberstam/* (accessed 17 November 2019).
10. McNally, *Monsters of the Market*, p. 213.
11. Rob Latham, *Consuming Youth: Vampires, Cyborgs, and the Culture of Consumption* (Chicago: University of Chicago Press, 2002), p. 31.
12. Stacey Abbott, *Undead Apocalypse: Vampires and Zombies in the 21st Century* (Edinburgh: Edinburgh University Press, 2016), p. 64.
13. S. M. Behuniak, 'The Living Dead? The construction of people with Alzheimer's disease as zombies', *Ageing and Society*, 31/1 (2011), 77.
14. McNally, *Monsters of the Market*, p. 273.
15. McNally, *Monsters of the Market*, p. 273.
16. Abbott, *Undead Apocalypse*, p. 81.
17. *World War Z*, Marc Forster, dir. (Skydance Productions/Hemisphere Media Capital/GK Films/Plan B Entertainment, 2DUX^2, 2013).
18. Behuniak, 'The Living Dead?'
19. Behuniak, 'The Living Dead?', 77–8.
20. G. Gordillo, 'The Killable Horde', Space and Politics Blog, 3 September 2014, *http://spaceandpolitics.blogspot.ca/2014/09/the-killable-horde.html* (accessed 14 September 2014).
21. Gordillo, 'The Killable Horde'.

22. Jeffrey J. Cohen, 'Monster Culture (Seven Theses)', in Jeffrey Jerome Cohen (ed.), *Monster Theory: Reading Culture* (Minneapolis: University of Minnesota Press, 1996), p. 7.
23. Mira Grant, *Feed* (London: Orbit, 2010), p. 553.
24. Grant, *Feed*, p. 37.
25. *In the Flesh*, 'Episode #1.1', Johnny Campbell, dir. (BBC Three, 17 March 2013).
26. *In the Flesh*, 'Episode #1.1'.
27. Carey, *The Girl*, p. 10.
28. K. W. Williams, 'The Girl with All the Gifts Race Analysis', BlackGirlNerds.com, 18 March 2017, *https://blackgirlnerds.com/girl-gifts-race-analysis/* (accessed 4 July 2017).
29. Haraway, Donna J., *When Species Meet* (Minneapolis: University of Minnesota Press, 2008).
30. Margrit Shildrick, 'Chimerism and *Immunitas*: The Emergence of a Posthumanist Biophilosophy', in S. E. Wilmer and Audronė Žukauskaitė (eds), *Resisting Biopolitics: Philosophical, Political, and Performative Strategies* (London: Routledge, 2015), pp. 95–108, 95.
31. O. Ergas, 'Mindfulness in education at the intersection of science, religion, and healing', *Critical Studies in Education*, 55/1 (2014), 58–72, 59.
32. Ergas, 'Mindfulness in education', 66.
33. Ergas, 'Mindfulness in education', 59.
34. *In the Flesh*, 'Episode #1.1'.
35. *In the Flesh*, 'Episode #2.6', Alice Troughton, dir. (BBC Three, 8 June 2014).
36. Carey, *The Girl*, pp. 132, 9.
37. Fred Botting and Dale Townshend, *Twentieth Century Gothic: Our Monsters, Our Pets* (London: Routledge, 2004), p. 4.
38. Jeffrey A. Weinstock, 'Invisible Monsters: Vision, Horror, and Contemporary Culture', in Asa Simon Mittman and Peter J. Dendle (eds), *The Ashgate Research Companion to Monsters and the Monstrous* (Farnham: Ashgate, 2013), pp. 275–89, 276.
39. Weinstock, 'Invisible Monsters', pp. 276–7.
40. N. Katherine Hayles, *How We Became Posthuman: Virtual Bodies in Cybernetics, Literature, and Informatics* (Chicago: Chicago University Press, 1999), p. 4.
41. S. G. Browne, *Breathers: A Zombie's Lament* (New York: Broadway Books, 2009); Warm Bodies, Jonathan Levine, dir. (Mandeville Films, 2013).
42. McNally, *Monsters of the Market*, p. 2.
43. E. J. Arnould and C. J. Thompson, 'Consumer Culture Theory (CCT): Twenty Years of Research', *Journal of Consumer Research*, 31/4 (2005), 868–82, 871.

44. Arnould and Thompson, 'Consumer Culture Theory (CCT)', 871.
45. Pierre Dardot and Christian Laval, *The New Way of the World: On Neoliberal Society* (New York: Verso, 2014), p. 4.
46. Dardot and Laval, *The New Way of the World*, p. 4.
47. Dardot and Laval, *The New Way of the World*, p. 2.
48. McNally, *Monsters of the Market*, p. 9.
49. *Santa Clarita Diet*, 'So Then a Bat or a Monkey', Ruben Fleischer, dir. (Netflix, 3 February 2017).
50. *Santa Clarita Diet*, 'So Then a Bat or a Monkey'.
51. *Santa Clarita Diet*, 'So Then a Bat or a Monkey'. This is a transformation that links the zombie strongly to its sexy undead cousin, the vampire. And as Abbott argues, these two figures are indeed 'increasingly integrated and intertwined' in twenty-first-century film and television, becoming progressively more difficult to distinguish (see Abbott, *Undead Apocalypse*, p. 4).
52. Isaac Marion, *Warm Bodies (The Warm Bodies Series)* (London: Random House, 2010), p. 3.
53. Cohen, 'Monster Culture', p. 7.
54. S. G. Browne, *Breathers: A Zombie's Lament* (London: Hachette UK, 2011), p. 204.
55. Erika L. Rosenberg, 'Mindfulness and Consumerism', in Tim Kasser and Allen D. Kanner (eds), *Psychology and Consumer Culture: The Struggle for a Good Life in a Materialistic World* (Washington: Psychological Association, 2004), pp. 107–25, 109.
56. B. Scherer and J. Waistell, 'Incorporating mindfulness: questioning capitalism', *Journal of Management, Spirituality & Religion*, 15/2 (2018), 1–18, 2.
57. Scherer and Waistell, 'Incorporating mindfulness', 2.
58. In one episode, Liv literally consumes the brains of a mindfulness coach: *iZombie*, 'Eat, Pray, Liv', Mairzee Almas, dir. (The CW, 18 April 2017). There are a handful of exceptions to the show's use of the zombie as a metaphor for whiteness and consumerism, including a third season story arc which sees zombies racialised as non-human others by Seattle's human population, and targeted as victims of xenophobic violence and hate speech.
59. Peter J. Dendle, 'The zombie as barometer of cultural anxiety', in Niall Scott (ed.), *Monsters and the Monstrous: Myths and Metaphors of Enduring Evil* (Amsterdam: Rodopi, 2007), pp. 45–57, 47.
60. *iZombie*, 'Spanking the Zombie', Tessa Blake, dir. (The CW, 2 May 2017).
61. *iZombie*, 'Spanking the Zombie'.
62. *iZombie*, 'Looking for Mr. Goodbrain, Part 2', Dan Etheridge, dir. (The CW, 27 June 2017).

63. *iZombie*, 'Live and Let Clive', John Kretchmer, dir. (The CW, 7 April 2015).
64. *iZombie*, 'Killer Queen', Jude Weng, dir. (The CW, 18 July 2019).
65. McNally, *Monsters of the Market*, pp. 260–2.
66. Hassler-Forest, *Science Fiction, Fantasy and Politics*, p. 174.
67. McNally, *Monsters of the Market*, p. 2.

8

Networks, Desire and Risk Management in Gay Contagion Fiction

Mica Hilson

A FEW YEARS AGO, when I lived in South Carolina, I would listen to the radio during my morning commute to work. One day, the two morning DJs, a man and a woman, were discussing this hypothetical question: if you could live in the fictional world of any TV series for a week, which TV series would you pick? Without hesitating, the female DJ picked *The Walking Dead*. 'But why?' her co-host wondered, 'Wouldn't you worry about getting eaten by a zombie?' 'No, I'd know what to do', she said confidently, 'I'd be the one killing all the zombies. I just think it would be fun.'

While I initially thought this woman's response was an anomaly, a weird misreading of the series, I have come to regard it as a perfect illustration of the appeal that zombie thrillers and other viral catastrophe narratives hold for many viewers. In much the same way that, as Carol Clover famously noted, slasher films build audience identification with the figure of the 'final girl' – the one character who, unlike her foolish peers, manages to use her intelligence and resourcefulness to evade the killer – fictions about zombie plagues and other epidemics invite us to identify with the survivors, the ones 'killing all the zombies'.[1] Counter-intuitively, even as these contagion narratives stoke our fears, they also serve to assuage anxieties, reassuring viewers that there are simple ways to manage the risk of contagion and to control whether we survive. However, this generalisation only holds true for the most popular zombie and contagion narratives; in this essay, I will contrast those mainstream contagion narratives with ones being produced by and for a minority group with a very different understanding of risk and self-management: gay men. In these gay erotic fictions, the risk of contagion is almost impossibly hard to manage, because the individual is trapped in a complex web of interlocking social, financial and technological networks through which contagion might spread.

In contrast, the zombie pandemic narratives that have comprised much of this century's most popular contagion-related media rely on a radically simplified, gamified model of contagion. Think about one of the works that helped kick off the current zombie boom, *The Zombie Survival Guide* (2003) by Max Brooks, who went on to write *World War Z*.[2] Wikipedia currently describes The Zombie Survival Guide as 'a survival manual dealing with the fictional potentiality of a zombie attack'.[3] Take a moment to focus on that one phrase – 'fictional potentiality'. On the one hand, it seems redundant; what is a 'potentiality' but a fiction, a series of events we imagine *might* happen? Yet perhaps *The Zombie Survival Guide* illustrates a fundamental difference between 'real potentiality' and 'fictional potentiality'. Real potentiality is boundless, and although we can to some extent predict and rank the most likely scenarios, we often have to juggle a staggeringly complex set of variables to do so. (Quick: ask yourself, 'Will I be happier if I sign for this 20-year mortgage?' and think about all the variables that might go into that prediction.) The fictional potentiality presented in a work like *The Zombie Survival Guide* is so much simpler; in fact, the zombie is defined by its lack of creativity, spontaneity, or cognitive complexity, making its behaviours all the more predictable and manageable. Brooks's guide came out in 2003, just months after the September 11 terror attacks, at a time when Americans were advised to plan for the real potentiality of another terrorist attack. But terrorists are unpredictable; their methods are varied, and their motives are often opaque. No wonder that so many Americans devoted more time thinking about what they would do in the fictional potentiality of a zombie outbreak rather than in the real potentiality of a terror attack or a natural disaster. In fact, in the United States in 2019, the Federal Emergency Management Agency (FEMA) launched a multimedia advertising campaign starring the cast of *Zombieland 2*, with the tagline 'Zombies don't plan ahead. You can. Make your emergency plan.'[4]

In both the FEMA advertisement and Brooks's survival guide, the reader is hailed as a neoliberal subject, her fundamental difference from the zombie lying in her capacity for risk management. In his introduction, Brooks writes, 'knowledge is only part of the fight for survival. The rest must come from you. Personal choice, the will to live, must be paramount . . . ask yourself one question: What will you do – end your existence in passive acceptance, or stand up and shout, "I will not be their victim! I will survive!" The choice is yours.'[5] Brooks is repeating one of the mantras of neoliberalism, the notion that one's existence is a matter of individual choice, of self-determination.[6] In this equation, the combination of knowledge and will-power is unstoppable. Another key component of neoliberal ideology is the notion that the individual is responsible for managing his or her own calculated risks. As Brown et al. write, 'concepts of risk are both generated by and used to reinforce a neoliberal agenda . . . risk may be used as a tool to advance ideals such as rational choice and individual responsibility'.[7] Furthermore, as Ellen Defossez observes, neoliberalism is responsible for a 'shift toward linking health with responsibility and agency [. . . leading] to reconfigured notions of what it means to be "healthy", what can and should be done in the pursuit of health, and who is ultimately responsible for promoting and securing health'.[8]

The COVID-19 pandemic has laid bare some of the problems with this purely individualistic mindset, as the person who takes a calculated risk by refusing to social distance or wear a mask in public can still be responsible for endangering the health of many others. Even before then, however, North Americans and Europeans had grown increasingly disillusioned with neoliberal ideology, in part because they found that the equation Brooks presents just doesn't add up; it is missing some important variables. In a deeply complex and interconnected world – one that is increasingly controlled by 'black box' algorithms whose mechanisms are mysterious and unpredictable – will-power plus knowledge alone is not enough. We also have to worry about many different forms of 'contagion', including social contagion, emotional contagion and financial contagion.

Admittedly, some of these fears have existed for decades; studies of mass hysteria date back at least as far as Charles Mackay's 1841 *Extraordinary Popular Delusions and the Madness of Crowds*.[9] What is slightly different about the current representation of social contagion is the way this scholarship gets recounted in the mass media as a set of prescriptive warnings. For instance, a 2018 study in the medical journal *JAMA Pediatrics* got reported widely in the mainstream press, inspiring headlines like

Newsweek's 'Weight Gain is Contagious and You Could "Catch" Obesity from Your Neighbors, Study Finds'.[10] Similarly, research on emotional contagion has served as the basis for articles like *Wired*'s 'Happiness and Sadness Spread Just Like Disease' and a host of more prescriptive pieces, like Elle Kaplan's article for *Medium*, 'Why Negative People are Literally Killing You (and How to Protect Your Positivity)'.[11] While the term 'financial contagion' has primarily been applied to macroeconomic processes like the phenomena that spurred the 2008 global financial crisis, there is also a whole genre of business reporting warning individuals that their continued financial health depends on avoiding close contact with financially unhealthy people. For instance, as *The Telegraph*'s 2013 article 'Your Facebook Friends Could Damage Your Credit Rating' warned, 'How you socialise online – and who with – could help or hinder your application for a loan or mortgage'.[12]

These articles about avoiding contagion are perfect clickbait for readers who have internalised neoliberal ideologies about risk and personal responsibility. But if you read enough of them, you get a sense that modern life is a minefield, where one must navigate a narrow safe path between the various contagious hordes who might infect you with their social or emotional or financial maladies. Despite the warnings we might read in the press, the sheer number of 'contagions' out there add up to more risk variables than any individual can conceivably manage. These are forms of contagion that the characters in *The Walking Dead* never have to worry about. They are living in a simplified world, where they only need to worry about avoiding one form of contagion, the zombie plague, and all the other low-level anxieties of modern life have disappeared. In fact, they are living in a gamified world, where the rules can be learned and mastered. No wonder, then, that some viewers want to escape into that world.

Although movies and stories featuring zombies have been around for many decades, the gamification of the zombie only emerged in the twenty-first century. Zombies have been the antagonists in a variety of popular video games, ranging from the *Resident Evil* series (1996–present) to the *Plants vs Zombies* series (2009–16).[13] Even several titles in the best-selling first-person shooter war game series *Call of Duty* include 'zombie modes', where players can shoot at a horde of zombies rather than a horde of enemy soldiers.[14] Most of the aforementioned games demand a combination of strategy and fast reflexes, making zombies the perfect antagonists; their movements are predictable enough that players can gradually learn the skills necessary to defeat the zombies, advance to the next level, and eventually win the game. If the zombies were too smart or spontaneous – or if they learned at a faster rate than the human players – then the games would be impossible to win. The game mechanics thus require the zombie antagonists to act in relatively simple and mechanical ways.

The gamification of the zombie has also begun to spill over into more serious academic research and public health initiatives. For instance, in 2009, four mathematicians from the University of Ottawa grabbed media attention for their research paper, 'When Zombies Attack!: Mathematical Modeling of an Outbreak of Zombie Infection'.[15] The various models they use are incredibly simplistic. The first simply divides the population into three groups: Zombies, Removed (i.e. killed zombies) and Susceptible (i.e. uninfected humans), making the assumption that all Susceptible individuals have the same rate of resistance to zombie infection.[16] The experiment at the heart of the 2018 BBC documentary *Contagion!* offered another vastly simplified (and gamified) model of disease transmission; 'in the small town of Haslemere, Surrey . . . volunteers were issued with apps that could become "infected" if they got too close to presenter Dr Hannah Fry's "Patient Zero"'.[17] Although actual disease transmission depends on far more than just cell phone proximity, data from the Haslemere study has already formed the basis for one academic article describing possible disease outbreak models.[18] These examples serve as potent illustrations of how the gamification of epidemics only exacerbates our tendency to confuse real potentiality (predictions drawn from an extremely complex set of interrelated variables) with fictional potentiality (predictions made according to a simplistic generic narrative).

Zombie games are not only popular in digital formats; there have also been a slew of live-action events such as Humans vs Zombies games. Ethnographer Heather Myers offers this description of a Humans vs Zombies game she attended in 2011:

> The game began with our two team guides presenting the safety and game play information. All human players wear colored flags on their person, zombies do not have flags. For player and staff protection there is no body on body contact, to get around this restriction the zombies in the game 'vomit' Nerf balls that they throw at players to spread the zombie plague. If a player is hit by a zombie twice they themselves become zombie and are able to use their Nerf guns to attack the remaining humans.[19]

The game thus operates under relatively simple rules, and all players have full awareness of how the zombie plague is spread, knowledge that can help them prepare their strategies for avoiding infection. Furthermore, the game is organised by staff members who explain and enforce the rules, intervening when bad actors might seek to violate the rules and monitoring the spread of zombie plague to prevent accidents.

From Myers's descriptions, it is easy to see why players find such games more thrilling than dispiriting. As players manage the risk of getting infected by zombie plague, they must weigh a relatively simple set of strategic concerns: should they play offensively, spraying the zombies with Nerf ammunition, or more defensively, conserving ammunition? When they run low on ammunition, should they go back to their supply bucket, or forge ahead?[20] The game also has a clear endpoint; it is over 'when either all human players are turned into zombies, or the objective of the human teams, to kill Subject Zero with a Nerf canon/bazooka, is achieved'.[21] That awareness of an ending – the sense that one is taking a temporary time-out from normal life, rather than living a ceaseless nightmare – helps explain why Humans vs Zombies players find the game to be a source of fun and excitement, rather than existential dread.

Activities like the Humans vs Zombies game fit the classic Bakhtinian definition of carnival; they allow for a temporary suspension of the drudgery of the daily routine, a short time where people can let off some steam, rather than exploding at the pressures of their everyday lives. However, the critiques of carnival could also apply here; as Terry Eagleton notes, 'Carnival, after all, is a *licensed* affair in every sense, a permissible rupture of hegemony'.[22] This is both a good thing and a bad one. From the standpoint of individual psychology, it is beneficial because the temporary release of carnival can help prevent stressed individuals from reaching their breaking point and reacting in explosive, destructive ways; indeed, many participants in Humans vs Zombies games describe the experience as therapeutic. On the other hand, those explosions of an angry, stressed populace can lead to a radical overturning of the status quo; in that sense, the licensed release valve of carnival can serve an insidious purpose, pacifying an oppressed population just enough that they decline to revolt. I would thus like to suggest that many of our most popular zombie narratives and other contagion narratives similarly work to re-contain the viewer's revolutionary sentiments. They allow their audiences to imagine an escape from the conditions that neoliberalism has wrought – a 'buyer beware' world where nearly all risk is imagined to be the individual's 'personal responsibility' to manage – yet still cling to that core neoliberal ideology of self-management.

At this point, it is important to note that not every recent narrative involving zombie plagues or other epidemics fits the paradigm I have been critiquing. Thus, I would like to use the second half of this chapter to discuss a little-known subgenre of contagion narratives that counter the trends I have been describing in a particularly pointed way. These stories, which I have termed gay erotic viral transformation fiction, also treat epidemic phenomena as a locus for both fear and desire. However, they critique the belief that the individual with superior risk-management skills can avoid contagion, and they often situate their fictional epidemics within real-world financial and social networks that engender viral transmission. It is worth noting that these are non-professional, non-profit stories, posted to erotic fiction archives and Tumblr pages devoted to specific fetishes like mind control, muscle growth or robotisation. Authors are motivated to share their work because of the positive reader feedback it garners, as well as the possibility that it will inspire other readers to author and share similar fantasies – to hopefully infect the reader with his own fetishes, so that he might read more stories catering to those fetishes.

To provide an illustration of this subgenre, I will offer a close reading of three stories posted online in the early 2000s – Absman420's 'Cycle One', Wrestlr's 'Infiltration' and Magus's 'Four Weeks Later' – paying special attention to how their main characters approach the notion of risk management. 'Cycle One' (2002) is narrated by Sam Bennett, a professional author of detective fiction for pre-teen readers, who gradually discovers a mysterious conspiracy at his local gym.[23] A company named Cycle One is giving away free samples of its eponymous energy drink to the (all-male) gym-goers. Cycle One not only enables its drinkers to work out more frequently, lift more weight, and gain more muscular definition; it also turns them into devotees and proselytisers for the product. Sam, who is very cautious about what he consumes, declines his free sample of Cycle One, but, on each visit to the gym, he is accosted by more and more men insisting he has to try it, delivering an elaborate sales pitch for the ostensibly 'free' product. Suspicious, but compelled to investigate further, Sam pretends to drink his free sample of Cycle One – in reality, he has poured out the contents and replaced them with tap water – and tries to imitate the vapidly enthusiastic and exhibitionistic Cycle One addicts around him, to go undetected amongst the zombies. He makes one more visit to the gym, planning to collect a sample of Cycle One and get it chemically analysed, so that he might solve the mystery of this seemingly magic potion and its effects; however, he gets caught and is forced to consume a bottle of Cycle One. By the end of the story, Sam tells the reader that he intends to head back to the gym as soon as it opens that morning: 'Okay, look, here's the plan: I'll drink the bottle of shit they offer me today voluntarily, so they won't think I'm on to them. Don't worry, I'm in control of my own mind. Another bottle isn't gonna hurt me – I'll be fine. Besides, I'm benching. I want that fuckin' pump for my chest, you know? Can you blame me?' He signs off by saying: 'I'm fairly confident that you'll hear from me again. Drop me an email at AbsMan420@aol.com if you don't – or if maybe you want me to snag you a bottle of Cycle One. I'm tellin' ya friends, it feels fuckin' awesome!'

Sam begins the story as a seemingly reliable and sympathetic narrator: a rational, perceptive, resolute and prudent individual quite unlike the foolish, weak-willed and impulsive men who are becoming Cycle One zombies. Sam himself seems aware of this distinction and is rather smug about it: 'Unlike Lou, and the boys, and the firemen, and the old guy on the treadmill, and Coach himself, I would sleep well that night, not crashing from caffeine withdrawal. That's what they got, I thought, for ducking the FDA.' By the end of the story, however, Sam's belief in his rationality, risk-management abilities and self-control becomes comical; he's clearly coming under the mental influence of the viral product Cycle One, and he's beginning to recite the same promotional catchphrases spouted by its other users (e.g. 'it feels fuckin' awesome!'). The story thus subverts the mainstream contagion narrative's convention that the focal character – our ostensible identification character – will use his intelligence and superior risk-management skills to stay immune to the contagion's effects.

In a sense, Sam is always already infected, already one of 'them'. Some of Cycle One's main symptoms are the ways that it turns its users into promoters for the product, compelled to display their desirable designer bodies as testimonials to the product, extensions of the product. Yet long before he tries Cycle One, Sam is doing the same thing with his books; he tells us that book signings were 'a great way to make some bank, meet your fans and all that [. . . but] having the physique I have makes people less-than sympathetic about my arm being tired, especially kids. To thirteen year-old boys, I'm Superman.' Sam is a perfect neoliberal subject – a successful, independent self-promoter who takes care of his body and rationally assesses risk – and, as such, is perfect prey for this virus, which thrives under the same conditions. The ending – where readers are invited to e-mail the real author Absman420 (and not the fictional author Sam) in order to 'snag a bottle of Cycle One' – suggests that we readers, linked into a networked online culture, would make similarly easy marks for the virus.

It is important to note here that in 'Cycle One', as in most gay erotic viral transformation stories, the infection is spread through social networks in private space, rather than through contact with random strangers in public space. In *Times Square Red, Times Square Blue*, his acclaimed memoir/essay mourning the disappearance of New York's public sex culture, Samuel Delany draws a key distinction between 'contact' and 'networking', claiming that 'Networking tends to be professional and motive-driven. Contact tends to be more broadly social and appears random [. . .] Contact is associated with public space and the architecture and commerce that depend on and promote it. Thus contact is often an outdoor sport; networking tends to occur indoors.'[24] For Delany, the paradigmatic spaces of urban contact in pre-AIDS-era New York included public restrooms, adult movie theatres and gay saunas – all spaces where men from very different social backgrounds would develop relationships, some momentary but others lasting for years. The AIDS crisis helped solidify a perception of such random, cross-class contact as unsafe and unclean, fundamentally less hygienic than sexual relationships fostered through networking (e.g. private clubs, workplaces, dating services). Delany's book was published in 1999, the same year as Michael Warner's *The Trouble with Normal*, which also bemoaned the disappearance of New York's public sex culture, which was then being accelerated by two factors: gentrification and the rise of the internet.[25] One key difference between traditional 'pick-up spaces' such as gay bars and 'hook-up apps' like Grindr and Scruff is that the latter allow users to filter out 'undesirables' according to predetermined criteria.

The metaphor of the filter – used in many online platforms, from dating apps to search engines – is powerful and seductive. Traditionally, filters have been used to purify the water we drink and the air we breathe; all the harmful contaminants in the stream thus end up on the other side of the filter. By appropriating this metaphor, online platforms give users a sense of security and control; when we apply filters, we can tell ourselves that we are taking precautions, avoiding contact with dangerous people or websites that might otherwise appear in our stream. Several authors of gay erotic viral transformation fiction, however, have created stories that run counter to this logic, wherein the filter itself serves as the vector of infection. In Wrestlr's 'InFiltration' series, for instance, a hypnotist known only as Doc infiltrates a university's elite fraternities and athletics programmes, first by offering a 'mental training' course for athletes, who trust that this trained professional will help them set up 'mental filters' that will enable them to ignore distractions and achieve their peak performance while competing at sports.[26] As he explains to Luke, the first story's protagonist, 'That's the core of my filter system: Until the goal is achieved, only the important things will matter. Everything unimportant will not even be noticed.' Of course, with Doc determining what information counts as 'important' and what counts as 'unimportant', the mental filters bring the young men under his control, as only his commands make it through the filters and all contradictory thoughts are flagged and blocked as distractions. In the later instalments of the 'InFiltration' series, Doc's filters begin to go viral, as the young men he commands act as recruiters for him, using their social networks to hypnotise other influential men (including their fathers, team-mates and fraternity brothers), install the same set of mental filters in them. Here, the very tactics that neoliberal ideology proscribes to keep us safe – sticking to a selective social network of affiliated individuals, filtering out potential contaminants – become the vulnerabilities that Doc exploits. And as in 'Cycle One', intelligent, well-informed men who feel confident in their ability to assess and manage risk are among the most susceptible. When he meets Doc, Luke is well-read on the subject of sports hypnosis, and he is even aware of the techniques Doc is using to mirror his body language; however, this education is inextricably connected with his neoliberal fixation on competition and maximising performance, which ultimately bring him under the control of the virus Doc implants in his mind.

So why does this gay erotic fiction take such a different attitude toward risk management and the potentiality of contagion than the neoliberal approach we find in mainstream texts like *The Zombie Survival Guide*? One reason is that these online authors are writing in an erotic mode, and risk tends to be viewed differently when it's framed in these terms; as demonstrated even by popular 'trash' like the *50 Shades* books, erotic risk can be perceived as something desirable, not just a negative factor to be rationally controlled and minimised. However, it is also important to note that viral transformation stories like 'Cycle One' and 'InFiltration' are primarily written by and for gay men, for whom the risk of contagion through erotic activities has a special resonance. Although AIDS is almost never directly mentioned in these stories, I would argue that most of them are haunted by the spectre of the AIDS epidemic and its aftermath.

In my generation, gay men grew up with constant reminders that sexual contact between men might lead to AIDS. Indeed, the message that gay men get AIDS was so strong that it tended to drown out the subtle but important distinctions between sexual activities that carried a relatively high risk of HIV infection and those that carried a relatively low risk. Instead of a discourse about acts, we got discourses about proper and improper identities and desires, including misleading messages that promiscuous gay men got AIDS, while monogamous gay men did not. Viral transformation stories like 'Cycle One' break down the dichotomy between promiscuity and monogamy. Sam never mentions having a girlfriend or a boyfriend or a sexual history of any kind; for the purposes of the story he is effectively celibate. Yet his participation in social networks, however minimal – even at his gym, he's a bit of a loner – is enough 'promiscuity' to cause Sam to become infected with the contagion and to convert from 'Cycle One negative' to 'Cycle One positive'. In this way, the story challenges the neoliberal assumptions of mainstream contagion narratives which reassure us that risk can be effectively managed by smart, sensible individuals; Sam is an exemplar of self-discipline and social distancing, and yet he still ends up catching the contagion.

One of the stories that most clearly expresses the AIDS-era mindset is Magus's 'Four Weeks Later', which was written in 2003, the year after Danny Boyle's influential zombie movie *28 Days Later* was released.[27] Here, rather than being infected with a virus called Rage, the zombies are infected by a virus called Lust. The story's protagonist is a slim young man named Corey, who is one of the few humans left uninfected by the Lust. He scavenges food and supplies from abandoned store shelves, carefully calculating when to take the risk of leaving his secure underground bunker; as the narrator notes, in the four weeks since the start of the outbreak, 'he'd had to learn a lot about survival'. Corey is not only a survivor, he has outlasted many of his friends, and this mood of mourning underlies the story; one of the first sentences reads, 'Too many times he'd thought he was safe, only to lose friends to the Virus, to the Lust, almost losing himself. And now there was just him.' Such sentiments were depressingly common in the gay literature of the late 1980s and early 1990s, as writers recalled the friends they lost to another sexually transmitted virus, AIDS, acknowledging how close they came to contracting the virus as well.

Despite all his careful safety procedures, Corey is infected when one of the Lust-infected men drips pre-cum into an open cut on Corey's hand. However, Corey does not realise this at first, and he misinterprets the first signs of his infection: his growing horniness. As he reflects, 'This was the worst part of living with the Virus. He was human, he still had human needs, and one of those was sex. Most times he barely even thought about it – getting off often takes a back seat to survival – but he'd found that after tense moments he was almost always horny. The first few times it had freaked him out – the first symptom of the Lust was, well, lust – and even while he told himself that getting a hard on every now and then was perfectly normal, it always gave him a sense of unease.' Corey's sex drive thus functions both as a sign of his 'human needs' and as a sign that he is becoming *inhuman*, transforming into a Lust-infected monster. Again, the parallels with writing from the AIDS epidemic are striking; both depict the 'sense of unease' that occurs when a healthy libido becomes associated with pathology. The phrase 'living with the Virus' is also telling, suggesting that in some sense Corey is always already infected, since the virus has such a defining impact on his self-image and behaviour. When Corey transforms from a man who is 'living with the Virus' by trying to cautiously control any exposure to it, into a beast who is 'living with the Virus' by *ceding* control to it, his conversion evokes both horror and relief. Corey begins the story a frightened, reedy young man hiding in a dark underground bunker, but once he succumbs to the infection, he gains muscle, strength and masculine sexual characteristics, then literally comes out of the closet. Bounding toward the 'fresh air' he senses above ground, 'He reached the sunshine and stopped, grateful for the freedom, breathing the air, taking it into his wide chest. He reached up and stroked it with his left hand, his right hand went to his cock. It felt so good, so very good. He felt his powerful muscles flex as he came, and he let out a violent, guttural roar. Pleasure washed his brain free of any thought as he shot his load.'

In his book *Unlimited Intimacy*, psychoanalytic scholar Tim Dean examines the cultures of gay male sexual risk-taking, particularly the cultures of 'barebacking' (condomless anal sex) and 'bug chasing' (HIV- men who seek out HIV+ partners with the goal of becoming infected).[28] Among the many factors fuelling the barebacking trend, one is the way that AIDS has gone from being a death sentence to a treatable chronic condition, at least for first-world citizens with adequate healthcare. For a few barebackers, seroconversion may even come as a relief, as it means they no longer have to worry about contracting HIV. The small fringe group of 'bug chasers' even represent themselves as masculine subjects making an empowering choice, men who aren't 'afraid of the big bad bug' (as one chaser website puts it). This 'choose to seroconvert' discourse is like the perverse twin of Max Brooks's 'choose to survive' discourse; both place agency and fate in the hands of the individual, not the complex network of contagions he encounters. The viral transformation fiction I have examined is very different, depicting the individual's lack of agency and presenting scenarios where the virus 'outsmarts' the rational individual (rather than vice versa). In online comments to these stories, readers often express that they're rooting for the virus. For instance, one of the comments underneath 'Four Weeks Later' is entitled 'Fantastic ... more!' and reads, 'That was a great story. Can't wait to see him infect someone by cumming on them. Encore!' Rooting for the viral conversion when reading these stories also involves rooting for homosexuality; the men who get converted develop an attraction to other men, particularly those who have not already been infected. The notion of homosexuality as a contagion is nothing new; it pervades much homophobic discourse. Little wonder, then, that gay male writers and readers may feel that they are always already infected, always already contagious – and thus might root for the spread of the contagion rather than for the individuals who seek to remain 'pure'.

Despite their major differences, there is one key theme that unites gay erotic viral transformation fiction and mainstream narratives about zombie epidemics and other contagious outbreaks: a desire for simplicity. In gay erotic viral transformation fiction, becoming infected is also a path to simplifying one's life, setting aside all the complex calculations of risk versus reward, of indulgence versus delayed gratification. The mindlessness that is a key symptom of infection in stories like 'Four Weeks Later' (where 'Pleasure washed [Corey's] brain free of any thought') is arguably no worse than the neurotic *mindfulness* that is a key symptom of non-infection.

To sum up, what makes gay erotic viral transformation fiction so distinctive is its complex ambivalence towards the contagion it represents and the individuals who seek to resist it. These stories provide a counter-narrative to the mainstream movies, television programmes and books depicting epidemics, which suggest that avoiding infection is a game with predictable rules simple enough to be mastered. That kind of mastery is impossible in gay erotic viral transformation fiction, which I would suggest is more honest about the world in which we actually live. It is not a clean, simple game in which the individual can maintain control, but rather a miasma of social contagions and a complex web of interwoven networks, ideal breeding grounds for the viral.

Notes

1. Carol Clover, *Men, Women, and Chainsaws* (Princeton, NJ: Princeton University Press, 1992).
2. Max Brooks, *The Zombie Survival Guide* (New York: Three Rivers Press, 2003); Max Brooks, *World War Z: An Oral History of the Zombie War* (New York: Crown, 2006).
3. 'The Zombie Survival Guide', *Wikipedia*, *https://en.wikipedia.org/wiki/The_Zombie_Survival_Guide* (accessed 21 June 2018).
4. FEMA, 'Ready Campaign Promotes Disaster Preparedness with "Zombieland: Double Tap"', Federal Emergency Management Agency (FEMA), 9 October 2019, *https://www.fema.gov/news-release/2019/10/09/ready-campaign-promotes-disaster-preparedness-zombieland-double-tap* (accessed 27 January 2020). For the tagline, see FEMA, 'Zombies don't plan ahead. You can', *https://www.facebook.com/watch/?v=1667596443374622* (accessed 27 January 2020).
5. Brooks, *The Zombie Survival Guide*, p. xiv.
6. For more on the intersection of the zombie narrative and neoliberal ideology, see chapter 7 in this volume: Megen de Bruin-Molé, 'Killable Hordes, Chronic Others and "Mindful" Consumers: Rehabilitating the Zombie in Twenty-First-Century Popular Culture', in Sandra Becker, Megen de Bruin-Molé and Sara Polak (eds), *Embodying Contagion: The Viropolitics of Horror and Desire in Contemporary Discourse* (Cardiff: University of Wales Press, 2021), pp. 159–78.
7. Sally Brown et al., 'Risk, Resistance, and the Neoliberal Agenda: young people, health, and well-being in the UK, Canada, and Australia', *Health, Risk, and Society*, 15/4 (2013), 333–46, 333.
8. Ellen Defossez, 'Health and personal responsibility in the context of neoliberalism: Cultivating alertness, autonomy and accountability through three contemporary health practices', *The International Journal of Communication and Health*, 9 (2016), 73–9, 74.
9. Charles Mackay, *Extraordinary Popular Delusions and the Madness of Crowds* (London: Richard Bentley, 1841).
10. Melissa Matthews, 'Weight Gain is Contagious and You Could "Catch" Obesity from Your Neighbors, Study Finds', *Newsweek*, 24 January 2018, *http://www.newsweek.com/weight-gain-contagious-and-you-could-catch-obesity-your-neighbors-study-finds-789547* (accessed 27 January 2020).
11. Brandon Keim, 'Happiness and Sadness Spread Just Like Disease', *Wired*, 14 July 2010, *https://www.wired.com/2010/07/contagious-emotions/* (accessed

19 June 2019); Elle Kaplan, 'Why Negative People are Literally Killing You (and How to Protect Your Positivity)', *Medium*, 14 November 2016, *https://medium.com/the-mission/why-negative-people-are-literally-killing-you-and-how-to-obliterate-pessimism-from-your-life-eb85fadced87* (accessed 19 June 2019).

12. 'Your Facebook Friends Could Damage Your Credit Rating', *The Telegraph*, 27 August 2013, *https://www.telegraph.co.uk/finance/personalfinance/borrowing/loans/10268408/Your-Facebook-friends-could-damage-your-credit-rating.html* (accessed 19 June 2019).
13. *Resident Evil* (Osaka: Capcom, 1996–present); *Plants vs Zombies* (Seattle: PopCap, 2009–16); See also Dawn Stobbart, *Videogames and Horror: From Amnesia to Zombies, Run!* (Cardiff: University of Wales Press, 2019).
14. *Call of Duty* (Woodland Hills: Infinity Ward, 2003–present).
15. Philip Munz, Ioan Hudea, Joe Imad and Robert J. Smith, 'When Zombies Attack!: Mathematical Modeling of an Outbreak of Zombie Infection', in Jean M. Tchuenche and Christinah Chiyaka (eds), *Infectious Disease Modeling Research Progress* (Hauppauge: Nova Science, 2009), pp. 133–50.
16. Interestingly, this study avoids making the neoliberal assumption that strong and resourceful individuals will survive at a higher rate than others. However, the study relies on such simplistic models that its utility is questionable, especially if it is meant to inform policy on real disease outbreaks.
17. Lucy Mangan, 'Contagion! review – an epidemic of tedium', *The Guardian*, 22 March 2018, *https://www.theguardian.com/tv-and-radio/2018/mar/22/contagion-review-an-epidemic-of-tedium* (accessed 17 November 2019).
18. Petra Klepac, Stephen Kissler and Julia Gog, 'Contagion! The BBC Four Pandemic: The model behind the documentary', *Epidemics*, 24 (2018), 49–59.
19. Heather Myers, 'Crawling Off the Screen: An Ethnography of Live Action Zombie Events in the United States' (unpublished MA thesis, Harvard University, Cambridge, 2011), 67, *https://www.academia.edu/2493358/Crawling_off_the_Screen_An_Ethnography_of_Live_Action_Zombie_Events_in_the_United_States* (accessed 17 November 2019).
20. Myers, 'Crawling Off the Screen', 68–9.
21. Myers, 'Crawling Off the Screen', 68.
22. Terry Eagleton, *Walter Benjamin, or Towards a Revolutionary Criticism* (London: Verso, 1981), p. 148.
23. A later Absman420 story, the superhero comic parody 'King Rex', reveals that the addictive and transformative special ingredient in Cycle One is actually the supervillain's semen, further underscoring the parallels to AIDS and

seroconversion. Absman420, 'Cycle One', *Erotic Mind-Control Story Archive,* 19 January 2002, *https://www.mcstories.com/CycleOne/index.html* (accessed 17 November 2019); Absman420, 'King Rex', *Gay Spiral Stories*, 28 February 2014, https://www.gayspiralstories.com/newStory/show/958 (accessed 2 June 2016).

24. Samuel R. Delany, *Times Square Red, Times Square Blue* (New York and London: New York University Press, 1999), p. 192.
25. Michael Warner, *The Trouble with Normal* (New York: Free Press, 1999).
26. Wrestlr, 'InFiltration', *Erotic Mind Control Story Archive*, 2001, *https://mcstories.com/InFiltrationWrestlr/index.html* (accessed 17 June 2002).
27. Magus, 'New Story: 4 Weeks Later', *The Evolution Forum: Male Muscle Growth*, 20 September 2003, *https://archive.muscle-growth.org/threads/413-p1.html* (accessed 15 June 2017); *28 Days Later*, Danny Boyle, dir. (DNA Films/UK Film Council, 2003).
28. Tim Dean, *Unlimited Intimacy: Reflections on the Subculture of Barebacking* (Chicago: Chicago University Press, 2009).

9

'This Long Disease, My Life'

AIDS Activism and Contagious Bodies in Larry Kramer's *The Normal Heart* and *The Destiny of Me*

Astrid Haas

IN HIS PERFORMANCE piece *The Night Larry Kramer Kissed Me* (1992), American actor David Drake powerfully shows how Larry Kramer's drama *The Normal Heart* (1985) inspired him to become an AIDS activist. Watching a performance of the play during its first run on Broadway alerted him to AIDS as 'the silent, unprintable killer' seemingly 'stalking' gay men.[1] Drake's depiction of AIDS also testifies to the mainstream media's coverage of the growing AIDS epidemic in the mid-1980s, which oscillated between moralising stories and ignoring the subject. In a similar vein, the YouTuber Simón El Mono (Simón Aguilar) in a rap song captures the popular anxiety about the COVID-19 pandemic ravaging the world in the spring of 2020: 'No one predicted this entire epidemic . . . / I have the entire planet in my grip . . . / I invade your territory and I won't slow down . . . / I arrive in full, I am the venom.'[2] Both Drake's play and El Mono's rap are tightly connected to the widespread societal perceptions of AIDS and COVID-19 at the time they entered public conscience. As a highly infectious droplet infection that has quickly moved around the world, COVID-19 is acknowledged as a threat to anyone, even though its origin in China has led to political scapegoating of the country. Moreover, in several countries, people perceived to be Chinese as well as healthcare personnel have reported abuse and discrimination for being seen as potential carriers of the virus.[3] AIDS is much more difficult to contract than COVID-19, as its viral carrier, HIV, needs to enter the human bloodstream. However, as it particularly affects gay men and intravenous drug users in the West, mainstream societies often view it as a 'disease of deviance'. This is based on the widespread perception of both homosexuality and AIDS in the 1980s as pathological conditions that caused and marked the 'deformed' identities and 'contagious' bodies of those who seemingly threatened the social and/or medical health of the nation.[4]

While COVID-19 in 2020 appears to have triggered primarily musical responses that can be easily circulated via online video platforms, stage plays were at the forefront of cultural interventions into hegemonic views of AIDS and homosexuality in 1980s' America. Among them, Larry Kramer's diptych of plays about a gay writer's struggle against AIDS and its social stigma, *The Normal Heart* (1985) and *The Destiny of Me* (1991), represents one of the most prominent examples of this body of writing from the United States to this day.[5] Although AIDS and HIV remain a subject of American literature, their role has shifted, owing to interconnected medical and societal changes. On the one hand, retroviral medical treatment has turned HIV/AIDS into a chronic, manageable disease in Western countries since the mid-1990s. On the other hand, gay and AIDS activism has increased the acceptance of gay men in Western countries. Resulting from this dual 'normalisation', American drama now tends to present AIDS either as an urgent issue of the recent past or as an integral part of contemporary American life or as an ongoing health threat in other world regions.[6]

Because of the shifting social perception and theatrical representation of HIV/AIDS in the United States, only a few AIDS dramas from the 1980s and early 1990s, especially Tony Kushner's two-part *Angels in America* (1991/1992) and Kramer's *The Normal Heart*, have retained a prominent place in the national theatre repertory and were further adapted for cinema and television.[7] This chapter analyses the depiction of the contagious gay male body and its connection to ideas of a deformed identity in *The Normal Heart* and *The Destiny of Me*. Based on close readings of the two plays against the backdrop of social discourses of contagion and monstrosity, I investigate how they employ images of a 'diseased' life, manifest in deformed identities and contagious bodies, to pursue an ambivalent political agenda. I argue that *The Normal Heart* and *The Destiny of Me* scrutinise society's disregard for gay men's lives based on their dual association with a pathological sexual identity and a lethal pandemic. However, I also show how the two plays simultaneously undermine their very social critique, as their parallels between AIDS and homosexuality and their striving for gay assimilation to heterosexual society somewhat confirm homophobic ideas of gay social, sexual and medical deficiency.

Contagion, Monstrosity and HIV/AIDS Discourses

'Contagion is the dominant horror of the 21st century', Dan Dinello writes, as it 'corrodes our sense of individual, national and global security'.[8] Originally meaning 'the communication of disease from body to body', the term also entails the spread of ideas, practices and emotions.[9] Fears of contagion articulate anxieties not only about communicable diseases but also about social change.[10] The power of contagion to escape human control and to transform entire societies has particularly triggered the desire to identify the living agents and vectors of infection, as can be seen in the current debates about identifying a 'patient zero' of COVID-19.[11] In line with traditional moral frameworks that tie social deviance to physical and/or moral deformation, both causes and carriers of contagion often figure in popular discourses as veritable monsters, whose distorted physical shape corresponds to their social transgressions.[12] Dinello points out:

> Emerging as dangerous invaders that want to penetrate physical borders, contagious monsters transform and mutate the body's genetic material to serve . . . the uncontrollable, exponential proliferation of these hungry, demanding predators that want to subvert civilization, turning us into them. Virulent contagion . . . suggests a subversive order of infiltration, takeover, and spread.[13]

This discourse builds upon the monster as a cultural figure which, according to Jeffrey Cohen, 'incorporates [the] fear, desire, anxiety, and fantasy' of a period and culture.[14] Its power lies in its ability to transform itself to respond to and further entice socio-cultural changes. The monster is a 'harbinger of crisis' whose hybrid body undermines notions of reason, order and social distinction.[15] Its distorted physical features and malignant intentions represent difference as a threat to society; they serve as a warning against trespassing the boundaries that define communities and thereby 'normalize and enforce' these borders.[16] As it not only arouses fear and loathing but also the desire for its freedom and alterity, the monster urges us to question our attitudes to alterity that manifest themselves in our very creation of monsters.[17]

In discourses of contagion, the monster has gained a particular momentum since the early 1980s, when medical practitioners in the United States publicised the first deaths from an unknown source later identified and labelled Acquired Immune Deficiency Syndrome (AIDS). The advent of AIDS not only represents the most severe global pandemic between the outbreaks of the Spanish Influenza in 1918 and COVID-19 in 2020 but it also shattered the widely held belief in Western industrialised countries that epidemics of infectious diseases in their territories were a matter of the past. The fact that AIDS was quickly understood as a lethal epidemic transmitted most frequently in the West through sexual intercourse among men or contaminated injection drug needles fundamentally shaped the public response to the syndrome.[18] Owing to their mutability, manipulation of host organisms, causing abhorrent symptoms and being difficult to treat, viruses often evoke notions of secret invasion, subversion and monstrous hybridity, as Simón El Mono's coronavirus rap poignantly shows. In the 1980s and early 1990s, discursive representations commonly framed HIV as a foreign invader or coloniser of the human body. Given the function of the body as a 'carrier of culture, values, and morality', Julia Epstein argues, the collapse of the immune system HIV causes and the virus's connection to gay male sex or IV drug use threaten not only the boundaries of the individual, physical body but also 'the borders of social and moral categories'.[19]

Building upon the paradox perception of the socio-cultural other as 'both abject weakness and powerful threat',[20] popular and even some scientific discourses commonly portrayed gay or bisexual men in a contradictory manner. On the one hand, these groups figured as responsible for their own (potential) HIV infection, as their presumably passive, feminised bodies 'allowed or even encouraged the virus's transmission'.[21] On the other hand, they simultaneously appear in these discourses as a menace to public health and national values, as they would 'lure' male youths into homosexuality and thereby expose them to HIV infection or even consciously spread the virus.[22] Especially popular discourses further tended to pit gay/bisexual men and drug injectors as 'guilty AIDS carriers' against the implicitly 'innocent victims' of the epidemic such as people infected with HIV through contaminated blood products or the heterosexual partners of bisexuals or drug users. Usually conceptualised as one-way receptors of infection, the latter groups were then used as signifiers of an endangered society to justify force and control against the socio-sexually deviant. Constructing clear categories of 'AIDS risk groups' against the background of a non-specified (but by implication white, heterosexual and middle-class) 'general population', Alan Peterson and Deborah Lupton point out, 'constitutes a way of defining the implicated from the immune, the pathological from the healthy, relying on social properties' rather than individual behaviour.[23]

AIDS and the Contagious Body in *The Normal Heart*

During the 1980s and early 1990s, theatre and drama were at the forefront among the cultural responses to the AIDS crisis in the United States. Especially dramatic works coming out of the already politicised and particularly affected gay male community scrutinised the homophobic public discourse and policies in the country, marked by disregard for the health of gay men and aiming at preventing the spread of HIV/AIDS among heterosexual society. Although many gay-authored and -themed AIDS plays address the gay male experience with the epidemic, few explore the impact of the dual stigma of homosexuality and HIV/AIDS on a person's entire life so deeply as Larry Kramer's *The Normal Heart* (1985) and *The Destiny of Me* (1992). Based on the playwright's personal experience as a co-founder of Gay Men's Health Crisis, the first gay AIDS activist organisation in New York, *The Normal Heart* chronicles the first three years of the AIDS crisis in that city from a gay activist point of view. Alerted by the physician Emma Brookner, the gay writer Ned Weeks attempts to incite the deeply frightened gay community of New York into action against a new epidemic ravaging among them. Ned's political quest is set alongside his private struggle for acceptance by his heterosexual brother and his relationship with the AIDS-afflicted journalist Felix.

Ever since its first production, *The Normal Heart* has met with critique for its political agenda, which targets gay male promiscuity as a key source of the spread of HIV/AIDS, the gay closet as a hindrance to effective AIDS activism and both as barriers to gay socio-sexual assimilation and mainstream acceptance.[24] However, the play crucially addresses a host of personal and societal responses to AIDS in the early 1980s with a particular focus on gay men living with AIDS. This is a common feature of gay-focused American AIDS drama from the mid-1980s to the late

1990s, which sought to counter the hegemonic societal discourse about the epidemic with its emphasis on disfiguring symptoms, often placed in a moralising explanatory framework of socio-sexual deviance leading to disease and death. Especially plays set in the first decade of the epidemic such as William Hoffman's *As Is* (1985), Cheryl West's *Before It Hits Home* (1991) or Kushner's *Angels in America* show gay men struggling with tell-tale symptoms of end-stage AIDS and their social stigma as signifiers of the 'gay plague', as AIDS was commonly labelled then.[25]

Set in a GP's surgery, the opening scene of *The Normal Heart* ties in with these works and informs audiences about some of the major symptoms of full-blown AIDS – night sweats, fevers, swollen glands and purple Kaposi's Sarcoma lesions – as well as the terror they evoked in gay men in the early 1980s as signifiers of doom. 'Did you see that guy in there's spots?', one man in the waiting room asks his companion and soon afterward admits, 'I'm tired all the time. I wake up in swimming pools of sweat . . . I'm all swollen, like something ready to explode.'[26] These striking symptoms not only mark people as AIDS-afflicted but also physically disfigure them. In so doing, they stigmatise gay men with AIDS as powerless social outsiders. As Peter Michael Pober observes, 'the marked body is the disempowered body. Stripped of its capacity to appear "normal", it is treated as . . . near death, untouched, diseased'.[27] A later scene in the play exemplifies how the physical change the AIDS-afflicted body undergoes also deforms a patient's sense of self. 'Don't touch me!', Felix urges Ned, 'I'm so ugly. I cannot stand it when you look at my body.'[28]

'The marked body', Pober continues, 'becomes both an indicator of contagion (physical and psychological) and a justification for homophobia'.[29] Already burdened with the triple stigma of communicable disease, physical disfiguration and sexual outsider status, gay men with AIDS and their social environments frequently faced social ostracism resulting from growing public fears of infection in the 1980s. At the time *The Normal Heart* is set, limited medical knowledge about the infection routes of HIV, paired with several highly mediatised cases of HIV infection among women and children, had raised anxiety within heterosexual society, which had previously deemed itself safe from the epidemic, about HIV transmission through casual contacts. It is no surprise then that early AIDS dramas like *As Is* and *Before It Hits Home* prominently address the subject. While they validate popular fears of infection from seropositive friends or family members, they criticise the discrimination many persons living with AIDS (PWAs) experienced at the time as a result of these fears.[30]

The Normal Heart articulates these different anxieties and their impact on public perceptions and treatments of gay men with AIDS most powerfully in the story Ned's friend Bruce relates about the last days of his partner, Albert:

> The pilot wouldn't take off and I refused to leave the plane . . . Then, after we take off, Albert loses his mind . . . and then, right there, on the plane, he becomes . . . incontinent . . . and all these people are staring at us and moving away in droves . . . And when we got to Phoenix, there's a police van waiting for us and all the police are in protective rubber clothing, they looked like fucking astronauts, and by the time we got to the hospital where Albert's mother had fixed up his room real nice, Albert was dead . . . The hospital doctors refused to examine him to put a cause of death on the death certificate, and without a death certificate the undertakers wouldn't take him away, and neither would the police. Finally, some orderly comes in and stuffs Albert in a heavy-duty Glad bag . . . and he puts him out in the back alley with the garbage . . . I paid him, and then his mother and I carried the bag to her car and we finally found a black undertaker who cremated him for a thousand dollars, no questions asked.

Dying from AIDS, this scene powerfully argues, means to be denied one's humanity, manifest in Albert's losing control over his mind and body, his being treated like a monstrous alien from outer space while he is alive and as a piece of contagious garbage after his death. His geographic journey home becomes the symbolic trip to hell homo- and AIDS-phobic society considers – and itself triggers – life as a gay man and person with AIDS to be. For the gay PWA, Phoenix does not entail the possibility of rising from the ashes but a clandestine cremation that leaves no space for his loved ones to publicly acknowledge his life and death.

While the play does not reiterate Albert's dehumanisation by having his suffering and death acted out on stage, it nevertheless reifies the PWA as the object of a tale told by another, non-afflicted man. And, indeed, exemplified in the figures of Ned and his friends and fellow activists, *The Normal Heart* mainly focuses on the ways (supposedly) HIV-negative gay men respond to the nascent AIDS epidemic. Typical for popular discourses and media images of contagion, mainstream American society has widely perceived asymptomatic carriers of communicable diseases as malevolent, one-way vectors of infection and often causally connected their medical condition to racial, social or sexual alterity. What further heightened the carriers particularly 'monstrous subversion' of American society was the inability to immediately recognise them as medical others as well, which undermines the idea of social distinction based on clear visual markers of difference.[32] In contrast to this view, the fear of unknowingly infecting a partner haunted the gay community in particular before the HIV antibody test became available by the mid-1980s.[33]

The Normal Heart validates gay men's anxieties about spreading HIV to their loved ones and presents asymptomatic carriers like Bruce as caring human beings rather than as uncontrollable threat.[34] In one scene of the drama, Bruce confesses, 'I'm so scared I'm some sort of carrier. [Albert's death] makes three people I've been with who are dead. I went to Emma and I begged her: please test me somehow, please tell me if I'm giving this to people.' Ned complements this personal testimony with a rhetorical question about the impact HIV carriership had on the entire gay community, 'When are we going to admit we might be spreading this?'[35] What renders this otherwise pivotal moment of self-reflection problematic, however, is its placement in the context of Ned's crusade against promiscuity, which he considers a barrier to gay assimilation to mainstream society. As he argues that giving up casual sex 'is not a civil-rights issue [but] a contagion issue',[36] Ned disconnects sexual practice from gay identity. In so doing, he not only ignores the crucial role promiscuity played for gay liberation and the development of a positive gay sexual identity in a homophobic environment. Instead of searching for a pragmatic solution to the dilemma, such as advocating safer sex measures, Ned's radical striving for heterosexual acceptance confirms mainstream society's vilification of gay men as monstrous health threat based on their 'spreading' the 'diseases' of homosexuality and AIDS.[37]

In addition to scrutinising discriminating personal responses to AIDS, *The Normal Heart* unmasks the homophobic fear of 'social contagion' through association with the gay community which informed the response of political authorities, the media and society at large to the epidemic in the mid-1980s. 'You have a mayor who's a bachelor and I assume afraid of being perceived as too friendly to anyone gay', Emma Brookner argues in *The Normal Heart*. Ned adds that the *New York Times* 'won't even use the word "gay" . . . To them we're still homosexuals.'[38] In another scene, he reproaches his brother Ben for refusing to support his AIDS activism. 'Aren't you afraid your corporate clients will say, "Was that your faggot brother I saw on TV?"', Ned asks rhetorically.

His conclusion from this encounter goes even further than the other examples: 'The single-minded determination of all you people to forever see us as sick helps keep us sick.'[39] In so arguing, he points out how viewing homosexuality as a disease became a kind of self-fulfilling prophesy, as mainstream society's homophobic reluctance to tackle the gay-coded AIDS epidemic crucially contributed to its spread among gay men and thus to the illness of their community.

What mars the power of Ned's critique of American homophobia in *The Normal Heart*, Pober points out, is his 'failing to destigmatize the image-laden gay body . . . that was marked before AIDS'.[40] When Ben characterises gay men as a kind of freak show – saying 'I open magazines and I see pictures of you guys in leather and chains and whips and black masks' – Ned does not defend the diversity of the gay community but distances himself from what he, too, perceives as their bodily and sexual aberrations.[41] Moreover, Ned's repeated attempts to obtain Ben's unconditional love articulates the play's persistent striving to prove the healthiness of homosexuality and its social sameness to heterosexuality. According to Jacob Juntunen, this was a crucial factor for the popularity of the drama among heterosexual viewers.[42] Thus, although the piece scrutinises the stigmatisation of gay men and PWAs, it simultaneously confirms the heteronormative social order and especially biased mainstream society's framing of gay men as weak, deficient, and/or diseased. In such a perception, AIDS only inscribes the 'monstrosity' of homosexuality visibly on the gay male body.

Deformed Identities in *The Destiny of Me*

The parallel perception of AIDS and homosexuality as disempowering diseases leaving their marks on the gay body and psyche also figures prominently in *The Destiny of Me*, the play with which Larry Kramer returned to his protagonist Ned Weeks seven years after *The Normal Heart*. While it did not attract as much attention as the earlier piece, this sequel met with a much more favourable reception, garnering praise especially for the way it blends political critique and family drama.[43] Now HIV-positive himself, Ned undergoes an experimental treatment at the National Institutes of Health (NIH). As he encounters his younger self, Alexander, there, he embarks upon an inner journey through crucial moments of his life as a gay Jewish American. In interweaving the two narrative threads – Ned's current AIDS treatment and the remembrance of his youth – the play integrates the AIDS crisis into the context of an individual life story, a family chronicle and recent American history. The parallels of physical and emotional suffering in past and present suggest a continuity of experience across time. In so doing, the drama employs AIDS 'as the catalyst for an exploration of [Ned's] life, sexual orientation, and sense of purpose'.[44]

Like *The Normal Heart*, *The Destiny of Me* looks at the then-current state of affairs concerning the AIDS epidemic in the United States from a gay activist and patient perspective. A key setting of the play, the hospital does not represent scientific progress but, on the contrary, a dehumanising force. It further signifies the ongoing failure of medical science in halting or curing the AIDS epidemic, despite its advanced technological means. As a hospitalised AIDS patient, Ned is reduced to a state of powerlessness that manifests itself in the play in two striking images. On the one hand, his treatment forces him into a physical symbiosis with the medical equipment, connecting his body to several technical apparatuses that serve as an extension of his blood circuit.[45] In contrast to hegemonic discourses of the cyborg as a particularly powerful version of the monster, Ned's hybrid body resulting from this symbiosis is forced into immobility and passivity, and he regains full social agency only when he disconnects from the machines in the final scene. Signifying on the words 'to excel' and 'accelerator', the tell-tale name of the key apparatus, Ex-Cell-Aerator, further captures the notion of unfulfilled promise when the machine fails to improve Ned's medical condition. On the other hand, Ned compares his social status to that of a laboratory animal. While he is cognitively above mice and apes, he enjoys less social protection than the actual animals used to test his treatment. As his nurse tells Ned, the medical researchers 'have to guarantee each chimp a thirty-thousand-dollar retirement endowment. Their activists are better than yours.'[46]

The Destiny of Me underlines this critique of the American medical establishment and its dealing with the AIDS epidemic in three scenes that focus on blood. In the first of these, the nurse enters Ned's hospital room right after AIDS activists drowned her in fake blood. Her stained clothes mark this representative of the medical system as a 'perpetrator' who has the blood of her patients on her hands.[47] In a later scene, Ned launches an angry diatribe against the 'tyranny of the blood test':

> We are being tested for the presence of a virus that may or may not be the killer. We are being tested to discover if this and/or that miraculous new discovery that may or may not kill the virus which may

> or may not be the killer is working. We live in constant terror that the number of healthy cells, which may or may not be an accurate indicator of anything at all and which the virus which may or may not be the killer may or may not be destroying, will decline and fall.

Although the passage does not address the physical disfiguration of AIDS patients, the notion of 'tyranny' and the angry litany of 'may or may nots' convey the tremendous psychic impact blood tests had on the life of PWAs and the still limited medical knowledge about the syndrome in the early 1990s. As a powerful tool to designate HIV serostatus, medical condition or treatment success, the blood test not only symbolises the volatile identity of HIV/AIDS patients but also evokes the 'blood testimony' of martyrdom.

The final scene of *The Destiny of Me* reinforces this notion of sacrifice. The concept of martyrdom turns a victim of violence into a hero who dies for a purpose, whose suffering is thus endowed with meaning for their community and who is immortalised through their collective memory.[49] When he hears about the failure of his AIDS treatment in the play, Ned throws around blood bags and disconnects his body from the medical tubes, gushing his blood across the stage.[50] By closing with the image of its protagonist as a martyr-like figure, the drama once again indicts the disregard the political and medical establishments, represented here by the NIH and its politically savvy medical director, showed for gay men's health. As it exposes actors and audiences to what represents the danger of HIV-contaminated blood, the drama forces spectators into the position the nurse found herself in earlier in the play and thus reminds them of their own implication as members of American society in the 'sacrifice' of gay lives. However, the scene simultaneously undermines its political critique, as Ned's symbolically placing the audience at risk for HIV infection confirms the homophobic stereotype of the gay PWA as a contagious threat to the health of the nation.

To viewers familiar with both of Kramer's dramas, the final scene of *The Destiny of Me* recalls an earlier passage in *The Normal Heart*, in which Ned, enraged about Felix's having given up the fight for his health, throws around a milk carton and food on stage.[51] While this is the only scene in the earlier play that shows Ned weak and desperate, *The Destiny of Me* explores the complexity of its protagonist in greater length. It connects the AIDS play to the family drama by setting Ned's hospitalisation for AIDS alongside Alexander's coming of age in a homophobic family.

The drama aptly captures what these plot lines have in common when Ned's nurse quotes Alexander Pope's famous phrase 'this long disease, my life'.[52] Originally expressing the eighteenth-century poet's lifelong struggle with chronic pain, a deformed body and professional controversies, the line can be equally applied to Ned's condition. It foregrounds the parallels in the way American mainstream society in the 1980s and early 1990s dealt with what it perceived to be the entangled 'diseases' of gay men: the pathological condition as which homosexuality had been framed and treated by American psychoanalysts from the 1940s through the 1970s and the gay-coded AIDS epidemic.[53]

The reluctant political concern of the American political, social and medical establishments with AIDS is accordingly presented as mainstream society's renewed attempts to rid itself from the 'ill(ness)' of homosexuality. The drama establishes this parallel most strikingly in setting the account of Alexander's undergoing years of psychotherapy to 'cure' his sexuality alongside Ned's medical treatment for his AIDS. In having the two protagonists of the piece comment upon not only their own but also each other's experiences from a perspective of either retrospective knowledge or youthful foresight, the play powerfully conveys the painful errors of judgment in past and present, heightened by the failure of both therapies. Moreover, the play recurs to the very imagery of homosexuality as a disease and of gay men as vectors of contagion that dominated the mainstream discursive framing of homosexuality and gay men as societal health threats in the first decade of AIDS. 'You little parasite', Ned calls his younger self in one scene. 'You're like the very virus itself, and I can't get rid of you.' Alexander, in turn, describes his sexuality in a way more befitting Ned's HIV/AIDS: 'It doesn't want to die. And fights tenaciously to stay alive, against all odds . . . no matter what anyone does to try and kill it.'[54]

Even though it scrutinises pathologising homosexuality and in particular the role of psychoanalysis played herein, *The Destiny of Me* is ripe with elements of psychoanalytical theory and the Weeks family appears like a case study of mid-twentieth-century psychoanalysis.[55] In an early flashback scene, Alexander's narration of how a neighbour bribed him for sex in early adolescence evokes the homophobic stereotype of gay men 'recruiting' boys to their 'lifestyle'. In a similar vein, his father Richard understands his son's difference as a kind of gender inversion resulting from a weak father and an overbearing mother. Once again, it is the body through which the gay youth's 'monstrous' alterity manifests itself in the play and which becomes the site of its oppression. For Richard, his son's socio-sexual deviance shows in the boy's shaving his pubic hair, love of theatrical performance and joy of dressing up, and the father's 'remedy' is corporal punishment.[56] While Alexander's body itself did not show any previous signs of otherness, the bruises resulting from Richard's beatings render his social transgression visible, turning him into the 'monster' that can be identified and duly coerced to restore social order.

In contrast to Richard's response, Ben views his sibling's homosexuality as a psychic illness that must be cured through psychoanalysis. However, Ben's forcing his brother to undergo a string of psychotherapies leaves lasting scars on Alexander's psyche that turn out to be as painful as Richard's paternal rejection of his younger son. 'Every social structure I'm supposed to be a part of . . . tells me over and over what I feel and think and do is sick', Ned sums up his lifelong struggle for self-acceptance.[57] Recurring one more time to the gay body, *The Destiny of Me* undermines the heteronormative view of homosexuality as a disease of otherness that shows in gay bodies' physical differences from mainstream society. Among others, Ned reflects upon his growing physical and psychic resemblance to his father. He tells his mirror image in one scene, 'You even look like Richard . . . I am more my father's child than ever I wanted to be. I fought so hard not to look like you. I've fought so hard not to inherit your failure.'[58]

The Destiny of Me further targets homophobic violence by placing Alexander's subjugation to beatings and psychotherapy alongside the Jewish experience in the twentieth century. In brief but compelling references, Ned suggests certain parallels between the work of his physician at the NIH, on the one hand, and the medical crimes of euthanasia and the Holocaust carried out under the German Nazi regime, on the other. Moreover, Kramer's drama sets Alexander's struggling with his environment's homophobia alongside his family's encounters with McCarthy-era American anti-Semitism and the pressure of conformity. Alexander's adolescent flight from his family also reiterates his mother's youthful immigration to the United States to escape anti-Jewish pogroms in Russia.[59] These analogies powerfully highlight the continuity of social prejudice inflicting suffering upon people. Yet, by limiting most of these references to the realism and domestic sphere of the Weeks family, the play limits their politically critical potential. Thus 'balancing' Ned's verbal outbursts against medical inefficiency and government homophobia in the hospital scenes, the domestic moments steer the piece into the 'safe haven' of bourgeois family drama, which allows audiences to experience the cathartic effects of personal tragedy without necessarily feeling personally affected or called to action.

Conclusion

In his essay 'Theatre and the Plague', Antonin Artaud reassesses the classical and early modern understanding of the theatre as a force of contagion working upon its audiences. Like the plague,

> Theatre is a disease because it is a final balance that cannot be obtained without destruction. It . . . reveals their dark powers and hidden strengths to men, urging them to take a noble, more heroic stand in the face of destiny than they would have assumed without it.[60]

Songs about COVID-19 or theatre about AIDS cannot stop the spread of the two afflictions, cure the sick, or alleviate trauma. Yet, both art forms can, and have been doing so, intervene in the societal discourses on and representations of these pandemics by providing spectators with biomedical knowledge, outlining forms and fields of political activism and critique, as well as creating a sense of community that validates the experiences of the affected.[61]

This chapter has shown that, and how, Larry Kramer's plays *The Normal Heart* and *The Destiny of Me* criticise the way mainstream social and medical discourses of the 1980s and early 1990s pathologised homosexuality as 'monstrous' aberration and AIDS as both its marker and its consequence. *The Destiny of Me* particularly targets the historical tradition of viewing same-sex desire as a disease in its own right as well as the physical or psychic violence unleashed upon gay men in an attempt to eliminate this 'ill'. Both dramas scrutinise how these discourses conflate and denigrate gay men and PWAs as threats to the social and/or medical health of the nation. They particularly expose the ways this vilification manifests itself in representations of gay (and) HIV-positive bodies as contagious and of gay male identities as deformed. The two plays validate not only popular fears of HIV infection but also gay men's concerns about contracting as well as spreading the virus. At the same time, they criticise the resulting discrimination of gay men and PWAs and they especially target the homophobically informed reluctance with which the medical and political establishments responded to the AIDS epidemic.

However, the two dramas absorb part of their critical potential through their argumentation and imagery. Both *The Normal Heart* and *The Destiny of Me* connect gay sexuality to illness as well as evoke the popular stereotype of gay men as 'monstrous' creatures who recruit boys to their 'lifestyle' and whose contagious bodies, resulting from their careless sexual risk-taking, expose others to HIV infection. Although meant to inspire critical reflection in viewers and counter homophobic discourses, these allusions may be taken to confirm the very biases they seek to undermine. Especially *The Normal Heart* partially blames anti-gay discrimination on gay male cowardice and sexual irresponsibility. Staying in the closet and engaging in promiscuous sex figure here exclusively as self-imposed barriers to gay men's assimilation to mainstream culture. Advocating marriage as the path to societal acceptance, the drama strikingly anticipates the de-radicalisation of mainstream gay political activism since the 1990s, as it moved from demanding sexual freedom toward civil rights claims, particularly marriage equality.[62] This approach may be one reason for the play's ongoing resonance with theatre audiences.

In addition to engaging in this discourse of gay social sameness to heterosexual society that affirms the prevailing socio-sexual order, both *The Normal Heart* and *The Destiny of Me* further subscribe to the American discourse of social mobility through individual self-management and improvement, which fits well into contemporary neoliberalism and is another likely source of the ongoing appeal of *The Normal Heart.*[63] Despite their admirable exposure of discriminatory discourses of sexuality and disease, the two dramas privilege individual psychological explanations and solutions over a systematic socio-political critique of structural homophobia in American society and its connection to prevailing ideologies of class, gender, family and nation. In so doing, they contribute to the very vilification of gay men as 'contagious monsters' they seek to undermine.

Notes

1. David Drake, *The Night Larry Kramer Kissed Me* (New York: Anchor Books, 1994), p. 14.
2. Simón El Mono, 'Rap del Coronavirus', *YouTube.com*, 6 March 2020, rpt. *Letras.com*, *https://www.letras.com/simonelmono/rap-del-coronavirus-2020/* (accessed 8 May 2020), ll. 7, 9, 16, 18, my trans.
3. Delan Devakumar et al., 'Racism and discrimination in COVID-19 responses', *The Lancet* 395, 1 April 2020, 1194, *https://www.thelancet.com/journals/lancet/article/PIIS0140-6736(20)30792-3/fulltext* (accessed 8 May

2020); Sophie Roborgh and Larissa Fast, 'Healthcare workers are still coming under attack during the coronavirus pandemic', *The Conversation*, 28 April 2020, *https://theconversation.com/healthcare-workers-are-still-coming-under-attack-during-the-coronavirus-pandemic-136573* (accessed 8 May 2020).

4. Astrid Haas, *Stages of Agency: The Contributions of American Drama to the AIDS Discourse* (Heidelberg: Winter, 2011), pp. 38–40, 43–5, 51–3; Sabrina Hüttner, '"No country for the infirm": Capitalism, AIDS, and American Drama', in Eva Boesenberg, Reinhard Isensee and Martin Klepper (eds), *American Economies* (Heidelberg: Winter, 2012), pp. 261–80, 266–7.
5. For an overview of recent book-length studies on American AIDS writing, especially drama, see Haas, *Stages of Agency*; Monica B. Pearl, *AIDS Literature and Gay Identity: The Literature of Loss* (New York: Routledge, 2013); Jacob Juntunen, *Mainstream AIDS Theatre, the Media, and Gay Civil Rights: Making the Radical Palatable* (New York: Routledge, 2016); Alyson Campbell and Dirk Gindt (eds), *Viral Dramaturgies: HIV and AIDS in Performance in the Twenty-First Century* (New York: Palgrave Macmillan, 2018); Aimee Pozorski, Jennifer J. Lavoie and Christine J. Cynn (eds), *Literary and Visual Representations of HIV/AIDS: Forty Years Later* (Lanham, MD: Lexington Books, 2019).
6. Stephen Farrier, 'Re-membering AIDS, Dis-membering Form', in Alyson Campbell and Dirk Gindt (eds), *Viral Dramaturgies: HIV and AIDS in Performance in the Twenty-First Century* (London: Palgrave Macmillan, 2018), pp. 155–72, 158–61.
7. Pearl, *AIDS Literature and Gay Identity*, pp. 112–13. For detailed discussions of these plays and their impact, see Haas, *Stages of Agency*, pp. 96–121, 154–74, 191–236; Juntunen, *Mainstream AIDS Theatre*, pp. 33–52, 60–87; Dirk Visser, 'Countering the Plague: AIDS Theatre as a Site of Memory', in Aimee Pozorski, Jennifer J. Lavoie and Christine J. Cynn (eds), *Literary and Visual Representations of HIV/AIDS: Forty Years Later* (Lanham, MD: Lexington Books, 2019), pp. 13–28.
8. Dan Dinello, 'The Contagious Age: Overwhelmed by Vampires, Viruses, and Zombies in the 21st Century', *Pop Matters*, 7 September 2011, *https://www.popmatters.com/148166-the-contagious-age-overwhelmed-by-vampires-viruses-and-zombies-2495957745.html* (accessed 28 November 2019).
9. Peta Mitchell, *Contagious Metaphor* (London: Bloomsbury, 2013), pp. 1–5, 7, 12.
10. Dinello, 'The Contagious Age'; Priscilla Wald, *Contagious: Cultures, Carriers, and The Outbreak Narrative* (London and Durham, NC: Duke University Press, 2008), pp. 2, 12–13.

11. Fernando Duarte, 'Who is "patient zero" in the coronavirus outbreak?', *BBC.com*, 24 February 2020, *https://www.bbc.com/future/article/20200221-coronavirus-the-harmful-hunt-for-covid-19s-patient-zero* (accessed 8 May 2020).
12. Haas, *Stages of Agency*, pp. 19–20.
13. Dinello, 'The Contagious Age'; see also Wald, *Contagious*, pp. 4, 10, 213, 257, 260–1.
14. Jeffrey J. Cohen, 'Monster Culture (Seven Theses)', in Jeffrey J. Cohen (ed.), *Monster Theory: Reading Culture* (Minneapolis: University of Minnesota Press, 1996), pp. 3–25, 4.
15. Cohen, 'Monster Culture', p. 6.
16. Cohen, 'Monster Culture', p. 16.
17. Cohen, 'Monster Culture', pp. 16–20.
18. Wald, *Contagious*, pp. 29–30, 213, 219–24.
19. Julia Epstein, 'AIDS, Stigma, and Narratives of Containment', *American Imago*, 49/3 (1992), 292–310, 296, 304.
20. Steven F. Kruger, *AIDS Narratives: Gender and Sexuality, Fiction and Science* (New York: Garland, 1996), p. 41.
21. Peter Michael Pober, 'Still Angry after All These Years: Performing the Language of HIV and the Marked Body in *The Normal Heart* and *The Destiny of Me*', *Theatre Symposium*, 5 (1997), 125–40, 138.
22. Wald, *Contagious*, pp. 4, 225, 230, 241.
23. Alan Peterson and Deborah Lupton, *The New Public Health: Health and Self in the Age of Risk* (London: Sage, 1996), p. 58.
24. Visser, 'Countering the Plague', pp. 13–14, 17–20, 26–7; Juntunen, *Mainstream AIDS Theatre*, pp. 43–4. Sabrina Hüttner interprets the play's critique of promiscuity and the closet as critiquing the ruthless individualism and consumerism of gay culture. However, her analysis does not address the fact that the drama's advocacy of gay monogamous marriage simultaneously endorses a similarly individualist, bourgeois way of life. Hüttner, '"No country for the infirm"', pp. 269–71.
25. Haas, *Stages of Agency*, pp. 42–3, 55, 82, 90, 140, 199.
26. Larry Kramer, *The Normal Heart and The Destiny of Me: Two Plays* (New York: Grove Press, 2000), pp. 19–20.
27. Pober, 'Still Angry after All These Years', p. 137.
28. Kramer, *The Normal Heart and The Destiny of Me,* p. 110.
29. Pober, 'Still Angry after All These Years', p. 137.
30. Haas, *Stages of Agency*, pp. 39, 51–4, 84–5, 146.
31. Kramer, *The Normal Heart and The Destiny of Me,* pp. 100–1, third ellipsis in the original.

32. Wald, *Contagious*, pp. 4, 10, 16, 33, 56.
33. David Román, *Acts of Intervention: U.S. Theatre and Performance, Gay Men and AIDS* (Bloomington: Indiana University Press, 1998), pp. 235–7.
34. Haas, *Stages of Agency*, pp. 122–9.
35. Kramer, *The Normal Heart and The Destiny of Me*, pp. 100, 94.
36. Kramer, *The Normal Heart and The Destiny of Me*, p. 95.
37. Kramer, *The Normal Heart and The Destiny of Me*, pp. 44–8, 70–2, 108–10.
38. Kramer, *The Normal Heart and The Destiny of Me*, pp. 24, 23.
39. Kramer, *The Normal Heart and The Destiny of Me*, p. 58, 60.
40. Pober, 'Still Angry after All These Years', p. 131.
41. Kramer, *The Normal Heart and The Destiny of Me*, p. 59.
42. Juntunen, *Mainstream AIDS Theatre*, pp. 42–3.
43. Haas, *Stages of Agency*, p. 154.
44. James Fisher, 'Larry Kramer', in Christopher J. Wheatley (ed.), *Dictionary of Literary Biography, vol. 249: Twentieth-Century American Dramatists, Third Series* (Detroit: Gale, 2002), pp. 195–208, 205.
45. Kramer, *The Normal Heart and The Destiny of Me*, pp. 190, 192, 229, 239, 251.
46. Kramer, *The Normal Heart and The Destiny of Me*, p. 141.
47. Kramer, *The Normal Heart and The Destiny of Me*, p. 188.
48. Kramer, *The Normal Heart and The Destiny of Me*, p. 215.
49. Haas, *Stages of Agency*, p. 161.
50. Kramer, *The Normal Heart and The Destiny of Me*, p. 251.
51. Kramer, *The Normal Heart and The Destiny of Me*, pp. 112–13.
52. Kramer, *The Normal Heart and The Destiny of Me*, p. 177; Alexander Pope, 'An Epistle from Mr. Pope to Dr. Arbuthnot' [1735], in Alexander Pope, *The Poems of Alexander Pope*, ed. John Butt (London: Methuen, 1965), p. 132.
53. David Bergman, *Gaiety Transfigured: Gay Self-Representation in American Literature* (Madison: University of Wisconsin Press, 1991), pp. 189–90.
54. Kramer, *The Normal Heart and The Destiny of Me*, pp. 217, 219.
55. Haas, *Stages of Agency*, p. 156.
56. Kramer, *The Normal Heart and The Destiny of Me*, pp. 185–7, 205, 234–5.
57. Kramer, *The Normal Heart and The Destiny of Me*, p. 225.
58. Kramer, *The Normal Heart and The Destiny of Me*, p. 226.
59. Kramer, *The Normal Heart and The Destiny of Me*, pp. 140, 144, 157, 165, 171, 175, 179, 182.
60. Antonin Artaud, 'Theatre and the Plague', in *The Theatre and Its Double: Essays by Antonin Artaud*, trans. Victor Corti (London: Calder & Boyars, 1970), pp. 7–22, 22.

61. Haas, *Stages of Agency*, pp. 285, 292; Pober, 'Still Angry after All These Years', p. 138. For popular music interventions into the COVID-19 pandemic, see Kimi Eisele, 'Sounds and Songs of the Pandemic: A Global Coronavirus Playlist', *Border Lore: Heritage & Culture of the U.S. Southwest and Northern Mexico*, Southwest Folklife Alliance, 3 April 2020, *https://borderlore.org/sounds-and-songs-of-the-pandemic-a-global-coronavirus-playlist/* (accessed 8 May 2020).
62. Kramer, *The Normal Heart and The Destiny of Me*, pp. 117–18; Pearl, *AIDS Literature and Gay Identity*, pp. 113, 126–7; Farrier, 'Re-membering AIDS', pp. 158–60.
63. On the American discourse of social mobility, see Hüttner, '"No country for the infirm"', pp. 262–5.

10

The Epidemic of History

Contagion of the Past in the Era of the Never-Ending Present

Elana Gomel

THE FOUR HORSEMEN of the Apocalypse traditionally comprise War, Famine and Pestilence, led by Death. Contagious diseases have played a significant role in history, often changing its course by wiping out or undermining entire civilisations. The Plague of Athens in the fifth century BCE; the Black Death; and the ravages of smallpox and other European diseases in the New World are only some of the best-known examples of the fundamental role of contagion in history.[1] And conversely, human-made historical disasters often trail epidemics in their wake: 'a whole variety of diseases' was associated with Mao's Great Leap Forward in China, while climate change is reviving old plagues like Ebola and encouraging the development of new ones.[2] The imagery of disease has been commonly used to represent various socio-political trends, from the 'epidemic' of cell-phone usage to the 'plague' of colonialism. And of course, the coronavirus pandemic is history unfolding in real time, impacting everything from the global economy to race relations in the USA.

But can history itself be imaged as contagion? And if yes, what does it say about the relationship between the historical imagination and the current socio-political moment? In this essay, I want to consider some of the ways in which historical memory becomes a source of physical disease in fantastic fiction. I will argue that fantastic tropes of monstrosity can do what ordinary historical fiction cannot: represent not just specific moments in the past but *pastness* itself.

In *The Varieties of History*, historian Franz Stern points out that 'history is the cognitive expression of the deep-rooted human desire to know the past . . . A discipline so close to life cannot remain fixed; it changes with time, with the impact of new hopes, thoughts, and fears.'[3] The narrative malleability of history, the way in which history is also a *story*, underlies Hayden White's scepticism about the veridical claims of history-writing. The ensuing debate is well-known and does not need to be rehearsed here. What interests me is the convergence, extensively discussed by White, between forms of the historical imagination and narrative genres.

Epidemics generate their own post-apocalyptic genre of fantasy, in which the continuity and inconclusiveness of infectious disease figure the continuous and inconclusive nature of the historical process.[4] But I would argue that recent socio-political and cultural developments have led to an interesting mutation in the narrative 'dramaturgy' or common plot of pestilence.[5] While previously the source of contagion was the polluted body of some enemy *du jour* – blacks, Jews, gays or what have you – more and more frequently it is located in the historical process itself. Time becomes a pathogen.

Ends of History

In 1992, one year after the collapse of the USSR, Francis Fukuyama published his influential book *The End of History*.[6] It has been misunderstood as forecasting the end of the historical process, which is absurd. In fact, it was about the end of History with a capital H: that is, the notion that this process has an inbuilt salvational or destructive directionality. Events, even momentous events such as 9/11, will keep happening. What has ended, though, is the belief that these events are inescapably building up toward some preordained goal, whether it be a communist society of equality and plenty, or a total collapse of civilisation.

The end of historical teleology has created the world in which 'late capitalism seems to have no natural enemies'.[7] Apart from its political implications, this foreclosure of utopian/dystopian alternatives paralyses the historical imagination itself. One of Jameson's most famous essays is subtitled 'How Can We Imagine the Future?' and the answer seems to be that we cannot. We live today not in the expectation or fear of the future but in what Hans Ulrich Gumbrecht calls the 'Chronotope of the Broad Present', the representation of time and space in our shared cultural discourse:

> Different from the ever shrinking and therefore 'imperceptibly short' present of the historicist chronotope, the new present (that continues to be our present in the early twenty-first century) is one in which all paradigms and phenomena from the past are juxtaposed as being available and ready-to-hand. For this present, instead of leaving the past behind, is inundated with pastness, and at the same time it is facing a future which, instead of being an open horizon of possibilities, seems occupied by threats that are inevitably moving towards us (think of 'global warming' as an example).[8]

Paired with the end of history, in Fukuyama's terms, is another trend that signifies a rupture between past and present: the ascent of randomness or contingency across all fields of social interaction. Ted C. Lewis offers a model of what he calls punctuated reality (by analogy with the evolutionary concept of *punctuated equilibrium*) to describe the historical process of the interconnected, global world. In this model, 'independent random events' are replaced with 'highly dependent conditional events'.[9] In other words, extreme events come in waves, amplified by the unpredictable interactions across the social and political field. These waves 'are pulled toward extreme values', statistically speaking, and thus cannot be described by the ordinary historical methods derived from the narratively continuous paradigm of the realistic novel, which is based on what might be called the literary regression to the mean.[10]

Both the ascendance of the 'broad present' and the establishment of 'punctuated reality' represent a significant shift in our perception of history. Instead of being haunted by the presence of the past, we are haunted by its absence. Or rather, we are haunted by the absence of *pastness*: that is, we can no longer distinguish between past, present and future by organising memories and premonitions into an orderly linear narrative. Gumbrecht describes this situation as being 'flooded' by inchoate and chaotic histories: 'Between the past that engulfs us and the menacing future, the present has turned into a dimension of expanding simultaneities.'[11]

Hegelian teleological history is denied or bracketed out. But, as we know, what is repressed comes back in the shape of a monster. And the particular morphology of its monstrosity mirrors the forms of repression that have created it in the first place. When the past was tangible, present and inescapable, as in the classic nineteenth- and twentieth-century Gothic, the monster appeared as tangible and discrete: a specific haunting, tied either to a particular location or to a particular person. Contemporary monsters, however, are plural, multiple and contingent: just like Lewis's 'highly dependent conditional events', they come in waves and are spread by a mechanism of contagion across the entire cultural field. If previously the historical imagination was spurred, as Stern argues, by the desire to remember, it may now be hobbled by the need to forget.

When history is represented as contagion in fantastic fiction, several common narrative strategies appear across a range of texts. Some of these strategies include pollution, proliferation and reproduction. In what follows I will give examples for each. I do not claim that this list is in any way exhaustive. Rather, I will try to show how a new narrative language of monstrosity has evolved to cope with the 'chronotope of the broad present'. What distinguishes this language from the familiar Gothic and post-Gothic tropes of monstrosity is its emphasis on multiplicity, uncertainty and non-linear expansion. In other words, time itself becomes an epidemic generating diseased and polluted bodies.

Utopian Pollution

All utopias are dystopias; and vice versa.[12] The genre represents a future that is radically different from the present; and this difference may be articulated in either positive or negative terms, depending on the ideological position of the implied author and/or narrator. Utopia/dystopia marks the terminus of history: the millennium or apocalypse.Precisely because utopia is situated *after* history, it is essentially defined in spatial terms. The original Utopia was an artificial island whose inhabitants separated it from the mainland by a deliberately dug ditch, to keep out the pollution of violence, inequality, stupidity and frivolity. Since then, utopias are under strict quarantine to keep their purity intact. Ursula Le Guin's utopian novel *The Dispossessed* (1974) opens with a description of the 'quarantine' wall that both hems in and separates the anarchist utopia of Anarres from its capitalist twin Urras (Le Guin 1974, 1). Indeed, one may argue that all the walls, ditches and other spatial barriers (including mental ones) are ways to separate utopian space from historical time; to prevent the contamination of the perfect world by the mutability, contingency and randomness of the historical process.

It is not surprising, then, that when the walls of utopia are breached, the flux of history is often imaged in terms of a disease. In George Orwell's *Nineteen Eighty-Four*, O'Brien tells Winston Smith that his opposition to Ingsoc is a form of mental illness in need of a cure. But there are utopias/dystopias that go much further in embodying history itself in a corporeal form of a contagion. I want to discuss one well-known, though in my view under-theorised example: Lois Lowry's *The Giver* (1993). Though the book is ostensibly a YA, it actually contains all the thematic and structural features of the twentieth-century utopia/dystopia in a condensed and highly self-conscious form.

The Giver depicts a regimented and regulated world, in which all differences are smoothed away by a combination of social engineering and biomedical intervention. Names, occupations, spouses and children are assigned; every citizen goes through predictable and uniform life-stages; sexual desire is tamped down by medication; and a form of eugenics is practised, in which less-than-perfect babies and old people are 'released' into Elsewhere, or, in less euphemistic terms, killed by a lethal injection. The short novel is narrated from the point of view of a young boy Jonas who gradually realises the horror of his society and escapes with a baby Gabriel whom his ostensibly caring and nurturing father is about to 'release'. The ending of the novel is ambiguous, as it is not clear whether Jonas and Gabriel die in the snow or indeed reach some better destination.[14]

The unusual aspect of this dystopian society, however, is the role of historical memory. Instead of being simply repressed, as in *Nineteen Eighty-Four*, history is entrusted to a single individual called the Receiver whose role is to advise the Elders of the community based on the knowledge derived from the collective memory of the past. Jonas is appointed the Receiver-in-training, absorbing memories of the past through a physical contact with the previous Receiver who, therefore, becomes the Giver. History in the dystopian imagination is often represented in the form of records: the old photographs and newspaper articles that Winston Smith falsifies in *Nineteen Eighty-Four*; or the burning books of Ray Bradbury's *Fahrenheit 451*. But in *The Giver* history is intensely physical. Not only does it have to be held in an individual's memory as an actual recollection but it is passed on by touch. History is literally a disease. And like any disease, it causes pain.

The memories that the Giver passes on to Jonas through laying of hands are not tidy narratives or general facts: they are raw emotions and sensations. When Jonas absorbs memories of war, he does not learn the dates of famous battles but experiences the death of a soldier on the battlefield:

> From the distance, Jonas could hear the thud of cannons. Overwhelmed by pain, he lay there in the fearsome stench for hours, listened to the men and animals die, and learned what warfare meant.[15]

The previous Receiver-in-Training, the Giver's daughter, could not stand the pain of history and asked for euthanasia. The Giver tells Jonas, 'I couldn't bring myself to inflict physical pain on her. But I gave her anguish of many kinds. Poverty, and hunger, and terror.'[16] History is not something you teach but something you infect others with. History is like flu: an insidious virus that is transmitted by physical contact. And while the Giver is wracked by remorse about the death of his daughter and Jonas's pain, he is also convinced that this is something that needs to be done. If historical memory in not contained in one person, it will spill into the community at large, contaminating and infecting everybody. The physicality of history is such that it sparks off corporeal changes in Jonas. Released from the pill regimen of the community, he goes through puberty. The inhabitants of the utopia perceive everything in black and white while Jonas acquires colour vision. This is emphasised in the rather pedestrian movie based on *The Giver*, in which the splash of rainbow colour onto the grey screen makes the audience accept Jonas's transformation as wholly positive. But the novel is more subtle in this regard. Jonas is happy to see that apples are red and grass is green; but he is also aware that his 'heightened feelings' include rage, mood swings and grief.[17]

Jonas's near-suicidal escape from the community is powered by his desire to save Gabriel, whom he regards as his brother. But it is also the result of his wholesale rejection of the utopia of Sameness:

> [T]he orderly disciplined life he had always known . . . The life where nothing was ever unexpected. Or inconvenient. Or unusual. The life without color, pain, or past.[18]

The ambiguity of the ending, however, emphasises that the alternative is not another form of perfection that embraces all that his community has rejected, while offering the same safety and equality it provides. The alternative to utopia is history; and history is filled with suffering:

> You have never been starving, he had been told. You will never be starving. Now he was. If he had stayed in the community, he would not be. It was as simple as that. Once he had yearned for choice. Then, when he had had a choice, he had made the wrong one: the choice to leave. And now he was starving.[19]

The subtlety of Lowry's novel lies precisely in her emphasis on the positive aspects of the utopia of Sameness: the elimination of pain, suffering and inequality. In that respect, it is significantly different from later-generation YA dystopias, such as Susanne Collins's *Hunger Games* (2008–10), in which the brutal society of the future has no redeeming qualities whatsoever. Lowry, on the other hand, balances the need for historical memories with the full awareness of their dangers. History can easily become a vampire: the past feeding off the future, infecting it with memories of unresolved conflicts and unsettled scores. History is a disease. But if violence is one symptom of this disease, choice is another.

A similar image of the diseased body of history occurs in Ursula Le Guin's meta-utopian story 'The Ones Who Walk Away from Omelas' (1973), in which the happiness and stability of a utopian society depends on the 'abominable suffering' of one child. This story juxtaposes the perfection of the utopian city of Omelas with the vividly described physical pain and degradation of the child's diseased body. No explanation is offered as to why this suffering is necessary, but it fits into the wider framework of symbolic dichotomies which define the relation of utopia and history: space/time, stability/change, health/malady. The putative health and stability of utopia are wholly dependent on the diseased mutability of history. And history is contagious. The conditions of the child prompt some of the inhabitants of Omelas to reject utopia in favour of an escape into the unknown and precarious future. Those who 'walk away', much like Jonas, are carriers of the virus of change.

Zombie Origination

The stunning popularity of zombies has engendered its own plague: that of critical texts about zombies that are trying to explain this phenomenon.[20] In this short section I am not going to offer a comprehensive overview of zombie culture. But I would like to consider one particular aspect of it: namely, zombies' origin. Compared to other signature monsters, such as the vampire, the zombie is astonishingly rootless. By this I mean that as opposed to, say, *Dracula* that creates an elaborate narrative of origin for the ur-vampire, most zombie texts, whether literary or cinematic, hardly bother with a fig leaf of even the most minimal justification of the plague. At best, some vague 'virus' is mentioned; at worst, nothing at all. Tony Monchinski's Eden (2008) is fairly typical in simply rejecting the issue of origin as irrelevant:

> Some survivors refer to the coming of the undead as 'the plague'. The more religious among us dub it 'the apocalypse' or 'end times'. No savior has appeared. The origins of the outbreak are unknown. The nature of the contagion, spread by bites, is unclear.[21]

The reason for this is the zombie's essential ahistoricity. The zombie is a monster of the present, not the past or the future. It is 'a cultural cypher for an ever-adaptive barrage of social anxieties and fears'.[22] Its contagion does not generate a narrative time-arrow but rather exists in the perpetual 'now' of the self-originating, self-sustaining and self-consuming proliferation of the electronic media. Zombies are fake news made (undead) flesh. But zombies by now constitute a whole ecology of monstrosity; and within this ecology, just about any permutation of meaning may be found. There are zombies who buckle the trend of recycling, repetition and ahistoricity. I want to discuss two texts that do engage with zombies' past and future. But in doing so, they also reflect the profound unease plaguing the contemporary historical imagination.

M. R. Carey's popular novel *The Girl With All the Gifts* (2014; made into a movie in 2016) is a zombie utopia, in which a fungal contagion that reduces adults to mindless predators also generates a new breed of post-human children who combine zombie ferocity with agency and sentience. This is not the static utopia of *The Giver* but rather what Tom Moylan defines as a *dynamic utopia*: a narrative that traces the emergence of a new form of society and a new form of subjectivity.[23] As Carey's novel reminds us, not all utopian subjects are positive (from our point of view) alternatives to the status quo. Indeed, most utopian subjects of the last century, from the Futurist 'Man-Machine' to the Nazi 'Ubermensch' and the Soviet 'New Man', would make an average zombie appear peaceful and harmless. However, a dynamic utopia, as opposed to its static counterpart, can at least point to the open-endedness of the historical process and evoke the idea of change.

In Carey's novel, it is the future that is the source of contagion. When Melanie the zombie protagonist releases the fungal spores that will infect the last remaining 'true' humans, she symbolically kills the past and ushers in the brave new world of posthuman monsters. The last sentence is not meant to be pejorative. The word 'monster', after all, comes from the Latin 'monere', a portent or a sign; and a 'hopeful monster' was a term used in nineteenth-century biology to describe a new and promising mutation. Melanie's zombiehood is a symbol of her historical newness. Yeats's 'rough beast slouching to Bethlehem' may be monstrous but it is also messianic.[24]

Another interesting feature of Carey's novel is its relationship with historical memory. As opposed to *The Giver*, in which the utopian/dystopian society is predicated on collective amnesia, the zombie utopia presents itself as a legitimate heir to Western culture and history. Melanie is metaphorically related to Greek Pandora ('the girl with all the gifts'); she is a ferocious reader and scholar; and the last words of the novel are an invitation to her beloved Miss Helen, spared from the zombie plague, to start a class on world history, in which the pupils have to be shackled in order not to eat the teacher. As grotesque as this may appear, it is in fact a positive image of historical continuity and the way in which a posthuman condition may be a fulfilment of the humanist tradition rather than its denial.[25]

There are other texts, in which a zombie plague arises out of the past rather than the future. Nicholas Wolff's *The Binding* (2016), for example, cleverly transforms the extra-textual origin story of the zombie myth into the intra-textual origin stories of zombies. The zombie myth originates in Haitian folklore (though traditional Haitian zombies are very different from the ravenous hordes of *The Walking Dead*). In Wolff's novel, the epidemic of the undead that strikes a small college town in Massachusetts originates in the shameful historical legacy of the US occupation of Haiti at the beginning of the twentieth century. This little-known episode of colonial history becomes a source of contagion, striking the descendants of the occupiers with a virulent supernatural form of Cotard Syndrome, in which a living person believes themselves to be dead. Zombie epidemic generates a liminal zone, in which the living dead and the dead living re-enact the tragedy of an unresolved and largely forgotten historical atrocity.

Zombies are agents of post-history and post-utopia, existing in the 'broad present' of global capitalism. But exceptions such as Carey's and Wolff's texts point to the implicit historicity of the trope itself. Whether as memory or premonition, the zombie may be used to figure the disquieting monstrosity of time. Some critics argue that zombies are perfect metaphors for 'a way of thinking that posits capitalism as the only viable system for social organization and geopolitical relations as well as for economic exchange'.[26] This is largely true; but at the same time, this 'way of thinking' is, in itself, a product of a very specific historical configuration. And no matter how timeless the zombie poetics of recycling appears to be, it can be turned around to represent the contagion of history.

Ghostly Reproduction

Ghosts, of course, are monsters of history, condensed repositories of historical memory. Every run-of-the-mill haunted house novel is rooted in some traumatic event of the past, which is replayed by the ominous apparitions within the decaying walls of the old mansion (or the suburban bungalow, as the case may be). It is interesting, though, that in what is perhaps the most famous non-fictional use of ghostly imagery, Karl Marx's *Communist Manifesto*, the spectre that is haunting Europe is of the future rather than the past.[27]

Despite the ubiquity of zombies, ghosts hold their own as our culture's most popular monsters. But the changes and mutations in their representation signify shifts in our uneasy relation with history. The most interesting of these mutations, in my view, is ghostly reproduction: that is, ghosts reproducing and multiplying in order to become agents of contagion. At first blush, the idea seems ridiculous. Zombies are bodies without minds: naturally, their figuration of bio-power is expressed in the perversion of the two main biological functions of the human body – feeding and reproduction. But ghosts are minds without bodies, removed from the reach of bio-politics and subjects to a different regimen of power: that of historical memory and forgetting. How can they reproduce? And if they do, what does it say about our relationship with history?

To answer the second question first, I would contend that ghosts-as-disease point to the same historical malaise as utopian epidemics and zombie plagues: the sense that history has lost its directionality, and that the past and the future indiscriminately 'bleed' into the present, contaminating it with indigested memories and inchoate premonitions. And as to *how* incorporeal spectra can accomplish the seemingly impossible task of becoming bodies of contagion, I would like to discuss briefly two recent novels: Simon Bestwick's *The Faceless* (2012) and F. G. Cottam's *The Waiting Room* (2010). It is not an accident that the history both invoke is that of the First World War: the 'forgotten' war, eclipsed by the clear ideological divisions of the Second World War. It is precisely because the First World War does not fit into the same storytelling mould as the Second World War, with its good-versus-evil narrative, that it becomes a source of historical contagion.

In Bestwick's novel, a small English mill-town becomes the stage for an invasion of the ghosts of First World War soldiers. Starting on Armistice Day, strange events begin to occur. First in a trickle and then in a flood, spectral figures crowd both individual homes and city streets. The fact that public and private spaces are equally subject to the ghostly invasion is significant. The traditional ghost story relies on the clear distinction between the two. The history that breeds monsters is strictly a history of private life; when social and political events intrude, as they do occasionally, it is in a mediated and indirect way through an individual victim. This 'singularity' of the genre is flouted in Bestwick's novel where first the entire town and then the entire country become engulfed by the busily multiplying incorporeal hordes.

The ghosts (also called the Spindly Men) are horrifically mutilated First World War soldiers. Their lost corporeality is gradually 'returned' to them as the description of contemporary events, focalised through a number of characters, is interrupted by first-person testimonies of the dead, graphically focusing on their pain and suffering:

> felt like there was a chicken bone in my mouth then realized it was part of my jawbone couldn't smell the trench either thought that was a blessing at the time all I could smell was copper blood.[28]

The masks worn by the disfigured soldiers in the pre-plastic surgery era become a synecdoche for this corporeality of the historical rage that has not been resolved or appeased by the following century. As the Spindly

Men take on increasingly physical shapes, they belie the traditional view of ghosts articulated by one of the characters: 'I've never heard of a spiritual being causing direct physical harm'.[29] These beings can be physically harmful, however, precisely because they are not 'spiritual' as ghosts are traditionally imagined to be. They are bodies torn apart by military violence that revolt against being buried under the layer of comforting platitudes about patriotism and the community. They are the past demanding accountability from the present. Their resurrection in the monstrous flesh represents the historical infection of unresolved conflicts, unsettled scores and distorted memories.

The plague of the Spindly Men spreads from one small town into the whole of the UK until the dead literally force the living out. At the end of the book, the British Isles are taken over by the ghostly soldiers. History has come back with vengeance:

> 'The glorious dead,' said Gideon. 'The fallen. So many names for them. For some, it's broken promises: a land fit for heroes, a war to end all wars. For others, it's decadence and immorality – interracial marriage and homosexuality. Others see hard-won rights and freedoms stripped away, saw a better world built in the years following their death, and now see it dismantled with no-one lifting a finger to stop it. Whatever your political or religious bias, there is ample food for your discontent. You've heard the saying: for our tomorrow, they gave their today. Well . . . some of them don't consider it a fair trade, and they want to cancel the deal.[30]

The dead have their politics, just like the living. The contagion they spread is the same kind you see in newspaper editorials and online forums: the contagion of history, in which conflicts of the past breed wars of the present and the future.

Cottam's *The Waiting Room* (2010) also resurrects ghosts of the Great War in a shockingly corporeal form. But in this novel, time itself is bent, as the abandoned waiting room of the title, in which soldiers waited for their train to the frontline, becomes a conduit to the past. Faulkner's saying that the past is never dead, it's not even the past, becomes literalised as the protagonist Julian Creed physically travels to the year 1916 to prevent 'the plague of death' spread by 'the soulless, growing ranks' of ghosts.[31] At the centre of the supernatural mystery of the novel is a dead soldier resurrected by some necromantic ritual who survives into the present, spreading the contagion of First World War violence, which is repeated and amplified in the Second World War Two and the Falklands War. He is a Typhoid Mary of history. The novel's time-loops, unusual in a supernatural thriller, dramatise the 'broad present', in which both chronology and teleology have broken down. Creed, who fought in the Falklands War, dismisses it at the beginning as 'ancient history . . . fittingly barbaric', and yet it is his skill with a bayonet acquired in the 1980s that enables him to survive in 1918.[32] Past and present bleed into and contaminate each other.

The contagious ghosts of these novels belie the common understanding of the literary ghost as a metaphor for persistence of memory. Rather, they become an image of the culture in which memory and experience, history and policy become muddled and indistinguishable. In a world with no future, there can be no past.

The Sense of No Ending

The contagion of history is one way in which the current crisis of the historical imagination expresses itself in popular culture. As Hayden White pointed out, narrativisation of history is what allows us to make sense of the chaotic and unruly progression of events.[33] Only when made into a story with a beginning, middle and end does history become part of the collective imagination. In order to create a future, one needs to understand the past. And this understanding expresses itself through narrative.

Contagion, however, rejects what Frank Kermode called 'the sense of an ending'.[34] The 'dramaturgy' of an epidemic is of an infinite duration, proceeding in heads and starts, receding and then starting again. An epidemic is never totally defeated. Albert Camus's celebrated ending of *The Plague* (1948) emphasises contagion's resistance to narrative:

> And, indeed, as he listened to the cries of joy rising from the town, Rieux remembered that such joy is always imperilled. He knew what those jubilant crowds did not know but could have learned from books: that the plague bacillus never dies or disappears for good; that it can lie dormant for years and years in furniture and linen chests; that it bides its time in bedrooms, cellars, trunks, and bookshelves; and that perhaps the day would come when, for the bane and the enlightening of men, it would rouse up its rats again and send them forth to die in a happy city.[35]

What 'never dies or disappears for good' can never be laid to rest either. If the past is never quite gone, the future is never quite born.

Fantastic images of contagion, from the utopian zombies to the infinitely multiplying ghosts, articulate the twin anxieties that haunt our post-historical era: longing for the past and fear of the future. Whether as the malignant politics of nostalgia or as the inability to imagine a viable alternative to the neoliberal order, the loss of history unleashes forces compared to which actual viruses and bacteria may appear positively benign.

This essay was written before the current pandemic; however, I believe that its emphasis on the peril of ahistoricity is only made more topical by the confusion, muddle and fear engendered by the coronavirus. Despite the media saturation of our environment, we seem to be no better at telling the comprehensive story of COVID-19 than we are at understanding the trajectory of global history in general. 'Punctuated reality' is only exacerbated by the randomness of a viral outbreak. As opposed to viruses, human beings live in historical time; and we need a narrative to steer us through an onslaught of unpredictable events. Victory over a biological contagion will be in vain unless we tame the contagion of history as well.

Notes

1. Terence Ranger and Paul Slack, *Epidemics and Ideas: Essay on the Historical Perception of Pestilence* (Cambridge (UK): Cambridge University Press,1992), p. 28.
2. Frank Dikötter, *Mao's Great Famine: The History of China's Most Devastating Catastrophe, 1958–62* (New York: Walker & Co., 2010), p. 276.
3. Franz Stern, *The Varieties of History* (New York: Random House, 1973), p. 24.
4. E. Gomel, 'The Plague of Utopias: Pestilence and the Apocalyptic Body', *Twentieth Century Literature*, 46/4 (2000), 405–33.
5. Ranger and Slack, *Epidemics and Ideas*, p. 3.
6. Francis Fukuyama, *The End of History and the Last Man* (New York: Simon & Schuster, 2006 [1992]).
7. Fredric Jameson, *Archaeologies of the Future: The Desire Called Utopia and Other Science Fictions* (London: Verso, 2005), p. 17.
8. H. U. Gumbrecht, 'Philology and the Complex Present', *Florilegium*, 32 (2015), 273–81, 273.

9. Ted G. Lewis, *Book of Extremes: Why the 21st Century Isn't Like the 20th Century* (New York: Springer, 2014), p. 1.
10. Lewis, *Book of Extremes*, p. 17.
11. Hans U. Gumbrecht, *Our Broad Present: Time and Contemporary Culture* (New York: Columbia University Press, 2014), p. xiii.
12. Krishan Kumar, *Utopia and Anti-utopia in Modern Times* (Oxford: Basil Blackwell, 1987), p. 16.
13. John Gray, *Black Mass: Apocalyptic Religion and the Death of Utopia* (New York: Farrar, Straus and Giroux, 2007).
14. *The Giver* is part of *The Giver Quartet*, composed of four novels – *The Giver* (1993), *Gathering Blue* (2000), *Messenger* (2004) and *Son* (2012). *Son* shows Jonas and Gabriel saved in a fisherman village, which, though far from perfect, is different from the utopian/dystopian inhumanity of t he first novel. However, *The Giver*, by far the best of the Quartet, stands on its own both thematically and generically, and is generally discussed alone. Louis Lowry, *The Giver Quartet* (New York: Houghton Mifflin Harcourt, 2012).
15. Lowry, *The Giver Quartet*, p. 110.
16. Lowry, *The Giver Quartet*, p. 130.
17. Lowry, *The Giver Quartet*, p. 120.
18. Lowry, *The Giver Quartet*, p. 152.
19. Lowry, *The Giver Quartet*, pp. 158–9.
20. See chapters 2 and 7 in this volume: Sara Polak, '"Preparedness 101: Zombie Pandemic" and the Ebola Scare: How the CDC's Use of Zombie Pop Culture Helped Fan a Nationalist Outbreak Narrative' and Megen de Bruin-Molé, 'Killable Hordes, Chronic Others and "Mindful" Consumers: Rehabilitating the Zombie in Twenty-First-Century Popular Culture', in Sandra Becker, Megen de Bruin-Molé and Sara Polak (eds), *Embodying Contagion: The Viropolitics of Horror and Desire in Contemporary Discourse* (Cardiff: University of Wales Press, 2021), pp. 41–59 and pp. 159–79. See also Sarah J. Lauro (ed.), *Zombie Theory: A Reader* (Minneapolis: University of Minnesota Press, 2017) and E. Gomel, 'Invasion of the Dead (Languages): Zombie Apocalypse and the End of Narrative', *Frame – Journal of Literary Studies*, 26/1 (2013).
21. Tony Monchinski, *Eden* (New York: Permuted Press, 2008), p. 25.
22. Lars Schmeink, '9/11 and the Wasted Lives of Posthuman Zombies', in Lars Schmeink (ed.), *Biopunk Dystopias: Genetic Engineering, Society and Science Fiction* (Liverpool: Liverpool University Press, 2016), pp. 200–36, 204.
23. Tom Moylan, *Demand the Impossible: Science Fiction and the Utopian Imagination* (London: Peter Lang, 1976 [2014]).

24. 'And what rough beast, its hour come round at last / Slouches towards Bethlehem to be born?', W. B. Yeats, 'The Second Coming', *The Dial* (1920).
25. See also the discussion of the 'mindful zombie' by de Bruin-Molé in chapter 7 in this volume. The relationship between posthumanism and humanism is one of the most vexing problems in posthumanist studies today. My argument would be that within the consumerist landscape of neoliberalism, Melanie's embrace of the humanist cultural heritage actually weakens her role as a utopian subject, while also making her palatable to the broad audience who may welcome a monster as long as she is not (too) transgressive.
26. Jen Webb and Samuel Byrnand, 'Some Kind of Virus: The Zombie as Body and as Trope', in Sarah J. Lauro (ed.), *Zombie Theory: A Reader* (Minneapolis: University of Minnesota Press, 2017), pp. 111–23, 116.
27. 'A spectre is haunting Europe – the spectre of communism. All the powers of old Europe have entered into a holy alliance to exorcise this spectre: Pope and Tsar, Metternich and Guizot, French Radicals and German police-spies', Karl Marx and Friedrich Engels, 'Manifesto of the Communist Party' [1848], *Marxists.org, https://www.marxists.org/archive/marx/works/1848/communist-manifesto/ch01.htm* (accessed 27 January 2020).
28. Simon Bestwick, The Faceless (Oxford: Solaris, 2012), Loc. 136.
29. Bestwick, *The Faceless*, Loc. 3211.
30. Bestwick, *The Faceless*, Loc. 7495.
31. Francis G. Cottam, *The Waiting Room* (London: Hodder and Stoughton, 2010), Loc. 4317.
32. Cottam, *The Waiting Room*, Loc. 83.
33. Hayden White, *Metahistory: The Historical Imagination in Nineteenth-Century Europe* (Philadelphia: Johns Hopkins University Press, 1973), p. 5.
34. Frank Kermode, *The Sense of an Ending: Studies in Theory of Fiction* (Oxford: Oxford University Press, 1967).
35. Albert Camus, *The Plague* [1948], trans. Stuart Gilbert, 24grammata.com, 150, *http://www.24grammata.com/wp-content/uploads/2013/06/The_Plague__Albert_Camus-24grammata.com_.pdf* (accessed 20 April 2019).

EPILOGUE

CONTAGION
CONTAGION

'Contagion Contagion'

Viral Metaphors, Lockdown and Suffering Economies in the COVID-19 Pandemic

Sandra Becker

No, listen, it's really, I mean – it's difficult, because we've got, in my mind, we've got three viruses that we are dealing with: The obvious one, the coronavirus that we're all trying to survive. But the second virus is the Trump virus that needs to be, ehm, eradicated, non-violently and legally, at the polls. And the third virus is what I call the virus – the pre-Trump virus, the one that we've had for many years, long before Trump. It's not Trump. Trump didn't fall out of the sky. We had a number of things that we hadn't quite fixed yet in this country. And they were causing us still a lot of pain and despair and whatever. And so, if we can get to that third virus, after we get rid of this – the coronavirus, the COVID-19 that we have right now, and if we can remove Trump from office in November, then I think – I think that a lot of people – those who have been fortunate enough to be at home, like I have been – . . . have been thinking about, like, how do we want to live after the pandemic?

(Michael Moore on the quarantine version of the *The Late Show* with Stephen Colbert, promoting his new documentary project *Planet of the Humans* (2020, with Jeff Gibson, dir.), 22 April 2020.)[1]

THIS EPILOGUE was first drafted in mid-May 2020, three weeks after this interview with Moore aired. Since then countries like Italy, France, the Netherlands, the UK, Germany, and thirty-one out of fifty US states have already started easing their varying lockdowns and coronavirus containment measures.[2] Like the documentary Moore is promoting in the above quotation, this collection was in 'post-production' when the COVID-19 epidemic started to spread.[3] Only one month after the official naming of this virus, the World Health Organization (WHO) declared it a 'pandemic' on 11 March 2020 with 113 countries confirming first cases of COVID-19.[4] Writing and revising this epilogue (as well as the collection as a whole) while the pandemic still continued felt like trying to hit a moving target. Through the acceleration of information and events around the coronavirus, and contagion more broadly, this epilogue risked returning to the common pattern of 'contagion, contagion' illustrated by Moore's excessive use of viral metaphors above. It is an outstanding example of how contagious 'vocabulary and metaphors from outbreak narratives have infiltrated how news media, policymakers and the general public view the world and the people within it', as Priscilla Wald postulated in her pre-COVID draft of the preface to this book. Next to keywords like 'flattening the curve', 'social distancing' and 'herd immunity', Moore's usage of the 'virus'-metaphor shows just how this real, ongoing pandemic invites one to fall victim to the twenty-first-century 'plague of self-referential contagiousness'.[5] His characterisation of the present moment in the United States as marked by a threefold virus of COVID-19 pandemic, Trumpism, and inequality caused by neoliberal capitalism, distract from his actual goal to promote his new documentary *Planet of the Humans* and the pressing topic of climate change. Overall, Moore's discussion obscures more than it reveals about these other issues.

Priscilla Wald rightly points out that this volume offers insights into how apocalyptic stories and fantasies 'titillate us' and 'shape experience', and this concluding analysis of our current, real life apocalyptic threat likewise allows for a timely understanding of 'who, what and where a culture locates . . . its definitions of "us" and "them", its response to other cultures and to the planet' and ultimately who and what is considered worth protecting.[6] While it is too early to speculate about how and in how far the life around the globe will be affected by the COVID-19 pandemic in the long-term, or what future fantasies of epidemic realities will look like, it is worthwhile to make some preliminary observations about how this pandemic has been framed and made sense of so far. The patterns in the following examples from European and US news media and politics reveal that the coronavirus pandemic is already being transferred into yet another contagion narrative that '[is] not about disease at all, but rather about the warring horrors and desires inherent in human and non-human embodiment, networks and contagion vectors in an increasingly risk-averse world' in late capitalism (introductory chapter).

As both Priscilla Wald (in her 2008 book *Contagious: Cultures, Carriers, and the Outbreak Narrative*) and Sara Polak (in chapter 2 in this volume) emphasise, the differentiation between us and the dangerous Other forms as much a part of any outbreak narrative as 'patient zero'. Due to the speed with which the coronavirus spread globally, and spread within the US at the beginning of 2020, it was the 'foreign virus' that president Donald J. Trump identified as threat in his 'Address to the Nation' on 11 March 2020, shortly after the WHO had declared the pandemic.[7] While Canadian flight attendant Gaëtan Dugas was framed as patient zero in the 1980s AIDS epidemic, and the Liberian Thomas Eric Duncan in the 2014 Ebola outbreak in West Africa, it was the whole Republic of China and Europe that were framed as 'threat to our citizens' by the US president in this address.[8] As the scholars Jérôme Viala-Gaudefroy and Dana Lindeman demonstrate in *The Conversation*, within a month Trump had switched from praise of China's leader Xi Jinping in February to calling COVID-19 the 'Chinese virus'.[9] Both phrasings 'foreign virus' and 'Chinese virus' are problematic in their own right and clearly express the need to blame an 'exotic other'.[10] Given the trade war between the US and Europe that started in autumn 2019, it was less of a surprise that Trump warned in his speech that 'a large number of new clusters in the United States were seeded by travelers from Europe'. This allegation criminalised Europeans by implying that they consciously 'seeded' the deathly 'foreign virus' in the United States to weaken the country, and served as a basis for the US president to declare a thirty-day ban for European travellers.

Media emphasis on the origin of the virus caused racist resentments towards China, the Chinese and 'Asian-looking' people on both sides of the Atlantic. In February and March, the news media were filled with cases of anti-Asian assaults, and xenophobic violence against Chinese and Asian expats and minorities around the globe.[11] In an interview with the *Leidsch Dagblad*, Polak reminded Dutch readers that videos also circulated in the Netherlands that showed Chinese people eating bat soup, perpetuating Western fantasies of the Chinese as a people with outlandish tastes and habits, and spreaders of lethal disease.[12] Two months before this interview, a 25,000-signature-strong petition under the banner 'We are not a virus!' helped ban a racist carnival song by Radio 10 broadcast, titled 'Voorkomen is beter dan Chinezen' [Prevention is better than Chinese]. The broadcast warned listeners about eating Chinese food, playing with the Dutch proverb 'Voorkomen is beter dan genezen' [Prevention is better than a cure].[13] In the UK, the government observed a 21 per cent increase in anti-Asian hate-crimes during the coronavirus crisis, while the US Homeland Security warned about '[v]iolent extremists . . . seeking to exploit public fears associated with the spread of COVID-19 to incite violence, intimidate targets and promote their ideologies'.[14]

The employment of the outbreak narrative in the coronavirus crisis goes further than the search for a 'patient zero', though, or a people as scapegoat for the pandemic. Although the COVID-19 pandemic differs from the extent of the spread of the virus and the monstrous discourses that were circulated during the 2014–16 Ebola epidemic, the 'outbreak was [yet again] employed politically . . . to advocate for isolationism and border closures' in the US and elsewhere.[15] Whereas 'most countries in the world have [had] imposed partial or complete border closures to foreign nationals due to coronavirus outbreaks' by 31 March 2020, according to data collected by the PEW Research Center, the US government decided to extend the '30-day restriction on all nonessential travel' enforced by the CDC on 21 March 2020 for another month.[16] The resulting closure of the US-Mexican border has widely been recognised as a move by the Trump administration to employ the health emergency in the pandemic 'to justify restrictive immigration policies, including halting flights of refugees, naturalization ceremonies and the issuance of many green cards to those outside the United States'.[17] This is not to say that suspensions due to the coronavirus crisis at the European borders do not similarly affect lives of immigrants and asylum seekers. As Megen de Bruin-Molé shows in chapter 7, migrants have long been equated with 'killable [zombie] hordes', a 'de-humanising metaphor for groups of people considered "threatening" to Western civilisation: immigrants, enemy combatants, the poor, and so on'.[18] Greece, Italy, Germany and France suspended or reduced migrant services, such as asylum-seeker hearings and integrational courses, and in March and April the closure of the US-Mexican border added yet another restriction to immigration into the US, following the extension of a travel ban in January 2020 to include Nigeria, Myanmar, Eritrea, Kyrgyzstan, Sudan and Tanzania.[19] Hidden under the cloak of viral 'contagion contagion'-rhetoric that Moore uses to interpret the current situation are yet more forms of inequality and facets of Trumpism.

The US is far from the only nation state to use the pandemic for drastic political action. China and Hungary also took advantage of the health emergency to extend state surveillance and the power of their autocratic leaders.[20] As with earlier viral outbreaks, such as the Zika virus in Brazil in 2018–19 discussed by Madison A. Krall, Marouf Hasian Jr and Yvonne Karyn Clark in chapter 3, the COVID-19 pandemic also fostered the 'use of military and security frames' to 'declare emergency'.[21] In his televised address to the nation on 16 March 2020, for example, France's president Emmanuel Macron emphasised seven times that 'we're at war' [*nous sommes en guerre*]. In the weeks after this speech he supported the introduction of a 'state-supported "StopCOVID" contact-tracing app' with central national data storage to facilitate identification of new infection chains.[22] Preliminary scientific studies like the Agent-based Social Simulation of the Coronavirus Crisis (ASSOCC), however, suggest that testing together with continuing hygiene measures and masks pose more successful lockdown exit strategies than the usage of apps.[23]

The coronavirus war metaphor resurfaced in other contexts and countries as well: in the UK, for instance, the media discourse around the valuation of the work of the NHS staff as 'the nation's "frontline" defenders' is framed via the 'Clap for our Heroes'-campaign.[24] The clapping campaign, as well as other forms of symbolic support like nationwide minutes of silence and window signs of solidarity, distract from missing financial compensation, a deficient supply of PPE equipment for the safety of doctors and nurses, and the disproportionate number of low-paid migrant NHS workers who have died in the pandemic.[25]

PPE masks have been a dominant figure in coronavirus media, framed as crucial for the lockdown exit and slow return to a 'new normalcy'. Data from 17 May 2020 showed that mouth coverage had become an obligatory requirement for individuals to be allowed to enter supermarkets and to participate in public life in over fifty different countries in Latin America, Asia, Europe and Africa.[26] As Yiğit Soncul and Jussi Parikka rightly indicate, however, masks had already been dominating media messages for over a year before the coronavirus outbreak: first in the form of oxygen masks of firefighters in the large-scale Australian bushfires, then in the pandemic with health-care workers, doctors and caricatures of the earth wearing PPE masks.[27] Thus, while the president of the US continues to avoid wearing a mask, showing off his superiority over the 'invisible enemy' (as discussed in chapter 6), the growing importance of masks and respirators has long since entered public awareness.[28]

This shift in outbreak awareness can be traced both in academic literature and pop cultural imaginations of 'the coming plague' – or, as has been the distinction throughout the book, 'Epidemic Fantasies in Reality' (Part I) and 'Epidemic Realities in Fantasy' (Part II).[29] The congeries of new virus pandemics since the 1990s and the new awareness of 'toxicity' (illustrated by this term being chosen as word of the year 2018 by the OED), have also led to a change in book covers on contagion. Monographs and collections on contagion from the early-2000s often attempted to visualise a microbial, invisible threat, or pointed out the animals that could serve as potential carriers, such as rats and apes, whereas a variety of masks have conquered book covers (including this one) in the last decade.[30] Contagion's symbolic relevance has likewise evolved beyond academia in the context of twenty-first-century dangers and survival due to the numerous pop cultural fictions of (post-)apocalyptic futures, ranging from *Book of Eli* (2010), *Mad Max: Fury Road* (2015) to the video game series *Fallout* (1997–2020).[31] In anticipation of the coming plague (as well as in the coronavirus crisis), numerous historic pandemics have been re-examined.[32] In this context, the beak-like masks of seventeenth-century plague doctors have found their way onto many twenty-first-century book covers and broadcasted documentaries.[33] PPE masks emphasise the embodiment of contagion in 'leaky bodies and boundaries'.[34] This not only reflects the horror of embodying contagion oneself, or the risk that others as potential contagious bodies pose to the self; masks also serve to 'visually mark and differentiate' people, and impacts 'their capacities to relate to one another' in our face-centric, globalised networked culture.[35] As an opaque medical device that covers the mouth and nose – and thus half of the human face – PPE masks interrupt technology-based networked communication, and render visible humanity's fragility in the face of natural, viral disasters.

But how much do media and political discourses actually revolve around humans in the current pandemic? On 29 June 2020, the number of confirmed COVID-19 cases globally exceeded 10 million – with a death toll of 500,000 – and the whole world feared the second wave to come.[36] As with other rhetorics of 'contagion contagion', discursive tokens of paroles of solidarity ('we are all in this together') too often obscure inequalities with regard to vulnerability (i.e. due to pre-existing conditions or disabilities), availability of tests and health care coverage, medical literacy, and housing. Examples from the UK showed a heightened risk for Black, Asian and minority ethnic (short BAME) pregnant women to contract COVID-19, and in the United States detailed statistics of infections and deaths in New York City, 'the epicenter of the U.S. coronavirus outbreak', revealed that low-income areas with large households were hit the hardest. A study from Germany – 'a country with universal welfare and health care access' as the authors emphasise – found that long-term unemployed people faced an 84.1 per cent higher risk of hospitalisation if contracting SARS-CoV-2.[38] This is not to say that BAME or poor people are inherently likelier to contract COVID-19, but that they are often less protected in other essential ways, and often form part of an ironically underpaid class of 'essential workers'.

From one perspective, the coronavirus crisis is understood as a global crisis because of its impact on white middle-class people. It also radically exposes and intensifies the extreme inequality that already existed in neoliberal capitalism. Up until the end of June, when the global death toll exceeded half a million and the International Energy Agency (IEA) announced its online summit on a 'green recovery' on 9 July 2020, human lives seemed to be of less interest than governmental pushes to 'reopen' their countries for the sake of the economy.[39] The coronavirus crisis has often been read as a kind of fire drill for climate change in its demand for global action and solidarity, but too often the economy has been the central body of concern. Ironically, as literary scholar Nicky Marsh pointed out after the global financial crisis in 2007–8, the 'diseased body' has, in fact, long served as 'a familiar figure . . . to narrate both the attacks upon and the potential recovery of, the holistically imagined economy'.[40] Those threatening the health of this holistic economy, such as the greedy, speculative stock market traders of the financial crisis, or the Dutch company Flow Traders who have been profiting from the pandemic, have been classed as an autoimmune disease: the 'AIDS of the world economy'.[41]

In the continued absence of global solidarity, economic stability, or long-term salary increases for essential workers, Kim Stanley Robinson's optimistic article on how 'The Coronavirus Is Rewriting Our Imaginations' seems like little more than a naïve utopian fantasy. Robinson envisions that the severe inequalities in neoliberal capitalism, laid bare by the pandemic, will lead to a post-capitalist world with 'rent and debt relief; unemployment aid for all those laid off; government hiring for contact tracing and the manufacture of necessary health equipment; the world's militaries used to support health care; [and] the rapid construction of hospitals'.[42] In stark contrast, conspiracy theorist Alex Jones has stated that he would feed his neighbours to his children before considering going to buy food.[43] Despite the worldwide, deadly coronavirus crisis and the major inequality and racism it uncovered, envisioning the apocalypse – as Fredric Jameson once stated – still seems to be easier than envisioning the end of neoliberal capitalism. We remain trapped in a contagion contagion, and it will take more nuanced rhetorics and strategies to move us towards a truly 'new' normal.[44]

Notes

1. The Late Show with Stephen Colbert, 'Michael Moore's Question For Americans: How Do We Want To Live After This Pandemic?' *YouTube*, 22 April 2020, *https://www.youtube.com/watch?v=wFKkVvUgUUk* (accessed 19 May 2020).
2. S. Mervosh, J. C. Lee, L. Gamio and N. Popovich, 'See Which States are Reopening and Which are Still Shut Down', *The New York Times*, 14 May 2020, *https://www.nytimes.com/interactive/2020/us/states-reopen-map-coronavirus.html* (accessed 22 May 2020).
3. The first 'Report on the Coronavirus Disease' of the WHO that listed cases outside Asia is Situation Report 5 from 25 January 2020, mentioning varying numbers of one to three confirmed cases in France, the US and Australia. WHO, 'Coronavirus disease 2019 (COVID-19): Situation Report – 5', World Health Organization (WHO), 25 January 2020, *https://www.who.int/docs/default-source/coronaviruse/situation-reports/20200125-sitrep-5-2019-ncov.pdf?sfvrsn=429b143d_8* (accessed 22 May 2020).
4. WHO, 'Coronavirus disease 2019 (COVID-19): Situation Report – 51', World Health Organization (WHO), 11 March 2020, *https://www.who.int/docs/default-source/coronaviruse/situation-reports/20200311-sitrep-51-covid-19.pdf?sfvrsn=1ba62e57_10* (accessed 22 May 2020).
5. See the introductory essay in this volume: Megen de Bruin-Molé and Sara Polak, 'Embodying the Fantasies and Realities of Contagion', in Sandra Becker, Megen de Bruin-Molé and Sara Polak (eds), *Embodying Contagion: The Viropolitics of Horror and Desire in Contemporary Discourse* (Cardiff: University of Wales Press, 2021), pp. 1–12.
6. The quote refers to the pre-COVID draft of the preface of this volume by Priscilla Wald. In its current version, the quoted text reads: 'As these stories titillate us, they shape experience: who, what and where a culture locates its threats, its definitions of "us" and "them", its response to other cultures and to the planet'. See Priscilla Wald, 'Preface' in Sandra Becker, Megen de Bruin-Molé and Sara Polak (eds), *Embodying Contagion: The Viropolitics of Horror*

and Desire in Contemporary Discourse (Cardiff: University of Wales Press, 2021), pp. xiii–xviii, p. xvii.

7. Donald Trump, 'Remarks by President Trump in Address to the Nation', 11 March 2020, *https://www.whitehouse.gov/briefings-statements/remarks-president-trump-address-nation/* (accessed 22 May 2020).
8. Trump, 'Remarks by President Trump'.
9. J. Viala-Gaudefroy and D. Lindeman, 'Donald Trump's "Chinese virus": the politics of naming', *The Conversation*, 21 April 2020, *https://theconversation.com/donald-trumps-chinese-virus-the-politics-of-naming-136796* (accessed 19 May 2020).
10. See Sara Polak in an interview with the *Leidsch Dagblad*: '[H]et liefst wijzen we dan naar een exotische 'ander' waar toch al vooroordelen over bestaan.' Quoted in Anike van de Wijngaard, 'Angst voor het gevaar dat schuilt in de samenleving', *Leidsch Dagblad*, 17 April 2020.
11. Z. Abbany, 'Corona-phobia: Like SARS, coronavirus fear feeds racism', *Deutsche Welle*, 4 February 2020, *https://www.dw.com/en/corona-phobia-like-sars-coronavirus-fear-feeds-racism/a-52252908* (accessed 22 May 2020); J. Mahncke, 'Campaign aims to #WashTheHate of coronavirus racism', *Deutsche Welle*, 2 May 2020, *https://www.dw.com/en/campaign-aims-to-washthehate-of-coronavirus-racism/a-53309233* (accessed 22 May 2020).
12. See Sara Polak in an interview with the *Leidsch Dagblad*: 'We zagen ook in de media filmpjes voorbij komen van mensen die vleermuizensoep aten. Dit draagt bij aan het beeld dat al in het Westen bestaat over dat Chinezen rare dingen eten en dat dit de bron is van de ziekte.' Van de Wijngaard, 'Angst voor het gevaar'.
13. J. Pieters, 'Online Petition against Anti-Asian Discrimination Signed 25,000 Times', *NLTIMES.nl*, 10 February 2020, *https://nltimes.nl/2020/02/10/online-petition-anti-asian-discrimination-signed-25000-times* (accessed 20 May 2020).
14. J. Grierson, 'Anti-Asian hate crimes up 21% in UK during coronavirus crisis', *The Guardian*, 13 May 2020, *https://www.theguardian.com/world/2020/may/13/anti-asian-hate-crimes-up-21-in-uk-during-coronavirus-crisis* (accessed 22 May 2020); A. Mallin and J. Margolin, 'Homeland Security warns terrorists may exploit COVID-19 pandemic', *ABC News*, 24 March 2020, *https://abcnews.go.com/Politics/homeland-security-warns-terrorists-exploit-covid-19-pandemic/story?id=69770582* (accessed 22 May 2020).
15. See chapter 2 in this volume: Sara Polak, '"Preparedness 101: Zombie Pandemic" and the Ebola Scare: How the CDC's Use of Zombie Pop Culture Helped Fan a Nationalist Outbreak Narrative', in Sandra Becker, Megen de Bruin-Molé and Sara Polak (eds), *Embodying Contagion: The Viropolitics of*

Horror and Desire in Contemporary Discourse (Cardiff: University of Wales Press, 2021), pp. 41–59.

16. P. Connor, 'More than nine-in-ten people worldwide live in countries with travel restrictions amid COVID-19', PEW Research Center, 1 April 2020, *https://www.pewresearch.org/fact-tank/2020/04/01/more-than-nine-in-ten-people-worldwide-live-in-countries-with-travel-restrictions-amid-covid-19/* (accessed 22 May 2020).
17. M. D. Shear and Z. Kanno-Youngs, 'Trump Administration Plans to Extend Virus Border Restrictions Indefinitely', *The New York Times*, 13 May 2020, *https://www.nytimes.com/2020/05/13/us/politics/trump-coronavirus-border-restrictions.html* (accessed 22 May 2020).
18. See chapter 7 in this volume: Megen de Bruin-Molé, 'Killable Hordes, Chronic Others and "Mindful" Consumers: Rehabilitating the Zombie in Twenty-First-Century Popular Culture', in Sandra Becker, Megen de Bruin-Molé and Sara Polak (eds), *Embodying Contagion: The Viropolitics of Horror and Desire in Contemporary Discourse* (Cardiff: University of Wales Press, 2021), pp. 159–78.
19. E. Wallis, 'Which migrant services in Europe are suspended or reduced due to COVID-19?' *InfoMigrants.net*, 18 March 2020, *https://www.infomigrants.net/en/post/23524/which-migrant-services-in-europe-are-suspended-or-reduced-due-to-covid-19* (accessed 19 May 2020); Z. Kanno-Youngs, 'Trump Administration Adds Six Countries to Travel Ban', *The New York Times*, 31 January 2020, *https://www.nytimes.com/2020/01/31/us/politics/trump-travel-ban.html?auth=login-email&login=email* (accessed 21 May 2020).
20. L. Kuo, '"The new normal": China's excessive coronavirus public monitoring could be here to stay', *The Guardian*, 9 March 2020, *https://www.theguardian.com/world/2020/mar/09/the-new-normal-chinas-excessive-coronavirus-public-monitoring-could-be-here-to-stay* (accessed 19 May 2020); S. Walker and J. Rankin, 'Hungary passes law that will let Orbán rule by decree', *The Guardian*, 30 March 2020, *https://www.theguardian.com/world/2020/mar/30/hungary-jail-for-coronavirus-misinformation-viktor-orban* (accessed 19 May 2020).
21. See chapter 3 in this volume: Madison A. Krall, Marouf Hasian and Yvonne Karyn Clark, 'The Zika Virus, Ebola Contagion Narratives and US Obsessions with Securitising Neglected Infectious Diseases', in Sandra Becker, Megen de Bruin-Molé and Sara Polak (eds), *Embodying Contagion: The Viropolitics of Horror and Desire in Contemporary Discourse* (Cardiff: University of Wales Press, 2021), pp. 61–82.
22. Emmanuel Macron, 'Adresse aux Français', 16 mars 2020, *https://www.elysee.fr/emmanuel-macron/2020/03/16/adresse-aux-francais-covid19* (accessed

22 May 2020); M. Rosemain, 'France's COVID-19 tracing app expected to enter testing in week of May 11', *Reuters*, 3 May 2020, *https://www.reuters.com/article/us-health-coronavirus-france/frances-covid-19-tracing-app-expected-to-enter-testing-in-week-of-may-11-idUSKBN22F0QW* (accessed 20 May 2020).

23. ASSOCC, Scenario: effect of track&trace apps, Agent-based social Simulation of the Coronavirus Crisis (ASSOCC). Understanding the effectiveness of containment policy responses to the coronavirus pandemic by social simulation and social reporting, *https://simassocc.org/scenario-effect-of-tracktrace-apps/* (accessed 20 May 2020).
24. Meghan Tinsley and Neema Beegum, 'Clap for Our Heroes: "Good" Migrants, Wartime Rhetoric, and Covid19', *Discover Society*, 21 May 2020, *https://discoversociety.org/2020/05/21/clap-for-our-heroes-good-migrants-wartime-rhetoric-and-covid-19/* (accessed 8 July 2019).
25. Tinsley and Beegum, 'Clap for Our Heroes'.
26. 'Which countries have made wearing face masks compulsory?' *Aljazeera News*, last updated 17 May 2020, *https://www.aljazeera.com/news/2020/04/countries-wearing-face-masks-compulsory-200423094510867.html* (accessed 17 May 2020).
27. Y. Soncul and J. Parikka, 'Masks: The Face between Bodies and Networks', *Paletten Art Journal*, 28 April 2020, *https://paletten.net/journal/masks-between-bodies-and-networks* (accessed 18 May 2020).
28. J. Shafer, 'Behind Trump's Strange "Invisible Enemy" Rhetoric', *Politico*, 9 April 2020, *https://www.politico.com/news/magazine/2020/04/09/trump-coronavirus-invisible-enemy-177894* (accessed 2 July 2020).
29. Wald, Preface.
30. O. Petter, '"Toxic" Named Word of 2018 by Oxford Dictionaries', *The Independent*, 16 November 2018, *https://www.independent.co.uk/life-style/toxic-word-of-the-year-oxford-dictionary-2018-gaslighting-gammon-a8636581.html* (accessed 1 July 2020).
31. For covers with microbial, invisible threats see: Alison Bashford and Claire Hooker (eds), *Contagion: Historical and Cultural Studies* (London: Routledge, 2001); Priscilla Wald, *Contagious: Cultures, Carriers, and the Outbreak Narrative* (London and Durham, NC: Duke University Press, 2008); Bruce Magnusson and Zahi Zalloua (eds), *Contagion: Health, Fear, Sovereignty* (Seattle: University of Washington Press, 2012). For covers with animals as potential carriers, see Mark Harrison, *Contagion: How Commerce Has Spread Disease* (New Haven: Yale University Press, 2012); Neel Ahuja, *Bioinsecurities: Disease Interventions, Empire, and the Government of Species* (Durham, NC: Duke

University Press, 2016). For covers featuring masks being on covers, see Dahlia Schweitzer, *Going Viral: Zombies, Viruses, and the End of the World* (New Brunswick: Rutgers University Press, 2018); Carlen Lavigne, *Post-Apocalyptic Patriarchy: American Television and Gendered Visions of Survival* (Jefferson: McFarland, 2018).

32. Annika Mann, *Reading Contagion: The Hazards of Reading in the Age of Print* (Charlottesville: University of Virginia Press, 2018). For the newly found interest in past plagues and plague literature, see M. Theroux, 'The end of corona virus: what plague literature tells us about our future', *The Guardian*, 1 May 2020, *https://www.theguardian.com/books/2020/may/01/the-end-of-coronavirus-what-plague-literature-tells-us-about-our-future* (accessed 20 May 2020).
33. Breanne Fahs, Annika Mann, Eric Swank and Sarah Stage (eds), *Transforming Contagion: Risky Contacts Among Bodies, Disciplines, and Nations* (New Brunswick: Rutgers University Press, 2018); *The Great Plague*, Timeline, 2017, *https://youtu.be/HPe6BgzHWY0* (accessed 22 May 2020).
34. See Margrit Shildrick, *Leaky Bodies and Boundaries: Feminism, Postmodernism and (Bio)ethics* (London: Routledge, 1997).
35. Soncul and Parikka, 'Masks'.
36. P. Beaumont, 'Global report: COVID-19 cases exceed 10m as anxieties rise over US', *The Guardian*, 29 June 2020, *https://www.theguardian.com/world/2020/jun/28/global-report-covid-19-cases-exceed-10m-as-anxieties-rise-over-us* (accessed 1 July 2020); J. Knodel, 'Texas Lt. Gov. Dan Patrick suggests he, other seniors willing to die to get economy going again', *NBC News*, 24 March 2020, *https://www.nbcnews.com/news/us-news/texas-lt-gov-dan-patrick-suggests-he-other-seniors-willing-n1167341* (accessed 2 July 2020).
37. A. Mohdin, 'BAME women make up 55% of UK pregnancy hospitalisations with COVID-19', *The Guardian*, 16 May 2020, *https://www.theguardian.com/world/2020/may/16/bame-majority-pregnant-women-hospitalised-covid-19-troubling-midwives* (accessed 22 May 2020); S. Mansoor, 'Data Suggests Many New York City Neighborhoods Hardest Hit by COVID-19 Are Also Low-Income Areas', *Time*, 5 April 2020, *https://time.com/5815820/data-new-york-low-income-neighborhoods-coronavirus/* (accessed 22 May 2020).
38. N. Dragano, C. J. Rupprecht, O. Dortmann, M. Scheider and M. Wahrendorf, 'Higher risk of COVID-19 hospitalization for unemployed: an analysis of 1,298,416 health insured individuals in Germany', *Medrxiv.org*, 19 June 2020, 1–17, 11, *https://www.medrxiv.org/content/10.1101/2020.06.17.20133918v1.full.pdf* (accessed 1 July 2020); S. Delfs and K. Kooroshy, 'Corona

trifft sozial Benachteiligte härter', *Tagesschau.de*, 15 June 2020, *https://www.tagesschau.de/inland/corona-sozial-schwache-101.html* (accessed 1 July 2020).

39. F. Harvey, 'US to join summit on global green recovery from COVID-19 crisis', *The Guardian*, 29 June 2020, *https://www.theguardian.com/environment/2020/jun/29/us-joins-summit-on-global-green-recovery-from-covid-19-crisis* (accessed 2 July 2020).
40. N. Marsh, 'Desire and disease in the speculative economy', *Journal of Cultural Economy*, 4/3 (2011), 301–14, 301f.
41. J. Witteman, 'Flitshandelaars verveertienvoudigen winst dankzij corona-pandemie', *de Volkskrant*, 21 April 2020, *https://www.volkskrant.nl/economie/flitshandelaars-verveertienvoudigen-winst-dankzij-coronapandemie~b32b6f4c/* (accessed 2 July 2020); Hans-Peter Martin and Harald Schumann, *The Global Trap: Globalization and the Assault on Prosperity and Democracy* (London: Zed Books, 1997), p. 47, quoted in Marsh, 'Desire and disease', p. 305.
42. J. Schindler, 'Die "Sparsamen Vier" sind der Inbegriff von Asozialität', *Der Spiegel*, 5 June 2020, *https://www.spiegel.de/politik/ausland/corona-und-europaeische-solidaritaet-die-sparsamen-vier-sind-schlicht-der-inbegriff-von-asozialitaet-a-7dcdc93e-2150-47a7-ae21-ea095748248d* (accessed 1 July 2020); S. Boseley, 'US secures world stock of key COVID-19 drug remdesivir', *The Guardian*, 30 June 2020, *https://www.theguardian.com/us-news/2020/jun/30/us-buys-up-world-stock-of-key-covid-19-drug* (accessed 2 July 2020); K. S. Robinson, 'The Coronavirus Is Rewriting Our Imaginations', *The New Yorker*, 1 May 2020, *https://www.newyorker.com/culture/annals-of-inquiry/the-coronavirus-and-our-future* (accessed 2 July 2020).
43. O. O'Connell, 'Alex Jones says he'd kill and cook his neighbours to feed his kids', *The Independent*, 1 May 2020, *https://www.independent.co.uk/news/world/americas/alex-jones-coronavirus-global-collapse-cook-neighbours-feed-kids-a9495201.html* (accessed 2 July 2020).
44. F. Jameson, 'Future City', *New Left Review*, 21 (2003), 65–79, 76.

Bibliography

#2AinNJ, Twitter post, 2 October 2015, *https://twitter.com/ReviveLiberty/status/517693226136768512* (accessed 2 October 2014).

28 Days Later, Danny Boyle, dir. (DNA Films/UK Film Council, 2003).

Abbany, Z., 'Corona-phobia: Like SARS, coronavirus fear feeds racism', *Deutsche Welle*, 4 February 2020, *https://www.dw.com/en/corona-phobia-like-sars-coronavirus-fear-feeds-racism/a-52252908* (accessed 22 May 2020).

Abbott, Stacey, *Undead Apocalypse: Vampires and Zombies in the 21st Century* (Edinburgh: Edinburgh University Press, 2016).

Abel, J., 'Like-Farming Facebook Scams', *Consumer Affairs*, 22 April 2015, *https://www.consumeraffairs.com/news/like-farming-facebook-scams-look-before-you-like-042215.html* (accessed 26 May 2018).

Abele, Elizabeth, 'Last Men Standing: Will Smith as the Obsolete Patriarchal Male', in Elizabeth Abele and John A. Gronbeck-Tedesco (eds), *Screening Images of American Masculinity in the Age of Postfeminism* (Lanham, MD: Lexington Books, 2016), pp. 187–202.

Absman420, 'Cycle One', *Erotic Mind-Control Story Archive*, 19 January 2002, *https://www.mcstories.com/CycleOne/index.html* (accessed 17 November 2019).

Absman420, 'King Rex', *Gay Spiral Stories*, 28 February 2014, *https://www.gayspiralstories.com/newStory/show/958* (accessed 2 June 2016).

Ahuja, Neel, *Bioinsecurities: Disease Interventions, Empire, and the Government of Species* (Durham, NC: Duke University Press, 2016).

Alien, Ridley Scott, dir. (20th Century Fox/Brandywine Productions, 1979).

Alonzo, K., 'Krokodil, The Drug that Eats You Alive [Graphic Images]', *Guardian Liberty Voice*, 30 September 2013, *http://guardianlv.com/2013/09/*

krokodil-the-drug-that-eats-you-alive-graphic-images/ (accessed 26 January 2020).

Alves, E. A., J.-P. C. Grund, C. M. Afonso, A. D. Pereira Netto, F. Carvalho and R. J. Dinis-Oliveira, 'The Harmful Chemistry behind "Krokodil": Street-like Synthesis and Product Analysis', *Forensic Science International*, 257 (2015), 76–82.

An, R., M. Ji and S. Zhang, 'Global Warming and Obesity: A Systematic Review', *Obesity Reviews*, 19/2 (2018), 150–63.

Anderson, Benedict, *Imagined Communities: Reflections on the Origin and Spread of Nationalism* (London: Verso, 1983).

Arendt, Hannah, *The Human Condition* (Chicago: The University of Chicago Press, 1958).

Arnould, E. J. and C. J. Thompson, 'Consumer Culture Theory (CCT): Twenty Years of Research', *Journal of Consumer Research*, 31/4 (2005), 868–82.

Artaud, Antonin, 'Theatre and the Plague', in *The Theatre and Its Double: Essays* by Antonin Artaud, trans. Victor Corti (London: Calder & Boyars, 1970), pp. 7–22.

ASSOCC, Scenario: effect of track&trace apps, Agent-based social Simulation of the Coronavirus Crisis (ASSOCC). Understanding the effectiveness of containment policy responses to the coronavirus pandemic by social simulation and social reporting, *https://simassocc.org/scenario-effect-of-tracktrace-apps/* (accessed 20 May 2020).

Avery's Angels Gastroschisis Foundation, 'Alert: Please Report This!!', *Facebook*, 8 January 2017, *https://www.facebook.com/averysangels/posts/10154957008249874* (accessed 9 April 2019).

Ayres, T. C. and Y. Jewkes, 'The Haunting Spectacle of Crystal Meth: A Media-Created Mythology?', *Crime Media Culture*, 8 (2012), 315–32.

Bacon, Simon, 'Toxic Fundamentalism: The Strain (del Toro and Hogan, 2014–17)', in Simon Bacon (ed.), *Toxicity: A Companion* (Bern: Peter Lang, forthcoming).

Bacon, Simon, '"This Is Something New . . . or – Something Very, Very Old": The Strain Trilogy in Context', in Deborah Shaw, Ann Davies and Dolores Tierney (eds), *The Transnational Fantasies of Guillermo del Toro* (New York: Palgrave Macmillan, 2014), pp. 63–82.

Basham, P., 'Who Are You Calling Fat?', *The Independent*, 23 October 2007, *https://www.independent.co.uk/life-style/health-and-families/health-news/obesity-epidemic-who-are-you-calling-fat-397647.html* (accessed 29 August 2019).

Bashford, Alison, and Claire Hooker (eds), *Contagion: Historical and Cultural Studies* (London: Routledge, 2001).

Baym, Nancy K., *Personal Connections in the Digital Age: Digital Media and Society Series* (Malden: Polity Press, 2015).

Beaumont, P., 'Global report: COVID-19 cases exceed 10m as anxieties rise over US', *The Guardian*, 29 June 2020, *https://www.theguardian.com/world/2020/jun/28/global-report-covid-19-cases-exceed-10m-as-anxieties-rise-over-us* (accessed 1 July 2020).

Behuniak, S. M., 'The Living Dead? The construction of people with Alzheimer's disease as zombies', *Ageing and Society* 3 (2011), 170–92.

Bekiempis, V., 'Report: Krokodil Concerns Lack Teeth', *Newsweek*, 28 October 2013, *http://www.newsweek.com/report-krokodil-concerns-lack-teeth-1123* (accessed 26 January 2020).

Bekiempis, V., 'Why You Don't Need to Worry about "Flesh-Eating" Drug Krokodil', *Newsweek*, 21 October 2013, *http://www.newsweek.com/why-you-do-not-need-worry-about-flesh-eating-drug-krokodil-613* (accessed 26 January 2020).

Belluz, J., S. Tubrin and G. Barton, 'The Zika Virus, explained in less than 3 minutes' [video], *Vox*, 2 February 2016, *https://www.vox.com/2016/2/2/10890210/zika-virus-explained* (accessed 15 May 2018).

Bennett, Jeffrey A., *Banning Queer Blood: Rhetorics of Citizenship, Contagion, and Resistance* (Tuscaloosa: University of Alabama Press, 2015).

Berger, J. and K. L. Milkman, 'What Makes Online Content Viral?' *Journal of Marketing Research*, 49/2 (2012), 192–205.

Bergman, David, *Gaiety Transfigured: Gay Self-Representation in American Literature* (Madison: University of Wisconsin Press, 1991).

Best, Joel, *Social Problems* (New York: Norton, 2008).

Bestwick, Simon, *The Faceless* (Oxford: Solaris, 2012).

Blakely, R., 'Florida swamped with Chinese "zombie' drug", *The Sunday Times*, 12 June 2015, *http://www.thetimes.co.uk/tto/news/world/americas/article4467603.ece* (accessed 26 January 2020).

Blank, Trevor J., *The Last Laugh: Folk Humor, Celebrity Culture, and Mass-Mediated Disasters in the Digital Age* (Madison: University of Wisconsin Press, 2013).

Bogado, A., 'Zika, tropical medicine, and infant monsters of the third world', *Grist Magazine*, 11 February 2016, *https://grist.org/science/zika-tropical-medicine-and-infant-monsters-of-the-third-world/* (accessed 16 May 2018).

Bolter, Jay D. and Richard Grusin, *Remediation: Understanding New Media* (Cambridge (MA): MIT Press, 1999).

Booth, R. E. '"Krokodil" and Other Home-Produced Drugs for Injection: A Perspective from Ukraine', *International Journal of Drug Policy*, 24 (2013), pp. 277–8.

Boseley, S., 'US secures world stock of key COVID-19 drug remdesivir', *The Guardian*, 30 June 2020, *https://www.theguardian.com/us-news/2020/jun/30/us-buys-up-world-stock-of-key-covid-19-drug* (accessed 2 July 2020).

Botting, Fred and Dale Townshend, *Twentieth Century Gothic: Our Monsters, Our Pets* (London: Routledge, 2004).

Boudia, Soraya and Nathalie Jas (eds), *Powerless Science? Science and Politics in a Toxic World* (New York: Berghahn, 2016).

Boyd, L. W., 'Zika Virus Adapts Itself for the USA', *Zombie Research Society*, 9 February 2016, *http://zombieresearchsociety.com/archives/28315* (accessed 15 May 2018).

Britt, R. R., 'Are Fat People Destroying Earth?', *Livescience.com*, 21 April 2009, *https://www.livescience.com/7704-fat-people-destroying-earth.html* (accessed 29 August 2019).

Broderick, M., 'Surviving Armageddon: Beyond the Imagination of Disaster', *Science Fiction Studies*, 20/3 (1993), 362–82.

Brooks, Max, *The Zombie Survival Guide* (New York: Three Rivers Press, 2003).

Brooks, Max, *World War Z: An Oral History of the Zombie War* (New York: Crown, 2006).

Brown, F., 'Utah Gov. Gary Herbert Signs Resolution Calling Porn a "Health Hazard"', *CNN*, 19 April 2016, *https://www.cnn.com/2016/04/18/health/utah-governor-porn-resolution-health-hazard/index.html* (accessed 31 May 2018).

Brown, Phil, *Toxic Exposures: Contested Illnesses and the Environmental Health Movement* (New York: Columbia University Press, 2007).

Brown, Sally et al., 'Risk, Resistance, and the Neoliberal Agenda: young people, health, and well-being in the UK, Canada, and Australia', *Health, Risk, and Society*, 15/4 (2013), 333–46.

Browne, S. G., *Breathers: A Zombie's Lament* (London: Hachette UK, 2011, New York: Broadway Books, 2009).

Bruin-Molé, M. de, 'Our Zombies, Ourselves: A Lecture with J. Halberstam', *Frankenfiction.com*, 4 February 2015, *http://frankenfiction.com/our-zombies-ourselves-a-lecture-with-j-halberstam/* (accessed 17 November 2019).

Butler, Judith, *Bodies That Matter: On the Discursive Limits of 'Sex'* (London: Routledge, 1993).

Butler, Judith, *Undoing Gender* (London: Routledge, 2004).

Call of Duty (Woodland Hills: Infinity Ward, 2003–present).

Campbell, Alyson and Dirk Gindt (eds), *Viral Dramaturgies: HIV and AIDS in Performance in the Twenty-First Century* (New York: Palgrave Macmillan, 2018).

Camus, Albert, *The Plague* [1948], trans. Stuart Gilbert, *24grammata.com*, 150, *http://www.24grammata.com/wp-content/uploads/2013/06/The_Plague__Albert_Camus-24grammata.com_.pdf* (accessed 20 April 2019).

Canavan, G., '"We are the Walking Dead": Race, Time, and Survival in Zombie Narrative', *Extrapolation*, 51/3 (2010), 431–53.

Carey, James, *Communication as Culture* (New York: Routledge, 1989).

Carey, Mike R., *The Girl With All The Gifts* (London: Orbit, 2014).

Carlson, Ashley Lynn (ed.), *Women in STEM on Television: Critical Essays* (Jefferson: McFarland & Company, 2018).

Cassidy, Joshua, Twitter post, 25 September 2014, *https://twitter.com/JoshCassidy84/status/515150910818111488* (accessed 17 November 2019).

CDC, '2017 Case Counts in the US', Centers for Disease Control and Prevention (CDC), 24 April 2019, *https://www.cdc.gov/ zika/reporting/2017-case-counts.html* (accessed 15 November 2019).

CDC, 'Zombie Preparedness', Centers for Disease Control and Prevention (CDC), Office of Public Preparedness and Response, 11 October 2018, *https://www.cdc.gov/phpr/zombie/index.htm* (accessed 30 January 2020).

Charles, C., 'Facebook Page "Sowter Daisy" Shows Why You Shouldn't Type Amen on a Post', *That's Nonsense*, 21 November 2016, *http://www.thatsnonsense.com/facebook-page-sowter-daisy-shows-why-you-shouldnt-type-amen-on-a-post/* (accessed 26 May 2018).

Christensen, J., 'To Fix Climate Change, Fix the Obesity and Starvation Epidemics, Reports Say', *CNN.com*, 27 January 2019, *https://edition.cnn.com/2019/01/27/health/obesity-climate-change-undernutrition/index.html* (accessed 29 August 2019).

Clare, Eli, *Brilliant Imperfection: Grappling with Cure* (Durham, NC: Duke University Press, 2017).

Clover, Carol, *Men, Women, and Chainsaws* (Princeton, NJ: Princeton University Press, 1992).

Cohen, Jeffrey J., 'Monster Culture (Seven Theses)', in Jeffrey J. Cohen (ed.), *Monster Theory: Reading Culture* (Minneapolis: University of Minnesota Press, 1996), pp. 3–25.

Cole, E., 'A Virus That Sure Sounds Like It Causes The Zombie Apocalypse Is Spreading Across The Americas', *Brobible.com*, 2016, *https://brobible.com/life/article/zika-virus-zombie-apocalypse-maayybe/* (accessed 14 May 2018).

Coleridge, Samuel T., 'Bibliographia Literaria', in Donald R. Stauffer (ed.), *Selected Poetry and Prose* (New York: Modern Library, 1951), p. 156.

Colls, R. and B. Evans, 'Making Space for Fat Bodies?: A Critical Account of "the Obesogenic Environment"', *Progress in Human Geography*, 38/6 (2014), 733–53.

Comentale, Edward P. and Aaron Jaffe, 'Introduction: The Zombie Research Center FAQ', in Edward P. Comentale and Aaron Jaffe (eds), *The Year's Work at the Zombie Research Center* (Bloomington: Indiana University Press, 2014), pp. 1–58.

Connor, P., 'More than nine-in-ten people worldwide live in countries with travel restrictions amid COVID-19', PEW Research Center, 1 April 2020, *https://www.*

pewresearch.org/fact-tank/2020/04/01/more-than-nine-in-ten-people-worldwide-live-in-countries-with-travel-restrictions-amid-covid-19/ (accessed 22 May 2020).

Connor, S., 'Pity Porn – It's a Headf**k, My Friend', *The Stringer*, 12 October 2014, *http://thestringer.com.au/pity-porn-its-a-headfk-my-friend-8822#* (accessed 1 June 2018).

Cottam, Francis G., *The Waiting Room* (London: Hodder and Stoughton, 2010).

Curtis, Claire P., *Postapocalyptic Fiction and the Social Contract: We'll not go home again* (Lanham, MD: Lexington Books, 2010).

Darabont, F. (2010–present), *The Walking Dead.*

Dardot, Pierre and Christian Laval, *The New Way of the World: On Neoliberal Society* (New York: Verso, 2014).

Darwin Awards, 'History & Rules', *https://darwinawards.com/rules/* (accessed 26 January 2020).

Davison, J., 'Krokodil hype: Is toxic "flesh-eating" street drug in Canada?', *CBC News*, 25 November 2013, *http://www.cbc.ca/news/health/krokodil-hype-is-toxic-flesh-eating-street-drug-in-canada-1.2435122?cmp=rss* (accessed 17 September 2014).

Dean, Tim, *Unlimited Intimacy: Reflections on the Subculture of Barebacking* (Chicago: Chicago University Press, 2009).

Defossez, Ellen, 'Health and personal responsibility in the context of neoliberalism: Cultivating alertness, autonomy and accountability through three contemporary health practices', *The International Journal of Communication and Health*, 9 (2016), 73–9.

Del Toro, Guillermo and Chuck Hogan, *The Fall* (London: HarperCollins, 2011 [2010]).

Del Toro, Guillermo and Chuck Hogan, *The Night Eternal* (London: HarperCollins, 2011).

Del Toro, Guillermo and Chuck Hogan, *The Strain* (London: HarperCollins, 2011 [2009]).

Delany, Samuel R., *Times Square Red, Times Square Blue* (New York and London: New York University Press, 1999).

Deleuze, Gilles and Félix Guattari, *Anti-Oedipus: Capitalism and Schizophrenia* (New York: Continuum, 2004).

Delfs, S. and K. Kooroshy, 'Corona trifft sozial Benachteiligte härter', *Tagesschau.de*, 15 June 2020, *https://www.tagesschau.de/inland/corona-sozial-schwache-101.html* (accessed 1 July 2020).

Delpeuch, Francis, Bernard Maire, Emmanuel Monnier and Michelle Holdsworth, *Globesity: A Planet Out of Control?* (London: Routledge, 2009).

Dendle, Peter J., 'The zombie as barometer of cultural anxiety', in Niall Scott (ed.), *Monsters and the Monstrous: Myths and Metaphors of Enduring Evil* (Amsterdam: Rodopi, 2007), pp. 45–57.

Devakumar, Delan et al., 'Racism and discrimination in COVID-19 responses', *The Lancet* 395, 1 April 2020, 1194, *https://www.thelancet.com/journals/lancet/article/PIIS0140-6736(20)30792-3/fulltext* (accessed 8 May 2020).

DigInTheCrates, 'Almost darwin award winner injects weird new drug into her genitals (graphic photos)', *ignboards.com*, 19 March 2015, *http://www.ign.com/boards/threads/almost-darwin-award-winner-injects-weird-new-drug-into-her-genitals-graphic-photos.454426543/* (accessed 26 January 2020).

Dijck, José van, *The Culture of Connectivity: A Critical History of Social Media* (Oxford: Oxford University Press, 2013).

Dikötter, Frank, *Mao's Great Famine: The History of China's Most Devastating Catastrophe, 1958–62* (New York: Walker & Co, 2010).

Dinello, Dan, 'The Contagious Age: Overwhelmed by Vampires, Viruses, and Zombies in the 21st Century', *Pop Matters*, 7 September 2011, *https://www.popmatters.com/148166-the-contagious-age-overwhelmed-by-vampires-viruses-and-zombies-2495957745.html* (accessed 28 June 2019).

Douglas, Mary, *Purity and Danger: An Analysis of Concepts of Pollution and Taboo* (New York: Routledge, 2002 [1966]).

Dragano, N., C. J. Rupprecht, O. Dortmann, M. Scheider and M. Wahrendorf, 'Higher risk of COVID-19 hospitalization for unemployed: an analysis of 1,298,416 health insured individuals in Germany', *Medrxiv.org*, 19 June 2020, 1–17, 11, *https://www.medrxiv.org/content/10.1101/2020.06.17.20133918v1.full.pdf* (accessed 1 July 2020).

Drake, David, *The Night Larry Kramer Kissed Me* (New York: Anchor Books, 1994).

Dredze, M., D. A. Broniatowski and K. M. Hilyard, 'Zika vaccine misconceptions: A social media analysis', *Vaccine*, 34/30 (2016), 3441–2.

Drezner, D. W., 'Metaphor of the Living Dead: Or, the Effect of the Zombie Apocalypse on Public Policy Discourse', *Social Research*, 81/4 (2014), 825–49.

D'Souza, Dinesh, *The Enemy at Home: The Cultural Left and Its Responsibility for 9/11* (New York: Doubleday, 2007).

Duarte, Fernando, 'Who is "patient zero" in the Coronavirus outbreak?', *BBC.com*, 24 February 2020, *https://www.bbc.com/future/article/20200221-coronavirus-the-harmful-hunt-for-covid-19s-patient-zero* (accessed 8 May 2020).

Eagleton, Terry, *Walter Benjamin, or Towards a Revolutionary Criticism* (London: Verso, 1981).

Ebben, H., 'The Desire to Recognize the Undesirable: De/Constructing the Autism Epidemic Metaphor and Contagion in Autism as a Discourse', *Feminist Formations*, 30/1 (2018), 141–63.

Ebola Zombies, Samuel Leong, dir. (Wild Eye, 2015).

Edwards, Justin D. and Agnieszka Soltysik Monnet, 'Introduction: From Goth/ic to Pop Goth', in Justin D. Edwards and Agnieszka Soltysik Monnet (eds), *The*

Gothic in Contemporary Literature and Popular Culture: Pop Goth (New York: Routledge, 2012), pp. 1–18.

Edwards, P. and I. Roberts, 'Population Adiposity and Climate Change', *International Journal of Epidemiology*, 38 (2009), 1137–40.

Egger, G., 'Dousing our Inflammatory Environment(s): Is Personal Carbon Trading an Option for Reducing Obesity – and Climate Change?', *Obesity Reviews*, 9 (2008), 456–63.

Egger G. and J. Dixon, 'Obesity and global warming: are they similar "canaries" in the same "mineshaft"?', *MJA*, 193/11–12 (2010), 635–7.

Egger, Garry and Boyd Swinburn, *Planet Obesity: How We're Eating Ourselves and the Planet to Death* (Crows Nest: Allen and Unwin, 2010).

Eisele, Kimi, 'Sounds and Songs of the Pandemic: A Global Coronavirus Playlist', *Border Lore: Heritage & Culture of the U.S. Southwest and Northern Mexico*, Southwest Folklife Alliance, 3 April 2020, *https://borderlore.org/sounds-and-songs-of-the-pandemic-a-global-coronavirus-playlist/* (accessed 8 May 2020).

El Mono, Simón, 'Rap del Coronavirus', *YouTube.com*, 6 March 2020, rpt. *Letras.com*, *https://www.letras.com/simonelmono/rap-del-coronavirus-2020/* (accessed 8 May 2020).

Epstein, Julia, 'AIDS, Stigma, and Narratives of Containment', *American Imago*, 49/3 (1992), 292–310.

Ergas, O., 'Mindfulness in education at the intersection of science, religion, and healing', *Critical Studies in Education*, 55/1 (2014), 58–72.

Escobar, H., 'Brazil's New President has Scientists Worried. Here's Why', *Sciencemag.org*, 1 January 2019, *https://www.sciencemag.org/news/2019/01/brazil-s-new-president-has-scientists-worried-here-s-why* (accessed 17 January 2020).

Evans, B., 'Climate Change and the Politics of Fatness', *Environmental Politics*, 21/2 (2012), 335.

Faergeman, O., 'Climate Change and Preventative Medicine', *European Journal of Cardiovascular Prevention and Rehabilitation*, 14 (2007), 726-9.

Fahs, Breanne, Annika Mann, Eric Swank and Sarah Stage (eds), *Transforming Contagion: Risky Contacts Among Bodies, Disciplines, and Nations* (New Brunswick: Rutgers University Press, 2018).

Fanatia, D., 'Fat People's Sweat is Changing Weather Patterns, Scientist Claims', *Weekly World News*, 30 August 2004, 47.

Farrier, Stephen, 'Re-membering AIDS, Dis-membering Form', in Alyson Campbell and Dirk Gindt (eds), *Viral Dramaturgies: HIV and AIDS in Performance in the Twenty-First Century* (London: Palgrave Macmillan, 2018), pp. 155–72.

FEMA, 'Ready Campaign Promotes Disaster Preparedness with "Zombieland: Double Tap"', Federal Emergency Management Agency (FEMA), 9 October

2019, *https://www.fema.gov/news-release/2019/10/09/ready-campaign-promotes-disaster-preparedness-zombieland-double-tap* (accessed 27 January 2020).

FEMA, 'Zombies don't plan ahead. You can', Federal Emergency Management Agency (FEMA), *https://www.facebook.com/watch/?v=1667596443374622* (accessed 27 January 2020).

Ferrara, J., '7 ways the war on Zika mosquitoes could be won', *Scienceline*, 2 February 2016, *http://scienceline.org/2016/05/an-easy-solution-to-the-war-on-zika/* (accessed 16 May 2018).

Ferrell, Jeff and Clinton R. Sanders (eds), *Cultural Criminology* (Boston: Northeastern University Press, 1995).

Ferri, B. A., 'Metaphors of Contagion and the Autoimmune Body', *Feminist Formations*, 30/1 (2018), 1–20.

Fischhoff, B., 'Risk Perception and Communication Unplugged: Twenty Years of Process', *Risk Analysis*, 15/2 (1995), 137–45.

Fisher, James, 'Larry Kramer', in Christopher J. Wheatley (ed.), *Dictionary of Literary Biography, vol. 249: Twentieth-Century American Dramatists, Third Series* (Detroit: Gale, 2002), pp. 195–208.

Flood, A., 'I Am Legend is named vampire novel of the century', *The Guardian*, 3 April 2012, *https://www.theguardian.com/books/2012/apr/03/i-am-legend-vampire-novel-century* (accessed 27 January 2020).

ForensicToxGuy, 'Krokodil ... not so fast, my friends!', The Dose Makes the Poison, 2 December 2013, *http://dosemakespoison.blogspot.nl/2013/12/krokodil not-so-fast-my-friends.html* (accessed 26 June 2015).

Foresight, *Tackling Obesities: Future Choices – Project Report*, 2nd edn (London: Department of Innovation Universities and Skills, 2007), *http://www.foresight.gov.uk/Obesity/17.pdf* (accessed 29 August 2019).

Foucault, Michel, *Discipline and Punishment: The Birth of the Prison* (New York: Vintage Books, 1975).

Fox Networks, 'About the Show' [The Strain], *https://fxplus.fxnetworks.com/the-strain/article/about-the-show-5b577c5b798f8c001a1bee3d/* (accessed 8 July 2019).

Frick, J. W., 'Anti-intellectualism and Representations of "Commonness" in the Nineteenth-Century American Theatre', *The Journal of American Drama and Theatre*, 9/2 (1997), 1–22.

Fritsch, K. and A. McGuire, 'The Biosocial Politics of Queer/Crip Contagions', *Feminist Formations*, 30/1 (2018), vii–xiv.

Fukuyama, Francis, *The End of History and the Last Man* (New York: Simon & Schuster, 2006 [1992]).

Gallagher, Mark, *Action Figures: Men, Action Films, and Contemporary Adventure Narratives* (New York: Palgrave Macmillan, 2006).

Gallar, M., 'Obesity and Climate Change', *International Journal of Epidemiology*, 39/5 (2009), 1398–9.

Gard, Michael, *The End of the Obesity Epidemic* (London: Routledge, 2011).

Gard, Michael and Jan Wright, *The Obesity Epidemic: Science Morality and Ideology* (London: Routledge, 2005).

Geraghty, Lincoln, *American Science Fiction Film and Television* (New York: Berg, 2009).

Gettys, T., 'Doctors confirm: Use of flesh-eating opioid drug krokodil is spreading in U.S.', *RawStory.com*, 15 November 2013, *https://www.rawstory.com/2013/11/doctors-confirm-use-of-flesh-eating-opioid-drug-krokodil-is-spreading-in-u-s/* (accessed 26 January 2020).

Gibbs, Anna, 'After Affect: Sympathy, Synchrony, and Mimetic Communication', in Melissa Gregg and Gregory J. Seigworth (eds), *The Affect Theory Reader* (Durham, NC: Duke University Press, 2010), pp. 186–205.

Gillborn, S., G. Rickett, T. Muskett and M. Woolhouse, 'Apocalyptic Public Health: Exploring Discourses of Fatness in Childhood "Obesity" Policy', *Journal of Education Policy*, 35/1 (2020).

Gitlin, Todd, *The Whole World is Watching: Mass Media in the Making and Unmaking of the Left* (Berkeley and Los Angeles: University of California Press, 2003).

Goddard, E. and I. Hamilton, 'The toxic impact of drug panics', *The Independent*, 6 November 2018, *https://www.independent.co.uk/news/long_reads/drug-panics-overdose-spice-monkey-dust-krokodil-mental-health-a8541036.html* (accessed 26 January 2020).

Godfrey, A. P., 'The Ethical Zombie', *The Comics Grid: Journal of Comics Scholarship*, 7/1 (2017), 1–9.

Godzilla, Gareth Edwards, dir. (Legendary Pictures, 2014).

Goffman, Erving, *Stigma: Notes on the Management of Spoiled Identity* (New York: Simon & Schuster, 1963).

Gogarty, C. and T. Davidson, 'Flesh-rotting "zombie" drug Krokodil "has arrived in the UK" – and it's 10 times stronger than heroin', *The Mirror*, 1 November 2018, *https://www.mirror.co.uk/news/uk-news/flesh-rotting-zombie-drug-krokodil-13519348* (accessed 26 January 2020).

Gojira, Ishirō Honda, dir. (Toho Studios, 1954).

Gomel, E., 'Invasion of the Dead (Languages): Zombie Apocalypse and the End of Narrative', *Frame – Journal of Literary Studies*, 26/1 (2013).

Gomel, E., 'The Plague of Utopias: Pestilence and the Apocalyptic Body', *Twentieth Century Literature*, 46/4 (2000), 405–33.

Good, C., 'Why did the CDC Develop a Plan for a Zombie Apocalypse?', *The Atlantic*, 20 May 2011, *https://www.theatlantic.com/politics/archive/2011/*

05/why-did-the-cdc-develop-a-plan-for-a-zombie-apocalypse/239246/ (accessed 14 May 2018).

Gordillo, G., 'The Killable Horde', Space and Politics Blog, 3 September 2014, *http://spaceandpolitics.blogspot.ca/2014/09/the-killable-horde.html* (accessed 14 September 2014).

Goriunova, Olga, 'The Force of Digital Aesthetics: On Memes, Hacking, and Individuation', *The Nordic Journal of Aesthetics*, 47 (2014), 54–75.

Graham-Leigh, Elaine, *A Diet of Austerity: Class, Food and Climate Change* (Winchester: Zero Books, 2015).

Grant, Mira, *Feed* (London: Orbit, 2010).

Gray, John, *Black Mass: Apocalyptic Religion and the Death of Utopia* (New York: Farrar, Straus and Giroux, 2007).

Grierson, J., 'Anti-Asian hate crimes up 21% in UK during coronavirus crisis', *The Guardian*, 13 May 2020, *https://www.theguardian.com/world/2020/may/13/anti-asian-hate-crimes-up-21-in-uk-during-coronavirus-crisis* (accessed 22 May 2020).

Grimm, Andy, 'Suspected krokodil a false alarm', *Chicago Tribune*, 27 October 2013, *http://articles.chicagotribune.com/2013-10-27/news/ct-met-krokodil-hunt-20131027_1_bath-salts-heroin-false-alarm* (accessed 26 January 2020).

Gross, D., 'On Facebook, Clicking "Like" Can Help Scammers', *CNN*, 22 January 2014, *http://www.cnn.com/2014/01/21/tech/social-media/facebook-like-farming* (accessed 8 August 2017).

Grossman, L., 'Zombies Are the New Vampires', *Time*, 9 April 2009, *http://www.time.com/time/magazine/article/0,9171,1890384,00.html?imw=Y* (accessed 10 September 2014).

Grund, J.-P. C., A. Latypov and M. Harris, 'Breaking Worse: The Emergence of Krokodil and Excessive Injuries among People who Inject Drugs in Eurasia', *International Journal of Drug Policy*, 24 (2013), 265–74.

Grusin, Richard, *Affect and Mediality After 9/11* (London: Palgrave Macmillan, 2010).

Gryka, A., J. Broom and C. Rolland, 'Global Warming: Is Weight Loss a Solution?', *International Journal of Obesity*, 36/3 (2012), 474–6.

Guerini, M. and J. Staiano, 'Deep Feelings: A Massive Cross-Lingual Study on the Relation Between Emotions and Virality', preprint version of WWW 2015 'Web Science Track' paper, *https://arxiv.org/abs/1503.04723* (accessed 26 May 2018).

Gumbrecht, Hans U., *Our Broad Present: Time and Contemporary Culture* (New York: Columbia University Press, 2014).

Gumbrecht, Hans U., 'Philology and the Complex Present', *Florilegium*, 32 (2015), 273–81.

Gurr, Barbara, 'Masculinity, Race, and the (Re?)imagined Frontier', in Barbara Gurr (ed.), *Race, Gender, and Sexuality in Post-Apocalyptic TV and Film* (London: Palgrave Macmillan, 2015), pp. 31–44.

Guthman, Julie, 'Excess Consumption or Over-Production?: US Farm Policy, Global Warming, and the Bizarre Attribution of Obesity', in Michael Watts, Richard Peet and Paul Robbins (eds), *Global Political Ecology* (London: Routledge, 2011), pp. 51–66.

Guthman, Julie, 'Neoliberalism and the Constitution of Contemporary Bodies', in Esther Rothblum and Sondra Solovay (eds), *The Fat Studies Reader* (New York and London: New York University Press, 2009), pp. 187–96.

Gutsche, R. E., 'Zombies, Drugs, and Florida Weirdness. "Imaginative Power" and Resonance in Coverage of Miami's "Causeway Cannibal"', *Journalism Studies*, 14/4 (2013), 555–67.

Haas, Astrid, *Stages of Agency: The Contributions of American Drama to the AIDS Discourse* (Heidelberg: Winter, 2011).

Haglage, A., 'Behind the Krokodil Panic', *Daily Beast*, 7 November 2013, *http://www.thedailybeast.com/articles/2013/11/07/behind-the-krokodil-panic.html* (accessed 26 January 2020).

Haller, Beth and Jeffrey Preston, 'Confirming Normalcy: "Inspiration Porn" and the Construction of the Disabled Subject?' in Katie Ellis and Mike Kent (eds), *Disability and Social Media: Global Perspectives* (New York: Routledge, 2017), pp. 41–56.

Hämmig, R., 'Krokodil' frisst Löcher in den Verstand', dgs-info Extra. 13 Oct-ober 2011 – Bochum: Info über Desomorphin/Krokodil für Drogenkonsumenten, Deutsche Gesellschaft für Suchtmedizin e.V., *http://www.dgsucht-medizin.de/fileadmin/documents/dgs-info_extra_20111013/R.Haemmig_%E2%80%9Ekrokodil%E2%80%9C_frisst_L%C3%B6cher_in_den_Verstand_.pdf* (accessed 26 June 2015).

Haraway, Donna J., *When Species Meet* (Minneapolis: University of Minnesota Press, 2008).

Harris, E. A., 'The Post-Apocalyptic Film Genre in American Culture: 1968–2013' (unpublished PhD thesis, University of Leicester, 2016), *https://lra.le.ac.uk/bitstream/2381/38758/1/2016HARRISEHPHD.pdf* (accessed 24 June 2019).

Harrison, Mark, *Contagion: How Commerce Has Spread Disease* (New Haven: Yale University Press, 2012).

Harvey, F., 'US to join summit on global green recovery from COVID-19 crisis', *The Guardian*, 29 June 2020, *https://www.theguardian.com/environment/2020/jun/29/us-joins-summit-on-global-green-recovery-from-covid-19-crisis* (accessed 2 July 2020).

Hasian Jr, Marouf A., *Representing Ebola: Culture, Law, and Public Discourse about the 2013–2015 West African Ebola Outbreak* (Madison: Fairleigh Dickinson University Press, 2016).

Hassler-Forest, Dan, *Science Fiction, Fantasy and Politics: Transmedia World-Building Beyond Capitalism* (London: Rowman & Littlefield, 2016).

Hastings, M., 'Modern life is blamed for obesity, but whatever happened to will-power?', *Daily Mail*, 18 October 2007, *http://www.dailymail.co.uk/debate/columnists/article-488238/Modern-life-blamed-obesity-happend-willpower.html* (accessed 29 August 2019).

Hayles, N. Katherine, *How We Became Posthuman: Virtual Bodies in Cybernetics, Literature, and Informatics* (Chicago: Chicago University Press, 1999).

Heffer, S., 'The humbling of Theresa May', *New Statesman*, 26 June 2017, *http://www.newstatesman.com/politics/uk/2017/06/humbling-theresa-may* (accessed 28 June 2017).

Heimer, R., 'Patterns of New Drug Emergence: A Comment in Light of "Krokodil"', *International Journal of Drug Policy*, 24 (2013), 275–7.

Hellboy, Guillermo del Toro, dir. (Columbia Pictures/Revolution Studios/Lawrence Gordon/Lloyd Levin Productions/Dark Horse Entertainment, 2004).

Hellboy II: The Golden Army, Guillermo del Toro, dir. (Relativity Media/Lawrence Gordon/Lloyd Levin Productions/Dark Horse Entertainment, 2008).

Henderson, Donald H., 'Surveillance Systems and Intergovernmental Cooperation', in Stephen S. Morse (ed.), *Emerging Viruses* (New York: Oxford University Press, 1993), pp. 283–9.

Henke, L. L., 'Breaking Through the Clutter: The Impact of Emotions and Flow on Viral Marketing', *Academy of Marketing Studies Journal*, 17/2 (2013), 111–18.

Hewitt, Chris, 'Sticks and Stones', in Bob Guter and John R. Killacky (eds), *Queer Crips: Disabled Men and Their Stories*, 2nd edn (New York: Routledge, 2014), pp. 14–15.

Higgins, P., 'Exercise-Based Transportation Reduces Oil Dependence, Carbon Emissions and Obesity', *Environmental Conservation*, 32/3 (2005), 197–202.

Hilgard, Joseph and Kathleen Hall Jamieson, 'Does a Scientific Breakthrough Increase Confidence in Science? News of a Zika Vaccine and Trust in Science', *Science Communication*, 39/4 (2017), 548–60.

Hoax or Fact, Twitter post, 9 October 2014, *https://twitter.com/HoaxOrFact/status/520167224628109312* (accessed 30 January 2020).

Hodges, C., 'Birthmarks and Laser Treatments', 19 April 2013, *http://www.thetravelinchick.com/2013/04/before-going-through-treatment.html* (accessed 28 May 2018).

Hodges, C., 'My Photo Went Viral on Facebook for the Wrong Reason', *The Mighty*, 21 May 2015, *https://themighty.com/2015/05/woman-responds-when-port-wine-stain-photo-goes-viral/* (accessed 26 May 2018).

Hodges, C., 'The Face that Went Viral', 24 August 2014, *http://www.thetravelinchick.com/2014/08/the-face-that-went-viral.html* (accessed 28 May 2018).

Hofstadter, Richard, *Anti-Intellectualism in American Life* (New York: Alfred A. Knopf, 1963).

'Houston girl, 17, is treated for rotting skin after "taking flesh-eating drug Krokodil" in Mexico', *Mail Online*, 3 January 2014, *http://www.dailymail. co.uk/news/article-2532996/First-confirmed-case-Krokodil-Mexico-17-year-old-Houston-treated-addiction-poor-mans-heroin-doctors-thought-STD-rotted-genitals.html* (accessed 26 January 2020).

Howard, R. G., 'Electronic Hybridity: The Persistent Processes of the Vernacular Web', *Journal of American Folklore*, 121/480 (2008), 192–218.

Howard, R. G., 'How Counter-Culture Helped Put the "Vernacular" in Vernacular Webs', in Trevor J. Blank (ed.), *Folk Culture in the Digital Age: The Emergent Dynamics of Human Interaction* (Boulder: University Press of Colorado, 2012), pp. 30–55.

HRW, 'Covid-19 Fueling Anti-Asian Racism and Xenophobia Worldwide', Human Rights Watch (HRW), 12 May 2020, *https://www.hrw.org/news/2020/05/12/covid-19-fueling-anti-asian-racism-and-xenophobia-worldwide* (accessed 25 June 2020).

Hume, Kathryn, *Fantasy and Mimesis: Responses to Reality in Western Literature* (New York: Methuen, 1984).

Hüttner, Sabrina, '"No country for the infirm": Capitalism, AIDS, and American Drama', in Eva Boesenberg, Reinhard Isensee and Martin Klepper (eds), *American Economies* (Heidelberg: Winter, 2012), pp. 261–80.

In the Flesh, 'Episode #1.1', Johnny Campbell, dir. (BBC Three, 17 March 2013).

In the Flesh, 'Episode #2.6', Alice Troughton, dir. (BBC Three, 8 June 2014).

Invasion of the Body Snatchers, Don Siegel, dir. (Walter Wanger Productions, 1956).

IPCC, *Global Warming of 1.5°C: An IPCC Special Report on the impacts of global warming of 1.5°C above pre-industrial levels and related global greenhouse gas emission pathways, in the context of strengthening the global response to the threat of climate change, sustainable development, and efforts to eradicate poverty*, Masson-Delmotte, V., P. Zhai, H.-O. Pörtner, D. Roberts, J. Skea, P. R. Shukla, A. Pirani, W. Moufouma-Okia, C. Péan, R. Pidcock, S. Connors, J. B. R. Matthews, Y. Chen, X. Zhou, M. I. Gomis, E. Lonnoy, T. Maycock, M. Tignor and T. Waterfield (eds), Intergovernmental Panel on Climate Change (IPCC), 2018, *https://www.ipcc.ch/site/assets/uploads/sites/2/2019/06/SR15_Full_Report_High_Res.pdf* (accessed 8 July 2019).

Irwin, William R., *The Game of the Impossible: A Rhetoric of Fantasy* (Urbana: University of Illinois Press, 1976).

iZombie, 'Eat, Pray, Liv', Mairzee Almas, dir. (The CW, 18 April 2017).

——, 'Killer Queen', Jude Weng, dir. (The CW, 18 July 2019).

——, 'Live and Let Clive', John Kretchmer, dir. (The CW, 7 April 2015).

——, 'Looking for Mr. Goodbrain, Part 2', Dan Etheridge, dir. (The CW, 27 June 2017).

——, 'Spanking the Zombie', Tessa Blake, dir. (The CW, 2 May 2017).

Jackson, B., 'Fatties Cause Global Warming', *The Sun*, 21 April 2009.

Jackson, Rosemary, *Fantasy: The Literature of Subversion* (London: Routledge, 1998).

James, Edward and Farah Mendlesohn (eds), *The Cambridge Companion to Fantasy Literature* (Cambridge (UK): Cambridge University Press, 2012).

Jameson, Fredric, *Archaeologies of the Future: The Desire Called Utopia and Other Science Fictions* (London: Verso, 2005).

Jameson, F., 'Future City', *New Left Review*, 21 (2003): 65–79, 76.

Jauregui, A., 'Mexican Teen Reportedly Injects Krokodil Into Genitals (UPDATED)', *The Huffington Post*, 6 December 2013, *http://www.huffingtonpost.com/2013/12/06/krokodil-mexico-teen-injected-drug-genitals_n_4398102.html* (accessed 26 January 2020).

Jeannel, Elizabeth, Twitter post, 23 April 2018, *https://twitter.com/jeannelzabeth/status/988468250576130048*.

Jenkins, Henry, Sam Ford and Joshua Green, *Spreadable Media: Creating Value and Meaning in a Networked Culture* (New York: New York University Press, 2013).

Jenkins, Philip, *Synthetic Panics: The Symbolic Politics of Designer Drugs* (New York: New York University Press, 1999).

Jennings, Ken, Twitter post, 22 September 2014, *https://twitter.com/KenJennings/status/514125105426071553*.

Jones, Robert P., Daniel Cox and Juhem Navarro-Rivera, *Believers, Sympathizers, & Skeptics: Why Americans are Conflicted about Climate Change, Environmental Policy and Science*. Findings from the PRRI/AAR Religion, Values, and Climate Change Survey (Washington (DC): Public Religion Research Institute, 2014), *http://www.prri.org/wp-content/uploads/2014/11/2014-Climate-Change-FINAL1-1.pdf* (accessed 8 July 2019).

Juntunen, Jacob, *Mainstream AIDS Theatre, the Media, and Gay Civil Rights: Making the Radical Palatable* (New York: Routledge, 2016).

Kakoudaki, Despina, 'Melodrama and Apocalypse: Politics and the Melodramatic Mode in *Contagion*', in Christine Gledhill and Linda Williams (eds), *Melodrama Unbound: Across History, Media, and National Cultures* (New York: Columbia University Press, 2018), pp. 312–24.

Kanno-Youngs, Z., 'Trump Administration Adds Six Countries to Travel Ban', *The New York Times*, 31 January 2020, *https://www.nytimes.com/2020/01/31/us/politics/trump-travel-ban.html?auth=login-email&login=email* (accessed 21 May 2020).

Kaplan, Elle, 'Why Negative People are Literally Killing You (and How to Protect Your Positivity)', *Medium*, 14 November 2016, *https://medium.com/the-mission/why-negative-people-are-literally-killing-you-and-how-to-obliterate-pessimism-from-your-life-eb85fadced87* (accessed 19 June 2019).

Katie, 'Sharing is NOT Caring: The Exploitation of Children on Facebook', Red Stick Moms Blog, 5 January 2017, *https://batonrouge.citymomsblog.com/sharing-is-not-caring-the-exploitation-of-children-on-facebook/* (accessed 1 June 2018).

Katselou, M., I. Papoutsis, P. Nikolaou, C. Spiliopoulou and S. Athanaselis, 'A "Krokodil" Emerges from the Murky Waters of Addiction. Abuse Trends of an Old Drug', *Life Sciences*, 102/2 (2014), 81–7.

Kay9x, 'Krokodil Drug (Rusia's Disaster)A drug that eats junkies', *YouTube*, 25 June 2011, *http://www.youtube.com/watch?v=cM6v-43-1PU* (accessed 26 January 2020).

Keim, Brandon, 'Happiness and Sadness Spread Just Like Disease', *Wired*, 14 July 2010, *https://www.wired.com/2010/07/contagious-emotions/* (accessed 19 June 2019).

Kent, Le'a, 'Fighting Abjection: Representing Fat Women', in Jana E. Braziel and Kathleen LeBesco (eds), *Bodies out of Bounds: Fatness and Transgression* (Berkeley: University of California Press, 2001), pp. 130–50.

Kermode, Frank, *The Sense of an Ending: Studies in Theory of Fiction* (Oxford: Oxford University Press, 1967).

Kirkland, A., 'The Environmental Account of Obesity: A Case for Feminist Skepticism', *Signs: Journal of Women in Culture and Society*, 36/2 (2011), 463–85.

Klepac, Petra, Stephen Kissler and Julia Gog, 'Contagion! The BBC Four Pandemic: The model behind the documentary', *Epidemics*, 24 (2018), 49–59.

Knodel, J., 'Texas Lt. Gov. Dan Patrick suggests he, other seniors willing to die to get economy going again', *NBC News*, 24 March 2020, *https://www.nbcnews.com/news/us-news/texas-lt-gov-dan-patrick-suggests-he-other-seniors-willing-n1167341* (accessed 2 July 2020).

Kramer, Larry, *The Normal Heart and The Destiny of Me: Two Plays* (New York: Grove Press, 2000).

Kristeva, Julia, *Powers of Horror: An Essay on Abjection*, translated by Leon S. Roudiez (New York: Columbia University Press, 1982).

'Krokodil crosses over to U.S. from Russia', CNN, YouTube, 11 October 2013, *https://www.youtube.com/watch?v=-xF1ejbShZ8* (accessed 26 January 2020).

'Krokodil, The Flesh-Eating Street Drug That Rots Skin From Inside-Out, Expands To Illinois', *The Huffington Post*, 9 October 2013, *http://www.huffingtonpost.com/2013/10/09/krokodil-drug_n_4073417.html?utm_hp_ref=krokodil* (accessed 26 January 2020).

Kruger, Steven F., *AIDS Narratives: Gender and Sexuality, Fiction and Science* (New York: Garland, 1996).

Kuhling, C. L., 'Zombie Banks, Zombie Politics and the "Walking Zombie Movement": Liminality and the Post-Crisis Irish Imaginary', *European Journal of Cultural Studies*, 20/4 (2017), 397–412.

Kumar, Krishan, *Utopia and Anti-utopia in Modern Times* (Oxford: Basil Blackwell, 1987).

Kuo, L., '"The new normal": China's excessive coronavirus public monitoring could be here to stay', *The Guardian*, 9 March 2020, *https://www.theguardian.com/world/2020/mar/09/the-new-normal-chinas-excessive-coronavirus-public-monitoring-could-be-here-to-stay* (accessed 19 May 2020).

Lakoff, George and Mark Johnson, *Metaphors We Live By* (Chicago and London: The University of Chicago Press, 1980, 2003).

Landau, E., 'Thinner is Better to Curb Global Warming, Study Says', *CNN.com*, 2009, *http://edition.cnn.com/2009/HEALTH/04/20/thin.global.warming/index.html* (accessed 29 August 2019).

Larson, Brendon M. H., Brigitte Nerlich and Patrick Wallis, 'Metaphors and Biorisks: The War on Infectious Diseases and Invasive Species', *Science Communication*, 26/3 (2005), 243–68.

Latham, Rob, *Consuming Youth: Vampires, Cyborgs, and the Culture of Consumption* (Chicago: University of Chicago Press, 2002).

Latour, Bruno, 'From Realpolitik to Dingpolitik: How to Make Things Public. An Introduction', in Bruno Latour and Peter Weibel (eds), *Making Things Public: Atmospheres of Democracy* (Cambridge (MA): MIT Press, 2005), pp. 1–31.

Lauro, Sarah J., *The Transatlantic Zombie: Slavery, Rebellion, and Living Death* (New Brunswick: Rutgers University Press, 2015).

Lauro, Sarah J. (ed.), *Zombie Theory: A Reader* (Minneapolis: University of Minnesota Press, 2017).

Lavigne, Carlen, *Post-Apocalyptic Patriarchy: American Television and Gendered Visions of Survival* (Jefferson: McFarland, 2018).

Lawrence, F., 'The Way We Eat is Killing Us – and the Planet', *The Guardian*, 28 January 2019, *https://www.theguardian.com/commentisfree/2019/jan/28/global-food-killing-humans-planet-climate-change-obesity* (accessed 29 August 2019).

Lazear, H. M., E. M. Stringer and A. M. De Silva, 'The emerging Zika virus epidemic in the Americas: Research priorities', *Journal of the American Medical Association*, 315/18 (2016), 1945–6.

Ledbetter, C., 'Ken Jennings Of "Jeopardy!" Fame Tweets Awful Wheelchair "Joke"', *Huffington Post*, 22 September 2014, *https://www.huffingtonpost.com/2014/09/22/ken-jennings-wheelchair-joke_n_5864374.html* (accessed 29 May 2018).

LeGuin, Ursula, 'The Ones Who Walk Away from Omelas' (1973), *http://www.mccc.edu/pdf/eng102/Week%209/Text_LeGuin%20Ursula_Ones%20Who%20Walk%20Away%20From%20Omelas.pdf* (accessed 20 June 2018).

LeGuin, Ursula, *The Dispossessed* (New York: HarperCollins ebooks, 2018 [1974]).

Lemon, T. I., 'Homemade Heroin Substitute Causing Hallucinations', *African Journal of Psychiatry*, 16/6 (2013), 411.

Lenz, L., 'That Viral Photo of a Baby with Disabilities is Likely a Money-Making Scam', *The Daily Dot*, 10 August 2016, *https://www.consumeraffairs.com/news/like-farming-facebook-scams-look-before-you-like-042215.html* (accessed 23 April 2018).

'Letters: Obesity and Climate Change', *The Independent*, 16 October 2007, *http://www.independent.co.uk/opinion/letters/letters-obesity-and-climate-change-396985.html* (accessed 29 August 2019).

Levin, D., 'Synthetic Drug Manufacturing Is an Open Secret in China', *The New York Times*, 23 June 2015, *http://www.nytimes.com/times-insider/2015/06/23/synthetic-drug-manufacturing-is-an-open-secret-in-china/?_r=0* (accessed 26 January 2020).

Levina, Marina, *Pandemics and the Media* (New York: Peter Lang, 2015).

Lewis, Ted G., *Book of Extremes: Why the 21st Century Isn't Like the 20th Century* (New York: Springer, 2014).

Lewis, Victoria A., 'Crip', in Rachel Adams, Benjamin Reiss and David Serlin (eds), *Keywords for Disability Studies* (New York: New York University Press, 2015), pp. 46–8.

Lindblad, K.-L., 'Bad News: People Are Taking Krokodil in Norway', *Vice*, 8 August 2012, *http://www.vice.com/en_uk/read/krokodil-norway* (accessed 26 January 2020).

Linnemann, T. and T. Wall, '"This is Your Face on Meth": The Punitive Spectacle of "White Trash" in the Rural War on Drugs', *Theoretical Criminology*, 17 (2013), 315–34.

Linnemann, T., L. Hanson and L. S. Williams, '"With Scenes of Blood and Pain". Crime Control and the Punitive Imagination of The Meth Project', *British Journal of Criminology*, 53 (2013), 605–23.

Linnemann, T., T. Wall and E. Green, 'The Walking Dead and Killing State: Zombification and the Normalization of Police Violence', *Theoretical Criminology*, 18/4 (2014), 506–27.

Losh, Elizabeth and Beth Coleman (eds), *Tweeting the Revolution: Networked Media, the Rhetorics of Activism, and Practices of the Everyday* (forthcoming).

Lowe, R., C. Barcellow, P. Brasil, O. G. Cruz, N. A. Honorio, H. Kuper and M. Sá Carvalho, 'The Zika Virus Epidemic in Brazil: From Discovery to Future Implications', *International Journal of Environmental Research and Public Health*, 15/96 (2018), 1–18.

Lowry, Louis, *The Giver Quartet* (New York: Houghton Mifflin Harcourt, 2012).

Lupkin, S., 'Here's What You Should Know About the Zika Virus', *Vice News*, 29 January 2016, *https://news.vice.com/article/heres-what-you-should-know-about-the-zika-virus* (accessed 15 May 2018).

Lusher, A., '"Zombie spice addicts plague" caused by everything we warned you about, claim legal highs ban critics', *The Independent*, 11 April 2017, *https://www.independent.co.uk/news/uk/home-news/spice-legal-highs-zombie-plague-walking-zombies-manchester-legal-highs-ban-psychoactive-substances-a7678931.html* (accessed 26 January 2020).

Lustig, Tim and James Peacock (eds), *Diseases and Disorders in Contemporary Fiction: The Syndrome Syndrome* (New York: Routledge, 2013).

Mackay, Charles, *Extraordinary Popular Delusions and the Madness of Crowds* (London: Richard Bentley, 1841).

Macron, Emmanuel, 'Adresse aux Français', 16 mars 2020, *https://www.elysee.fr/emmanuel-macron/2020/03/16/adresse-aux-francais-covid19* (accessed 22 May 2020).

Magnusson, Bruce and Zahi Zalloua (eds), *Contagion: Health, Fear, Sovereignty* (Seattle: University of Washington Press, 2012).

Magus, 'New Story: 4 Weeks Later', *The Evolution Forum: Male Muscle Growth*, 20 September 2003, *https://archive.muscle-growth.org/threads/413-p1.html* (accessed 15 June 2017).

Mahncke, J., 'Campaign aims to #WashTheHate of coronavirus racism', *Deutsche Welle*, 2 May 2020, *https://www.dw.com/en/campaign-aims-to-washthehate-of-coronavirus-racism/a-53309233* (accessed 22 May 2020).

Mallin, A. and J. Margolin, 'Homeland Security warns terrorists may exploit COVID-19 pandemic', *ABC News*, 24 March 2020, *https://abcnews.go.com/Politics/homeland-security-warns-terrorists-exploit-covid-19-pandemic/story?id=69770582* (accessed 22 May 2020).

Mangan, Lucy, 'Contagion! review – an epidemic of tedium', *The Guardian*, 22 March 2018, *https://www.theguardian.com/tv-and-radio/2018/mar/22/contagion-review-an-epidemic-of-tedium* (accessed 17 November 2019).

Manlove, Colin N., *The Impulse of Fantasy Literature* (London: Palgrave Macmillan, 1982).

Mann, Annika, *Reading Contagion: The Hazards of Reading in the Age of Print* (Charlottesville: University of Virginia Press, 2018).

Mansoor, S., 'Data Suggests Many New York City Neighborhoods Hardest Hit by COVID-19 Are Also Low-Income Areas', *Time*, 5 April 2020, *https://time.com/5815820/data-new-york-low-income-neighborhoods-coronavirus/* (accessed 22 May 2020).

Marion, Isaac, *Warm Bodies* (The Warm Bodies Series) (London: Random House, 2010).

Marsh, N., 'Desire and disease in the speculative economy', *Journal of Cultural Economy*, 4/3 (2011), 301–14.

Martin, Hans-Peter and Harald Schumann, *The Global Trap: Globalization and the Assault on Prosperity and Democracy* (London: Zed Books, 1997).

Marx, Karl and Friedrich Engels, 'Manifesto of the Communist Party' [1848], *Marxists.org*, *https://www.marxists.org/archive/marx/works/1848/communist-manifesto/ch01.htm* (accessed 27 January 2020).

Matheson, Richard, *I Am Legend* (London: Hatchette UK, 2011 [New York: Fawcett Publications, 1954]).

Matthews, Melissa, 'Weight Gain is Contagious and You Could "Catch" Obesity from Your Neighbors, Study Finds', *Newsweek*, 24 January 2018, *http://www.newsweek.com/weight-gain-contagious-and-you-could-catch-obesity-your-neighbors-study-finds-789547* (accessed 27 January 2020).

Matthews-King, A., 'International Treaty Needed to Stop "Big Food" Industry Driving Obesity and Climate Change, Report Says', *The Independent*, 28 January 2019, *https://www.independent.co.uk/news/health/big-food-treaty-agriculture-industry-obesity-climate-change-sugar-tax-a8747176.html* (accessed 29 August 2019).

Mayer, J. D., 'Big Daddy Trump', *The American Interest*, 25 August 2016, *https://www.the-american-interest.com/2016/08/25/big-daddy-trump/* (accessed 28 June 2019).

Mayo Foundation for Medical Education and Research, 'Microcephaly', *Mayo Clinic*, 26 April 2018, *https://www.mayoclinic.org/diseases-conditions/microcephaly/symptoms-causes/syc-20375051* (accessed 14 May 2018).

McCabe, Janet and Kim Akass (eds), *Quality TV: Contemporary American Television and Beyond* (New York: I.B. Tauris, 2007).

McDonald, Keith and Richard Clark, *Guillermo del Toro: Film as Alchemic Art* (New York: Bloomsbury, 2014).

McNally, David, *Monsters of the Market: Zombies, Vampires and Global Capitalism* (Chicago: Haymarket Books, 2012).

Melley, Timothy, *The Covert Sphere: Secrecy, Fiction, and the National Security State* (Ithaca: Cornell University Press, 2012).

Meredith, C., '"Krokodil" Trend Of Flesh-Rotting Drugs Hits UK (GRAPHIC PICTURES)', *The Huffington Post UK*, 26 October 2013, *http://www.huffington*

post.co.uk/2013/10/24/krokodil-drug-graphic-pictures-uk_n_4156584.html (accessed 26 January 2020).

Mervosh, S., J. C. Lee, L. Gamio and N. Popovich, 'See Which States are Reopening and Which are Still Shut Down', *The New York Times*, 14 May 2020, *https://www.nytimes.com/interactive/2020/us/states-reopen-map-coronavirus.html* (accessed 22 May 2020).

Michaelowa, A. and B. Dransfeld, 'Greenhouse Gas Benefits of Fighting Obesity', *Ecological Economics*, 66/2–3 (2008), 298–308.

Miles, T. and B. Hirschler, 'Zika virus set to spread across Americas, spurring vaccine hunt', *Reuters*, 25 January 2016, *https://www.reuters.com/article/us-health-zika-idUSKCN0V30U6* (accessed 15 May 2018).

Miller, B. L., J. M. Stogner, L. E. Agnich, A. Sanders, J. Bacot and S. Felix, 'Marketing a Panic: Media Coverage of Novel Psychoactive Drugs (NPDs) and its Relationship with Legal Changes', *American Journal of Criminal Justice*, 40/3 (2015), 523–41.

Mitchell, David T., Susan Antebi and Sharon L. Snyder (eds), T*he Matter of Disability: Materiality, Biopolitics, Crip Affect* (Ann Arbor: University of Michigan Press, 2019).

Mitchell, Peta, *Contagious Metaphor* (London: Bloomsbury, 2013).

Mitman, G., 'Ebola in a Stew of Fear', *The New England Journal of Medicine*, 371 (2014), 1763–5.

Mittell, Jason, *Complex TV: The Poetics of Contemporary Television Storytelling* (New York: New York University Press, 2015).

Mohdin, A., 'BAME women make up 55% of UK pregnancy hospitalisations with COVID-19', *The Guardian*, 16 May 2020, *https://www.theguardian.com/world/2020/may/16/bame-majority-pregnant-women-hospitalised-covid-19-troubling-midwives* (accessed 22 May 2020).

Monchinski, Tony, *Eden* (New York: Permuted Press, 2008).

Morton, Seth, 'Zombie Politics', in Edward P. Comentale and Aaron Jaffe (eds), T*he Year's Work at the Zombie Research Center* (Bloomington: Indiana University Press, 2014), pp. 315–40.

Motta, M., 'The Dynamics and Political Implications of Anti-Intellectualism in the United States', *American Politics Research*, 46/3 (2018), 465–98.

Moylan, Tom, *Demand the Impossible: Science Fiction and the Utopian Imagination* (London: Peter Lang, 1976 [2014]).

Mullins, M. E. and E. S. Schwarz, '"Krokodil" in the United States Is an Urban Legend and Not a Medical Fact', *American Journal of Medicine*, 127/7 (2014), e25.

Munz, Philip, Ioan Hudea, Joe Imad and Robert J. Smith, 'When Zombies Attack!: Mathematical Modeling of an Outbreak of Zombie Infection', in

Jean M. Tchuenche and Christinah Chiyaka (eds), *Infectious Disease Modeling Research Progress* (Hauppauge: Nova Science, 2009), pp. 133–50.

Murray, Ray, Twitter post, 20 April 2020, *https://twitter.com/praymurray/status/1252243718725423105/photo/1*.

Myers, Heather, 'Crawling Off the Screen: An Ethnography of Live Action Zombie Events in the United States' (unpublished MA thesis, Harvard University, Cambridge, 2011), *https://www.academia.edu/2493358/Crawling_off_the_Screen_An_Ethnography_of_Live_Action_Zombie_Events_in_the_United_States* (accessed 17 November 2019).

Nagle, Angela, *Kill All Normies: Online Culture Wars from 4chan and Tumblr to Trump and the Alt-Right* (New York: Zero Books, 2017).

Neiwert, David, *Alt-America: The Rise of the Radical Right in the Age of Trump* (New York: Verso Books, 2017).

Nerlich, Brigitte, Carmen McLeod and Steven Burgess, 'Frankenflies Sent To Defeat Monster Mosi: Zika in the English press', *PLOS*, 15 March 2016, *http://blogs.plos.org/blog/2016/03/15/frankenflies-sent-to-defeat-monster-mosi-zika-in-the-english-press/* (accessed 16 May 2018).

Ní Fhlainn, Sorcha, *Postmodern Vampires: Film, Fiction, and Popular Culture* (London: Palgrave Macmillan, 2019).

Nichols, Thomas M., *The Death of Expertise: The Campaign against Established Knowledge and Why it Matters* (New York: Oxford University Press, 2017).

Nilges, Matthias, 'The Aesthetics of Destruction: Contemporary US Cinema and TV Culture', in Jeff Birkenstein, Karen Randell and Anna Froula (eds), *Reframing 9/11: Film, Popular Culture and the 'War on Terror'* (New York: Continuum, 2010), pp. 23–33.

Nye, J., 'Horrific images of drug-users eaten alive by flesh-eating illness caused by homemade heroin substitute that has arrived on American shores in Arizona', *Mail Online*, 26 September 2013, *http://www.dailymail.co.uk/news/article-2432802/Drug-users-eaten-alive-flesh-eating-illness-caused-homemade-heroin-substitute-Krokodil.html#reader-comments* (accessed 26 January 2020).

'Obesity "As Bad As Climate Risk"', *BBC News*, 14 October 2007, *http://news.bbc.co.uk/1/hi/health/7043639.stm* (accessed 29 August 2019).

'Obesity Causes Global Warming, Say Scientists', *Mail Online*, 21 April 2009, *https://www.dailymail.co.uk/sciencetech/article-1172249/Being-fat-causes-global-warming-say-scientists.html* (accessed 29 August 2019).

'Obesity Crisis "On the Same Scale as Global Warming"', *The Times*, 15 October 2007, *https://www.thetimes.co.uk/article/obesity-crisis-on-the-same-scale-as-global-warming-q8zkk53vnjh* (accessed 29 August 2019).

O'Connell, O., 'Alex Jones says he'd kill and cook his neighbours to feed his kids', *The Independent*, 1 May 2020, *https://www.independent.co.uk/news/world/americas/*

alex-jones-coronavirus-global-collapse-cook-neighbours-feed-kids-a9495201.html (accessed 2 July 2020).

O'Leary, Stephen D., 'Apocalypticism in American Popular Culture: From the Dawn of the Nuclear Age to the End of the American Century', in John J. Collins, Bernard McGinn and Stephen J. Stein (eds), *The Encyclopedia of Apocalypticism*, vol. 3 (New York: Continuum, 1998), pp. 392–426.

Oliver, J. Eric, *Fat Politics: The Real Story Behind America's Obesity Epidemic* (Oxford: Oxford University Press, 2006).

Oliver, T., S. J. Gheevarghese, U. Gandhi, Z. Y. Bhat and U. Pillai, '"Krokodil" – A Menace Slowly Spreading Across the Atlantic', *American Journal of Therapeutics*, 22/3 (2015), 231–3.

Olson, G., '"Like a Dog": Rituals of Animal Degradation in J. M. Coetzee's Disgrace and Abu Ghraib Prison', *Journal of Narrative Theory*, 44/1 (2014), 116–56.

Osborne, H., 'Russia's Flesh-Eating Krokodil Drug an Urban Legend in UK, US and Canada', *International Business Times*, 21 November 2013, *http://www.ibtimes.co.uk/krokodil-flesh-eating-drug-spreading-usa-canada-524200* (accessed 26 January 2020).

Oteri, Michaela, Twitter post, 24 April 2018, *https://twitter.com/Ogrefairy/status/988860783865065472.*

Outbreak, Wolfgang Petersen, dir. (Warner Brothers, 1995).

Owen, L., 'Monstrous Freedom: Charting Fat Ambivalence', *Fat Studies*, 4/1 (2015), 1–13.

Oyler, L. 'When Did Everything Get So "Toxic"?' *The New York Times*, 2 October, 2018, *https://www.nytimes.com/2018/10/02/magazine/when-did-everything-get-so-toxic.html* (accessed 5 August 2020).

Page, S., 'Monkey Dust mayhem: the English city reportedly at the centre of a drug-fuelled "epidemic"', *The Conversation*, 6 September 2018, *https://theconversation.com/monkey-dust-mayhem-the-english-city-reportedly-at-the-centre-of-a-drug-fuelled-epidemic-102066* (accessed 26 January 2020).

Palmer, J., 'Don't Blame Bat Soup for the Coronavirus', *Foreign Policy*, 27 January 2020, *https://foreignpolicy.com/2020/01/27/coronavirus-covid19-dont-blame-bat-soup-for-the-virus/* (accessed 2 July 2020).

Pan's Labyrinth, Guillermo del Toro, dir. (Telecinco Cinema/Estudios Picasso/Tequila Gang/Esperanto Filmoj/Sententia Entertainment, 2006).

Parikka, Jussi, *Digital Contagions: A Media Archaeology of Computer Viruses*, 2nd updated edition (New York: Peter Lang, 2016).

Parsons, S., W. Simmons, F. Shinhoster and J. Kilburn, 'A Test of the Grapevine: An Empirical Examination of Conspiracy Theories among African Americans', *Sociological Spectrum*, 19/2 (1999), 201–22.

Pearl, Monica B., *AIDS Literature and Gay Identity: The Literature of Loss* (New York: Routledge, 2013).

Peeren, Esther, *The Spectral Metaphor: Living Ghosts and the Agency of Invisibility* (New York: Palgrave Macmillan, 2014).

Peters, J., 'Don't Believe the Hype about the "Flesh-Eating" Drug Krokodil', *Slate*, 18 November 2013, *http://www.slate.com/blogs/crime/2013/11/18/krokodil_desomorphine_don_t_believe_the_hype_about_flesh_eating_drug_krokodil.html* (accessed 26 January 2020).

Peters, M. A., 'Anti-intellectualism is a virus', *Educational Philosophy and Theory*, 51/4 (2019), 357–63.

Peterson, Alan and Deborah Lupton, *The New Public Health: Health and Self in the Age of Risk* (London: Sage, 1996).

Petter, O., '"Toxic" Named Word of 2018 by Oxford Dictionaries', *The Independent*, 16 November 2018, *https://www.independent.co.uk/life-style/toxic-word-of-the-year-oxford-dictionary-2018-gaslighting-gammon-a8636581.html* (accessed 1 July 2020).

Pheasant-Kelly, Frances, *Fantasy Film Post 9/11* (New York: Palgrave Macmillan, 2013).

Phillips, Whitney and Ryan Milner, *The Ambivalent Internet: Mischief, Oddity, and Antagonism Online* (Malden: Polity Press, 2017).

Pieters, J., 'Online Petition against Anti-Asian Discrimination Signed 25,000 Times', *NLTIMES.nl*, 10 February 2020, *https://nltimes.nl/2020/02/10/online-petition-anti-asian-discrimination-signed-25000-times* (accessed 20 May 2020).

Plants vs Zombies (Seattle: PopCap, 2009–16).

Plumer, B. and C. Davenport, 'Science Under Attack: How Trump Is Sidelining Researchers and Their Work', *The New York Times*, 28 December 2019, *https://www.nytimes.com/2019/12/28/climate/trump-administration-war-on-science.html* (17 January 2020).

Pober, Peter Michael, 'Still Angry after All These Years: Performing the Language of HIV and the Marked Body in *The Normal Heart* and *The Destiny of Me*', *Theatre Symposium*, 5 (1997), 125–40.

Poell, T. and J. van Dijck, 'Social Media and Activist Communication', in C. Atton (ed.), *The Routledge Companion to Alternative and Community Media* (London: Routledge, 2015), pp. 527–37.

Polak, Sara and Daniel Trottier (eds), *Violence and Trolling on Social Media: History, Affect and Effects of Violence and Trolling* (Amsterdam: Amsterdam University Press, 2020).

Pope, Alexander, 'An Epistle from Mr. Pope to Dr. Arbuthnot' [1735], in Alexander Pope, *The Poems of Alexander Pope*, ed. John Butt (London: Methuen, 1965).

'Porn in US "A Public Health Crisis"', *The Telegraph*, 16 May 2014, *https://www.telegraph.co.uk/news/worldnews/northamerica/usa/10835994/Porn-in-US-a-public-health-crisis.html* (accessed 31 May 2018).

Pozorski, Aimee, Jennifer J. Lavoie and Christine J. Cynn (eds), *Literary and Visual Representations of HIV/AIDS: Forty Years Later* (Lanham, MD: Lexington Books, 2019).

Puar, Jasbiar K., *Terrorist Assemblages: Homonationalism in Queer Times* (Durham, NC: Duke University Press, 2007).

PumpingMiddleAge, 'ZIKA ZOMBIES CONFIRMED IN AFRICA', *YouTube*, 25 February 2016, *https://www.youtube.com/watch?v=jqjAm8F7BBM* (accessed 30 April 2019).

Ramsey, L., 'A wacky conspiracy is circulating about Zika and GMOs – and it needs to stop', *Business Insider*, 30 January 2016, *http://www.businessinsider.com/zika-virus-conspiracy-theory-2016-1* (accessed 15 May 2018).

Ranger, Terence and Paul Slack, *Epidemics and Ideas: Essay on the Historical Perception of Pestilence* (Cambridge (UK): Cambridge University Press, 1992).

'Regering voert strijd tegen "legal highs" op', *Het Laatste Nieuws*, 26 April 2013, *http://www.hln.be/hln/nl/957/Binnenland/article/detail/1622571/2013/04/26/Regering-voert-strijd-tegen-legal-highs-op.dhtml* (accessed 26 January 2020).

Reinarman, Craig and Harry G. Levine, 'The Crack Attack: America's Latest Drug Scare, 1986–1992', in Joel Best (ed.), I*mages of Issues: Typifying Contemporary Social Problems* (New Brunswick: Transaction, 1995), pp. 147–86.

Resident Evil (Osaka: Capcom, 1996–present).

Rezac, M., 'What Can Priests Practically Do to Combat the Porn Epidemic?' *Catholic News Agency*, 19 December 2017, *https://www.catholicnewsagency.com/news/what-can-priests-practically-do-to-combat-the-porn-epidemic-44881* (accessed 31 May 2018).

Ribeiro, Barbara, Sarah Hartley, Brigitte Nerlich and Rusi Jaspal, 'Media coverage of the Zika crisis in Brazil: The construction of a "war" frame that masked social and gender inequalities', *Social Science & Medicine*, 200 (2018), 137–44.

Rich, E. and J. Evans, 'Fat Ethics – The Obesity Discourse and Body Politics', *Social Theory and Health*, 3 (2005), 341–58.

Rigney, D., 'Three Kinds of Anti-Intellectualism: Rethinking Hofstadter', *Sociological Inquiry*, 61/4 (1991), 434–51.

Roberts, I., 'Say no to global guzzling', *New Scientist*, 194/2610 (2007), 21.

Roberts, Ian and Phil Edwards, *The Energy Glut: The Politics of Fatness in an Overheating World* (London: Zed Books, 2010).

Robinson, K. S., 'The Coronavirus Is Rewriting Our Imaginations', *The New Yorker*, 1 May 2020, *https://www.newyorker.com/culture/annals-of-inquiry/the-coronavirus-and-our-future* (accessed 2 July 2020).

Roborgh, Sophie and Larissa Fast, 'Healthcare workers are still coming under attack during the coronavirus pandemic', *The Conversation*, 28 April 2020, *https://theconversation.com/healthcare-workers-are-still-coming-under-attack-during-the-coronavirus-pandemic-136573* (accessed 8 May 2020).

Román, David, *Acts of Intervention: U.S. Theatre and Performance, Gay Men and AIDS* (Bloomington: Indiana University Press, 1998).

Rose, Frank, 'Henry Jenkins on "Spreadable Media" why fans rule, and why "The Walking Dead" lives' [interview with Henry Jenkins], *Deep Media*, 17 January 2013, *http://www.deepmediaonline.com/deepmedia/2013/01/henry-jenkins-on-spreadable-media.html* (accessed 31 May 2018).

Rosemain, M., 'France's COVID-19 tracing app expected to enter testing in week of May 11', *Reuters*, 3 May 2020, *https://www.reuters.com/article/us-health-coronavirus-france/frances-covid-19-tracing-app-expected-to-enter-testing-in-week-of-may-11-idUSKBN22F0QW* (accessed 20 May 2020).

Rosenberg, Erika L., 'Mindfulness and Consumerism', in Tim Kasser and Allen D. Kanner (eds), *Psychology and Consumer Culture: The Struggle for a Good Life in a Materialistic World* (Washington: Psychological Association, 2004), pp. 107–25.

Roskam-Kwint, H. M., S. P. Kruizinga, M. J. H. Kaal and H.-P. R. Bootsma, 'Gevaarlijke Designer Drug "Krokodil" voor het Eerst in Nederland Gesignaleerd. Casuïstische Mededeling', *Pharmaceutisch Weekblad Wetenschappelijk Platform*, 7 (2013), a1328.

Russell, C. et al., '"Fatties Cause Global Warming": Fat Pedagogy and Environmental Education', *Canadian Journal of Environmental Education*, 18 (2013), 15–33.

'Russische Todesdroge: Bochumer Junkies spritzten doch kein "Krokodil"', *Focus Online*, 14 October 2011, *http://www.focus.de/gesundheit/ratgeber/psychologie/news/russische-todesdroge-bochumer-junkies-spritzten-doch-kein-krokodil_aid_674807.html* (accessed 26 January 2020).

Rutherford, Jennifer, *Zombies* (New York: Routledge, 2013).

Ryan, F., 'Surprised to See a Hot Woman in a Wheelchair?' *The Guardian*, 7 May 2018, *https://www.theguardian.com/society/shortcuts/2018/may/07/surprised-to-see-a-hot-woman-in-a-wheelchair-if-so-examine-your-prejudices* (accessed 28 May 2018).

Santa Clarita Diet, 'So Then a Bat or a Monkey', Ruben Fleischer, dir. (Netflix, 3 February 2017).

Schaefer, M. T., *Bastard Culture! How User Participation Transforms Cultural Production* (Amsterdam: Amsterdam University Press, 2011).

Scherer, B. and J. Waistell, 'Incorporating mindfulness: questioning capitalism', Journal of Management, *Spirituality & Religion*, 15/2 (2018), 1–18.

Schindler, J., 'Die "Sparsamen Vier" sind der Inbegriff von Asozialität', *Der Spiegel*, 5 June 2020, *https://www.spiegel.de/politik/ausland/corona-und-europaeische-solidaritaet-die-sparsamen-vier-sind-schlicht-der-inbegriff-von-asozialitaet-a-7dcdc93e-2150-47a7-ae21-ea095748248d* (accessed 1 July 2020).

Schmeink, Lars, '9/11 and the Wasted Lives of Posthuman Zombies', in Lars Schmeink (ed.), *Biopunk Dystopias: Genetic Engineering, Society and Science Fiction* (Liverpool: Liverpool University Press, 2016), pp. 200–36.

Schuetze, Sarah, 'The Zika Virus: What We're Really Talking About', *The Society Pages*, 2 February 2016, *https://thesocietypages.org/girlwpen/2016/02/02/the-zika-virus-what-were-really-talking-about/* (accessed 16 May 2018).

Schwartz, I., 'Chuck Todd: Are Republicans "Overdoing" Rhetoric on Ebola?' *RealClearPolitics*, 19 October 2014, *http://bit.ly/1FqnQd5* (accessed 26 January 2020).

Schweitzer, Dahlia, *Going Viral: Zombies, Viruses, and the End of the World* (New Brunswick: Rutgers University Press, 2018).

Segarra, Annie, Twitter post, 21 April 2018, *https://twitter.com/annieelainey/status/987846312761675776*.

Sell, T. K., C. Watson, D. Meyer, M. Kronk, S. Ravi, L. E. Pechta, K. M. Lubell and D. A. Rose, 'Frequency of Risk-Related News Media Messages in 2016 Coverage of Zika Virus: Risk-Related News Media Messages about Zika', *Risk Analysis* (2018), 1–11.

Seltzer, E. K., E. Horst-Martz, M. Lu and R. M. Merchant, 'Public sentiment and discourse about Zika virus on Instagram', *Public Health*, 150 (2017), 170–5.

Servitje, Lorenzo and Sherryl Vint (eds), *The Walking Med: Zombies and the Medical Image* (University Park: The Pennsylvania State University Press, 2016).

Shafer, J., 'Behind Trump's Strange "Invisible Enemy" Rhetoric', *Politico*, 9 April 2020, *https://www.politico.com/news/magazine/2020/04/09/trump-coronavirus-invisible-enemy-177894* (accessed 2 July 2020).

Shah, Nayan, *Contagious Divides: Epidemics and Race in San Francisco's Chinatown* (Oakland: University of California Press, 2001).

Shapiro, Joseph, *No Pity: People with Disabilities Forging a New Civil Rights Movement* (New York: Three Rivers Press, 1994).

Sharfstein, J. M., 'On Fear, Distrust, and Ebola', *JAMA Forum*, 24 February 2015, *http://jama.jamanetwork.com/article.aspx?articleid=2130303* (accessed 26 January 2020).

Shaviro, S., 'Capitalist Monsters', *Historical Materialism*, 10/4 (2002), 281–90.

Shear, M. D. and Z. Kanno-Youngs, 'Trump Administration Plans to Extend Virus Border Restrictions Indefinitely', *The New York Times*, 13 May 2020, *https://www.nytimes.com/2020/05/13/us/politics/trump-coronavirus-border-restrictions.html* (accessed 22 May 2020).

Shepherd, T., 'Social Media Stole My Daughter's Identity', *News.com.au*, 26 October 2012, *http://www.news.com.au/technology/facebook-stole-my-disabled-daughters-identity/news-story/9f77d1cd91ff00363a5c21f9a5bc1bc6* (accessed 14 May 2018).

Shifman, Limor, *Memes in Digital Culture* (Cambridge (MA): MIT Press, 2014).

Shildrick, Margrit, 'Chimerism and Immunitas: The Emergence of a Posthumanist Biophilosophy', in S. E. Wilmer and Audronė Žukauskaitė (eds), *Resisting Biopolitics: Philosophical, Political, and Performative Strategies* (London: Routledge, 2015), pp. 95–108.

Shildrick, Margrit, *Embodying the Monster: Encounters with the Vulnerable Self* (London and Thousand Oaks: Sage, 2002).

Shildrick, Margrit, *Leaky Bodies and Boundaries: Feminism, Postmodernism and (Bio)Ethics* (London: Routledge, 1997).

Sinclaire, J., 'Watch the Doomsday Clock Announcement', *The Bulletin of the Atomic Scientists*, 23 January 2017, *https://thebulletin.org/2017/01/watch-the-doomsday-clock-announcement/* (accessed 8 July 2019).

Smedley, T., 'The Poisons Released by Melting Arctic Ice', *BBC.com*, 17 June 2019, *http://www.bbc.com/future/story/20190612-the-poisons-released-by-melting-arctic-ice* (accessed 8 July 2019).

Smith, Angela M., 'Dis-Affection: Disability Effects and Disabled Moves at the Movies', in David T. Mitchell, Susan Antebi and Sharon L. Snyder (eds), *The Matter of Disability: Materiality, Biopolitics, Crip Affect* (Ann Arbor: University of Michigan Press, 2019), pp. 118–43.

Smith, H., 'Flesh-eating drug krokodil "could sink its teeth into British addicts", health workers warned', *Metro*, 23 March 2014, *http://metro.co.uk/2014/03/23/flesh-eating-drug-krokodil-could-sink-its-teeth-into-british-addicts-health-workers-warned-4674343/* (accessed 26 January 2020).

Sobchack, Vivian, *Screening Space: The American Science Fiction Film* (New Jersey: Rutgers University Press, 1999).

Soncul, Y. and J. Parikka, 'Masks: The Face between Bodies and Networks', *Paletten Art Journal*, 28 April 2020, *https://paletten.net/journal/masks-between-bodies-and-networks* (accessed 18 May 2020).

Sorenson, A. E., R. C. Jordan and S. LaDeau, 'Reframing communication about Zika and mosquitos to increase disease prevention behavior', *Cogent Environmental Science*, 3 (2017), 1–10.

Spooner, Catherine, *Post-Millennial Gothic: Comedy, Romance and the Rise of Happy Gothic* (London: Bloomsbury Publishing, 2017).

Sprayberry, T., 'The Can-I-Pray-For-You Encounter', *The Mobility Resource*, 23 September 2013, *https://blog.themobilityresource.com/blog/post/the-can-i-pray-for-you-encounter* (accessed 26 May 2018).

Squalli, J., 'Is obesity associated with global warming?', *Public Health*, 128/12 (2014), 1087–93.

Stern, Franz, *The Varieties of History* (New York: Random House, 1973).

Stobbart, Dawn, *Videogames and Horror: From Amnesia to Zombies, Run!* (Cardiff: University of Wales Press, 2019).

Stobbe, M., 'Study Finds Little Bang for the Buck in Zika Blood Testing', *Associated Press*, 9 May 2018, *https://www.usnews.com/news/us/articles/2018-05-09/study-finds-little-bang-for-the-buck-in-zika-blood-testing* (accessed 29 April 2019).

Stoker, Bram, *Dracula* (London: Signet Classics, 1996 [1987]).

Straw, J., 'Survivors of Zika Virus Mutate into Zombies Want to Eat Doctors', *YouTube*, 6 March 2017, *https://www.youtube.com/watch?v=lVNVYe7tJ4k* (accessed 30 April 2019).

Swinburn, B. et al., 'The Global Syndemic of Obesity, Undernutrition, and Climate Change: The Lancet Commission Report', *The Lancet*, 393 (2019), 791–846.

Tesfaye, S., 'America hits peak anti-intellectualism: Majority of Republicans now think college is bad', *Salon*, 11 July 2017, *https://www.salon.com/2017/07/11/america-hits-peak-anti-intellectualism-majority-of-republicans-now-think-college-is-bad/* (accessed 4 July 2019).

The Bookloft, 'In case you need a laugh . . .', *Facebook*, 10 November 2016, *https://www.facebook.com/434847149875233/photos/a.469008116459136.122829.434847149875233/1501154866577784/?type=3&theater* (accessed 8 July 2019).

The Day of the Triffids, Steve Sekely, dir. (Security Pictures Ltd, 1962).

The Girl with All the Gifts, Colm McCarthy, dir. (UK, Warner Bros. Pictures, 2016).

The Great Plague, Timeline, 2017, *https://youtu.be/HPe6BgzHWY0* (accessed 22 May 2020).

The Late Show with Stephen Colbert, 'Michael Moore's Question For Americans: How Do We Want To Live After This Pandemic?' *YouTube*, 22 April 2020, *https://www.youtube.com/watch?v=wFKkVvUgUUk* (accessed 19 May 2020).

The Real Truth Movement, 'The Effects of Krokodil – Real Life Zombies', *YouTube*, 23 November 2013, *https://www.youtube.com/watch?v=8HLYnl7vEoYT* (accessed 26 January 2020).

The Representation Project, Twitter post, 23 April 2018, *https://twitter.com/TheRepProject/status/988510175542759424*.

The Strain, 'BK, NY', Gregory Hoblit and Guillermo del Toro, dirs (FX, 17 September 2015).

——, 'By Any Means', T. J. Scott, dir. (FX, 24 September 2015).

——, 'Creatures of the Night', Guy Ferland, dir. (FX, 23 September 2015).

——, 'Do Or Die', Vincenzo Natali, dir. (FX, 12 June 2017).
——, 'For Services Rendered', Charlotte Sieling, dir. (FX, 16 September 2015).
——, 'Fort Defiance', Guy Ferland, dir. (FX, 1 October 2015).
——, 'Loved Ones', John Dahl, dir. (FX, 8 October 2015).
——, 'Madness', Deran Sarafian (FX, 29 May 2017).
——, 'Night Train', Vincenzo Natali, dir. (FX, 10 November 2016).
——, 'Night Zero', Guillermo del Toro, dir. (FX, 29 July 2015).
——, 'Occultation', Peter Weller, dir. (FX, 9 September 2015).
——, 'Runaways', Peter Weller, dir. (FX, 26 August 2015).
——, 'The Box', David Semel, dir. (FX, 5 August 2015).
——, 'The Disappeared', Charlotte Sieling, dir. (FX, 30 September 2015).
——, 'The Last Stand', J. Miles Dale, dir. (FX, 6 October 2017).
——, 'The Master', Phil Abraham, dir. (FX, 29 October 2015).
——, 'The Silver Angel', J. Miles Dale, dir. (FX, 8 October 2015).

The Thing from Another World, Christian Nyby, dir. (Winchester Pictures Corporation, 1951).

The Twilight Saga: Breaking Dawn, Part I and II, Bill Condon, dir. (Temple Hill Entertainment/Sunswept Entertainment, 2011/2012).

——, *Eclipse*, David Slade, dir. (Temple Hill Entertainment/Maverick Films/Imprint Entertainment/Sunswept Entertainment, 2010).

——, *New Moon*, Chris Weitz, dir. (Temple Hill Entertainment/Imprint Entertainment/Sunswept Entertainment, 2009).

The Walking Dead, 'Wildfire', Ernest R. Dickerson, dir. (AMC, 13 May 2012).

'The War on Mosquitoes: Bayer Researchers Aim to Stem Zika, Malaria and Dengue', *The Bayer Scientific Magazine*, 30 (2016), 94–9.

'The Zombie Survival Guide', Wikipedia, *https://en.wikipedia.org/wiki/The_Zombie_Survival_Guide* (accessed 21 June 2018).

Thekkemuriyi, D. V., S. G. John and U. Pillai, '"Krokodil" – A Designer Drug from Across the Atlantic, with Serious Consequences', *American Journal of Medicine*, 127/3 (2014), e1–e2.

Theroux, M., 'The end of corona virus: what plague literature tells us about our future', *The Guardian*, 1 May 2020, *https://www.theguardian.com/books/2020/may/01/the-end-of-coronavirus-what-plague-literature-tells-us-about-our-future* (accessed 20 May 2020).

Thibodeau, P. H. and L. Boroditsky, 'Metaphors We Think With: The Role of Metaphor in Reasoning', *PLoS ONE*, 6/2 (2011).

Tinsley, Meghan and Neema Beegum, 'Clap for Our Heroes: "Good" Migrants, Wartime Rhetoric, and Covid19', *Discover Society*, 21 May 2020, *https://discoversociety.org/2020/05/21/clap-for-our-heroes-good-migrants-wartime-rhetoric-and-covid-19/* (accessed 8 July 2019).

TmarTn, Twitter post, 15 October 2014, *https://twitter.com/TmarTn/status/522442071907774466* (accessed 30 January 2020).

Todorov, Tzvetan, *The Fantastic: A Structural Approach to a Literary Genre* (Oxford: Blackwell Publishers Inc., 1977).

Tomkins, Silvan, 'Script Theory and Nuclear Scripts', in Eve Kosofsky Sedgwick and Adam Frank (eds), *Shame and Its Sisters: A Silvan Tomkins Reader* (Durham, NC: Duke University Press, 1995), pp. 179–95.

Trappett, Geoff, Twitter post, 28 April 2018, *https://twitter.com/InclusionMoves/status/990441385093312512.*

Trump, Donald J., 'Remarks by President Trump in Address to the Nation', 11 March 2020, *https://www.whitehouse.gov/briefings-statements/remarks-president-trump-address-nation/* (accessed 22 May 2020).

——, Twitter post, 3 October 2014, *https://twitter.com/realDonaldTrump/status/517805743056359424* (accessed 30 January 2020).

——, Twitter post, 15 October 2014, *https://twitter.com/realdonaldtrump/status/522394479429689344* (accessed 30 January 2020).

Turner, Patricia A., *I Heard it Through the Grapevine: Rumor in African-American Culture* (Berkeley and Los Angeles: University of California Press, 1993).

Twilight, Catherine Hardwicke, dir. (Temple Hill Entertainment/Maverick Films/Imprint Entertainment/DMG Entertainment, 2008).

Unlocked, Michael Apted, dir. (Di Bonaventura Pictures/SRA Productions/Silver Reel/Bloom/Lipsync Productions, 2017).

Ustad Stav, T., 'Ingen beslag av «krokodil» i Tromsø', *nrk.no*, 19 October 2012, *http://www.nrk.no/nordnytt/ingen-beslag-av-_krokodil_-1.8364552* (accessed 26 January 2020).

Van Helsing, Stephen Sommers, dir. (Sommers Company/Stillking Films, 2004).

VanDerWerff, E. T., 'The Strain was supposed to be FX's Walking Dead. What happened?' *Vox*, 30 July 2017, *https://www.vox.com/culture/2017/7/30/16059374/the-strain-episode-2-recap-blood-tax-dutch* (accessed 6 July 2019).

Van de Wijngaard, Anike, 'Angst voor het gevaar dat schuilt in de samenleving', *Leidsch Dagblad*, 17 April 2020.

Viala-Gaudefroy, J. and D. Lindeman, 'Donald Trump's "Chinese virus": the politics of naming', *The Conversation*, 21 April 2020, *https://theconversation.com/donald-trumps-chinese-virus-the-politics-of-naming-136796* (accessed 19 May 2020).

Vice, 'Krokodil: Russia's Deadliest Drug (NSFW)', *YouTube*, 17 May 2012, *https://www.youtube.com/watch?v=JsUH8llvTZo* (accessed 26 January 2020).

Visser, Dirk, 'Countering the Plague: AIDS Theatre as a Site of Memory', in Aimee Pozorski, Jennifer J. Lavoie and Christine J. Cynn (eds), *Literary and Visual Representations of HIV/AIDS: Forty Years Later* (Lanham, MD: Lexington Books, 2019), pp. 13–28.

Vital Signs: Crip Culture Talks Back, David Mitchell and Sharon Snyder, dirs. (Fanlight Productions, 1998).

Vogel, G., 'One year later, Zika scientists prepare for a long war', *Science*, 354/6316 (2016), 1088–9.

Wald, Priscilla, *Contagious: Cultures, Carriers, and the Outbreak Narrative* (London and Durham, NC: Duke University Press, 2008).

Walker, S., 'Krokodil: The drug that eats junkies', *The Independent*, 22 June 2011, *http://www.independent.co.uk/news/world/europe/krokodil-the-drug-that-eats-junkies-2300787.html* (accessed 26 January 2020).

Walker, S. and J. Rankin, 'Hungary passes law that will let Orbán rule by decree', *The Guardian*, 30 March 2020, *https://www.theguardian.com/world/2020/mar/30/hungary-jail-for-coronavirus-misinformation-viktor-orban* (accessed 19 May 2020).

Wallace, K., 'Mathematicians Use Zombies to Learn About Swine Flu', *The Star*, 18 August 2009, *https://www.thestar.com/life/health_wellness/2009/08/18/mathematicians_use_zombies_to_learn_about_swine_flu.html* (accessed 17 November 2019).

Wallace-Wells, D., 'Time to Panic', *The New York Times*, 16 February 2019, *https://www.nytimes.com/2019/02/16/opinion/sunday/fear-panic-climate-change-warming.html* (accessed 8 July 2019).

Wallis, E., 'Which migrant services in Europe are suspended or reduced due to COVID-19?' *InfoMigrants.net*, 18 March 2020, *https://www.infomigrants.net/en/post/23524/which-migrant-services-in-europe-are-suspended-or-reduced-due-to-covid-19* (accessed 19 May 2020).

Wang, Y. A. and M. Barry, 'Zika outbreak bears an eerie resemblance to the spread of Ebola', *Los Angeles Times*, 9 February 2016, *https://www.latimes.com/local/lanow/la-oe-0209-wang-barry-zika-ebola-20160209-story.html* (accessed 29 April 2019).

Wann, Marilyn, 'Foreword', in Esther Rothblum and Sondra Solovay (eds), *The Fat Studies Reader* (New York: New York University Press, 2009), pp. xii–xiii.

Warm Bodies, Jonathan Levine, dir. (Mandeville Films, 2013).

Warner, Michael, *The Trouble with Normal* (New York: Free Press, 1999).

Watercutter, A., 'Guillermo del Toro Talks Vampires, Giant Monsters and the "Arrogance of Science"', *Wired*, 16 November 2011, *https://www.wired.com/2011/11/interview-guillermo-del-toro/* (accessed 28 June 2019).

Webb, G. and G. Egger, 'Obesity and climate change: can we link the two and can we deal with both together?', *American Journal of Lifestyle Medicine*, 8 (2014), 200–4.

Webb, Jen and Samuel Byrnand, 'Some Kind of Virus: The Zombie as Body and as Trope', in Sarah J. Lauro (ed.), *Zombie Theory: A Reader* (Minneapolis: University of Minnesota Press, 2017), pp. 111–23.

Wehling, E., 'Daddy is Home', *Kronen Zeitung*, 22 January 2017, *https://static1.squarespace.com/static/555908b8e4b02f3bca056c41/t/58868241bebafb413c1156de/1485210185741/KRONE.pdf* (accessed 24 June 2019).

Weinstock, Jeffrey A., 'Invisible Monsters: Vision, Horror, and Contemporary Culture', in Asa S. Mittman and Peter J. Dendle (eds), *The Ashgate Research Companion to Monsters and the Monstrous* (Farnham: Ashgate, 2013), p. 275–89.

Weisman, A., '"Jeopardy!" Champ Ken Jennings Under Fire for Insensitive Wheelchair Tweet', *Business Insider*, 23 September 2014, *http://www.businessinsider.com/jeopardy-champ-ken-jennings-awful-wheelchair-tweet-2014-9* (accessed 29 May 2018).

Westlake, C., 'Why You Shouldn't "Type Amen and Share" Posts of Sick Children', Courtney Westlake (blog), 7 January 2016, *http://www.courtneywestlake.com/why-you-shouldnt-share-posts-of-sick-children/* (accessed 1 June 2018).

'Which countries have made wearing face masks compulsory?' *Aljazeera News*, last updated 17 May 2020, *https://www.aljazeera.com/news/2020/04/countries-wearing-face-masks-compulsory-200423094510867.html* (accessed 17 May 2020).

White, F. R., 'Fat, Queer, Dead: "Obesity" and the Death Drive', *Somatechnics*, 2/1 (2012), 1–17.

White, Hayden, *Metahistory: The Historical Imagination in Nineteenth-Century Europe* (Philadelphia: Johns Hopkins University Press, 1973).

White, R., 'Undesirable Consequences? Resignifying Discursive Constructions of Fatness in the Obesity "Epidemic"', in Corinna Tomrley and Ann K. Naylor (eds), *Fat Studies in the UK* (York: Raw Nerve Books, 2009), pp. 69–81.

WHO, 'Coronavirus disease 2019 (COVID-19): Situation Report – 5', World Health Organization (WHO), 25 January 2020, *https://www.who.int/docs/default-source/coronaviruse/situation-reports/20200125-sitrep-5-2019-ncov.pdf?sfvrsn=429b143d_8* (accessed 22 May 2020).

WHO, 'Coronavirus disease 2019 (COVID-19): Situation Report – 51', World Health Organization (WHO), 11 March 2020, *https://www.who.int/docs/default-source/coronaviruse/situation-reports/20200311-sitrep-51-covid-19.pdf?sfvrsn=1ba62e57_10* (accessed 22 May 2020).

WHO, 'The history of the Zika virus', World Health Organization (WHO), 2019, *http://www.who.int/emergencies/zika-virus/timeline/en/* (accessed 15 May 2018).

WHO, 'IHR Procedures concerning public health emergencies of international concern (PHEIC)', World Health Organization (WHO, 2019), *https://www.who.int/ihr/procedures/pheic/en/* (accessed 29 April 2019).

WHO, 'Statement on the 1st meeting of the IHR Emergency Committee regarding the Ebola outbreak in 2018', World Health Organization (WHO), 2018, *https://www.who.int/news-room/detail/18-05-2018-statement-on-the-1st-meeting-of-the-ihr-emergency-committee-regarding-the-ebola-outbreak-in-2018* (accessed 29 April 2019).

'Why Do We Feel So Bad', *Quora*, *https://www.quora.com/Why-do-we-feel-so-bad-when-seeing-handicapped-people-or-animals-How-can-that-terrible-and-exhausting-feeling-be-overcome* (accessed 30 April 2018).

Williams, K. W., 'The Girl with All the Gifts Race Analysis', *BlackGirlNerds.com*, 18 March 2017, *https://blackgirlnerds.com/girl-gifts-race-analysis/* (accessed 4 July 2017).

Williams, Linda, 'World and Time: Serial Television Melodrama in America', in Christine Gledhill and Linda Williams (eds), *Melodrama Unbound: Across History, Media, and National Cultures* (New York: Columbia University Press, 2018), pp. 169–83.

Williams, Raymond, 'Film and the Dramatic Tradition', in Raymond Williams and Michael Orrom (eds), *Preface to Film* (London: Film Drama Ltd, 1954), pp. 25–41.

Wilson, C., '7 ways the war on Zika mosquitoes could be won', *New Scientist*, 2 February 2016, *https://www.newscientist.com/article/2076078-7-ways-the-war-on-zika-mosquitoes-could-be-won/* (accessed 16 May 2018).

Witteman, J., 'Flitshandelaars verveertienvoudigen winst dankzij coronapandemie', *de Volkskrant*, 21 April 2020, *https://www.volkskrant.nl/economie/flitshandelaars-verveertienvoudigen-winst-dankzij-coronapandemie~b32b6f4c/* (accessed 2 July 2020).

Wolff, Nicholas, *The Binding* (New York: Gallery Books, 2016).

Woolf, M., 'Obesity is as Serious a Threat as Climate Change, says Minister', *Independent on Sunday*, 14 October 2007, *http://www.independent.co.uk/news/uk/politics/obesity-is-as-seriousa-threat-as-climate-change-says-minister-396842.html* (accessed 29 August 2019).

World War Z, Marc Forster, dir. (Skydance Productions/Hemisphere Media Capital/GK Films/Plan B Entertainment, 2DUX², 2013).

Wrestlr, 'InFiltration', *Erotic Mind Control Story Archive*, 2001, *https://mcstories.com/InFiltrationWrestlr/index.html* (accessed 17 June 2002).

Yeats, W. B., 'The Second Coming', *The Dial* (1920).

Yong, E., 'How Zika Conquered the Americas', *The Atlantic*, 24 May 2017, *https://www.theatlantic.com/science/archive/2017/05/how-zika-conquered-the-americas/527961/* (accessed 15 May 2018).

Young, S., 'I'm Not Your Inspiration, Thank You Very Much', *TED Talk*, April 2014, *https://www.ted.com/talks/stella_young_i_m_not_your_inspiration_thank_you_very_much* (accessed 18 May 2018).

Young, S., 'We're Not Here for Your Inspiration', *ABC News*, 2 July 2012, *http://www.abc.net.au/news/2012-07-03/young-inspiration-porn/4107006* (accessed 14 May 2018).

'Your Facebook Friends Could Damage Your Credit Rating', *The Telegraph*, 27 August 2013, *https://www.telegraph.co.uk/finance/personalfinance/borrowing/loans/10268408/Your-Facebook-friends-could-damage-your-credit-rating.html* (accessed 19 June 2019).

'Zelfmaakdrug Krokodil nu ook in Duitsland', *NOS.nl*, 13 October 2011, *http://nos.nl/op3/artikel/303658-zelfmaakdrug-krokodil-nu-ook-in-duitsland.html* (accessed 26 January 2020).

Index

also in series

Sandra Becker, Megen de Bruin-Molé and Sara Polak (eds), *Embodying Contagion: The Viropolitics of Horror and Desire in Contemporary Discourse* (2021)

Lindsey Decker, *Transnationalism and Genre Hybridity in New British Horror Cinema* (2021)

Stacey Abbott and Lorna Jowett (eds), *Global TV Horror* (2021)

Michael J. Blouin, *Stephen King and American Politics* (2021)

Eddie Falvey, Joe Hickinbottom and Jonathan Wroot (eds), *New Blood: Critical Approaches to Contemporary Horror* (2020)

Darren Elliott-Smith and John Edgar Browning (eds), *New Queer Horror Film and Television* (2020)

Jonathan Newell, *A Century of Weird Fiction, 1832–1937: Disgust, Metaphysics and the Aesthetics of Cosmic Horror* (2020)

Alexandra Heller-Nicholas, *Masks in Horror Cinema: Eyes Without Faces* (2019)

Eleanor Beal and Jonathan Greenaway (eds), *Horror and Religion: New Literary Approaches to Theology, Race and Sexuality* (2019)

Dawn Stobbart, *Videogames and Horror: From Amnesia to Zombies, Run!* (2019)

David Annwn Jones, *Re-envisaging the First Age of Cinematic Horror, 1896–1934: Quanta of Fear* (2018)